The Quisling Factor

J.L.Oakley

J.L. Oakley/Fairchance Press
Bellingham, WA State

Publisher's Note: This is a work of fiction. Names, characters, places, and incidents are a product of the author's imagination. Locales and public names are sometimes used for atmospheric purposes. Any resemblance to actual people, living or dead, or to businesses, companies, events, institutions, or locales is completely coincidental.

Book Layout © 2017 BookDesignTemplates.com
Cover Design by j.allen fielder
Maps by Visual Results
Permission to use excerpt from the poem, Telavåg, by publisher

The Quisling Factor/J.L Oakley. -- 1st ed.
ISBN: 9780997323740

DEDICATION

The Quisling Factor is work of fiction, but it deals with the real traumatic aftermath of the five year German occupation of Norway. During the first year of liberation, the country not only released thousands of prisoners and foreign POWs from the concentration camps, rebuilt bombed out buildings and infrastructure, but also sought to immediately restore Norway's former justice system. Known as the Legal Purge, from the summer of 1945 to 1947, war crime trials were held all over the country.Some 30,000 Norwegians were arrested and put on trial. Quislings all. The most famous and sensational trial was the trial of Henry Oliver Rinnan and his gang in Trondheim.

Many thanks to those who shared their stories of what life was like during the war and the years after. It is not always easy to recall painful stories when so many just wanted to forget. Contrary to fiction, a war does not end on Liberation Day. There are consequences both physically and emotionally

I dedicate this novel to those who worked in the Resistance and lost their lives or lived and sufferered the consequences of traumatic experiences the rest of their lives. I also dedicate this work to those ordinary people who lost loved ones or had been traumatized by events in their communities, yet picked up their lives and moved on.

ACKNOWLEDGEMENTS

Tusen takk to the following museum professionals and historians who helped me on my research trip to Trondheim, Norway: Knut Sivertsen, police advisor at Justismuseet (Museum of Justice), for his help on the Henry Oliver Rinnan Trial and policing in 1946; Frøde Lingjerdet, historian at the Rustkammeret on the Resistance in the Trondheim region as well as Rinnan history; Idar Lind, songwriter, crime writer, and playwright who met me at Café Muser in Trondheim to share his knowledge of the Rinnan war crime trials and Rinnan's organization; and the staff at the National Museum of the Deaf.

A special thanks to Tore Greiner Eggan whom I met on-line in a WWII in Norway chatroom 20 years ago. He has been collecting photographs taken by members of German occupying force and posting them for that long a time. These photos helped me to understand the impact of 400,000 soldiers posted to Norway during the five years of occupation. We finally met in person on my trip at Café Muser. Afterwards, he led me on a tour of the many hideouts Rinnan and his gang used to meet and plan.

Tusen takk to Hilde Meadow for correcting all my Norwegian words and expressions; Christine Meloni, Thomas Barber, and Tom Stuen for typo hunting and to Andrew S. McBride, my first editor who always helps me get the story straight by his editing and insight. A shout out to J. Allen Fielder who always gets my covers right.

And last, but not least, tusen takk to Angar and Ingebjørg Melling who gave me an unexpected homestay in Trondheim and introduced to me to friends and places affected by the war years. I am so incredibly humbled. So funny, that we are both familiar with Kalamazoo, Michigan. Who knew?

The definition of quisling:

A person who betrays his or her country by aiding an invading enemy, often serving later in a puppet government. The word originates from the surname of the Norwegian war-time leader Vidkum Quisling, who betrayed his country and collaborated with the German occupiers during World War II. Traitor.

Just out of hatred
Take a child from its mother,
Butcher sixty cows
For one dead soldier.

Take the old men and kill them
With torture that drives you mad,
Burn down poor people's houses –
All that they ever had…

…When the prison boat pulled away:
Everything that the children got
Is deep in them, to stay.

Behind the seductive face,
The traitor's outstretched hand,
They shall see in a glimpse their dead father and Televåg that burned.

..In these whispers of children
The dream takes on its power,
And our Norway lives
Waiting its hour.

"Televåg," by Sigmund Skar

EUROPE

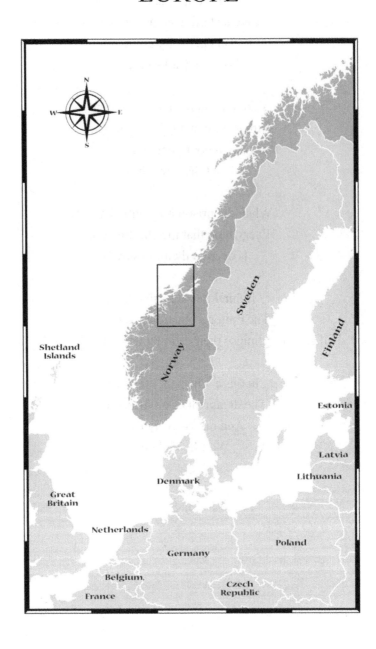

TRONDHEIM & SURROUNDING AREA

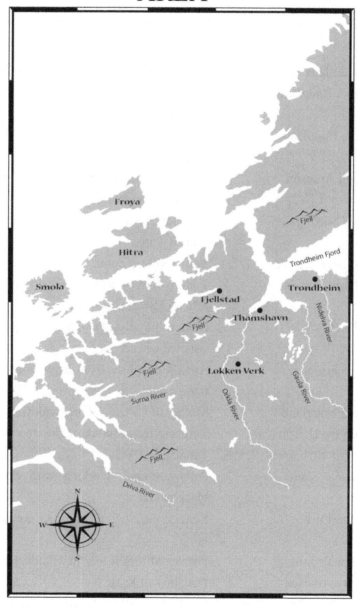

LIST of CHARACTERS

Tore "Jens" Haugland	Former intelligence agent SIS and XU
Anna Haugland	Tore's German-American wartime lover, now his wife
Lars Haugland	Oldest brother of Tore, formerly Milorg leader
Kjell Arneson	Local fisherman and Tore's wartime contact in the Resistance
Odd Sorting	Member of Rinnan Banden, has vendetta against Tore
Tommy Renvik	Tore's Milorg contact during the war
Margit Renvik	Tommy Renvik's wife, formerly of SOE office in Sweden
Ella Bjornson	Owner of Fjellstad *konditori* and past resistance worker
Lisa Fromme	Anna's daughter from a previous marriage
Inga Haugland	Mother of Lars and Tore; widowed
Solveig H. Tangen	Tore's sister, survivor of Gestapo raid on Telavåg in 1942
Gunnar Skele	Petty criminal, working with Rinnan; blackmarketeer
Aage Pilskog	Former manager of German controlled mine
Axel Tafjord	Former Milorg leader in Trondheim
Kitty Arneson	Daughter of Kjell
Bette Gudderson Norsby	Worked in Ella's *konditori* ; raped by Sorting; mother of his son

BOOK 1

BOOK I

Chapter 1

"Do you recognize this place?" The prosecutor held up a large photograph.

Tore Haugland looked at the photograph and saw a room with pine floor, large wine caskets and bottles on the walls.

"*Ja*. That's the Cloister."

"What was the Cloister?"

"That's where Rinnan interrogated resistance workers."

"And why are you familiar with it?"

"I was taken there after being arrested by the Gestapo. Just before Christmas 1944."

"And what happened?" The prosecutor gave him a sympathetic look as the onlookers in the courtroom leaned forward to listen. Some of the attendees were the good citizens of Trondheim. Some were members of the press from Norway and from all over the world. Like the on-going Nuremburg trials in Germany, this was no ordinary war crimes trial.

Haugland swallowed. To his right was the large holding gallery where the accused sat with large numbers printed on placards around their necks. He avoided looking at Number One.

"I was interrogated."

"Say louder."

"I was...tortured."

"Why?"

"For information. I was an intelligence officer in the Resistance. I ran a line that served SOE-Norway in England and our Home Forces."

"How long were you there...in the Cloister?"

"Over a week."

"And the extent of your injuries?"

Haugland described an amputated finger and broken hand, the damage to his back, and partial loss of hearing from the beatings. The horrific swastika brand.

"Were you released?"

"Nei. I was left for dead in the forest."

Some attendee in the gallery gasped as the lights grew dimmer.

"Can you identify any of your interrogators here in this courtroom?"

Haugland's voice grew smaller. *"Ja.* In the box over there. Number Five, Number Seven and... Number One."

"Are they all here?"

"Nei. Two others are dead. Died around capitulation."

The courtroom became darker, like a storm was approaching. Haugland looked into the gloom and thought the room had become smaller. Off to his right, he could distinctly hear the drip of water into an empty sink. The faces in the crowd began to fade. The prosecutor turned away.

"Point them out to the court."

Haugland turned and stared into the area where the accused sat and saw instead two posters on the wall. One of them made his skin crawl. It was a caricature of a skeleton with a scythe. Written below it were the words, *Velkommen til fest.* Welcome to the party.

"You didn't respond," the prosecutor said in a low resonant voice.

"I don't understand. They were there a moment ago." Haugland began to fidget as the place where he stood to testify began to lower to the floor, forcing him back on a stool on the pine floor. The sides of the docket dropped away.

"Then let me refresh your memory." The black-haired prosecutor had shrunk in size to that of a boy. Waving into the gloom, two men stepped forward, their sleeves rolled up. The largest one, a heavyset bully, had blood on his hands, but it did not correspond to the donut hole in his head. He came around and seized Haugland by his hair while the other shook out a whip.

"What are you doing?"

"Say the names," the little prosecutor said, then nodded for the thugs to begin.

"What? No, wait!" Haugland cried out, but it was too late. The whip ripped into his back like a white hot wire, causing him to jerk and scream. His back ran with blood and soaked his tattered shirt.

The sound of the dripping water grew louder.

"Oh, God," he cried out. "I can't do this again."

The whip hand came down again and again. Haugland writhed help-lessly until he remembered his tooth with its poison pill. Twisting the tooth, he bit down on the rubber-coated capsule. Instantly, there was silence, the only sensation of intense humidity and inadequate air. He no longer felt the insidious blows and he wondered if he was dead. Something moved in front of him. Curious, he opened an eye.

"Eh, what's up Doc?" The prosecutor was gone. So was the air. All that remained was Bugs Bunny.

"Party's over," Bugs said as he chomped his carrot.

***

Gasping, Tore Haugland sat up in the dark, stifling room and sought his bearings. When he moved his hand, he cried out at the pain. It was encased in a heavy gauze bandage and throbbed like hell. *Where the Devil was he?* Then he remembered. *Johns Hopkins Hospital. Balti-more, America.* He'd come here by ship all the way from Norway ten days ago to get movement in his crippled left hand restored.

Bracing himself with his arms, Haugland looked for a clock. He knew he went into surgery mid-morning, but the anesthesia must have put him out for hours. Through the dark he could see a long oval mirror above what Americans called a chest of drawers. It caught the moon-light outside but it also caught the ghostly outline of his body. He swallowed hard, his throat parched. His torso was covered with sweat, soaking his opened pajama top, his short dark hair plastered to his fore-head. The humid April air coming through the slightly ajar window was hot enough to suffocate a displaced Norwegian.

Haugland rubbed his eyes with his right hand, still shaken by the dream. It had been absurd. Only the week before he had seen such a cartoon rabbit at a motion picture show with his young stepdaughter, Lisel, in Baltimore. It made his nightmare even more ludicrous because most of his dark dream was true.

During the war, Haugland had been an intelligence officer with XU, the Norwegian intelligence branch of the Resistance, working closely with Britain's Secret Intelligence Servce. While managing a secret line that supported the Shetland Bus, a clandestine special operations group of fishing boats that brought arms and agents from the Shetland Islands to the West Coast of Norway, Haugland was betrayed. He *was* tortured by the Gestapo and Henry Oliver Rinnan's gang, *Rinnan Banden,* for nearly a week, then left for dead. He had survived, but was left with partial loss of hearing, a damaged hand and nightmares. Most of the fishermen who did secret work with him had been captured and shot.

In a month, Haugland would testify against Rinnan in Trondheim, the most important war crimes trial in Norway's history. The criminal indictment against Rinnan was so massive, it had taken six hours to read at the opening of the trial just days ago.

Haugland settled back on his pillows against the metal headboard and moved his bandaged hand high on his chest. The hand throbbed hard and relentless. He was grateful for the surgery made possible by the kindness of an American flier Haugland had rescued a year and a half ago in Norway. Captain John Trumball had raised the funds to bring Haugland and his family over to meet with one of the top ortho-pedic surgeons at Johns Hopkins. Haugland hoped the surgery would at least restore some flexibility to his fingers caused by the torture he had gone through. There was nothing he could do about the missing ring finger, but he would be glad for any improvement in the hand.

Haugland rubbed his forehead with the back of his good hand. This was his first visit to America. He had been enjoying his time here, though he could do without the heat and humidity. The Americans he met were friendly and energized by the war's end. Their soldiers were coming home in boatloads from Europe since the Germans surrendered, eleven months earlier.

In Norway, the Allies were still processing the remaining German soldiers down from a top force of 400,000 that had once been stationed throughout the country of three million people. In addition, there were 100,000 Allied POWs—mostly Russians—the Germans had used for slave labor being repatriated back to the Soviet Union and other countries. Though the Americans Haugland talked with were sympathetic about Norway's plight under the five year-long German occupation, few understood the depths of depravity and terror the average Norwegian endured: the SS and Gestapo *razzias* on villages that harbored members of the Resistance or British agents; the massive roundups of hostages, executing many on the slightest whim; the deportation and murder of Norway's small Jewish community; the tens of thousands of Norwegians languishing or dying in prisons and POW camps in Norway and Germany; the restrictions on movement and food.

Worse, there were the *quislings*—traitors—who betrayed their own countrymen. Some were opportunists. Many were members of Norway's Nazi party, the *Nasjonal Samling,* who worked closely with their German occupiers, some wearing the uniforms of the SS or the Stapo, the Norwegian State Police. Since the German capitulation, 90,000 Norwegians had been charged with treason. Their trials were ongoing as Norway, weary and in ruins, sought to bring back order and the pre-war laws of justice.

Out in the hall, Haugland heard movement. The door opened, backlighting a nurse with a pert winged cap. In the door frame, she appeared like a hazy white angel. Behind her stood another figure that glowed like golden dust motes caught in the sun, but Haugland couldn't make the person out. *Anna?*

"It's good to see you awake, Mr. Haugland. Are you in pain?" the nurse asked. She walked into the room, her starched clothing cool rustling in the muggy night. She turned on a light next to his bed. "Shall I ask for morphine?" Before he could answer, she stuck a thermometer in his mouth and checked his pulse. "Dr. Allen said the surgery went very well, but you might experience discomfort for a week or so. He'll want to talk about therapy before you are discharged." She read the thermometer and placed it into an enameled pan.

"Is my wife still here?" he asked groggily.

"Nothing could keep me away, Jens." The glowing figure from the hallway came forward to his bedside and laid a hand on his shoulder. She kissed his forehead.

Beautiful golden-haired Anna. She smelled of rosewater and milk. His wartime lover, now his wife and anchor in this crazy, shattered post-war world.

Chapter 2

Oslo, Norway. April 1946

"When did Tore get the first one?" Lars Haugland asked. He stood with Captain Tommy Renvik in a third floor office of Victoria Terrasse in Oslo. Both men had served in *Milorg*, the military branch of the Norwegian Resistance during the German occupation. The irony of being here was not lost on them. A little more than a year ago, it had been Gestapo headquarters in Norway. Now it was restored to its original use—the Royal Norwegian Ministry of Foreign Affairs.

Tommy scratched the side of his head, his reddish-blonde hair cut military style. "Tore told me about it a month and a half ago."

Tommy Renvik had been Tore Haugland's Milorg contact during the war. Since Lars got to know him, he thought Tommy was a dependable and first class military man. Tommy was the same age as Tore—twenty-six—but like Tore, seemed older than his age. *The war did that to me, too.* Tommy had stayed on in the armed forces as his country sought to never again let any aggressor catch it off guard and overpower it.

Lars turned the note over, wanting to rip it in half. "This one is horrifying. Despicable. Why the hell didn't Tore tell me?"

"Your brother didn't want to alarm anyone. Especially Anna."

Lars swallowed. The note made him feel sick. He gave it back to Tommy. A British-trained intelligence agent, his brother Tore Haugland had suffered terribly at the hands of the Gestapo and Rinnan. Why would anyone threaten him now? Lars rubbed his mouth. Unless… Rinnan's war crimes trial in Trondheim. Tore would be a chief witness at it in May. He had been one of the few survivors of Rinnan's notorious Cloister.

Lars nodded at the note. "You said this is the second. When did it come?"

"It came just before Tore and Anna left with the children for America."

Lars walked over to a window looking out toward Oslo Fjord. Tommy joined him. VT, as some called the massive building, once had torture chambers on the fourth floor, prisoner cells in the basement. Working here often gave Lars an eerie feeling, because one of his best friends had jumped from one of its windows after being tortured by the Gestapo over a two-day period. Rather than give up information on associates in security and XU, Torstein had killed himself. Remembering that was one of the empty echoes of the war.

Though it was mid-April, there had been frost last night and the streets at nine a.m. looked like they were dusted with opaque crystal glass when the sun struck them. Across the way Lars could see American soldiers in their jeep talking to some kids. Arriving a year ago to help secure the capital after capitulation and process the nearly 400,000 German soldiers and military personnel in the country, a few of the American units stayed on after the Germans had been repatriated, but were due to leave any time. He watched the Americans give the boys some candy, then drive off.

Tommy cleared his throat. "When the second one showed up, Tore came to see me and asked me to look into it. He didn't want to spoil their trip. He saw it as a honeymoon—albeit with kids and surgery— but he really wanted things to go well. He's been pretty happy, you know."

Lars smiled at Tommy before looking away. "I'm glad to hear that. I wasn't sure," he mumbled. "There has been some unpleasantness in the family."

"I heard. Tore confided in me. Some trouble with your sister."

"Damn war. Capitulation has not meant the end to all hostilities. There are the hostilities of the heart that linger on. Solveig lost her husband and children because of the *razzia* at Telavåg."

"I thought her children were living—"

"They are, but they were taken away from her by the Gestapo and sent to a reeducation center. A couple adopted them. For three years. They were so young that they barely remember Solveig. She has not forgotten or forgiven."

"I'm sorry. I truly am."

Lars acknowledged the comment, then resumed talking about the notes. "This third note. When did it arrive?"

"Yesterday. I found it when I went to collect their mail. Same type of envelope."

"What do you think? Does it have to do with the trial? Is it Rinnan?"

"I honestly don't know, but I don't think it's just a prank. I think it— and all of the notes— should be taken seriously."

The whole matter distressed Lars, but he was also angry. He picked up one of the sheets of paper, and shook his head. "What's the purpose of these notes?"

"If they are from Rinnan, it's all about preventing Tore from testifying. Your brother knows too much about Rinnan's infiltration of local resistance groups in the Trondheim region."

"Rinnan. That little Norwegian prick is a sadistic monster. It's hard to fathom how much damage he did to the Resistance. Heard his gang killed at least one hundred Norwegian patriots and British agents at that Cloister of his, not to mention torturing thousands. What he did to Tore…" Lars looked at the note, wanting to tear it up, but it was evidence of a possible plot to disrupt the trial. "I want the war to be over for my brother. He's been through enough to have to go through this garbage. I don't know how much more he can take."

Silence hung between the men. Lars was sure they shared the same sense of disillusionment.

Finally, Tommy said. "Your brother's stronger than all of us think. I was pretty upset when I first saw him that terrible winter. His back, his whole body was one repulsive wound. The shock of seeing him like that—" Tommy shook his head. "None of us in the export team thought he would be strong enough to go over the mountains to Sweden. Except for Gunnerson, the old logger who found him. He said that Haugland had already been through the worst of it. What were a few more mountains?"

Lars Haugland put the note down. "I think I'll hold onto this. I'm going to have photographs taken. The prosecutors in Trondheim will want to know."

"Good idea. I'll make you a file. Just in case. Tore would see the sense in that."

Lars stared down at the street. There were more people since they first looked. People were wearing spring coats and hats, some in styles that were outdated. After five years of occupation, things were still being rationed. Probably would be for a few more years.

"I'd like to send him a cable warning him about the third note," Lars said. "There's no doubt that whoever sent it knows something about my brother and his treatment in the Cloister. Someone who was there."

"Let me take care of that. I have a contact living in the Maryland area. We worked together during the war. He can take the telegram to Haugland and check out security at the same time." Tommy frowned. "Has anyone made a head count of who's in jail in Trondheim? After all, Rinnan escaped last Christmas, however briefly."

"The bastard. Can you believe it? A top war criminal and he was free for a least a day. Good thing someone turned him in. We still don't know how he did it."

"But since then security is tighter?"

"I think all's well," Lars replied, "but I'll have someone call up there and check."

"And I'll get on the cable to Tore," Tommy said.

"*Takk.* I appreciate it very much. You're a good friend," Lars said. "To both of us." He extended his hand and Tommy shook it. "Look," continued Lars, "I'll make that call to Trondheim, and then let's meet at your office at Akershus. I've got some things to work on, then I'll see about an early *middag* for us."

Tommy said he'd be happy to. He hadn't eaten yet.

***

Tommy took off and left Lars to clean up the papers. Lars stacked the notes on top of each other and prepared to put them in his briefcase when the top one got away from him. It glided to the floor under the table.

"Bastard," he said as he retrieved it. "Why don't you leave him alone?" He looked at the sketch with disgust and sinking dread. It was a crudely drawn picture of a man with dark hair. Lars guessed it was supposed to be his brother. The man was hanging from arms tied above him. There were cuts with dripping blood all over his body. On one side, a swastika was drawn, smoke rising from it. Underneath was a hastily written caption:

THE PARTY ISN'T OVER – YET.

Chapter 3

Baltimore, Maryland USA. April 1946

Two days after his surgery, Haugland was released from the hospital.

"Are you ready?" Anna spoke in English as she pushed him in his wheelchair to the elevator.

"As soon as I can get out of this contraption," he answered. "Apparently, it's orders I stay put until I'm downstairs." He spoke in English as well, his accent with a British clip to it. "Where are Nils and Lisel?"

"Downstairs, waiting for you. Now behave and do what you're told."

Down at the main entryway, Anna's uncle, Charles Howard, a vigorous man in his mid-fifties, greeted them. Slightly shorter than Haugland, he wore a linen suit. With his sleek brown hair and a sporty mustache, he looked to Haugland something of a British country squire. With him was Anna's seventy-five-year-old grandmother, Elizabeth Howard, a proud and well-groomed silver-haired matron. She held Haugland's infant son, Nils, in her arms. Lisel, his six-year-old step-daughter, was waiting in the car.

"*Pappa Jens!*" Lisel called out, making Haugland grin. His left arm in a sling, he got up from the wheelchair and welcomed her when she ran into his arms. Sweet, he signed when he stepped away. Lisel signed back, I miss you.

Me too.

Lisel was Anna's daughter from her first marriage. The little girl had always assumed Haugland couldn't hear at all. His cover had been a deaf-mute fisherman when Lisel met him in Fjellstad. After the war ended, Lisel learned that it had all been a game. Haugland could always speak and hear. He was pleased when Lisel said she liked the game. Could they still play? Of course. Lately, she had started calling him Pappa Jens. Her New Pappa.

"We better hurry," Howard said. "Must make that ferry or else we'll be stuck in Annapolis for the night." He opened the front door and helped Haugland in even though he didn't need it.

"You're looking good, Haugland. Hope it's working out for you."

Haugland murmured that it was, but by the time they reached the Howard home across the Chesapeake Bay hours later, his hand was aching and his back sore. He fell sound asleep as soon as he lay down.

He dreamed of Anna. She walked out of the woods toward him through a field of summer flowers. Below was an old farmhouse. Her hair flashed golden in the afternoon light, gently stirred by a breeze off the fjord. She laid a blanket down on the grass, sat down and set out a picnic. Lisel curled up next to her. When Anna looked at Haugland, he stirred deep inside, his heart full of love. But when he tried to tell her that, he couldn't speak, only sign. *DANGER. Don't give yourself away*, a voice said. Lives depended on it. She lay down on the blanket, her arms waiting for him, then the old farmhouse exploded into flames and collapsed into ashes. I'm sorry, she mouthed.

Haugland sat up abruptly and looked around the dim room that had been their private quarters since arriving here in Maryland two weeks ago. *Damn anesthesia.* The doctor had warned him that it could linger like a bad headache, but it should be going away by now. He reached for Anna and realized she was not sleeping next to him. He wondered if she had gone to check on Nils, their three-month-old son.

He moved his bandaged hand over her pillow and breathed in her scent. Rosewater. He smiled in the dark. Thinking of her always steadied him. In the other room, Haugland heard movement. They were staying in guest rooms built over a garage constructed in the 1930s. The house was owned by Anna's American grandmother and had once been the home of Anna's mother, Margaret Howard, when she was a girl. Old and stately, the main house sat on land deeded in the late 1660s on the Eastern Shore of Maryland. Haugland liked it for its privacy. He slipped out of bed and located his boxer shorts, finishing off with a mid-length silk robe Anna's grandmother had given him as a personal wedding gift.

Stepping across the Oriental rug to the door, he opened it slightly and saw Anna sitting on a small floral sofa with her back toward him. Her curly blonde hair was tied on her slender neck with a pink satin ribbon that matched the cotton nightgown she wore. The loud smacking and grunting sounds told him she was nursing Nils. Haugland came softly into the room and went around behind her.

"Jens!" Anna said softly. "We didn't wake you?" She spoke in Norwegian.

"*Nei*." He came around and sat down on the opposite end of the sofa and placed her feet on his lap. She was wearing soft slippers. He took one off and began rubbing the arch of her foot with his good hand.

"Uhmm..."

"You're up early or rather he is..."

"He's always up. Generally, I just roll over so you don't notice. I didn't want to disturb you this time. You were exhausted when we got here. Out like a light." She looked at him curiously. "Does your hand hurt?"

"It's tender, but the pills are helping."

She held the baby in her left arm and reached over and touched his shoulder. He released her foot and stretched out his hard six-foot plus frame.

The baby grew quieter. Haugland looked Anna's way, amazed at her patience. She was looking at Nils, her hand pressed on her breast. The baby's fuzzy blonde head seemed surrounded in the folds of her pink gown. The two of them made quite a picture and he felt tightness in his throat. His torture in the Cloister had been agonizing, but waiting out the twelve hours for the boy to be born had almost been as bad. He was terrified of losing Anna.

"Anna..."

She didn't hear him, so he ran a finger down her instep and she jerked back her bare foot. She beamed at him, then scowled playfully.

"You'll disturb him. I want him to go back to sleep."

Curious, he leaned over and looked. He pulled the nursing gown away from the baby's mouth and saw that Nils was still sucking.

"Can I have some?"

"Jens!" She batted his arm and gave him a mock look of shock.

He smiled at his tiny son. "He's something, isn't he?" He touched one of the hands with a finger. "Amazing..."

"Yes," Anna said, looking at Haugland. She brushed his hair off his forehead.

He leaned over farther and kissed her. He put a hand on her slender shoulder and pulled her closer. Underneath, Nils began to doze. Haugland pulled back and saw Nil's little bud mouth disengaged, a bubble of milk on the lips. Anna's nipple looked ripe and full. He looked at her, his eyes full of love.

"What time is it?" she asked. Outside the dimly lit room, the balcony glowed in the moonlight.

"Four-thirty in the morning." Haugland brushed a tendril of hair away from Anna's forehead.

"When is Trumball coming?"

"Ten."

"I'll put Nils to bed."

While Anna slipped into the small room where Lisel slept, Haugland got up and went over to the French doors. It felt odd being here, but since arriving from Norway, they had been welcomed by Anna's American relatives. Anna was an orphan now. Her American mother had died in Germany in 1933. Her German father had been killed in Berlin in a bombing raid in the last weeks of the war. The only surviving member of her immediate family was her twenty-two-year-old brother who had been a POW in France. He was now back in Germany, but due to come over in the fall to pursue school.

Haugland pulled aside the long sheer curtains. Outside, an old moon shone on the Chesapeake, its light caressing the tall reeds that rimmed a part of the beach. Haugland knew Anna was happy staying here. He was too. The Howards had welcomed him with open arms. He wished his family would do the same for Anna. His mother and brothers had welcomed Anna, but his sister Solveig had not. Her hatred of Germans was unrelenting. Too much had happened to Solveig for her to forgive.

Haugland let the curtain go. It was a source of contention in the Haugland family that he could no longer ignore. Desiring peace and harmony in his own growing family, Haugland had begun to stay away from gatherings at his mother's home.

Equally, he was becoming tired of the carping after the war and the finger-pointing. Over ninety thousand Norwegians had been arrested after capitulation for collaborating with the Germans, thirty thousands went on trial. As the trials continued, many were sentenced to hard labor at Falstad or at the former concentration camp, Grini, now named Ilebu. Others with serious crimes such as working for the Gestapo as inform- ants or agent provocateurs, were also on trial. As to those people who benefited greatly from a working relationship in German controlled in- dustry, Haugland wasn't too hopeful they would see justice.

With the strain in his family and the ruined economy in Norway, Haugland often thought of immigrating to America. With the Howard family's sponsorship, it would be fairly easy but what would he do? Although he spoke English fluently, here in America he might only be able to become a laborer and realistically, he would never completely be able to do some types of work ever again due to his hand and back.

Anna came into the room and turning off the floor lamp by the sofa, joined Haugland.

"Is Nils all right?"

"Sound asleep." Leaning against his right shoulder, she put her arm around him and hugged him. He hugged her back. Together they stood quietly and watched the moon over the water. Through the glass panes they could hear the call of Canada geese as they flew north. Like inno- cents abroad they tried to locate this new wonder. They opened the doors and stepped onto the balcony and were immediately hit with pred- awn humidity.

"*Aiiyeh...*" Haugland said. "Let's go back in."

"*Nei*, listen. Do you hear that? I remember those sounds from when I was little girl." Anna switched to English. "Spring peepers—frogs—make that noise."

Haugland spoke in English in turn. "I thought it was the bugs, the ones with the light bulbs."

"Oh. You're impossible."

"You're beautiful. I want you." Haugland signed it, Want you.

"You have a one-track mind."

He held her close and rocked her for a moment. He felt her relax against him.

Suddenly she said, "Oh, dear. I'm leaking. You're all wet." She sounded half-embarrassed, but she was half-challenging him.

She pushed away, but he would only let her go so far. They had little time together since Nils had been born and he missed her. He pulled her back toward him by the open doors and kissed her mouth. Slipping his hand inside the slit on her nursing gown, he caressed one of her breasts and felt the wetness. "Anna..." he said, "I love you." Haugland looked at her moonlit face and thought he would die for wanting her.

"I love you." She smiled sweetly when he took her hand and led her back inside.

Chapter 4

Trondheim, Norway. April 1946

The metal door creaked open and a guard put a tray of food on the bench.

Odd Sorting wanted to see who it was, but the door closed before he could turn. The cart carrying the pots creaked as it was pushed down the hall. The door next to his cell banged as it opened and shut. He heard a few voices in the hall, but he didn't recognize anyone. In an effort to keep the prisoners off balance, the guards were changed so no attachments could be made. Everything else was the same routine, day in and day out. It was driving him mad.

Sorting turned away from the wall and slid off his cot's hard mattress. There was a steaming bowl and some hunks of bread on the tray. *Stinking soup again.* He hated soup, but his stomach growled so he took the tray and brought it back to his bed. It didn't look too bad. There were potatoes in it and some sort of fish sausage. Today, it wasn't runny.

He wondered if there were going to be visitors. He gazed up at the window high up in the wall and tried to figure what kind of day it was turning out to be. He'd find out later when he was taken out of his cell and over to the *Tinghus* where the trial was going on. Some twenty-nine co-defendants of Rinnan were involved and he was one of them. The trial had begun on April 13, less than a week ago. By the looks of it could go on for months. Sorting made a face. This wasn't how it was supposed to work out.

Sorting joined *Rinnan Banden* in the winter of 1941. He had known Rolf Rinnan, the younger brother of Henry Oliver Rinnan, for some time and joined at his urging. It was a lark and there was money involved. It certainly beat having to report to the labor jobs the Germans and *quisling* government workers in the *Nasjonal Samling* forced on the local male population. All he had to do was to befriend ordinary Norwegians and uncover any kind of resistance activity and report. As Sorting got drawn farther into the organization, however, he saw how cunning and ruthless Rinnan was in running his operation. Sorting's boss was more successful than the Gestapo in rooting out resistance organizations because he used a system that employed unsuspecting loyal Norwegians to do his dirty work. Negative agents, Rinnan called them. *Sure got a fine one from Fjellstad. The Arneson girl.* Sorting thought of another name associated with that little fishing village on the west coast of Norway—Jens Hansen.

Sorting rubbed his left shoulder. The ache in it matched the bitterness he felt toward Hansen. Fjellstad might have been an isolated and inconsequential fishing village, but it nevertheless harbored a highly organized resistance cell that received arms and agents via the Shetland Bus. Sorting had been sent to Fjellstad in the summer of 1944 to locate the group and its leader.

Hansen had been that leader. Eventually through the use of their negative agent and information gathered from various *razzias*, the cell was crushed, and Hansen captured. Brutally interrogated by Rinnan himself, the gang had left Hansen for dead under snow-laden brambles wrapped in a blanket.

I thought you were deader than a doornail.

During the last months of the war, Sorting thought about leaving *Rinnan Banden* and plotted going to Sweden where he would hide out as a refugee with his girlfriend Freyda Olsen. Instead, the war came to an abrupt end after Hitler's suicide. Sorting was forced to flee with Rinnan to the Soviet Union where Rinnan had contacts. They never made it, but were hit by a May blizzard which forced them to look for shelter on the Norwegian side of the Swedish border.

Then you showed up like a bright krone.

Sorting massaged his shoulder a final time, then spit onto the floor. He was caught a few days later after a fierce gun battle with Hansen who had appeared alive and well. As they struggled over Hansen's sub-machine gun, Hansen shot him.

Sorting closed his eyes, the thought of food no longer important. He should have been grateful, he supposed, to be alive, but he felt only emptiness. He was not only being tried along with other members of Rinnan's gang with much more serious accusations against them, he was also having to face the trial alone. The one person he cared about—sweet, voluptuous Freyda—was gone. And for that he blamed Jens Hansen.

Sorting hated the man. After Hansen shot him, Sorting had taunted Hansen to kill him. For some reason, the agent didn't do it. As Sorting lay in the slush bleeding away, Hansen dropped a blood-stained scarf that once had been Freyda's into his hand. And then Hansen walked off. Sorting would never forgive him for that. He'd see him dead.

Because I know your real name, Tore Haugland.

Chapter 5

Eastern Shore, Maryland. April 1946

Anna Haugland rolled quietly to the edge of the bed and sat up. For a moment she listened to the sounds of the house, still in disbelief that after more than a decade of living in fear in Europe, she was once again safe in America. Home with family.

Mutti. Her American mother was born and grew up in this house. One brisk fall day in 1914, she met a German student, Heinrick von Schauffer, who had limped to the back door after twisting his ankle while duck hunting. They fell in love and married. When the war broke out in Europe, they stayed here.

I was born in this house. My little brother was born in this house.

The family lived in Maryland until 1930 when Anna's parents decided to move to England where her father could further his work in chemistry. In 1932, they moved to Germany to look after his own father who had lost everything in the 1929 Crash. Then Hitler came to power.

Anna closed her eyes. Outside the house, through the slightly ajar screened window, she could hear the *cheer-cheer* of a cardinal out in the garden. It brought back memories of fireflies, sparklers, and Fourth of July picnics down by the water. Her father's laugh. Her mother's adoring eyes on Pappa. Her sensible, aristocratic grandmother, Elizabeth Howard, who reigned over all.

Anna sighed as she put on her robe over her nightie. That was a long time ago, in a different world. A different reality. For the past five years, her reality in Norway had been terror, hunger, and aching loss. Despite all their love and affection, her American relatives would never fully understand, even those with gold stars in their windows. To live in fear and not trust anyone day after day, year after year wore on her. To be accused of something foul and untruthful wore her down. Anna hoped that in this year,

1946, her sense of hopelessness would end. That she would know joy again. The only ones who gave it to her now were her children and the man sleeping next to her, his breathing slow and steady. Anna turned. A strand of Haugland's dark hair had fallen over his forehead. She was tempted to lift it back, but she didn't want to wake him. It was going to be a long day.

She gently set the cotton sheet high over his exposed bare shoulder and back with its multitude of scars made with a whip and *totenschläger* and the swastika brand mark on his hip. She remembered the shock the first time she saw them. *Jens. Dear Jens.* Her lover and protector in Norway, now her husband. He had suffered. She had suffered. Somehow they still found love in the world.

Haugland stirred slightly, his long bare legs stretching toward the end of the bed. Earlier, assured that Nils and Lisel were asleep, they returned to their bed and made love. She still ached from his attentions, surprised he was little troubled by his heavily bandaged left hand and the lingering effects of the anesthesia. She throbbed everywhere. In a good way. She would let him sleep a bit longer while she bathed and got ready for Nils's seven o'clock feeding. And then coffee. The smell of it drifted under the door to their room. Real coffee, not rationed.

She started to get up, when Haugland made a sound in his throat. His hands twitched, the fingers on his right hand forming letters she recognized. His breathing grew ragged.

Another nightmare. They seemed to come often lately. The damn trial. She understood how important it was that he testify at such a major trial, but it was taking a toll on him. Was there something he wasn't telling her?

Anna leaned over and kissed his shoulder.

"Mmm."

"I'm here, Jens," Anna said.

Wondering if he really couldn't hear well out of that ear, she finger spelled against his shoulder. I here. You fine. Sleep. She gently stroked his cheek.

"Hmm." His breathing smoothed again. When she was sure he was asleep, she got up for the day.

Chapter 6

Two hours later, the entire household assembled in the living room of the old manor. As Haugland and Anna came in with the children, Anna's grandmother, Elizabeth Howard, walked over to greet them.

"You're wearing your uniform, Tore. It looks very smart. Just like the ones I've seen British soldiers wear in the newsreels, except for that Norwegian flag on your shoulder. Did you wear this in Norway?"

Haugland glanced briefly at Anna, who held their baby Nils in her arms. She nodded back at him. "Only once for a formal occasion. And now mysteriously, for this luncheon we're going to. Can't figure out why John Trumball insisted I bring it."

"John's father was in the Army Reserves. He's indebted to you for saving John's life." Elizabeth motioned to Anna that she would take Nils. "Was that formal occasion when you met King Haakon of Norway? Charles told me. You must be very proud."

"I am, but I wasn't the only one present. The Norwegian officers and crew from the Shetland Bus were also being honored."

Elizabeth smiled down at Nils who had grabbed onto her gold chain. "You are too modest, Tore." She bounced Nils gently and clucked at him. He opened his gummy mouth and squealed. "Sweetie," Elizabeth said, then carefully peeled his fingers off the chain.

"Will you excuse me?" Haugland nodded at Charles Howard who was busy stuffing a pipe as he stood by the colonial fireplace. Haugland thought Howard could be given a shotgun and easily transported to Norway's autumn fields rife with ptarmigan and pheasant. No one would miss a beat. He gave Anna a wry grin as he stepped past her.

"How far away is this place we're going?" Haugland asked Howard.

"Not far. About twenty minute drive. It's an impressive place."

"Strange that of all the people I should pull out of the *fjell* and export over to the Shetlands one would be an acquaintance of yours. John Trumball told me he had an uncle who was a lawyer in Baltimore. Incredible that his uncle's law partner was you."

Charles tamped the tobacco down, then put the metal tamp away in his blue linen jacket. "Small world. I knew, of course, that John had been trained as an aviator and stationed in Scotland, but that's about it. I didn't hear he had crash landed in Norway and nearly captured until recently. John talked of nothing else than how he was going to help the village of Fjellstad and you for saving him. After the war, when John learned of the awful raid on Fjellstad and the executions that followed, he assumed you were dead. Always felt guilty thinking he and his crew might have brought on the raid and your capture."

"They shouldn't worry about that because they didn't." Haugland smiled softly. He felt his face warm. *Was it the humidity or remembering details that always caught him off-guard?*

Charles lit his pipe, then puffed it to get it going. The sweet smell of Virginia tobacco immediately reminded Haugland how it was often smuggled into Norway during the occupation as a gift, but one had to be careful where they smoked it. The scent was a dead giveaway. Receiving goods from the black market or worse, a parachute drop, was a crime.

Charles continued. "John wanted to find out what happened to you. Through one of the villagers in Fjellstad, he learned that you were alive. That's when he got the ball rolling on getting you over here."

"I'll never be able to thank him for arranging for me to come over to see the doctors at Johns Hopkins about my hand."

"One of the best orthopedic hospitals in the world. The best doctors." Charles used his pipe to emphasize his point. "How is the hand coming along? Splendid, I hope."

Haugland stared at his heavily bandaged hand sticking out of his sling. "I'll have to undergo some therapy after the bandages come off. I'm to see the doctor again in a week. Stiches out a week after that."

Charles put his hand on Haugland's shoulder. "Good man, Torrey." He took a puff on his pipe and blew out a perfect smoke ring. "I know you're keeping it from the ladies, but how difficult is it in Norway now? King is restored, you just had elections last fall, and that traitor Prime Minister Vidkun Quisling gone to his just reward. How will it affect you and my wonderful niece? I heard the Germans were still there and everyone is on rations."

Haugland accepted Charles's offer of a sip of whiskey and set him straight on the facts until their ride showed up.

***

While Haugland talked with her uncle Anna made last-minute arrangements for Nils. He would be staying at the Howard home.

"You be a good boy," Anna said as she handed him over to her grandmother's colored maid, Rose. "Rose, are you sure it's no trouble?"

"No trouble, Mrs. Haugland. I think this one is real special. So good-natured."

"He'll be fine, Anna," Elizabeth said. "If you wish, Rose can bring him over later. Come and have a good time. You've been cooped up the last few days." She adjusted the neckline on Anna's light blue flower-patterned dress. It was in the latest style, the first new thing Anna had in six years.

Being here in the United States was sometimes overwhelming. There was an overpowering sense of wealth. Everyone looked so healthy and well-fed, something she had noticed in the American soldiers stationed in Oslo where they lived. Material goods seemed to abound here in the States. Anna gently squeezed her grandmother's hand.

Anna kissed Nils and thanked Rose. She joined the other women by the tall windows. They watched Charles outside talk to the driver of the first car and then come back in.

"They're ready for us," Charles said. "Tore, you, Anna and the children can go in the first car with Mother."

***

The ride passed through freshly turned fields and quaint countryside dotted lightly with colonial and Civil War-era structures. The trees were beyond their new-leaf stage.

Haugland listened to Elizabeth Howard talk about the history of some of the places they passed by, but he thought there was a sleepiness to the place, as though it had never been touched by the events of the past five years in Europe and in the Pacific. He settled back against the seat. Out the window, he caught a glimpse of the water on the Chesapeake Bay and saw a fishing boat making its way out. Gulls trailed behind it. The sight struck a chord within him.

"See you, Jens." A memory of a special wartime friend came to him: Kjell Arneson, fisherman and Haugland's contact in Fjellstad during his assignment there. Kjell had been "exporting" people in the Resistance for a couple of years. When Haugland came, Kjell's role was to house Haugland and help him organize a group of fishermen to move a large shipment of arms. For nearly ten months they had been a closely matched team and would always have that special bond between mates that came from war. As part of his cover Haugland had fished with Kjell and found he enjoyed it very much. Since then whenever Haugland saw a fishing boat, he thought of Kjell, often with a longing like a childhood lost.

I'll never be the same. I might talk of school, but I think I'm looking for something else.

Elizabeth turned the car onto a private graveled road and up to circular drive of a colonial-style home. A man in an Army Air Corps uniform with a fly-boy scarf thrown in for effect stepped out to greet them. *John Trumball.* Haugland had liked him since their first harrowing encounter at his snowbound hut outside of Fjellstad and was enjoying the deepening of their friendship. Trumball had just turned twenty-three, reminding Haugland how young many of the pilots had been during the war. Trumball was of medium build with brown hair and a slim mustache.

"Welcome. So glad you're here," Trumball said as Haugland helped Anna out. "How are you feeling, Jens?"

"Much better. I see the surgeon next week for one last appointment."

"And how's the weather treating you?"

Haugland laughed. "I haven't melted yet. We'll see with this uniform. I suppose you'll eventually explain the mystery about wearing it."

Trumball grinned, then turned to Anna.

"You look lovely."

"Thank you," she answered. She smiled when he took her hand and clicking his heels, bowed over it.

"Oh," she said and blanched.

"Did I do something wrong?" Trumball asked.

"Looks too Prussian to the both of us," Haugland said.

"Oops. My apologies." Trumball turned his attention to Lisel hugging Anna's dress. "And who is this young lady?"

"My daughter, Lisel," Anna said. "Our daughter."

"Welcome. My mother has a cat. Would like to see it, Lisel?"

Anna translated for her. Lisel's face brightened "Uh-uh."

"That would be very nice, John. You have a cat too, don't you, Munchin?" Anna asked.

"*Ja*." Lisel leaned her head into Anna.

"Well, we'll see if you can meet Barney. Head mouser." Trumball waved to the second car as it came in and helped to unload the rest of the group. "Please, come in."

They stepped into the small foyer of the well-appointed home with a polished wood floor furnished with oriental rugs. A stairway with a curving banister led to the upstairs. "Your parent's home?" Haugland asked Trumbull.

"Yes. I grew up here." Trumball led the group down a long hallway with doors that opened to rooms filled with antique furniture and bookcases. One room had a piano. At the end of the hall, through its screened doors, French doors opened to a view of green trees and lawn. Anna followed alongside Haugland with Lisel and when her aunt and uncle and John Trumball stopped at the screened doors, she bunched up with Haugland. Her grandmother smiled at them.

"Why don't you go out, Tore?" Elizabeth said.

Haugland pointed to himself. Me?

"Yes," Trumball replied.

With his good ear, Haugland could hear rustling on the other side. He turned to Anna, then shrugged. Trumball had been mysterious for the past week. Haugland opened the door and stepped out onto a wide covered veranda. A blast of humidity hitting him as he passed from the cool house to the outside again.

"Atten-shun."

To his surprise, a group of men in Army Air Corps uniforms snapped to attention in front of their patio chairs. They were strangers to him, but yet oddly familiar. They saluted him sharply, then stood at ease on command. Behind him Trumball came through and stood alongside Haugland.

"We're all here, except Scottie, God bless him. All here thanks to you."

Haugland was incredulous. These were the fliers he and Tommy Renvik had rescued from a frozen *fjell* near Fjellstad. The airmen beamed back at him, then suddenly broke loose *en masse* to welcome him. They mobbed him with good will and jokes, each eager to shake his good hand.

"This is Fred Squires from Lansing, Michigan," Trumball said gesturing. "Dalton Graves from Bennington, Vermont, Jimmy Ekberg from Ballard, Washington and Eddie Conway from Toronto, Canada."

Eddie. No wonder he looked familiar. He had been critically injured in the crash. Haugland had done what he could to help make the Canadian comfortable while they waited to be exported out to Scotland. He wasn't expected to make it.

Haugland shook Eddie's hand warmly, then asked how they had managed to pull this reunion off.

"Been working on it since John said you were coming," Eddie explained. Haugland thought Eddie was a bit on the thin side and wondered if he was still convalescing. "All of us guys talked about it before, but weren't sure if we could ever go back to Fjellstad, so decided to do this if you should ever come over."

"Well..." Haugland grinned at Trumball. "I guess I was lured over."

Trumball laughed. "Precisely. Now if you would be so kind to introduce your lovely wife to everyone, I think we can get this show on the road. There's more, I'm afraid."

The "more" was an elegant brunch buffet. Through the windows into the large dining room, Haugland could see tables set up with American and Norwegian flags. Out on the veranda, to his surprise, there were more guests arriving from out on the lawn. About twenty-five in all, including representatives from both the American State Department and the Norwegian Embassy. He turned to Anna and asked if she was aware of this. She whispered in Norwegian that she was aware that a brunch was to be given, but not the scope. She was as surprised as he was. Sensing his unease, she squeezed his good hand.

The brunch began with drinks on the veranda. Haugland mingled with the fliers and the other invited guests. A conversation nearby came to his attention. Jimmy Ekberg was talking about fishing in his state. When Haugland asked where that was, he got an earful about the mountains and islands of the Pacific Northwest, especially Washington. It was in some ways like Norway.

"My grandparents emigrated there at the turn of the century," Ekberg said. "In fact, a lot of Norwegians and Swedes did. Some got involved in logging, others in the fishing industry."

"What kind of fishing?" Haugland asked.

Like a proud father, Ekberg brought some pictures of salmon out of his wallet.

Other people came to talk to Haugland. Anna had stayed by him for a while, then got pulled away by her aunt to meet someone's wife. There was a man from the Norwegian Royal Information Office who had been stationed in Washington, D.C. during the war and a man who had been in Stockholm working with the British Legation which meant some sort of resistance work.

Eventually all were called inside to eat. Anna was by the linen-covered buffet tables talking to some ladies. She turned and smiled sweetly at him.

Who you? he signed to her.

Your girl, she signed back.

Marry me.

You did.

He winked at her and smiled clear to his eyes. I love you.

I know. I love you.

Haugland sat with Anna and patiently endured the speeches and toasts made on his behalf throughout the meal. He never thought of himself as a hero. Others that had done equally dangerous things and had paid with their lives, but the American fliers were so well meaning, he couldn't help but be caught up in their genuine gratitude and good humor.

Coffee and dessert were served. The atmosphere became more serious. The representatives from the Norwegian embassy and the State Department both gave short speeches, then John Trumball asked Haugland to stand. A third man who had joined them late came forward and presented Haugland with a medal on behalf of the United States Army Air Corps. For his rescue of the fliers, for valor under wartime conditions. Congratulating him, he shook Haugland's hand to the flash of a photographer's camera while the rest of the room stood up and applauded.

"Hear, hear," one of the flyers called out.

"Speech," said another.

Haugland looked to Anna, then waved everyone to sit down. "Thank you all. I'm terribly flattered and honored. You should know that there were others involved, in particular Petter Stagg, who guided the group out to our waiting boat along with my compatriot, Tommy Renvik. A local fisherman, Helmer Stagg, helped the town doctor, Dr. Grimstad, rendezvous with the fliers at sea making sure everyone had medical treatment before they were exported out. They all risked their lives." He picked up his drink and raised it. "To them I say, *Skål*."

Everyone stood up and raised their glasses. "*Skål*" reverberated around the room.

After the brunch, the guests began to disperse, some to admire a 1938 Fiat in the garage, others the formal garden on the side of the house. Anna stayed back for a tour of the house's antiques with John Trumball's mother and other ladies in the group.

Haugland gave Anna a kiss, then went outside to catch up with the fliers. As he stepped down onto the brick walkway lined with pungent-smelling boxwood hedges, a stranger in a beige linen suit appeared from the side of the house.

"*Hei*, Haugland," the man said in Norwegian, "*Vær så snill*. May I have a word?"

Instantly, the old wariness came back to Haugland. For a brief moment, his right hand hovered over his uniform pocket.

"My name's Storvik," the man said. "You don't know me, but we have a mutual friend: Tommy Renvik. Could we meet over at the greenhouse? I have something for you."

Haugland moved his hand away. "You'll have to give me more. What's Tommy's wife name? Maiden name?"

Storvik answered without hesitation. "Margit. Maiden name is Eidsvoll. Her code name was `Sister.' She was the lead secretary at the British Legation in Sweden." Storvik stepped closer. "Tommy and I trained together in Scotland for *Linge Compani,* I eventually got in with the Oslo Gang."

Haugland knew about the highly decorated sabotage group stationed in Oslo. "So, what do you have?"

"A telegram."

Haugland kept his face straight, but he felt like he had been hit in the gut. *Was it his mother? Something from the prosecutor's office in Trondheim?* Tommy wouldn't contact him unless it was serious. "All right. I'll meet with you inside, but I'll go first." They were alone on the pathway.

Haugland found the red brick greenhouse nestled among late flowering rhododendrons. It was a large glass structure that looked as ancient as the house. He stepped inside to a space that smelled of rich, damp dirt and lilies past their prime. He visually checked for all the exits. He was facing the main door when Storvik came in.

"This came last night," Storvik said.

Haugland took the telegram aside and studied it. From what he could see, it hadn't been tampered with. He had no way of knowing if Storvik had seen the contents, but trusted that he was just the deliverer. Haugland slit it open. He had a hollow feeling in his stomach. Tommy wouldn't have gotten in touch with him unless it was important.

SORRY TO BURST IN BUT ANOTHER NOTE CAME. STOP. DANGER IS REAL. STOP. CONTACT ME AS SOON AS POSSIBLE. STOP. WILL ASK FOR SECURITY ON SHIP. STOP.

He read Tommy's message about the third note, showing no emotion. When he was finished, he folded it up and asked Storvik for a match. He burned the telegram and finding a trowel, dug a hole in a planter box and buried the ashes.

"Thanks," Haugland said, switching to English—just to keep the man on his toes. "You're an American, aren't you?" Haugland asked.

"Yeah. There were many like me who got caught up in the war. I was born in Sandefjord, but immigrated with my family to New York when I was two. It wasn't difficult to go back. I spoke Norwegian in my home. When France collapsed, I made my way over to England and volunteered for the first group of operational agents to be put together. Getting there was another matter, but then you know about the Shetland Bus." He paused, then went on. "I saw Tommy not long after capitulation. My group was assigned to protect the Crown Prince on his return to Oslo. I came back to the States in August of last year, but we've been in touch. I was briefed on you before I came out with the telegram. I understand you're going back in three weeks to testify in the Rinnan trial."

"Yes." Haugland left it at that. He didn't want to talk about Rinnan.

"Do you have any other plans when you get back?" Storvik asked.

"I've got some exams at the university. I'm trying to finish my thesis. I'm about five years behind."

Storvik extended his hand. "Well, nice meeting you. The medal, by the way, is genuine. These American flyboys lived a grand life, sometimes ignoring the danger locals were put into trying to get them out of the occupied lands. Not Trumball's group. They've worked on this for months." He wished good luck to Haugland and his family, then said he'd leave first. A few moments later, Haugland was alone.

Haugland went back into the house, moving like a silent ghost as he looked for Anna. Trouble was coming and he wanted to be sure she was safe.

***

The rest of the day was hot, but pleasant. Some of the fliers went for a walk along the water, then up a lane running through some grassy fields. The sky was hazy with the heat, yet the sounds of a cardinal traveled far across the flowery meadows. The tang of Chesapeake Bay scented the light breeze. Haugland and Anna went along, with Lisel tagging behind. A few of the fliers had brought along wives and girlfriends. As they sauntered on, the women fell farther back as they chatted, giving the men some space. Walking along in their shirt sleeves, Dalton Graves and Jimmy Ekberg talked about fishing. Haugland wanted to know more about this Seattle and the salmon.

"You should come," Ekberg said. "Seattle has some fine schools. Great university. If you want to finish up or pursue a career. It's a good place. With postwar growth, it's starting to boom. And as I said, there is a large Scandinavian community."

"What about those boats? This Alaska. Boats go up from there? From Seattle?"

"Yeah, there's a large fleet."

The country dirt lane dipped and for a moment the women were out of sight. Eddie and Trumball stopped to light cigarettes, then caught up with Haugland.

"You talk to that guy from Stockholm?" Trumball asked. "He looked like a spy or something."

"You think so? Maybe he was." Haugland hesitated. Because of his work as an intelligence agent there were things he couldn't or wouldn't say. Haugland finally added. "If he did work out of Stockholm, it would have been tricky. Hush-hush. Officially, the Swedes weren't too enthusiastic about our resistance operations being planned in their city. Equally difficult, there were some in the royal family who were pro-German, even though Sweden was neutral. Things changed after Normandy."

"You ever go to Stockholm during the war?"

"Sorry, I can't answer that. But I can say that no one wanted to go back to England. It might be months before you got another chance to go to Norway. If you stayed out of trouble with the Swedes and Gestapo spies in the capital, you had it made."

Eddie and the others asked more questions, their voices in awe. Haugland tried to make it sound as boring as possible because sometimes it really was. On the flip side it was full of tension. No one could understand the tension unless you really experienced it. It could be very boring, but also very dangerous. You had to have steady nerves all the time.

"I can't imagine it." Ekberg said.

Haugland smiled softly. "Well, I can't imagine flying around in a tin can."

Trumball laughed. "You're right there. Not quite like the movies. I count myself very lucky."

Haugland nodded in agreement. He didn't have to close his eyes to remember the Cloister. "Life is very precious, yet at the same time inconsequential as a moth flying at a light. I have my life and I just want to live it. It's the little things that count."

The fliers became silent, perhaps remembering their own terror in the skies. They stopped at the bottom of the hill and looked back up. The women had come into view, their voices shimmering like music on the humid air. Anna was swinging Lisel's hand in one hand and holding a bunch of wildflowers in the other. A slight breeze tugged at her soft cotton dress caressing her hips and legs. The sun hit her hair and she was laughing.

Anna, Haugland thought, transfixed by her. He almost didn't hear Ekberg say he ought to come to Seattle.

Chapter 7

Three weeks later, Haugland and Anna left Baltimore for New York. While they waited for their boat to London, they were able to take in museums and their first baseball game as guests of Uncle Charles. Yankee Stadium was packed and Haugland was intrigued by the rules of the game. Used to playing cricket when he was in school at Cambridge, England, he found this American cousin a faster moving game. Bowlers and overs gave way to pitchers and outs. He was amused that for a time during the war, there had been only female professional baseball teams. The men had been drafted. In occupied Norway, playing sports was a little more serious, because if you played on a city or college team you were a *quisling*, a traitor. All the teams had been replaced by Nazi sports organizations. Some national sport heroes who refused to join were beaten or worse, shot.

Before they left for Norway, Haugland sent a telegram to his mother letting her know their arrival time in Oslo. It would take seven days to get to London if they avoided storms. That meant seven days cramped in a small cabin with two small children. Uncle Charles thought it intolerable and arranged for them to have a suite. In addition, a young woman returning to Norway was hired to look after the children in exchange for her passage. With such options, Haugland was beginning to look forward to this last segment of time before he would have to go to Trondheim to testify in Rinnan's trial.

Henry Oliver Rinnan.

He lay awake on the top berth in their cabin. He hadn't seen Rinnan since nearly a year ago in May when he went with a party of Milorg soldiers to capture the monster. The war in Europe on the continent had ended on May 6, 1945, but Norway's German occupying forces did not capitulate until the following day. When Rinnan tried to escape to the

Soviet Union through the mountains to Sweden, Haugland was there when he was caught.

Now Haugland would have to face Rinnan again, this time in a courtroom. He wondered if he would be able to answer the prosecutor's questions as though he were an observer of Rinnan's operations, not a victim.

Victim. The very word implied weakness, the outcome fatal. It meant prey.

"Jens?"

It was early, he knew, and he regretted waking Anna. The children were asleep below them, the baby in a bassinet attached to the lower bunk so it would not move in a storm.

"Hmmm?"

"Are you all right?" Anna spoke in Norwegian.

"*Ja,*" he answered. Anna rustled next to him, turning on her side. "You don't need more medicine, do you?"

"*Nei,* I'm fine. Go to sleep. I'm sorry I woke you."

"Are you anxious about returning home?"

"Well, there's the trial, of course, but I'd also like to get the matter of my studies underway. I'd like to finish, so I can feel like I'm amounting to something."

"You amount to something." Anna curled up against his bare back and massaged it. With a finger, she traced the long hash mark welts and puckers on his skin. Her touch was gentle. He wanted to forget what was on his back and was often ashamed to take off his shirt even around his family. Only Anna could see and touch, reminding him that she loved him no matter what.

"It's not your sister, Solveig?"

"I'm not lying here thinking of her. She doesn't keep me awake."

"I'm sorry for coming between the two of you."

"It's not you, Anna. It's the damn war. For some, it's just not over."
He examined his statement and realized that it applied to him. He

wanted it to be over, but someone or some people wanted him never to forget. Maybe not testify. *Why the threatening notes?*

Anna murmured something and Haugland asked her to repeat it. "I don't blame her, really," she went on. "How terrible to have your village razed, the men taken away and your children ripped out of your arms. I— I could understand her feelings against me..."

Haugland turned around and faced her in the dim space. A full moon outside was squeezing bright light in through the porthole and it angled up to the corner of their sleeping area. It was like Anna to say that and mean it truly, despite the fact that she had suffered, losing her first husband, Einar, to a *razzia* masterminded by Rinnan.

"My mother accepts you, so do my brothers. Solveig will take a little more time. In the meantime, forgive me for putting you through all this. We can move out of the house if you wish." He could see the features of her face and caught the frown. He changed the subject. "What did you think of that Jimmy from Ballard?"

"I thought he was nice. They all were. How kind they are to think of you and Fjellstad."

"I'm curious about this place he was talking about. I even looked it up on a map. Did you know they have Indians? They fish for salmon and herring. I read that they used to hunt whales in canoes made out of a single tree. Now that's a feat a Viking would take notice of."

Anna put a hand on his arm and rubbed it gently. "Didn't he say something about a fishing fleet?"

"He did." Haugland shared what he said. Anything to get her mind off the sticky dilemma with his sister. He had honestly thought that there wasn't going to be any problem, but he had been wrong. Because Anna was half-German, Solveig deeply resented her. There had been an ugly scene over two months ago and he had felt guilty for not protecting Anna more and for not helping his sister.

"Do you want to emigrate there?" Anna was asking. "We can go back to my grandmother's house until we're settled."

"I wondered about it, but I'd like to give things a chance at home. I want to help my mother. She went through so much during the war. She deserves to have all of us around for a little while. We'll get a place of our own. As soon as I can get enough money." He reached out and brushed her curly hair. "What about you? What do you want?"

"I'll go wherever you go. We'll manage." Anna stroked his hair. He relaxed.

"Umm." he said dreamily and chuckled when she bent into him and kissed him on his bare chest. He felt her stir, then pull her nightgown up to her chin before snuggling against him. "Ummm." Her nipples touched his skin. He kissed her and they quietly embraced and nuzzled, whispering little things into each other's ears that made them laugh softly. For a moment they paused and listened together for any stirring of children down below.

"It's safe," Anna whispered. "Kristin won't hear us in the other room, either."

"Just like guerrilla warfare. Sly."

"But much more enjoyable. Besides, weren't you in the underground?"

They both were laughing helplessly under their breaths when she pushed him over and rolled on top of him, pulling the covers over their heads.

Book 2

Bad is called good when worse happens.

~Norwegian saying

Chapter 8

Oslo, Norway, May 1946

Tore Haugland and Anna were met at the Oslo docks by Haugland's oldest brother, Lars. Once making it through customs and arranging for several boxes of clothing and food to be sent to the local branch of the American Relief for Norway, they said good-bye to their babysitter and piled into the car. While Anna sat in the back with Nils and Lisel, Haugland sat up front with his brother. Speaking in Norwegian, they visited back and forth between seats, happy with the news of all the things they had seen, but Haugland could feel his brother's tension and wondered when they could go off and talk.

"Who's at the house?"

"Alex came down with his girlfriend. Solveig's there, of course." Alex was Haugland's second eldest brother. During the war he had lived in England where he was in a fighter squadron made up of Norwegians. "Margit and Tommy are coming over later."

The car pulled out into the wide street and started through the heart of Oslo. The trees along the street sported the greens of spring. A wide variety of flowers blossomed in the parks, but they could not hide the scars of the war: the bombed-out areas caused by RAF bombs on German factories and rubble caused by the bombs of the Resistance. During the war, those Norwegians engaged in fighting the Germans and Norwegian Nazis called their secret battle "illegal work." All around the city there were examples of it.

"They still working on the railway station?" During the last days of the war, it had been blown up by the Resistance.

"Yes," answered Lars. "City Hall's getting finished and the clean-up's moving along in jerks and starts. Out in the waters, though, it's going to take years. A little girl up in Tromsø lost her life when she stepped on a mine a couple of days ago."

Haugland stiffened. He looked in the back to see if Lisel had heard the comment but his step-daughter was looking out the window.

"It's a nightmare for the shipping lanes with all the German mines still to collect."

"I'm sure it is." Haugland leaned forward to look at some of the department stores they were passing. They looked bare compared to those in New York and Baltimore. One of the stores had a mannequin dressed in the uniform of an American G.I., a reminder of their once high presence after the German capitulation here. As he looked on the corners, he saw one such example chatting to a pretty Norwegian girl. "They still here?"

"A couple of units. My American counterpart is quite nice. Had him over for dinner just the other night. Of course, things are bit spare. I doubt he realized that it was our monthly ration for meat." Lars made a left turn and began to head out of the city to the northwest. The car chugged along on its ration of gasoline. A year ago, it would have run on fuel produced by burning charcoal or wood in a furnace on the back of it. Only the Germans and members of the *Najional Samling* (NS), Norway's Nazi party, were permitted to have gasoline driven cars. Most citizens took the trains, trolleys or buses sporting *knottgenerator* furnaces on their backs.

They arrived at the wooded grounds of the Haugland home forty minutes later. Built on an open meadow in the middle of a thick pine forest, the villa wasn't quite as grand as it sounded. It was just a large home Haugland's parents had bought in 1920 to accommodate their family of four boys and a daughter. Haugland knew the house and its grounds intimately because as the youngest, he had literally grown up in it. He looked for his favorite climbing tree and smiled when he caught his mother out in her flower garden. She was an attractive white-haired woman in her early sixties. Slim and graceful, she was a lady every inch of her. As Inga Haugland waved to them as they drove up, Haugland felt a pang of tenderness mixed with anger. During the war, the Germans had confiscated the house and property, forcing his recently widowed mother to go to Bergen for the duration of the occupation. Inga had been back in the house a scant six months. When Haugland got out of the car, his mother put down her shears and ran to him.

"Oh, Tore, you're home at last!" Inga embraced him, trying not to squeeze too hard with his arm in the sling. She stepped back and gently touched his hand sticking out. It was encased in a soft leather brace. "How is your hand? Is it better?"

"*Ja*, Mamma." Carefully, he showed her how he could bend his fingers into his palm and then release them nearly flat. "Still tender, but I'm to start therapy soon. I'll pick up where I left off in the States." He kissed her on her cheek. Beyond her, Alex stood in the front doorway dressed in a tennis outfit. He nodded to Haugland and jammed a pipe into his mouth before coming out. Just like Lars.

Inga slipped out of his arms and clucked at Anna who getting out now with Nils and Lisel. Lisel slid along the car shyly, then came forward at the older woman's coaxing. Inga had told Haugland that she was very fond of Anna's daughter. "Having raised so many boys, it's nice to have a little girl again."

"Have you've been a good big sister? Did you help Momma?" Lisel nodded seriously, then giggled at the hug. "Why don't you go look for *Tante* Mari? She has a treat for you." Inga straightened up and looked at Anna. Anna wore a stylish new traveling suit, a summery blue that complemented her blonde hair and clear complexion. She held Nils close to her.

"How's that grandson of mine?" Inga asked as she pulled apart the light blanket around the baby's head. She embraced Anna and much to his satisfaction, the conversation around Haugland dissolved into women talk. He was anxious to get settled and talk to Lars.

Once the travelers were established back in their rooms and a light *middag* served where his sister was noticeably absent, Haugland changed into a pair of light pants and pullover and went outside to meet his brothers near the forest. He located Alex by the scent of his tobacco back in the woods. Alex had been enjoying Virginian tobacco ever since care packages were initiated last year from America. It was distressful having to rely on the packages, but clothing and other amenities were difficult to get. Anna's family had shipped more along with Haugland and Anna's belongings.

"Your family's looking well, Tore." Alex pointed his pipe at the house.

"*Takk*. Nils is getting big, isn't he? Of course, I'm just the father. Anna says that babies grow like this all the time. He's outgrowing clothes before he even gets them on. He just started lifting his head and trying to roll. Anna says he's very advanced for an old man of his age. Now if we could only fix his leaky plumbing."

Alex chuckled. He was six years older than Haugland, a man in his early thirties who missed most of the terror here during the war. He had experienced his own in the skies on raids over Germany. He was a tall man, lean like Haugland with the same long Nordic head, but like Lars, he was a blonde, though darker. Since the war, Alex had returned to school and was now preparing for a career as a geologist like their father.

"How did the surgery go?"

"I think it went very well. Better than I hoped for," Haugland answered.

"You have to be in that sling forever?"

"I was told six weeks, but I'm more than halfway there. I use it when I'm tired."

They talked about Haugland's trip to America and Anna's family. Alex was interested in the American flyboys who had hosted Haugland in Maryland and their stay in New York City. Alex had gone down there on leave once from Toronto, Canada where he trained as a pilot.

"How is Anna managing?" It was a quiet question that made Haugland look closer at Alex.

"She's fine. She's healthy since Nils's birth and that's all I care about."

"She's lovely, Tore. Smart. You're lucky. How did you get so fortunate?"

Haugland shrugged and grinned. "Secret agent stuff. Women were naturally attracted."

Alex rolled his eyes, then grew silent, stroking the side of his pipe.

"Which means you are happy for me," Haugland said, "but there has been trouble again with Solveig while we were gone."

Alex sighed. "Our poor sister. She's having a lot of trouble adjusting to the loss of her husband. And the children. They are more accepting of her, but having been raised in a home not of their own making…"

Haugland's heart ached for his sister. After the *razzia* on Telavåg in 1942, not only had her husband Ole been sent to the Sachsenhausen concentration camp in Germany where he died, but her two-year-old daughter and infant boy had been taken away and placed in the home of a German official and his Norwegian wife. At capitulation, the couple tried to leave the country with the children, but was stopped through the diligent work of the government. The children were returned to Solveig in that summer of freedom, 1945.

"Solveig's not...stable," Alex continued. "At best, her bitterness clouds her thinking, but Momma feels that it is the loving environment of the home that will heal her. Most days, Solveig is all right, but she can be difficult."

"You warning me?"

"It might be best you and Anna look for another place. Lars and I have talked about it—"

"Without talking to me? God, stop tiptoeing around me like I'm some emotional cripple. I'm *not.*"

"We've never meant that, Tore" Lars said coming up to them in the little clearing in the pine and birch stand. "Nor would we act without talking to you first. I'm just concerned about you and Anna and the emotional toll this could have on your marriage." Lars cleared his throat. "There is another reason as well. Security for you and your family."

The Trial. That stopped any further comment from Haugland. He stole a glance at Alex.

"I know about the threatening notes," Lars continued. "Tommy Renvik's coming up here any time. He's alarmed enough to want to provide security for you and I just might do it. We both have friends here in Milorg—"

"Wait a minute," Haugland said. "I haven't even seen the latest installment and you've got me under house detention?"

"Nei, you haven't. Nor have you or Renvik seen this." Lars took a small box out of his jacket pocket. "It came yesterday. Postmarked Trondheim. First, look at the last note."

The party's not over. The picture over the words was crude, but he got its meaning. The letter in the box was different. Like some of the other notes, the text had been patched together from words and letters cut from newspapers and magazines, but there were no suggestive pictures to go with it. It just came to the point:

"BEEN THINKING ABOUT YOU. HOW'S THE HAND?"

"This came with it." Lars reached into his pocket and took out a small pair of pliers.

Haugland let out a deep breath and stepped away. He felt the blood drain from his face. In the Cloister, one of Rinnan's thugs had pulled some of Haugland's fingernails out with pliers. Even after a year, the nails were still tender.

"The notes have got to be from someone in Rinnan's gang," Lars said. "How else the knowledge and detail? All the notes suggest the Cloister and to what happened to you there. I might add that will be part of your testimony when you go to Trondheim the next week."

Haugland didn't say anything. Distantly, he took his hand out of the sling and gently removed the brace. He looked at it. Red scars ran down from his fingers into the palm where stitches had been recently removed. The surgeons in Baltimore had used some radical new techniques that released the tendons that had held his fingers in a cup-like position, like a rounded garden rake. Some grafting onto the tendons brought back strength and mobility to the crippled fingers. A year and a half after they had been smashed in the Cloister, Haugland had use of his left hand back.

"Where's Sorting?" Haugland asked.

"I thought you might ask. I had a friend look into that right after Tommy alerted me to the first note," Lars answered. "He's in jail along with the others. Doesn't have any outside contact."

"Are you sure?"

"Reasonably. I had him checked. He's pretty much of a loner. Keeps himself separate from most of those on trial with Rinnan."

"Does he have a lawyer?"

"Someone has been assigned to him."

"Check him out." Haugland felt himself coming under control, old instincts kicking in.

"You're convinced Sorting did this?" Lars asked.

"Berger Strom and two of the others that interrogated me are dead. That leaves just Rinnan and Sorting."

"I thought Sorting didn't participate in the actual sessions."

"That's right, but he was there as sympathizer, a go-between."

Next to Haugland, Alex cleared his throat and suddenly got busy lighting his pipe. His eyes avoided the uncovered hand.

Haugland flashed his eyes at Alex. "That tobacco choking you?"

"*Nei*, but—"

"You can go on back, Alex. You don't need to hear this." Very carefully, Haugland slipped the brace back on and snapped it closed.

"I just wanted to know what I can do for you, brother, that's all. I have friends too that can help. Especially if you should have to move."

"*Takk.*" Haugland looked around the forest and out at the back of the house. He sighed. "Really don't want to move Anna and the kids. This is a good place for Lisel."

"What about when you're in Trondheim for the trial, Tore?" Lars wondered.

"They'll go with me and stay with Kjell in the city. His daughter Kitty is coming to be with them."

"Must you take them?"

"Anna insists that she be near me. I want her to be with me, too. Kjell's friends, the Nissens, have a home just outside of town. It's a lovely, country-like place. Anna will be happy there."

Lars shrugged. "If you say so. I'm still going to have an escort put together for you. Renvik will oversee it." Out in the front of the house, a car pulled up by the stone fence. "That must be him now. After you guys catch up, we'll talk some more."

Haugland shook his head in exasperation, but knew that he would have to agree—for Anna's sake.

Chapter 9

In the small fishing village of Fjellstad out on the west coast of Central Norway, Kjell Arneson gave his tie one last tug then stepped away from the mirror and went into the kitchen.

It'll have to do. The tie was the only new piece of clothing he'd owned in the last five years. He went to the sink and filled a glass with water.

Outside the second story apartment window, he could see the stone facade of the sea wall below and beyond the boats riding high in the water in the little harbor. He wondered if he would ever get over the Germans blowing up the boats, including his old fishing boat, the *Otta,* and later executing some of the village's leaders in retaliation for harboring a spy in their village. Remembering those days of terror and sacrifice still caused his heart to pick up a beat. Now, a year and a half later, it haunted him. At least the centuries-old warehouse of the Arneson family that lay alongside the long wharf had not been destroyed. Other families had not been so lucky. It was painful to see the remains of some of the boats still anchored out in the water.

At forty-six, Kjell had spent all of his growing years here in Fjellstad. The worst years were when his wife, Kristine, died of cancer and left him with their two young daughters and the brutal five-year occupation of Norway.

Kjell took a sip and sighed. *Hard, hard years.* By all rights he should be dead, shot by the Germans for aiding the young agent, Jens Hansen. Providence had intervened in the most unexpected way—the most hated person in the village, the young German widow Anna Fromme, turned out to be an ally. During the district-wide search for him, Anna hid him and another fisherman. She was the reason he and many others lived.

"Humpf," Kjell said out loud. And now she was married to that very agent. *I didn't see that coming*, he chuckled. "You rascal, Jens." Everyone still called the agent "Jens Hansen," even though a few had learned his real name after the war—Tore Haugland.

"That you, Kjell?"

"In the kitchen, Ella. How much time do we have?"

"We need to be down for the christening in fifteen minutes."

"I'll be out in a minute."

Thanks to the generosity of strangers in America, he was the first in his village to have his boat replaced. Even though he brought on Helmer Stagg, a local fisherman in his late twenties, as a partner and invited others to fish with him, he felt guilty sometimes. Not just over the new boat, but for what had happened to his village.

It's what you know about the razzia that attacked Fjellstad. It was Rika, his beautiful, twenty year-old patriotic daughter who caused the *razzia* to happen.

"Kjell?"

Ella's voice broke the shadows of his mind. Her pretty light brown hair and bright turquoise eyes belied a backbone of strength and resolve. During the war years, she had continued to hold onto the only *konditori* in the area, making the best pasteries in the area despite rationing. Widowed early on in the occupation, she also held the community together. Secretly, she worked on committees that found ways to resist the Germans and the Norwegian Nazis that plagued their isolated region. Kjell had known her many years and accepted her friendship as a matter of course. It came as a surprise at war's end to discover that he loved this strong-willed woman very much.

"Pastor Helvig is here. We are ready to begin."

Kjell tugged at his dark Sunday jacket that hung off his thin shoulders—food was still rationed a year after war's end—then gave in without much of a protest when Ella came and adjusted his collar.

"There..." She looked nice herself in a new dress or maybe one worked over. She was very clever with the needle. She glowed these days. Kjell beamed, knowing that he was to blame. It made him feel young again and full of hope. Kjell reached over and kissed her on her cheek. "I guess it's now or never. I wish Jens was here, though."

"So do I." For the people of Fjellstad, Tore Haugland would always be Jens. It had been his code name while he lived among them and people just continued to use it. His presence here, after all, was a shared memory, a history of their place during a terrible time and they wanted never to forget.

"Do you remember when Jens jumped into the freezing water to rescue that little daughter of Anna Fromme's?"

"I remember when Jens first showed me his cache of arms..."

"I'll never forget when Jens..."

"Oh, I got a postcard from him," Kjell said. "From America." Kjell took the card of out of his pocket. On the front was a picture of a crab boat in the Chesapeake Bay. On the back Haugland wrote:

Saw several types of boats on waters here. Crab and

rockfish typical catches. What do you know about

Seattle? Home soon. Anna and kids well.

Hilsen, JENS.

"Does he know about the boat?"

"I didn't get a chance to tell him. It came sooner than we both expected. I'm going to take a picture and develop it as soon as possible so I can show it to him when he comes to Trondheim."

"He always talks about boats. When is he going to finish school?"

Kjell shrugged. He didn't know. What he did know and appreciated was the depth of his young friend's restlessness, a condition the local doctor, Hans Grimstad, said was just being recognized as a medical condition, a response to the difficult and stressful lives many had gone through during the war. Jens's life as an agent certainly had been stress-ful, but his experiences in Rinnan's Cloister in Trondheim may have made him even more vulnerable to mood swings and spells of unquiet.

Most of his countrymen, Kjell knew, just thought that you forgot what happened to you and moved on. You shouldn't be dwelling on the past. But tell that to those who had been in the concentration camps at Grini and Falstad or the 10,000 men who served on boats on the deadly runs to Murmansk and other convoys. They had difficulties in adjusting. Sometimes the mind didn't want to forget.

"Maybe after the trial," Kjell said. "The trial is in his thoughts a lot and I know he would like to get it past him so he can go on with his life."

He smiled at her. He wanted to get his past behind him. Rika was lost. While he hadn't asked her yet, Ella was going to be part of his future. That is why he wanted the Lutheran pastor to bless his new boat and invite his friends and neighbors to the christening. After that, he would prepare for his trip to Trondheim with his surviving daughter, Kitty, and give support to his former comrade and friend who was like a son.

Chapter 10

"Will that be all, *Herr* Professor?" the housekeeper asked.

"*Ja. Takk.*" He waited until the young woman was out of the room and going down the back stairs, then turned to the large full-length oval mirror standing on the bedroom floor.

At fifty, Aage Pilskog was a man of cultured tastes: he enjoyed good music, beautiful women, aquavit, and the occasional glass of French wine. His lower middle-class background didn't keep him back from improving himself and attending the technical Institute in Trondheim with further study at the Oslo University and the Colorado School of Mines in the United States. His success led to buying this property. He prided himself in his international achievements, but remained a proud, patriotic Norwegian. He publicly eschewed the politics of the NS when they rose in the 1930s, but privately he agreed with their emphasis on race purity and Norwegians first.

As he stood in front of the mirror, Aage Pilskog brushed back his hair with manicured hands and commended himself for having come through the long war and occupation largely unscathed. He had cooperated with the Germans, but it was necessary to keep the mines running for the sake of the nation. People need to work. He also had to keep his wife Elisabet pleased. Marrying into a well-off family before the war meant keeping up appearances. They were discreet, of course, when so many suffered under the strict wartime rationing, but they had access to certain food items that made life more tolerable. They were able to keep a maidservant in Oslo who had a way with the needle, so Elisabet's clothing always looked smart. When he was asked to manage one of the German-controlled mines up near his boyhood home, he left his position in the geology department at Oslo University. They took their teenage daughter and the maid, settling into a comfortable house on the company grounds. If he was invited to gatherings of German Wehrmacht officers stationed nearby, he attended only to protect his family.

At the mine, Pilskog was to see that production was kept at a high level. Pyrite and copper were needed for war production in Germany. But it also meant walking a fine line protecting Norwegian employees at the mine and dealing with efforts by the Resistance to sabotage mine operations. The German response was harsh. Sometime innocent people got hurt or worse. Pilskog didn't like to think about that.

"Aage, dear. Are you ready?"

Pilskog turned around and looked at his wife standing in the door. Elisabet was in her early forties, but the occupation had not worn her down. She was fashionably dressed in a blue linen suit and real silk stocking for her trip to Oslo. A small hat with pheasant feather was perched on her dark hair.

"*Ja, ja.* I'll get you to the train at Melhus on time."

"Are you sure you can't come now?"

"*Ja.* I have a few things to finish up here. It will take a couple of days." He came over and gave her a kiss on her lips. "Our daughter is a sturdy young lady. She will be in good hands at the best hospital in Oslo when the baby comes." Their daughter was expecting their first grandchild in less than a week.

Elisabet put on her blue kid gloves and gently lowered the half veil over the end of the hat. "I'll be downstairs. My suitcases are ready to go. Our new housekeeper has seen to that."

After Elisabet left, Pilskog went over to the tall window that looked back onto the orchard. Beyond the trees and the barn, forested hills rose up to the west. Higher still was the rugged *fjell* that wove in and out like fingers along the coast. Pilskog sighed. The place had always given him peace, but it had been occupied by the Germans as a retreat during the war. Pilskog and his family had just settled back in ten months ago.

Pilskog frowned. The prospect of being a grandparent was something to look forward to, but he was finding war's end trying on the family finances, especially after the mine had been returned to the former owner. Pilskog was no longer manager. He hoped his research, teaching, and his father-in-law would see them through—if the "Legal Purge," as the judicial accounting of crimes committed during the war was called, didn't expose him. He hadn't been forthcoming with Elisabet about the fines that could be levied on him for working with the Germans.

A door closed downstairs, making Pilskog turn away from the window. On the bed was the day's newspaper. As they had been reporting for the past month, headlines and articles focused on the Rinnan trial in Trondheim. Though he had nothing to do with Rinnan and his monstrous gang, Pilskog discovered that he knew someone who was going to testify at the trial. That person might know about his past in the early days of the occupation in Olso. He wondered if he would have to do something about that.

Chapter 11

At the Haugland family home, Tommy Renvik was all smiles when he came up to shake Haugland's hand at the garden gate. He knew that it was only for show for the wives and family. Tommy was worried, but hid it well. "How's the world traveler?" he asked in Norwegian, then switched to English. "Everything OK?"

Haugland smiled. "Fine," he said in English. They had pretty much spent the war talking in English because of their time and training in England. Tommy always said he knew it as well as Norwegian since one of his grandfathers had come from the Shetland Islands.

Margit Renvik came forward next and gave Haugland a hug before taking Anna's hand warmly and looking down at Lisel. "Look at you, Lisel," Margit said. "How you've grown. Are you taking good care of your little brother?" Lisel went behind Anna's skirt until Margit showed her a present, a brightly-painted wooden horse.

"What do you say, Lisel?" Haugland asked.

"*Tusen takk, Tante* Margit."

"*Vaer så god.*"

Tommy watched with his hands in his pockets as Haugland visited with the women and children. His friend's ease with family matters amazed him. *Like nothing is going on,* he thought. Eventually though, Haugland excused himself and said he wanted to talk with Tommy. "See you in a bit," he said to Lars. Tommy thought he had timed it like a professional.

Inside the study built by his geology professor father, Haugland poured a couple glasses of whiskey and caught up with his friend of long standing. It was a restful space that looked out over the patio and the vibrant flower beds through large French doors. The walls were covered with shelves of books and an extraordinary collection of rocks and minerals. On a small cabinet there were pictures of the Haugland family when the children were younger and a fine picture of the son who was lost— Per—who had been shot before a firing squad back in 1942. Along with his father, Per had helped to arrange the collection of geological finds. Tommy paused to look at a picture of a group of men on skis.

"That you?"

"*Ja*. I was on the University of Oslo varsity cross-country team."

"Huh. I knew you were on the soccer team. Didn't know this."

"It got disbanded pretty quickly when the Germans showed up."

Tommy faced him. "You look rested, Scarlett." An old nickname for Haugland from the war.

"I should hope so. I was waited on hand and foot while over there, though a hospital stay isn't my idea of a good time. Still, it went well." He grinned at his friend. "I can wiggle my fingers."

Tommy skoaled him with his glass. "Bravo. That's great. How about Anna? What's her family like?"

"They're very nice. Welcomed me warmly. I was surprised by how well-off they were, but very nice."

Tommy took a drink. Haugland followed suit. "And our flyers?" Tommy asked.

"All in good health and eternally grateful."

"What's Maryland like? That's where Anna is from, right? Is it crowded with cities?"

"The Eastern Shore, as they call it, is actually very rural. Has a sleepy country charm with farms and quaint villages from their colonial past. It felt untouched by the war. I'm not sure that it's someplace that I would like to live. Not mountainous enough for me and full of mosquitoes. Fishing's superb, however. They have an excellent blue crab."

Tommy shook his head. "You and your fish."

"Never fear, it's just a pipe dream. Not sure I could do all the physical stuff anyway."

Tommy nodded in understanding. The damage to Haugland's back. And his hand.

They talked quietly for a while, content to be reunited again. Their wartime experiences together made them close. They found that they could be apart for some period of time and still resume their friendship where the last conversation dropped off. There was no pretension. They spoke freely to each other at all times. During the war, Kjell Arneson had once told Tommy it was what true freedom was all about: to be able to speak freely without the fear that someone would turn you in for saying the wrong thing. Haugland and Tommy figured that they had accomplished that long ago.

On one of the wingback chairs there was an opened newspaper. Tommy brushed it aside to sit down, then saw the headlines and blanched. Across the front page was the latest news out of Trondheim about the trial. All its drama, all its gruesome atrocities were there as more evidence was presented against one of the worst monsters of the war, Henry Oliver Rinnan. It seemed to both fascinate and repel Norwegians that a native son such as Rinnan could collaborate with the Germans and be as vicious as they were. Tommy tried to hide the paper from Haugland, then blushed with embarrassment when he caught his friend looking at him.

"It's impossible to ignore, Tommy," Haugland said, "so why bother to hide it?"

Tommy sputtered something, then asked when he was leaving for Trondheim.

"I leave next week. In the meantime, I thought I'd catch up with some old friends."

Tommy looked nonplussed. "Haugland, you're not taking those notes very seriously."

"I take them very seriously. I just can't let the trial rule my life. I'm only concerned about Anna and the children. That's why I want them to stay here. I think they'll be safer."

"I have some old friends," Tommy said. "They've spent the last six months weaseling out *quislings*, those little Nazi bastards who pretended to be such great patriots during the war. My friends have had their ears to the ground for months. I think they should watch out for you and your family."

Tommy sensed Haugland wanted to decline, but was glad common sense took hold.

"All right, how soon?" Haugland asked.

"Give me twenty-four hours. It'll be done quietly so not to alarm Anna and your mother.

They can also watch out for any new notes and try to trace them."

"If you get any more pliers, put them in Alex's tool box." Haugland would not be moved by the threats.

Chapter 12

The door clanked open and Odd Sorting shuffled into his cell. Someone higher up in the prison administration had decided he could share a cell with one of the other *Rinnan Baden* members on trial, Gunnar Skele. Sorting didn't know him all that well, but he had seen Skele a couple of times in the Cloister at Johannvaniens 64. He knew Skele had been involved in the abduction and murders of a couple of resistance workers and a British flier who had been captured behind the lines. Might have infiltrated some of the black market groups. In the two weeks they had been cellmates, they didn't talk much about what they did during the war. They talked about breaking out.

The trial had been going on since last month. Sorting had already heard the charges against him. He was surprised, however, to hear the prosecutor say that more than a hundred patriots had been killed by Rinnan and his gang. He had nothing to do with that, but he *had* been there during interrogation sessions.

Sorting knew that qualified him for the mess he was in. He would occasionally rough up a prisoner, but didn't take part in torture. He was more useful as sympathetic friend who could negotiate for anything leading to the alleviation of pain. He used to enjoy doing that, but now he didn't want anything to do with Rinnan and the others at all and when he thought why, he felt sick. That bastard Jens Hansen had been right. Sorting *had* lost the one person he cared about: lovely Freyda Olsen.

"How sweet you were, Freyda," Sorting said out loud as he settled down on the lower bunk's dank mattress. They had met during the first days of the occupation and stayed together to war's end. Sorting rubbed his scratchy face. He hated Hansen with a passion, blaming him for what happened to Freyda, but he also feared the former agent for what he could say at the trial. Hansen could place Sorting in Fjellstad trying to infiltrate the local resistance group; place Sorting in the Cloister as Rinnan tortured Hansen, forcing Hansen to reveal the coordinates of the incoming Shetland Bus. For that, Sorting could face a life sentence at hard labor with no parole. That's why he had been sending notes, trying to scare Hansen off. Sorting was so deep in thought that when the door to the cell opened and Skele came in, he startled.

"Hey, Sorting! Why so jittery?"

"I'm not jittery," he growled. He picked up a wash cloth and hung it over the metal end of his bunkbed.

"Good. I got that information that you wanted. My stoolie just slipped it to me while I was getting my hair cut." The big hairy brute scratched his arm and handed over a packet that looked like a rolled up cigarette.

"*Takk.*" Sorting was sitting up now. When he unrolled it, he found several layers of toilet paper with handwriting.

"Pretty clever, huh?"

Sorting mumbled, "This come from the court records?"

"*Ja.*"

Sorting read:

"The subject you are seeking. Tore Haugland, returned to Oslo today with his family. He is married and has two small children. Has apparently been out of country."

Haugland. Sorting was trying to get used to the name. In Fjellstad, the agent had been known as Jens Hansen. It took some work to get some official information on him, gleaned in part from the list of witnesses who were going to testify, but Sorting had known his true name now for a while. "What does 'apparently' mean here? I thought I had you send out a package for me."

"*Ja,* sure. My source had it delivered to that official in the Defense Department five days ago. His brother, wasn't it? He confirmed it. Your man's been out of the country."

When Sorting heard that, he panicked. He didn't want Haugland to ever get away to where he couldn't be reached. "Your source said he was married. Is that absolutely correct? He's been working overtime if he has two kids already. Last time I saw him was in May of last year. He wasn't in the best of health as I recall. Unless he met some wench when he was working as an agent..."

"Should say on one of those sheets," Skele said. "I asked my contact to find out everything he could. There's an Oslo phone number. I'm taking you seriously on your offer—Sorting. I do this and we get out together."

Sorting separated the sheets and found more writing on the next layer.

Spouse: Anna Howard Fromme

Children: Lisel Fromme, adopted, age 6 Nils, age 4 mos.

Sorting let out a big gasp that made Skele jump.

"What the Devil?" the man spat.

"Surprise, that's all." Sorting chuckled and thought of dirty jokes. "My, the politics of war." He could see Anna Fromme. He had seen her enough in Fjellstad where he had been doing undercover work for Rinnan. Slim and golden, a lovely woman in every way. She had been a widow then, a German despised by all in the village except for a few *quislings*. A beautiful widow. Sorting laughed again, a high nervous laugh. He had entertained enough thoughts of screwing her on his own, but it seemed that Jens Hansen had beat him to it.

How did he manage that? Everyone thought Hansen was some deaf mute. Had the woman known about his secret background? Sorting continued to shake his head and laugh. Suddenly he stopped, a deep sadness falling over him. As he envisioned the ill-matched lovers tangled in an erotic position, he knew that he had no such luck. Freyda was dead. Near the end of the war, she had vacillated and had begun to see people who could ease her out of involvement with *Rinnan Baden*. Rinnan had been furious and had her beaten. Sorting had dissuaded him, he had thought, from killing her. Apparently when they had fled for safety toward the Soviet Union at the capitulation of German forces in Norway, Rinnan—not pleased with Sorting's interference or lack of control over her—personally killed Freyda. Sorting only recently learned of this betrayal

Freyda, he thought. It was Haugland's fault. Rinnan had never forgiven Sorting for letting the critically injured agent cheat him out of valuable information by playing a deadly mental game. The co-ordinates were wrong. The Shetland Bus had been warned off by some code Haugland had given them to transmit. Despite all of Sorting's work over the months in Fjellstad, they never did find the main cache of arms. When Haugland was presumed dead all the major details about his operation went with him. Rinnan used to reprimand Sorting for that. When Freyda got careless, Rinnan's displeasure with him exploded.

Sorting looked at the names on the paper, staring at that of Anna and the little boy. So Haugland had a son.

"This the guy who's going to testify against you? That's how my contact got his information."

Sorting rolled the toilet paper back up. "*Ja.* That's why I want him out of the way." Sorting looked at Skele. "So when do we get out?"

"I'm working on it. We don't have much time. Frankly, I'm not sure if we can chance getting another note out. We think we may be watched."

Chapter 13

Haugland's eyes snapped open in the dark. Cocking his head toward the direction of the sound he had thought he heard, he listened long and hard. The house was utterly still and the room deep in inky shadows. Next to him, Anna was sound sleep on her side, her cotton nightie brushing against his bare legs. All a normal and perfectly safe feeling, but the war years had trained him to sleep lightly and something had disturbed him. Carefully, he moved away from her and slipped out of bed.

From a chair, he removed a pullover and put it on over his boxer shorts. He stood still for a moment and listened again. It was frustrating to have to check and recheck. Before his beating, his hearing had been excellent as required for an agent in the field, but now, his left ear played tricks on him. Sometimes he could almost hear normally, it seemed, but often any input was wiped out by the slightest background noise, so it was practically useless. His instincts weren't. His sixth sense for survival was still in high gear and it told him that something was wrong. Near the door, he quietly reached into a drawer and took out a flashlight and his Colt.38. He opened the door to the hallway and treaded lightly onto the strip of oriental carpeting that made a path around the U-shaped bannister built around the home's wide stairs and landing to the upper floor. On all sides there were bedrooms where guests and his sister slept. At the end of the hall on the left was his mother's. He opened the door nearest to their room and looked in on Lisel and Nils. Both were asleep and undisturbed.

Downstairs, Haugland went silently from room to room without using the flashlight, creeping through the large *stue* or living space and into the kitchen and dining room. Nothing unusual. He returned to the hall that led out to the front door and worked his way back to the study by the garden. At the French doors, there was a faint light from a new moon caressing the glass panes. Haugland listened. He heard nothing, but his eyes caught an irregularity with the doors and going over, he discovered that they had opened and shut, but not completely. Moving as softly as smoke, he gently opened the door and looked out.

The pine forest beyond the grounds was dark and impenetrable. There was no wind, no call of night animals. He cocked his head again, straining, then heard a sound to his right. Easing back the hammer on his gun, he went forward stealthily, then stopped. A cat emerged from a bush close to the house and came out to serenade him. It was Tomsin, his mother's cat.

Disgusted, Haugland drew back and returned to the door to the study. At the patio's edge, he turned the flashlight on and shined it on the flagstones. There in the light's yellow pool, he found two partial prints. Looking closer, he saw that they had been made by wet boots, probably a man's. He straightened up and pushing the doors into the room, looked for signs inside on the wood floor, but found none. They only appeared to be outside going *in*. He knelt down and looked closer for any depressions in the Oriental rug in the center of the study, but he could only see his own feet in passing. Further investigation in the hallway revealed nothing more. It was as though a ghost had come and drifted into the house, dissipating through the roof. He went back and closed the door. He was positive that something had been moving in the house, probably outside his door upstairs, but whatever it was, it was gone.

Upstairs, he paused outside the children's door, then on impulse went in. Lisel was still sleeping in the same position he had seen her last, her mouth slightly open as she slept. He pulled the summer blankets higher up on her, then gave her a kiss. Next he checked on Nils in his crib, remembering that he had not actually seen him the first time he had looked in. Shining the light near the baby's face, Haugland was relieved to see that he was all right. The sweet blonde face was quiet, his thumb stuck into his mouth and from time to time he sucked as he slept on his stomach with his little fanny sticking up into the air. Haugland chuckled and wondered if the position was normal. He reached over and tried to unplug the thumb and discovered that the hand was grasping something.

Haugland put a hand on his tightening chest. The baby's little fingers were gripping tightly onto what appeared to be a piece of newsprint. Gently, Haugland unrolled the fingers and slipped the paper out. It had been folded several times. It opened out into an eight by nine inch scrap. On one side there was text from several news items. On the other side—

Haugland gasped. The noise in the house had been real. As he turned the paper around, he stared into a newswire photo of a scene from the Cloister. It had only been published yesterday, but it was old news to him. He did not look at the men demonstrating some torture method for the press. He only saw the poster of the skeleton on the wall. Above its bony frame in vaguely familiar printing were the words:

"I'M COMING."

Stepping away, Haugland's face turned warm. He felt lightheaded. He had to get out and think. The study door had been left open. He had heard a sound. He held himself in check for just a moment more to look for any signs of disturbance, but found none. He went out into the hall. Taking a big breath, he leaned his head against the wall.

This isn't happening. It isn't real. He felt the adrenaline rush of danger once again and the desire to flee and hide himself. Only he couldn't do that now. He had Anna and the children. And the war was over.

To his left, the door to his mother's room opened. "Tore?" Ingrid whispered. "Is everything all right"

"*Ja,* Mamma," Haugland answered, working hard to keep his voice calm. The note felt like a hot coal in his hand.

"You're not ill, are you?"

"*Nei,* Mamma. I'm fine. I was only checking on the children. Go back to bed."

"*God natt.*" Ingrid closed the door leaving the upstairs deserted.

Down the hall to the right, a light in his sister's room went on. Since his arrival here, Haugland had only seen her once. She had avoided him all day, coming out only to get something in the kitchen. When Haugland asked after her, Solveig hissed and said she couldn't stand being around his German slut. "Why is she here and not my husband, Ole?" Solveig left the kitchen leaving him speechless and sad, wishing there was something he could do to restore their once harmonious relationship.

Now, out in the hallway, Haugland watched the shadows of her feet under the door walk across the floor as Solveig paced in her room. He felt no emotion when she opened the door and found him in the hall.

"Tore. What are you doing out here with a flashlight?" Her voice was normal, quite sane.

"Just checking on the kids. *God natt.*"

"Is everything all right?"

"*Ja, takk.*" He didn't know why he said that. But he did and even smiled at her. "How are your children?"

"Asleep."

"Bjarne is a fine boy. Tine so sweet..."

Solveig smiled wistfully. For a moment, her smile lit her eyes and made her weary face attractive again. She had been a beautiful young woman with light brown hair and fine, rosy complexion, but the war years had strained her face. She looked older. Her face suddenly filled with remorse. "Tore...I'm sorry for what I said."

"I know you are. I love you, Solveig. *God natt.*" He sighed. Making sure the gun was hidden, he went back into his room. He kept the door slightly ajar and watched her in the dim hall. She stayed near her room and appeared to be listening in his direction. After what seemed a long time, she closed the door. Haugland stared at the door long after the glow under it had disappeared.

Chapter 14

The sanctuary of Oslo's Deaf Church was deserted when Haugland stepped in. He made his way down to the front of the altar where a large, painted image of Christ looked down on him from the wall. He nodded at it out of habit and then went over to the side door that would take him down to the church offices. He found the room he wanted a few moments later. A young woman was at the typewriter, but she did not hear Haugland come into the room nor did she look up until he slapped the desk where she was working.

"Oh, *Go' dag,*" she said in a flat voice.

"*God dag,*" he answered in a loud voice. "Is CBS in?" He signed while he talked to her and she beamed.

Ja, she signed back. She got up and returned with a middle-aged cleric with wire rimmed glasses. Conrad Bonnevie-Svendsen, minister to the deaf. He smiled when he saw Haugland and came over to embrace him.

"Tore, how wonderful. I was worried that you had become so busy that we wouldn't be seeing much of you these days. How is your family? And how was the trip?"

Haugland answered fine on both counts, but he could tell the pastor was not fooled. Conrad invited him into his office where he offered Haugland a cup of coffee.

"*Takk.*" Haugland accepted the offer knowing it was an item still rationed in Norway. Such a contrast to his recent experience in America where everything was plentiful. He stood for a moment and studied the collection of photos on the wall, most of them dealing with Conrad's involvement with the deaf in Norway.

Since the mid-1930's, Conrad Bonnevie-Svendsen had been the leading priest for the deaf in Norway. This was their special church in

Oslo. A man in his late forties, the priest had been a Haugland family friend of long standing because Haugland's *Onkel* Kris had been deaf. What was not common knowledge was that during the war, Conrad had been a top leader in *Sivorg*, the civilian branch of the Resistance and that was where he and Haugland had special interests.

"Sit. Sit. Tell me about your hand. Your mother said that things went well."

Haugland gingerly flexed his fingers still encased in the half glove. "Getting better every day. Still have to arrange some therapy sessions with a doctor here, but I'm happy."

"And Anna? The children? You have a little boy."

While Conrad poured the coffee, Haugland obliged him, telling about some of their adventures in America, describing the countryside and weather.

Conrad sat down at his desk with his cup. "I hope to go to California someday to visit the John Tracy Clinic there." When Haugland looked at him blankly, Conrad added. "It's a famous clinic started by the American actor Spencer Tracy. His son is deaf."

"Ah."

"And yourself?" Conrad went on. "You haven't talked about yourself, Tore. I've been your confessor too long not to know that you have come for some reason other than church. You're such a poor believer."

Haugland made a harrumphing noise in his throat. During the war, his mother thought he had been killed and for security reasons he was not allowed to see her, but Conrad was different. Haugland often sought him out, catching up on news about his family and talking about things that troubled him. It was a dangerous life, but Haugland admired Conrad for his dedication as he traveled around the country visiting his deaf parishioners and holding secret meetings on the side until January of '45 when the Gestapo caught wind of him. After that, Conrad had to flee to Sweden for the remainder of the war.

"I'm glad to hear about the hand," Conrad said, "but what about the other injuries? What do the doctors say?"

To the point, Haugland thought. "My back has healed pretty much. I'm working on ways to strengthen it."

"And your hearing problem?"

"I'm waiting for the eardrum to heal. I was originally told six months to a year, but it seems to be taking its time. I'm hoping the damage isn't permanent."

"Tore... I'm sorry. Truly. There is nothing? Ringing in the ear?"

"Oh, there is something. My hearing comes and goes, sometimes very clear, other times like someone muttering in a tin can." Fortunately, no ringing in the ear." He looked away and scowled.

"Ah," CBS leaned back and took a sip of his coffee. "Have you considered a hearing aid? They are quite good these days."

"If I wore a hearing aid, its cord and battery would stick out like a sore thumb. For now, I'm relying on my skills at lip-reading. I found it very handy when I was assigned to Fjellstad."

When CBS cocked his head at Haugland, Haugland laughed. "Seriously. You forget that my *Onkel* Kris not only signed, but lip read."

"*Ja*. He was one of the first students at the Deaf School years ago."

"*Onkel* Kris gave me pointers on lip-reading when I was a little boy. We made up a game using it. I was to watch the lips of the villagers in Telavåg, then sign to him what they are saying. I was quite good."

"So you believe that a hearing aid would be so obvious. A weakness. Better not to let anyone know."

Haugland set his mouth. "Especially at this time. Someone has been stalking me and my family."

"*Nei*." Conrad got up and closed the office door.

He has the old wartime wariness. Haugland knew there was no hearing staff in the building at the present.

"God keep you. Why?"

"The trial, most likely." Haugland reached into his pants pocket and brought out the clipping that had been clenched in Nils' little fist. "I found this in my little son's hand last night."

Conrad adjusted his glasses for a better look, then gasped. "This is terrible. Who would do this?"

"Someone who doesn't want me testifying at the war crimes trial of Rinnan and his gang."

Conrad leaned forward. "You suspect someone with Rinnan who is working from the outside?"

"*Ja*, for sure."

The horror on Conrad's face assured Haugland that he was taking the threat seriously. "Have you asked for security?"

"Lars is arranging something. I *am* worried for Anna and our children. I'd be a fool not to. This was too close. I checked around the house this morning for the newspaper that the photo was published in, but our paper is intact. The clipping was introduced from outside."

Haugland stood up and paced restlessly, running his fingers through his hair. "With the criminal trials in Germany, I accept there is intrigue around them, but I've been naive to think that it's not going on here as well."

Conrad agreed. "It's an uncomfortable business, but these trials of *quislings* and their ilk in our country are necessary. I worry, though, that after a year the public is tiring of it all, except for the Rinnan trial. It's becoming harder to accept that there are still loose elements about that have not come to trial and probably never will."

Haugland stopped pacing. His face was grim. "Rinnan must be prosecuted for what he has done. Testimony so far, I've been informed, has been taken from a number of people who were negative agents for Rinnan or who had suffered at the hands of Rinnan, such as my friends, the Haraldsens. Other testimony has come from some of Rinnan's own underlings in hopes of lighter sentences. My testimony is different. I not only knew his operations, but I am one of the few to come out alive from the Cloister. I was a victim myself."

Haugland stiffened when he said the word "victim." It hurt him that some in his organization had not survived when he had.

"How much does Anna know about the threats?"

"I haven't told her."

Conrad cleared his throat, showing his disapproval. "Why?"

"I don't want her to worry and in particular, to become involved with the trial's daily trauma. It's because I've wanted to protect her from the truth about her first husband, Einar, and what happened to him at the Cloister."

The pastor shook his head. "I can understand that. I never heard of anything so cruel."

Haugland looked at his bad hand. Out of old habit he opened and closed it to test its strength. "Anna doesn't know what had happened to Einar. She's always hoped that after the war his body would be located like so many others and given proper burial. I finally had to tell her that he had been buried at sea. What I haven't told her was that Einar died in the Cloister and in order to dispose of him, they chopped him up into pieces and then took him out into the *Trondheimsleia* in a box and threw him overboard." Haugland picked up his coffee cup and sipped some of the brew as an image formed in his head:

The Cloister. Himself lying on the cold floor of the Cloister's laundry room, chained one-handed to the sink. Bloodied and delirious. Cigarette smoke blowing in his face. Odd Sorting, hovering, trying to be a friend. And the words, "Chopped up like cord wood" because Einar wouldn't fit into the coffin.

Haugland looked at his hand around the cup. It was shaking.

"Tore?"

"I'm all right. I sometimes see things. The Cloister. Dead companions. Just going to take some time."

"You have my prayers."

"I know. And my back." He smiled at Conrad. "I just don't want Anna to know. When I said I would go and give testimony for this trial last year, I asked one of the prosecutors to suppress the information about Einar in exchange."

"Are you worried it will get out?"

"*Ja*. Rinnan is supposed to have done something similar to three other people near the end of the war, one of them an XU intelligence agent. So it could come out that way."

"Are you concerned for Anna or yourself?"

Haugland frowned. Conrad was acting more like a devil's advocate and it was making Haugland uncomfortable, but he was also touching on a truth. Lately, Haugland had been thinking of Einar. Knowing how Einar died would hurt Anna so much, but would knowing also hurt their marriage? After all, when Haugland first met Anna it had been less than a year since Einar's arrest and murder. Grief, Haugland knew, did not go away on some time frame. It could put down roots and go down deep for years.

"Are you afraid it could bring up her old feelings toward him?"

"*Ja*." Haugland sighed. "Dumb isn't it? I suppose I am feeling a bit insecure. Einar was a good man, you know. I knew him since the day I was born." Haugland paused. "I guess I worry that Anna and I met and married too soon." He looked at Conrad. "The last thing I want is for this to be some wartime love affair that falls apart after a few years of marriage because things didn't get settled. And yet, I truly want to spare her the painful details."

Conrad leaned back, like he was about to deliver some theology point to his most intractable student. He put his fingers together like a church steeple and said thoughtfully, "Love is a beautiful thing. When it is given unconditionally out of trust and mutual respect, it never dies. I never met Anna until you brought her here for a visit last summer, but I did meet Einar once at your parents' home. I think when he was studying to be a teacher at the University. Knowing her now, I can see them together."

Haugland swallowed. "I love her so much. She keeps me grounded. I'm not sure if I could face the trial without her."

"You are stronger than you think. And she loves *you*. That I know. Would it comfort you to know that I had a long talk with her before I married you? I admire her greatly. She is a strong, brave woman. When she told me many stories of your kindness to her when she was so alone in Fjellstad, accused of betraying Einar, her love for you came through. Anna is a woman of faith and devotion. She's devoted to you."

Haugland grew quiet. He picked up his cup of nearly cold coffee, but drank it anyway.

Conrad cleared his throat. "Now back to the notes. This latest one is dangerous. You must reconsider."

"I have. I wanted to see you, though, first. I have a favor to ask of you."

"Of course."

"I need to find a safe place for Anna and the children. I want no one to know, but I will make some excuse so my mother won't be alarmed. I want it to be like a vacation before I go to Trondheim. Only I will go and leave her."

Conrad came forward. He was no longer a cleric with a parish concern. He was *Sivorg* again. The Resistance. "What have you said to Lars? Surely with his Milorg experience..."

"Lars is aware of the notes. In fact, he is the one who has insisted on some sort of escort for us. Until last night, I was only half-convinced of the need."

"And Tommy Renvik? He is informed, of course." Conrad was well aware of Haugland's old comrade, having married them both in a double ceremony last year.

"He's in on it."

"Good. So what are you waiting for? I will find the place you want. A safe place until your testimony is over. It will alarm no one and can be guarded by as many as you like. All of you will be safe."

Haugland corrected him. Anna and the children would be safe. He would remain at large going about his duties like normal. If everyone insisted, he could have a shadow. He leaned over and finished off his coffee. It was supposed to put an end to this conversation for now, but he should have known better. His confessor would not be moved off the subject until all the details were worked out. In the end, Haugland was grateful. Haugland's sixth sense might be active, but his heart hadn't been in the Resistance business anymore. He just wanted to finish school and be with his family. Unlike others he knew, the glamour of being a secret XU agent in the King's service held no sway over him. He wanted a normal life, since he had nearly lost it the first time around on the floor of Rinnan's Cloister.

Chapter 15

The day is perfectly lovely, thought Inga Haugland as she came down the hall to the study. Her head was filled with the plans she would do today now that all her children and grandchildren were here. There would be feathers to smooth again, she knew, between Tore and Solveig, but despite the disturbing realization that things might never mend, she had to try. For both their sakes. They had been through so much.

Outside on the patio, she could hear the sound of Solveig's children playing with their step-cousin Lisel. After a year's time back in their mother's care, Bjarne and Tine both seemed happy and well-adjusted here. Tine, who had no real memory of her mother, spoke less German now and seemed more accepting of her real mother because her brother did remember. Bjarne's story broke Inga's heart.

About six months after he and Tine were reunited with the Haugland family, Bjarne told Inga that he thought he had done something bad to be taken away from his mother and father by the soldiers. He did not remember the *razzia* on Telavåg very well except he saw soldiers with helmets and heard booms around them as he was herded along with the rest of the village children to a big boat.

Inga wondered what he really saw. *Did he see the Germans slaughter the cattle and burn the fishing boats? See his father taken away, never to come home again?* When he asked about his father, it broke her heart to remind her grandson that he was in Heaven. Someday, many years from now, he would see his father again. In the meantime his uncles Alex, Lars and Tore would be there for him.

She stepped into the study and smiled as Lisel and Bjarne rushed past the French doors, squealing in childish delight at some game. *The sweet sound of healing.* She stayed there for a minute, lost in thought about an earlier time when her own children were small and when Jens Nils, her husband and dearest companion, was alive. The boys had run out there like that too, chasing Solveig with chubby Tore toddling behind. *The purest sound.* She saw herself younger, stepping back into the coolness of the room from the summer heat of the afternoon, holding a babe in her arms. She smelt the sweet no-scent of the child and felt the heavy weight of its bottom in her hand as she supported it against her breast. The light hair was just wisps that rose up like tuffs of down feathers....

"Mamma, look what I found."

"Solveig?" Inga's daydreaming stopped at the shock of seeing her daughter secretly backing into the room, watching outside as though she were hiding from some terror. Solveig stiffened at her name and for what seemed a long time, waited. When she did turn finally, Inga's heart sank.

Solveig held Nils in her arms. A plump hand clutching Solveig's dress front. A range of emotions flicked across Solveig's face, most of them unsteady or unpleasant. "Isn't he sweet? Silly kids, they just left him in the baby buggy. I thought I should bring him in."

"Where's Anna?" Inga asked carefully. She knew Anna had taken the baby out to sun. She had to be close by.

"I don't know, do you?"

Inga swallowed, then held out her hands. "Here, I'll take him off your hands. She must be around here somewhere."

"Oh, it's all right, Mother. Look, see how happy he is with me. Isn't it funny? He looks like Tine when she was that age."

"He does have the Haugland look. Like Tore, except fair." Inga came closer and stroked the baby's head. He opened wide his engaging mouth and squealed with delight, before lapsing into a long series of coos that ended with bubbles. The little arms pumped up and down.

"Oh silly," Solveig said when he lost his balance and fell out from her embrace.

Inga instinctively reached out and supported the baby's back. "Here. I'll take him." She took Nils and held him against her shoulder. "Was there a blanket?"

"I don't remember." Solveig watched the baby quietly.

Inga wondered what she was thinking. For a moment, she didn't want to know.

"There wasn't a bottle," Solveig said dully. "He won't take one, I noticed. Tine was like that. I nursed her until I ached. She was so demanding. When the soldiers took her away, my breasts swelled and gave me a fever. Worse, my baby was gone...."

"Shh... Solveig." Inga reached out and stroked her daughter's hair. How could she ever comfort her? How horrible to have your infant taken away and placed in a stranger's home. How cruel. It was the worst kind of torture for a mother. "Sophia's fine, *lille jente*. She knows you're her mother now. Listen to her play with her cousins. She's a sweet girl."

Solveig didn't seem to hear Inga. "I used to sit at the window and look out over the water. I always wondered where she was." She looked at Nils bobbing his head against Inga's shoulders as he worked to straighten his back. He smiled at Inga. "He's very sociable, isn't he? Not alarmed when his mother is away. I hoped Sophia howled and sobbed for me when she was taken. Never giving into another woman's love."

Inga couldn't find words to answer.

Solveig sighed. "My Ole loved her. When he came home from fishing each night..."

Inga thought this should stop. It made no sense for Solveig to torture herself over and over what was done. She shouldered Nils better and announced that she was going outside to look for Anna.

"Where is Tore?" Solveig asked.

"He's gone to the city to see some friends." *But you knew that,* thought Inga. She watched with cold fascination as Solveig collected her thoughts, then ask softly,

"What's wrong with me, Mother? Why can't I be happy for Tore?" She touched the baby's head and smiled wistfully, but before Solveig could answer, the smile had slipped and a harsher tone come into her voice. The swift change alarmed Inga as Solveig continued. "Nils is sweet, Mother, but I can't stand the thought of Tore making him with *her*. I can't stand him being with *her*. Lying with *her*. It isn't right. It isn't right." She wiped the side of her mouth several times with the flat of her hand. Her eyes went unfocused. "He betrayed us, Mamma." Solveig turned and looked at Inga with eyes full of tears. "Make her go away." Her voice got pinched and weepy.

"Oh, *lille jente*, don't make it hard for Tore. *Vær så snill*. It's so hard as it is."

Solveig swallowed and again her face seemed to change, like clouds trying to make up their mind whether to rain or not to rain on a blustery day. The calm, in-control Solveig returned, but she looked bewildered, afraid of her words that were so full of venom. She leaned into Inga and the baby and whispered, "Help me. I think I'm going crazy."

Chapter 16

After Haugland left Conrad Bonnevie-Svendsen, he had one more stop to make before he returned home— the Viking Ship Museum in Bygdøy. It was an old haunt since he was a boy. After parking his car, Haugland slipped into the deserted main hall from a side door where the Osberg ship rose above the stone floor. The fiddlehead carving high on its brow pointed right at him. That brought a smile to Haugland as he remembered the first time he came here at eight years of age.

Haugland had taken the trolley down from his parents' home and snuck past the attendant. He followed the guide around sketching the things he saw: the ships, the wagons, the funerary jewelry. The curator, Ave Starheim, discovered him without his ticket, but he knew Haugland's father, a professor at the university and allowed him to stay. Impressed with his juvenile sketches, Starheim told Haugland he could come back if he liked and wrote out a note as his pass. Over time, they became great friends, Starheim, the mentor, Haugland the student—until the Germans invaded. The ships sparked Haugland's early interest in history and literature.

Now, after a long five years, Haugland was returning, but for a different reason. Starheim had called and left a message, telling him it was urgent. Haugland started for the offices when someone called out to him.

"My God! Where have you been? All this time and you haven't been to see me!" Ave Starheim came out into the hall and shook his finger at Haugland. "Does it take a note to get you to come see an old man?" He winked, then laughed. "How did you get in?"

"The usual way. I used to be able to sneak in quite easily, remember? Are the guards as old as you are?"

"*Ja, ja.*" Ave Starheim laughed, his gray mustache drooping, then rising back up in his mirth. Except for deeper lines around his eyes and a receding hairline, Starheim hadn't changed much. The wiry man gave Haugland a hug, then stepped back to admire him. "So good to see you, Tore. Such stories. Your father would be very proud."

"I'm not sure what you've been listening to, but don't believe all you hear." Haugland removed his battered fishing cap. He wondered how much Starheim really knew about his war activities. Only his brother Lars and Tommy Renvik knew he worked with the Shetland Bus.

Starheim noticed Haugland's left hand in its brace, especially the missing end of a finger. "You hurt your hand."

"Fishing accident. Did some fishing around Hitra during the war. Doing fine now."

Starheim let out a sigh. "*Vaer så snill.* Come back to my office. I think you know the way."

Haugland nodded at the Osberg ship. Its dark form looked as though it was preparing to rise up on an imaginary wave toward him. "I'm glad some things haven't changed. I've always admired her."

Starheim shook his head. "We came very close to losing her. Spent most of the war trying to keep all the ships out of SS hands."

"Why? What did they want with them?"

"Those crazy Nazis." Starheim spat to the side. "Nordic mythology was almost a religion with them. They made several attempts to move the ships to Germany, but I foiled every one. The ships are *our* history. It would have been a scandal, an assault on our national pride if they were removed. Oddly, Norwegian Nazi party officials wouldn't hear of it."

Haugland shook his head. "That would be the only time I've heard anything good about the *Nasjonal Samling*"

Starheim led Haugland back into his office. The walls were plastered with posters of Viking ships. Bookshelves heavy with books and artifacts. Starheim pointed to a stool for him to sit on, but Haugland pulled over a chair by the window instead. Since his torture in the Cloister, he couldn't stand sitting on a stool.

"Where have you been hiding, Tore?" Starheim retrieved a bottle of aquavit and two shot glasses out of a desk drawer. "I heard that you were married and have children. Congratulations." He filled up his glass and then Haugland's. "Of course, this does not excuse you from not seeing me. *Skal.*"

"*Skal.*" Haugland took a sip, then laughed. If he tried, he could almost believe it was like the old days. The place was certainly the same, as well as was the kindness of this old friend. He felt the pull of history and the wanting to know about things he had forever asked since a child. But he was not a child. He was a man, confounded by the war's end and what he should do with the rest of his life. *If he was going to keep his life.* Someone wanted him out of the picture.

He took another sip, then cautioned himself not to hurry and drink too much. He needed all his senses now, especially with his hearing problem. He needed to be alert.

Haugland opened his wallet and showed Starheim a group photo taken in Baltimore, a gift of Anna's grandmother who wanted a picture of them all.

"That's my wife Anna."

"Beautiful. She's Norwegian?"

"American." He decided to let the half-truth stand since it was easier.

"And this little fellow?"

"My son Nils." Starheim smiled at the name in honor of Haugland's father. "The little girl, Lisel, is my wife's child," Haugland went on. "She lost her first husband during the war."

"Illegal work?"

"Milorg. A true *jøssing*. He was Norwegian."

Starheim raised his glass again. "To all *jøssings*, may they rest in peace. And to all who returned. My son Tomas was at Grini."

"He survived?"

"*Ja.*"

Haugland raised his glass "To Tomas." He took a sip, then froze when from far off a metal door clanked. His good hand strayed to his coat pocket. "Anyone still working here?"

"Oscar Mortensen. You remember him. One of the security guards. Any reason why?"

Haugland shrugged. "War time jitters. Not easy to dismiss."

"God bless you, boy. I'm sure it's fine. We closed early for cleaning."

Haugland's hand relaxed, but his heart still pounded. He finished off the rest of his aquavit. "You said in your message that you had something for me."

"*Ja, ja.*" Starheim got up and walked over to a file cabinet. He unlocked the bottom drawer and took out a small black day journal. "I almost forgot I had this." He set it on the desk in front of Haugland. He sat down with a sigh. "This was your father's. He gave it to me a few days before he was arrested."

Haugland felt a jolt of sadness go through him. His father had been arrested for resisting the changes the Germans wanted at the University of Oslo. He died of a massive heart attack the day after he was released. Haugland picked up the day book.

"I felt I had to keep it hidden," Starheim said. "Especially after his arrest. I hid it so well that I only found it a week ago. I felt you should have it."

Haugland pulled at the rubber band that closed it. The brittle band broke in his hands. He opened it. Written either in black ink or pencil, the words of each entry were scrawled across the pages in a hand so familiar to him. It brought another stab of memory.

When his father was arrested in September of 1940, the Gestapo searched for Haugland and his brothers Per, Alex and Lars. He went into hiding in a mountain cabin with a group of university students only to be ambushed by German soldiers. Haugland was wounded, but manage to escape to Conrad Bonnvie-Svendsen's deaf school. When he was well enough, Haugland made it to the west coast and got on a boat to England. He never saw his father again.

"Tore?"

"Sorry." Haugland looked up, his eyes stinging. "He was grand man, my father. I wish he was here."

"*Ja, ja.* He was a good friend. One of the first *jøssings.* Did I do right in keeping it?"

Haugland nodded that he had done the right thing. Out in the hall something metal clanked again. "You sure it's just Oscar?"

"I'm sure it is, but we can go look. Are you sure you're all right?"

Haugland stood up. "I'm sorry. I should go. I've got a lot on my mind." He put the journal into his coat pocket. "I'll look at this later."

"Tore. You're not in some sort of trouble, are you?"

"*Nei.* It's an awkward time. We just got back from America and I am going to have to tell my mother that I've found a new place to live. You know my mother. Very romantic about her sons going away during the war years. I think she feels we owe her for all the sleepless nights. In terms of grandchildren, that is. She'd happily put them all up for the rest of their growing years."

Out in the main hall behind the Osberg ship, they saw Oscar mopping the stone floor. His metal bucket on wheels clanked again when he dipped the mop into it. Haugland still wasn't satisfied. He looked beyond the rainbow arched ceiling over the ship to the two viewing balconies behind it. *Empty.*

He looked back at the ship, its dark planks shimmering in the summer eve light bouncing off the white washed walls. The Osberg always stirred Haugland's imagination. Like it was just waiting for the right wind before it would slip across the stone floor and out the door to Oslofjord where modern motorcraft picked their way around some predestined course. The Osberg ship would know no boundary. It was wild and free.

Haugland turned and shook Starheim's hand. "*Takk* for the visit and the drink." He patted his coat pocket. "And *takk* for this. My father's papers were destroyed by the Germans when they ransacked our house. This will be precious."

The curator walked with Haugland to the outside and followed him to his car. He watched curiously as Haugland appraised his surroundings before driving off. Ave Starheim shivered in the warm air. The war was over, but he thought somehow it was not for his young friend.

Chapter 17

Back home, Haugland found the family gathered out on the stone patio, over by the wall across the lawn. Lars Haugland and his wife Siv visited with Alex Haugland. Two strangers stood near them. A quick appraisal of the men made Haugland think ex-Milorg. There were a lot of them these days. These were probably Lars or Tommy's war chums. He suppressed his continuing unease from last night and joined them.

"Just in time," Inga Haugland said. "We're having iced tea before supper. Lars has invited some of his friends from the university."

Haugland kissed her, told her she looked nice, and took the glass offered him.

"Did you get your appointments squared away?" Inga asked.

"*Ja*, Mamma. *Takk*. Conrad says hello." Haugland looked for Anna.

She was by Nils who was on the grass where he was examining things eye level with his mouth. Haugland watched Anna swoop their baby up and kiss him loudly on his belly before planting him back on his blanket. Nils howled with pleasure, and started pushing on his elbows as soon as he was put down. Lisel sat down beside him with her cousin Trygve to corral him.

"He started to roll this morning, Tore," Inga said. "I remember when you rolled the first time. You kept going."

"Was it up at the seter? The floors are uneven. You could roll a ball across it." Haugland caught Anna's attention and with glass in hand signed, Hello, Beautiful.

Anna smiled and signed back, Same you. Where you go? At the patio's edge, she stopped to brush some grass off her summer dress, then walked over.

She slipped her hand into Haugland's free hand. He pecked her on her cheek and pulled her close to his side.

Lars joined them and introduced his guests as Polsen and Øyen. Haugland shook hands, but was distracted when Nils squealed.

"He's definitely not an office type," Lars said. "Always on the go."

Everyone laughed. With the children on the lawn and the adults bantering happily around the patio, it was a pleasant family setting in the long Nordic spring light, enjoyed by all except some watchful eyes on the second floor. Having seen enough, someone snapped the curtains shut.

Supper was served. Before going into the dining room with the rest of the family and their guests, out in the hall, Anna stopped and signed to Haugland, I want see you.

"Go on ahead, Lars," Haugland said as Anna took him by the hand and pulled him into the study.

What wrong? he signed as he shut the door. They only signed when they had a private message between them or if something urgent needed to be said.

Wait, Anna signed. She looked behind him. When the hall was quiet, she finally spoke. "Why are you so secretive, roaming the halls at night? Why are you afraid? I've been so happy, but is my happiness a dream and your fears my waking hours?"

Haugland started, a puzzled look on his face. "I don't know what..."

"You were awake last night. I heard you go downstairs and then you came back up and went into the children's room. You were upset, then I heard you talking to Solveig. When you came back, you stood at the door a long time. A long time. What are you afraid of?"

"Anna..."

Stop, she signed. "I told you in Maryland not to hide things from me. My God, it was a little over a year that I thought you were dead, gone forever from me. Whatever it is, the trial, family problems, don't hide them from me." For emphasis, she came at him and struck his chest several times until he took her hands and forced her to stop. He drew her to his arms.

"Why did you go into Oslo?" she cried into his bad ear. "And who are those friends of your brother's? They remind me of Tommy Renvik. Resistance men." Haugland held her tighter. He had heard her.

Lars knocked on the door. "You folks coming? Mamma's waiting."

"In a moment. We'll be along." Sorry, Haugland signed to Anna. He sat her down on the arm of one of the chairs. Clearing his throat, he ran his hands through his hair, but he couldn't speak immediately.

He took a breath and said, "You're right, of course. I have been pre-occupied, but I didn't want to alarm you. I wanted you to have a good time with your family in America. I should have told you while we were coming back. I was wrong to keep it from you." He reached into his wallet and brought out the newspaper clipping. He watched her face as it turned pale when she saw the photo and the printed words.

"Oh, Jens... Who would do this?"

"Someone with a sick mind or someone connected to the trial. It's been going on since before we left for America. Could possibly be Odd Sorting."

Anna gasped. "Odd Sorting?" Haugland knew Sorting's name made her cringe. He had been the one who betrayed her first husband, Einar. "But he's in jail." Her voice became a hollow whisper.

"*Ja*, but I think he's behind the notes."

"There are more? Oh, Jens."

"I wanted to tell you about the notes last night," he explained, "but I was afraid—"

Anna interrupted. "—This note. Where did you find it? Was it in the house? That's why were upset?" Anna's eyes grew wide. She hunched her shoulders. She clenched the news clipping tight. "*Nei,* don't tell me." Her voice was so low, Haugland had to cock his head to hear. There was a thunderous pause.

Haugland cleared his throat. "I called Lars first thing when he got into town this morning. I told him everything."

"Those men?"

"Friends of Lars. They'll be watching us from now on. Until the trial is over."

Anna's face was pale and drawn, but she straightened her shoulders and got up as if she was prepared to resolve the conflict once and for all.

"Will we stay here?"

"*Nei.* I'm making arrangements for a place for all of us to stay. Maybe Margit Renvik can give you a hand. She's used to intrigue and would make an interesting nanny. Once you are settled, I'll go."

"You're not staying with us?"

"*Nei.* It's for the best, Anna. Whoever it is will be busy watching me."

"But you will tell me from now on. Everything."

"*Ja.*" Haugland gave her his word and this time, he promised he would never lie to her ever again. The note had frightened him more than he admitted. Wanting to protect her and the children, he had forgotten how brave she had been last year when the SS and *Wehrmacht* hunted for him and his village friends, Kjell Arneson and Helmer Stagg. He knew her beauty belied courage and fortitude underneath.

Anna stood up and came into his arms. Haugland rocked her, then kissed her lightly. "Just take care of the kids. And yourself. That's all I ask. When the trial's over, we'll go somewhere."

"We can't go to Trondheim and see Kjell and Ella, can we?"

"We'll see."

***

It was late, but still light when Lars said "*God natt.*" His friends accompanied him down to his car along with Haugland. They stood talking in the driveway for a few moments like they were old war horses swapping tales. From any window, it would appear that all were returning to the city.

"Where will you be?" Haugland asked Polson.

"I'll be in the back, in the woods," Polson said. "Øyen will be near the front."

"You can rest easy tonight, Tore." Lars smiled at him encouragingly. "No one will get past these guys. We'll get you moved as soon as feasible." He put a hand on his brother's shoulder and patted it smartly. "Get some sleep. After that long boat ride home, you've barely gotten settled."

Haugland did manage to get a good night's sleep. The next day, he kept his mood from turning black by keeping busy. He took phone calls from various friends and with Anna's help, quietly filled some suitcases for their departure. During this time, Anna stayed close to him, careful to keep an eye on the children. She spent time with Inga frequently, giving no hint that they might be leaving soon. She saw little of Solveig. The two young women met only once during the evening meal. Anna sensed her animosity, but worked hard to maintain a cordial relationship with her for the family's sake. If Anna was aware of her mother-in-law's hovering around Nils, she thought it was only the older woman's delight in him. If Anna had thought about it, she would have noticed the baby was never left alone in the house when Solveig was there. She began to relax and take her cue from Haugland because he appeared to be less tense as well.

"Where are Lars's friends?" she asked once.

Haugland replied, "In the trees."

***

Inga Haugland was not fooled, however. She realized that something was wrong and her worst fears were realized two nights later when the phone rang late at night. Tore got up and went down to the landing to answer it. He was on the phone for a long time. Finally, he came back upstairs and went back into his room. She listened for any more sounds in the hallway, but was relieved that Solveig hadn't stirred. She had taken some medication to soothe her headaches and apparently was sound asleep. Thank God. Since the incident with the baby, Inga had begun to realize the fragility of her daughter's mental state and possible tragic consequences if she was not watched. She was not sure if the baby had been in danger, but she was sure of her daughter's hatred of Anna.

Inga lay back on her pillows and must have drifted back to sleep because she was suddenly jolted awake when she realized that someone had sat down on her bed. Very gently, a hand was laid over her mouth and a light next to the bed turned on.

"Shhh...Mamma, I don't mean to alarm you, but I couldn't just go. Something has happened and I must leave. I'm taking Anna and the children with me." Haugland took his hand away.

"In the middle of the night?" Inga sat up abruptly. "Why?"

"It's the trial. They thought it wise that we go somewhere out of the public eye until I give my testimony." Haugland looked pained, but he would give no other explanation.

Inga's white hair was undone around her shoulders. She found her silk ribbon and bunched her hair back. "Must you?"

Haugland put his hand on her shoulder and squeezed it. "I have to, Mother, but perhaps it's for the best. For all of us. We both know that things are strained. This will be a good excuse to leave gracefully."

"Oh, Tore...I never wanted this to happen."

"It's no one's fault, Mor." He leaned over and kissed her.

"You will at least let me know where you are?"

"I'm sorry... No one must know. No one. Lars can keep you informed on how things are going. Tell people that we will gone for a few weeks. Blame it on the prosecutor if you like, but don't discuss it. If I feel it warranted, I will contact you."

"But it's more than that, isn't it? Something has happened as you said yourself."

Haugland made a face. Yes, he had said that. He shook his head. "It's just best we're away."

Inga wanted to say something strong to her youngest son, but held her tongue. Instead, she told him to watch over her newest grandson and for him to take care of himself.

Her heart sank when Haugland looked straight at her and said, "*Takk* for being the strongest one in the family. We'll make it up to you. You can teach Nils how to play the piano. That'll take a lifetime, won't it?" He started to go.

"I won't come out," Inga said.

"*Nei*. It wouldn't be such a good idea. Some friends will take us. And Mother... don't be alarmed if you should see *Herrene* Polson or Øyen around. It's just a precaution."

***

The children were bundled out, Nils with Anna and Lisel half asleep in Haugland's arms. Outside in front, a car was waiting in the light of a sun that had never slept during this season. They could see clearly up and down the forested road for nearly a half mile. Which made Lars and the other man nervous. Øyen came out of his car which he had kept hidden off the road and kept an armed watch while the youngsters were settled. Nils stirred and began to fuss. Anna quieted him in the back with a breast, cradling Lisel against her side. Their few belongings were stacked next to them. Anna sat back quietly, her face strained and pale. She had obeyed him without question, but when Haugland was finally settled into the front seat with Lars, she could not stay silent any longer. As the baby tugged vigorously at her and clenched the breast between his little hands as he nursed, she leaned forward and asked in hushed voice,

"Why Jens? What has happened?"

Haugland turned around and looked at her grimly. "It's Sorting. He escaped from jail."

Chapter 18

"Let's go over the plan one more time," Sorting said, sticking his head out from under the top bunk in their tight jail cell. "Only risk I see is getting out of here in broad daylight."

"It's evening," Skele answered sitting above him. "And springtime. People will be out after work. We'll just be workers going home. It's a good plan."

"*Ja, ja.* I agree the plan seems sound, but are you sure about this Anse Nilson?" Nilsen was the jail keeper for their floor.

"I'm sure. He thinks he's so pure," Skele said, "but I told you during the war Nilsen did a little bit of informing in exchange for keeping his job at a lumber mill. During the work day, Nilsen was just an average man keeping his head low and minding his own business. At night and on weekends, he would compile fact sheets on neighbors and acquaintances that he eventually turned over to a contact." Skele laughed. "That contact was me. When I threatened to expose him, he agreed to help us escape."

Sorting stood up and paced around. Outside their solid steel door, gray and rusted, he could hear movement in the hall as keys jangled and a lock turned. Someone was led down the hall. It gave him the chills. For an unsettling moment he could almost feel the terror he had instilled in resistance workers and political prisoners when he worked with Rinnan at the Mission Hotel where men and women were tortured by the Gestapo. Worse, the basement at the Cloister. He quickly dismissed it. *Relax,* he thought as he made another turn in the cell.

"So you're OK with this?" Skele asked Sorting.

"So far."

"Good. During dinner, when Neilson brings the food cart around, he'll hide a set of keys on my tray, then leave our cell door unlocked.

To make sure of our escape, he's arranged for the jailers to be tied up in a friendly game of cards."

Sorting stopped. "You said the jailers always play while we eat. What if they end their game quickly?"

"*Ja*, but Nilsen is bringing some *aquavit* since it's his birthday. While they celebrate, he'll leave a cart at the end of the corridor and stow away some staff uniforms and street clothes. He'll get us identification documents, just in case."

"What else did that prick have to say?" Sorting had no respect for those who gave away information to save their necks.

"Nilsen said we were fortunate we weren't at Fort Kristiansand but here in the county jail. Said it would be easier to blend into the evening crowd. When we get out we'll find two bicycles for you a block away."

"What about the wall?"

"Nilsen's got that covered, too."

Sorting sat back down on his bunk bed. All they had to do was wait.

At 6:00 the meal cart clattered down the hall. Their trays were passed through the food slot. After a pause, Sorting heard a shuffling sound. When someone inserted a key into the lock, Skele mouthed "Nilsen." They froze until they heard the cart continue down the hall to the next cell.

"Better eat while we can," Sorting said. "Might be our only meal for a while." He downed his food with a spoon. Afterward, he took a leak in the corner, then sat down on his bunk to listen for noises outside their door. Skele joined him in silence.

At the agreed time, Sorting swung open their cell door and stepped out. Skele followed and left trays on the outside near the food slot so not to arouse suspicion until bed check. Then, locking the cell door behind them, they slipped past the locked cells to the end of the hall where a meal cart was waiting. Underneath, were a haversack and two sets of coveralls and two caps worn by the jail staff who cleaned the cells. They went through the door to the back stairs and on the landing hurriedly pulled the coveralls over their prison outfits. They crept down the stairs to the exit to the outside.

At the door, Sorting stopped. "Give me the key," he said. "I'll take care of it."

Skele handed it over. "What are you worried about? Nilsen said he'd put a duplicate set of keys on the board inside the office. Make them think our escape came from the outside."

"Let's call it insurance." Sorting opened a handkerchief and told Skele to put the key in it. He carefully slipped the cloth package into his coat pocket.

"Ready?" Skele asked.

"Get it over with."

Skele took a deep breath, opened the door and then they were out.

Chapter 19

As their car sped through the streets of Oslo, Anna huddled in the backseat with the children. Cradling sleeping Nils in one arm and holding tight to Lisel in her other, her thoughts raced to another time when she was forced to flee. Two years ago, after the death of Einar, her first husband, she left Lillehaven in a panic to get away from the false accusation that she betrayed him. Now she was on the run again. When will the war be over?

Anna straightened up and looked out the window. The late evening sun glowed as bright as daytime as they passed gardens, apartments and people out for the sun. Eventually, they entered the countryside. When she looked back through the narrow rear window, there was no one else on the road. She touched Haugland on his shoulder.

He turned around and signed, I love you. We'll be fine. He squeezed her hand.

Anna squeezed back, gathering strength from his words but also pulling on her own reserves. She was a survivor. She knew she had the courage to see this new terror through. Had she not faced Rinnan himself in Fjellstad and emerged humiliated, but with the dignity that won the admiration of all the women in the village who had hated her before?

"We're here," Haugland said.

The car pulled up to a tall wooden gate. Letting the car idle, Lars got out and knocked on a side door. A man in blue coveralls came out and after speaking to Lars opened the gate. Lars drove through into what appeared to Anna as some sort of park.

"Where are we, Jens?" She asked Haugland.

"Folklife Museum. We'll stay here until we get that window of dark, then we'll go."

Anna knew his smile meant to reassure her, but she wasn't comforted. "Go where?" She struggled to keep her voice from being sharp.

"Fjellstad. Tommy and Lars think it's a good move as Sorting knows where we live here in Oslo. I agree. You'll be with Kjell and Ella. Margit Renvik is coming, too. She'll watch over you and the kids."

Anna had no time to ask *how* they were getting to Fjellstad, hundreds of miles away, when the car came from under a canopy of trees and stopped. Rising from a grassy knoll was the dark shape of a stave church. Its ancient form rose up into the pale sky with multiple-peaked roofs with wooden shingles shaped like dragon scales. Dragon head appendages at the top gave the huge wooden structure a fairy tale feel, but to Anna, it was foreboding.

Haugland helped Lisel and Anna out. "Let me take Nils." He took the sleeping baby from Anna. She watched Haugland's face soften as he cradled Nils. For a brief moment the tension she had felt in him vanished.

Anna took Lisel's hand. "Are we are staying in the stave church, Jens?"

"*Nei*, the old pastor's house over there. Lars has promised coffee. There are *dyne* for you and the children to curl up in."

Anna looked down, afraid of tears threatening to come.

"Anna," Haugland said softly, "we'll be well away in a couple of hours. When it is dark, a friend of Lars will fly us by seaplane out to the coast. Kjell and Ella are waiting for us."

"Am I going? Lisel asked.

Holding Nils against his chest, Haugland leaned down and said, "Of course, you are, *lille jente*. We wouldn't leave you." Lisel tugged on Anna's hand. "Will I see my kitty?"

"I'm sure he will be fine." Anna hoped that was true. They couldn't find him before they left for Oslo. Winters in Fjellstad could be harsh.

Lars came around with a lit lantern. "It will be dark inside."

With that they followed Lars into the ancient building. Haugland settled Lisel in a *dyne* on a wide plank wall seat and gave her a kiss.

Anna lay down facing Lisel, holding Nils in her arms. He stirred briefly, rooting for a breast, then putting a fist in his mouth and going back to sleep.

Haugland tucked the *dyne* around Anna. "I'll be out front with Lars. Try to rest." He picked up the lantern. As he walked across the room, light splashed across the solid beams, exposing old *rosemaling* patterns on thick posts. He closed the heavy door behind him.

"Momma. Is Pappa Jens coming back?"

Anna sighed. "*Ja*. Why don't you sleep too?"

"Uh-huh." Lisel's voice faded away. Her breathing quieted.

Now if only I could sleep.

For a long time, Anna watched the light outside the only window in the thick walled space grow dim. Finally, she drifted, dreaming of a mail boat taking her to a village wrapped in mist.

"Anna." She woke with a jerk. Haugland stood over her, his figure outlined by a lantern. The room was black as tar, but beyond the window, darkness seemed to have a tenuous hold.

"Time to go," he said.

Chapter 20

Damned light, Sorting thought for the thousandth time. He would try to make a break as Norway's spring season raced toward the lightest time of the year. As he straddled his bicycle, he pulled his jacket's collar up around his chin, grateful that the stolen article had a Norwegian flag on the arm. It made him look more patriotic. Maybe someone would see that before they tried to look at his face. He pulled his fisher cap over his ears.

So far their escape had gone well. That jailer Nielson had thought of everything, but while Skele had confidence in him, Sorting did not. Instead of taking the incriminating keys with him, Sorting dropped them in a ground floor window shaft next to the jail. This was the very reason he had asked for the keys and put them in the handkerchief. He hoped only the fingerprints made by Neilson and Skele would show. As soon as they found the bicycles on the far side of the park opposite the prison, Sorting insisted that they separate.

"I think we should meet outside of the city instead of staying together as planned," Sorting told Skele.

"Why?" Skele hissed. "I thought we were to stay together. You're not trying to ditch me, are you?"

"*Nei.* Look around. Alarm is sure to be sounded sometime this evening. With worse luck, sooner. See you in Heimdal." With that, Sorting got on his bicycle and rode off, blending into the light evening crowd, a mix of students and workers getting off work.

Ten miles south of the city, Sorting stopped to catch his breath and get his bearings on the country road heading to Melhus. It was harder than he thought taking on the rolling hills. He hadn't been on a bike in years. Being jailed for over a year didn't help either, though every time the jailers let them out in the yard, he found ways to exercise and keep his strength up.

Sorting looked back down the way he came. He had gained altitude since leaving the outskirts of Trondheim, the road skirting around forested mountains rising a couple of thousand feet to the east. Now as he rested, Sorting could see occasional farms scattered among the extensive marshland and forests, but so far no signs of activity. He listened for sirens. He heard none. Only a cow in a pasture across the road calling to her calf. Relaxing, Sorting leaned against a stone fence post. He took out a paper package that contained two cigarettes and lit one.

Now what? Wait for Skele? Or just go? He reasoned that the authorities would be watching the Swedish border to the northeast—it was only sixty miles away—because it was logical that he would try to get into Sweden and from there into the Soviet Union. Since their occupation of Finland to the north in the fall of 1944, Russia now butted up against Norway in the northern province of Nordmarka. What he was going to do was not logical. He would go south to Oslo where Haugland was last reported.

Sorting dragged on the cigarette a couple of times, letting the smoke fill his lungs before he blew it out into the late spring air. A couple more drags, then he put the precious cigarette out. Sorting used to get cigarettes all the time when he was with Rinnan. He couldn't believe they were still luxury items in Norway and rationed like during the war years.

Better get moving. Sorting had made up his mind about escaping at the very last moment after he uncovered Skele's plans. Common sense had been telling him for weeks that he should bolt while he could, but it was a short notice in the Trondheim paper, *Advissen*, that made him reckless. Several days old, it had been slipped to him by the barber who believed in God's forgiveness for certain sorts of war crimes. Though alarmed by the cruelties of *Rinnan Banden*, he had told Sorting that he was on the fence about whether every member on the fringe should be damned to hell. Sorting made sure the barber knew that he regretted getting caught up in the excesses of war. He had fallen into bad company. His charges weren't too serious—he was no murderer—*except for the unfortunate agent*—and surely Sorting could be redeemed. So the barber sent newspapers and in this particular issue, Sorting saw the announcement concerning the engagement of Kjell Arneson to *Fru* Ella Moen Bjornson of Fjellstad.

At first, Sorting thought it sort of comical, like his discovery of Haugland and the Fromme woman together. As the short announcement sank in, he became angry. Why did life seem to go on? Why couldn't it be him and Freyda? The unfairness galled him. They didn't deserve it.

"Morkdal!" someone called to him down the road. Pedaling hard and huffing, Skele dashed toward Sorting, his bicycle leaning left and right as he pumped.

Sorting glowered. "Have you lost your mind?" he hissed. "I said no meeting until *after* Heimdal." He looked around for any sign of traffic, but the single country road was deserted. That didn't mean they weren't watched. In such a rural country such as Norway, the passing of anything was noted. "And don't call me Morkdal. The name's Sorting. My true name."

Skele came to an abrupt halt and nearly fell off his bike. Bracing his legs, he regained his balance and said, "You passed Heimdal."

How did I miss that? "You don't have to come. This is my affair. You can turn around and get to Sweden in a couple of days on foot and into Russia."

Skele spat. "Those stories are overrated. All there is over there are Bolsheviks. And maybe worse. Why do you suppose those Russian POWs the Germans dragged up here for slave labor weren't too happy about being repatriated? Rinnan always talked of joining the KGB, but frankly all I think we'd get is a bullet in the back of the head."

"Isn't that what you're facing now?"

"You're not so lily white yourself—Odd. Oh, you pretend to be, but you're not. That intelligence officer testifies and you're in shit." Skele looked up sharp at a bird twittering in the brush, then muttered that he had nothing else to do. "I thought I'd go along for the fun of it." He took out a long sausage provided by Nielson and tore off a piece with his yellow teeth. "What do you intend to do anyway?"

"I haven't decided yet. I've got to locate Haugland first. Assume he's at that address in Oslo your friend got."

"I might know someone."

Sorting stared at Skele. The man annoyed him, but he had the most astonishing connections, most of whom seemed to be doing fine outside of prison. It was like the criminal element in the country had been culled out over the past year and jailed. Now the remainders were resurfacing. "Why should you care?"

Skele shrugged. "The woman. You said she was beautiful."

"I said nothing about her."

"That's right. So she must be lush." He outlined a woman's body in the air and, laughing, set the sausage on his groin. He made an obscene gesture with it, then bit off a piece and leaned on the handlebars of the bike. "When's this train coming?"

"What time do you have? Nielson didn't give me a watch."

"Because he gave it to me." Skele pulled back his jacket sleeve. "Eight-thirty."

Damn. It took me two hours to go twelve and half miles?" Sorting frowned, the calves on his legs suddenly aching fiercely. "That gives us a half hour to get to Melhus. Train's at nine fifteen. My source said they added it after the war. We can ditch the bikes, then board."

"They're going to look."

"No Gestapo, remember? No I.D. cards. We just have to convince them we're workers going home."

Sorting felt in his pocket for the envelope of money. At least Nilsen had been thorough in that respect. He could buy a watch later. What Sorting needed to do, though, was get access to an account with the Bank of Norway under one of his many names, one that he felt sure the authorities didn't know about. No one in *Rinnan Banden* knew. He had put a sizeable amount away for a reason he realized no longer mattered. It could serve him now.

"Where's this friend of yours?"

"Lillestrom, north of Oslo. That close enough?"

Sorting glowered, then said it would do. "Let's move."

Chapter 21

The cat with yellow eyes sat down on a chair opposite Haugland and waited for him to wake. Outside the hut, snow fell. Haugland could see everything clearly, even though his eyes were closed.

"Don't tell anyone I'm here," he told the cat. "I'm hiding." The cat tucked his front paws in and began to purr loudly. Haugland pulled the wool blanket over his bare shoulders, preparing to disappear into its warmth when the wooden bed bumped and dropped.

Haugland sat up in an instant, his eyes staring into the dim quarters of the seaplane. The purring sound was only the loud drone of the plane. It faded in and out in his left ear with its mending eardrum. Anna was sound asleep in a seat across the tight aisle from him with Lisel nestled against her. In the seat in front, Nils was strapped into a traveling bassinet. Behind them Margit and Tommy Renvik slept, also oblivious to the mild air pocket they were passing through.

Haugland took his arm out of the sling and clenched and unclenched his hand, in part to make the dull ache in his palm and fingers go away. *Damn dream.* He used to dream it a couple of times a month, but lately he had been dreaming of that cabin up in the mountains almost every night. The cat and the snow and his first understanding that he was still alive, safe from Rinnan, thanks to the logger who found him.

Why that dream? he wondered. Why not the cabin where he had reunited with Anna months later? Her intimate acceptance of his damaged body was his first true step to healing.

Haugland pulled the wool blanket around him. The cabin in the old Junkers seaplane was chilly. He was surprised the airline kept it. After the war, the Norwegian government destroyed most of the Junkers seaplanes as if to wipe away another ugly reminder of the German occupation. This one was still serviceable. At least that is what Ave Starheim said.

He took out a small stone from his pocket. When he turned it, the ribbed shape of a trilobite presented itself. To his surprise, Ave Starheim from the Viking Ships Museum had greeted them at the seaplane launch and had given the fossil to him.

"You arranged our flight?" Haugland said as he shook his friend's hand.

"Lars asked me. Remember," Ave said, laughing. "I know all things maritime. What did you think I did during the war? Not just protecting the Viking ships."

"I'm afraid to ask."

Starheim laughed again and patted Haugland on the shoulder. He nodded at the aircraft floating next to the dock. "It's an old tub, but reliable. Here, I want to give this trilobite to you. Something else your father left with me."

The plane bumped one more time, then smoothed out. Haugland rubbed the trilobite with his thumb. *Pappa. What are you trying to tell me? The notebook, of course.*

Under the seat in front of him, he pulled out the small black journal from his canvas rucksack. He weighed it his hand and then, taking a breath, opened it.

When Ave had handed it to him, Haugland had only noted the familiar handwriting, not the content. Now as he flipped through the pages, he saw not only journal entries, but discovered a list. Not about geology, but about people. He searched the rest of the journal and found two more lists with notes.

Was this why Pappa had given it to Starheim? The summer and fall of 1940 were dangerous times for Norway as it was pressed deeper under the German thumb. Europe had fallen. England was on its own. Terboven, appointed *Reichskommissar* by Hitler in the spring, began cracking down on labor unions, newspapers and the universities. It was dangerous to object, but Haugland's father had. As he read the names on the first list, Haugland didn't recognize anyone, but then he was a university student at the start of the war, playing soccer on the university team, sticking to his studies. These names could have been contacts in the scientific world his father passed through. Maybe they didn't mean anything.

Haugland flipped through the pages to the second list, one of the lists with notes and sat up straight. Next to each name printed in pencil, there was a note. Its purpose was very clear. These were names of professors and people in industry who were colluding with the Germans or the Nasjonal Samling (NS), the Nazi party in Norway. Haugland recognized several of them. Though the occupation by the Germans was only a few months old, already people were taking sides. *Quislings.* Each notation had a date, where seen, and a comment on the person's affiliation. *Pappa. Who were you keeping it for? What made you start in the first place?* Something had triggered this accounting.

Haugland pushed back the cloth curtain on the little window next to him. Light had returned to the sky. Down below, he could see the end of the vast *fjell* and the beginning of the western coastline. Their pilot was taking them north up to Molde on the coast. There they would refuel and go on to a landing spot south of Hitra and the entrance to the fjord that led to Fjellstad.

Haugland returned to the journal, going down the list of names with a finger, then stopped. *Aage Pilskog.* Pappa had underlined the name twice. Here was someone Haugland did know. At one time, Pilskog had been a visiting lecturer at the University of Oslo and had been hosted by Haugland's parents on several occasions before the war. Haugland tapped the entry with his finger. Tall man, blonde, with a stubborn jaw and light colored eyebrows that rose over his wire-rimmed glasses. His background was geology and some other interest Haugland couldn't remember. Not a native of Oslo. Next to Pilskog's name was the note: *I'm beginning to distrust Aage's position on the faculty acquiescing to German dictates. Seen with NS men. Possibly Gestapo.*

Haugland leaned back in his seat, trying to recall what Conrad Bonnevie-Svendsen had said about Norwegians in industry and intellectual groups who had collaborated with the Germans, but so far had received only fines for their participation. He wondered about Pilskog. Why was his name underlined? For a moment, he wondered if Pilskog had something to do with Pappa's arrest. Was Pilskog still alive? Haugland tapped his lip, then sighed. Maybe it was time Pilskog came under scrutiny.

Chapter 22

Just outside of Melhus, Sorting stopped and stared at the village nestled in a valley between rolling green hills and forests below him. He could see the occasional small farm farther off, but what drew his attention were a number of wooden buildings that appeared to be factories. Having grown up in a rural area many miles north of Trondheim, this was unknown territory and it made him uneasy.

"What?" Skele skidded to a stop next to him.

Sorting waved toward Melhus. "I wasn't expecting to see mills. That's means a lot of people."

Skele nodded at one of the large wooden buildings in the distance. "Closed. Used to make furniture, but the owners didn't recover from the war. There were sawmills here too, but everything is old and out of date. Not a lot of money to put into new equipment." Skele looked at his watch. "Look, it's almost nine. Most people are back on their farms, settling down for the night. If you want to see, Nilsen gave me a piece of a map." Skele took a folded piece of paper out of his knapsack. "The station's here. The village is beyond. They shouldn't even notice us." Skele got back on his bike and began to pedal away. "Come on. Looks good to me."

Sorting wasn't so sure. Skele may have been up to no good in the black market during the war, but Sorting had developed a sixth sense for trouble while working his way into resistance groups. He knew when it was necessary to back out. It had been hours since they had escaped. Surely, there was an all-points alert by now. Cautiously, he followed Skele.

To the west the sun was brushing the tops of mountains, sending gold pollen light on the land. To the south, hills, more forest, and rising mountains. From the map, the Gaula River was supposed to come in around Melhus. If that were true, the high grassy embankment that followed the road prevented him from seeing it. The long twilight was approaching. If he wasn't suddenly so tense, Sorting might have enjoyed this scene of freedom full of memories long ago before the war.

On the side of the road, a sign announced the approach to the Melhus Station. "There," Sorting pointed. He slowed down, then stopped

Skele had to turn around and pedal back. "Why'd you stop?"

"Something's not right."

"How the Devil would you know?"

Sorting didn't answer. He lay his bike against the grassy knoll and climbed up, then lay down on the rim. As he suspected, the hill hid the railway bed running from a curve to the north and down south. To the north, the track lay empty with no sign of life. Farther down the track a yellow two-story building stood silent. No sign of anyone waiting on the train platform. He ignored Skele grumbling as he climbed up and joined him. "Keep your damn head down," Sorting growled.

"I don't see anything. We'll miss the train if we wait here."

Sorting didn't answer. His eyes were focused on a window in what was most likely the waiting room. He thought he saw movement. "Shh." His heart pounding, he held his breath, then to his unhappy instinct, two men stepped out onto the narrow platform. There was no denying their uniforms.

"That the police?" Skele asked.

"*Ja.* You better think fast, because we're not getting on that train." Sorting lowered his head farther when another man came out and joined the police officers. He wore plain clothes. He talked with them for moment, at one point gesturing in Sorting's direction, then went back inside.

Sorting backed down the hill and picked up his bike. Skele scrambled down after him. Standing in the road, Sorting looked in both directions. Empty, which made him think they could ride farther south and try for another station. If the police were at the Melhus train station, more could be in the village. What took him hours to get here from

Trondheim, a police car could do in short order. Sorting didn't like their prospects. And he didn't like relying on Skele. For a brief moment, he wondered if he could find one of his wartime contacts not in jail. Could he trust him?

"I know someone," Skele said. "And he owes me big time."

Sorting straddled his bike. *Of course you do.* "Where?"

"We'll have to go back north and then cut over to the coast. We don't have to be on this road."

"Why do you think he'll help?"

"Because he's one of those big fishes that never got caught. I know his secrets. He'll do whatever I tell him to."

Which is why hours later in the deep twilight of late Nordic spring, Sorting arrived exhausted and hungry at the stone gate to the home of Skele's contact. In the murky light, Sorting could make out a gravel road leading down to a manor house set among a cluster of pine trees and formal gardens. A newly planted field in front of the house looked like a minefield. Sorting felt uncomfortably exposed. He also wondered who this person was. No ordinary one. Parked in front of the house was a new car. Regular Norwegians didn't have new cars let alone old ones. Most cars were destroyed during the war. Whoever Skele's contact was, he could be a help or a dangerous quisling with enough power and money to turn the tables on them.

Chapter 23

"Say, again,." Standing in the kitchen of Ella's *konditori,* Kjell pressed the wall phone's receiver hard against his ear. He strained to hear his friend's voice.

"I'm telling you, Kjell. I saw him riding on a bike down near Orkdal, heading for the coast. It was Odd Sorting." The fisherman's words were followed by more crackling.

"For sure? He's in Vollan Prison along with the rest of the trash." The phone connection in the *konditori* was pretty good considering the mountains between them.

"He was going south?"

"*Ja.*"

"Let the Trondheim police know where you last saw him." Kjell didn't tell Sverre he already knew that Sorting was out. He rubbed his eyes in attempt to stay awake.

"It's two in the morning."

"Call them." Kjell looked out the *konditori*'s windows. It was growing light again after the brief curtain of dark. "I'll do the same on my end."

"He wasn't alone."

"The Devil you say. All the more to let them know. This is really bad if he is getting outside help."

There was silence on the other end, followed by more crackling. Finally, Sverre asked. "Have you heard from Jens?"

"*Ja.* He's back home."

"Good to know. Tell him to be careful. I'll call the police." Sverre signed off, his worried voice echoing in Kjell's ear.

For a moment, Kjell held the phone's receiver to his chest. Hearing the man's fear from seeing Sorting—and Kjell believed that he had—

sickened him. Sverre Haraldsen came from a God-fearing family of fishermen who lived out in the nearly treeless islands off the coast. In the spring of 1944, Sverre, his father, and his brothers secretly joined Jens in his operation to store arms and materiel brought over on the Shetland Bus. When the line was exposed by Sorting, all the Haraldsen adult males except for Sverre had been captured, taken to Trondheim for interrogation and torture, then shot. Sverre was the only survivor from Jens' cell.

Kjell put the phone on its hook on the wall and looked out into the dark tea room. This *konditori* and *landhandel* had been Ella's place of business since before the war and during the occupation. She now ran it with the help of Kjell's youngest daughter, Kitty. He could make out the lace curtains at the windows and the little flowers in jars on the tables. Soon it would smell of sweet bread and cinnamon rolls fresh out of the oven when Ella came downstairs for the day.

The scene cheered him. He had had an uneven year since capitulation, some of it financial, due to the loss of his boat and home blown up for his part in working with Jens. Kjell stayed with various friends while his house was rebuilt and occasionally crewed on other fishing boats. Sometimes their kindness tormented him because he knew another reason why the village had suffered under Rinnan's *razzia*. Odd Sorting wasn't the only one who had caused Jens' line to be exposed. Kjell's daughter Rika had been responsible,too.

Beautiful, headstrong Rika. Only nineteen, she had gone to Trondheim in the summer of '44 to fulfill a dream of working in the city. Unknown to Kjell, she secretly joined an illegal group as a courier. Somehow, she came into Rinnan's sphere of influence. At war's end, Rika discovered that she had helped to bring about Haugland's arrest and the deaths of so many, including a man she loved and planned to marry. She killed herself.

Kjell's heart was broken. He had just brought her remains home this April to rest next to her mother in the little cemetery by the church.

The year had been hard and bitter. Ella's love and practical nature had saved him. So too the kindness of friends who admired his courage and leadership during the war years. More than anything, Kjell wanted them to forgive Rika—for Kitty's sake. He did not want the years of occupation and Rika's unknowing betrayal to bury the rest of his lively seventeen-year-old daughter Kitty's life.

Out in the *landhandel* portion of the shop, Kjell heard a light knocking at the door. Soon the bell over it jingled as someone came in. That would be Helmer Stagg, an old comrade from the Resistance. Together, they would go out in the *Kristine* to meet Jens and his family.

"Boat's loaded, Kjell." Helmer said. "Just waiting on your orders."

"Then let's move. We've only a couple of hours to meet them." Kjell grabbed his coat and cap, then follow Helmer out into the crisp spring air. Though the war was over, Jens' team of fishermen was being reunited once again. They would make sure his testimony at Rinnan's trial would finally bring justice to those who had destroyed their village and murdered their friends.

Chapter 24

Despite dropping out of the sky at a sharp angle that made its wings teeter back and forth, the old Junkers seaplane settled gently on the sea and taxied to a stop next to the *Kristine*'s starboard side.

"Did you see that?" Helmer called out from the boat's bow. The wiry blonde-haired fisherman pointed to the seaplane in awe.

"*Ja*, Helmer. Let's get ready to transport them over." Kjell didn't add it reminded him of a German bomb attack he had witnessed at the beginning of the war in 1940. The planes dropped out of the sky just like that and bombed Molde's harbor. He waited for the Junker's propellers to stop spinning and the water to calm down before he left the wheelhouse to join Helmer.

Through the plane's small curtained windows, Kjell could see movement as people shifted around. Eventually, the pilot opened the door and stepped out on to the plane's pontoon.

"*Hei, hei,*" Kjell called out. "Ready to send the dinghy over?"

"*Ja.* Everyone's lined up and waiting."

Kjell motioned for Helmer to open the boarding gate, then together they lowered the rowboat. While Helmer stayed on board, Kjell rowed over.

Tommy and Margit Renvik came out first. Once in the dinghy, Tommy helped Anna and the children get settled. Haugland came out last. When Kjell saw him, he couldn't hide his pleasure. At war's end a year ago May, Haugland had been thin and worn down. *Now you look like the day I first met you.* Tough, hale and hearty, even tanned. Kjell was anxious to know how his hand was healing.

Kjell helped Haugland in. "Jens," he said, his voice thick with emotion. "Kjell."

No other words needed. They understood each other very well.

Once everyone was settled in, Kjell rowed them over.

While Tommy helped Anna, the children and Margit board the fishing boat, Kjell turned to Haugland and said in a low voice, "As soon they are settled down in the crew quarters, I need to speak to you. It's Sverre. He's seen Sorting."

Haugland stared at Kjell. "Sorting? Where?"

"Orkdal area. Southwest of Trondheim. There's a road that goes down through there to Vinje. Come. I'll tell you about it in a bit. Let's go get the rest of your stuff."

Back at the seaplane, the pilot handed down their luggage and several boxes containing clothing and food from America, then said goodbye. There were final words to the pilot, then the seaplane door closed. As Kjell rowed over to the *Kristine,* the plane taxied way, causing the dinghy to rise and fall in its wake. Some distance away, it gathered speed and took to the air.

Down below in the *Kristine*, hot coffee and biscuits waited on a table in the tight galley. It was nearly five in the morning and they had another ninety minutes to Fjellstad.

"You're welcome to claim a bunk and sleep in," Kjell said to the women. "Blankets are stacked at each end."

Margit looked at Anna holding a sleeping Nils and said it was a capital idea. "I could use another hour. I'm sure Anna agrees."

"Look, Mamma," Lisel said. "I want this one."

Anna said that she could take it, then chose the bunk next to her. "But first, coffee sounds delicious."

"Good," Kjell said. "We'll leave you ladies to it."

Up on deck, the men joined Helmer Stagg in the wheelhouse. They sat down on stools. While Kjell started up the boat, Haugland came immediately to the point. "So what did Sverre say?"

"Sverre Haraldsen?" Tommy scowled. "What's going on?"

Kjell went on to describe his conversation with Sverre. "I believe him. Puts Sorting about where he should be after you were notified that he escaped."

Haugland frowned. "Did he alert the authorities?"

"Sverre said he would tell the police. I made my own call. I'm sure any attempt of Sorting to board a train will be blocked."

"Where was Sorting headed?" Tommy asked.

"Sverre said he was going south. He wasn't alone."

Tommy looked at Haugland. "He must think you are in Oslo."

"Let him." Haugland let out a puff of air.

"We'll get you settled soon enough, Jens."

"*Takk*." Haugland grew silent and stared out the wheelhouse window. Kjell and the other men became silent. The *tonka-tonka-tonka* of the boat's engine was the only sound filling the wheelhouse.

The sky was overcast with no hint of rain. As Kjell steered, he watched Haugland take it all in: the steep rocky shores of the coastline rising up several hundred feet; the forests and the occasional red shack; the scattering of skerries to the west. Despite the danger during wartime, he and Haugland had had good times together fishing, waiting for the Bus.

"Miss it?"

"The sea? *Ja*, it got into me, though I don't miss our required poster saying 'Contact with the enemy is death."

Kjell chuckled. "*Ja*, there's that."

Tommy shook his head. "Never understood the appeal of being stuck out on water. I prefer the mountains."

Haugland clapped Tommy on his shoulder. "Don't worry. You're in good hands."

Kjell hoped that he would be those good hands while Haugland waited to testify at the trial. It was not only a matter of friendship, but another nail to put on the coffin of what was the harrowing war years. Yet, while it troubled him that Sorting had escaped, Kjell feared larger conspiracies were at work. Even in his cell at Mission Hotel Rinnan wanted Haugland dead.

Chapter 25

Lars Haugland felt like he had barely made it back to bed in his apartment in the west end of Oslo when the phone rang out in the *stue*. He sat up and glared at the clock on the lamp table. It read 1 AM. He carefully rose so as not to disturb Siv sleeping next to him and putting on his bathrobe, went out to answer the incessant ring.

"*Hallo?*" Lars could barely make out the voice. The man sounded like he was calling through a tin can.

"*Herr* Haugland, this is Hammar Stilsen in Trondheim. I'm sorry to call so late, but I'm with the prosecutor's office."

"*Ja?* Have you found Sorting?"

"The authorities are working on it."

"It's not enough to say you're working on it. This is a serious security breach." Lars let loose a string of expletives loud enough to rouse the dead.

The phone on the other end went silent. Lars wondered if the connection had been dropped.

Finally, Stilsen answered. "Police do have one clue that it was an inside job. A search outside the grounds turned up a set of keys. They match keys left inside the office."

"So you have no idea where Sorting is. But you call me at this hour." Lars made an attempt to keep his rising temper under control.

"Like I said, we're working on that." Stilsen paused. "Where is your brother?"

"Based on the prison staff's blundering, I'm not going to tell you." With that, Lars slammed the phone down on its receiver. He closed his eyes. He felt sick to his stomach.

"Lars? What is wrong?" A light turned on in the bedroom.

Lars swore, regretting that his shouting had wakened Siv. Lars took a deep breath and walked to their bedroom door. Siv sat on the edge of the bed, her breasts heavy; her swollen belly straining against her nightgown. Her flaxen hair was unbound, caressing the top of her thin shoulders. There were circles under her eyes. For a moment Lars panicked that she was not getting enough to eat. Expectant mothers were given a higher ration, but not some of the things she craved.

"Sorry, I didn't mean to wake you."

"I wasn't really asleep. It's getting harder to find a comfortable position." Siv braced herself on the bed before looking at Lars. "Who called?"

Lars was about to make up some white lie so not to worry her further, but he couldn't do it. "It was someone from the prosecutor's office in Trondheim."

"Is everything OK? You left so abruptly after dinner. Is Tore OK? Why call at this hour?"

Lars sighed. "He's OK for now. There's been a complication."

Siv patted the bed. "Come here."

Lars sat down and pulled her to him. He considered himself the luckiest man in the world. In order to protect her and their small son, at the beginning of the German occupation in 1940, Lars had divorced Siv so that the Gestapo would not tie her to any of the illegal activities he was undertaking. Now they were together again and expecting their second child in July. He would never forget how utterly faithful she had been all that time.

"Are you going to tell me or do I pull it out of you?"

"Hmph." Lars laid his head on hers. "Don't worry. We have things well in hand."

Siv looked up at him and stroked his cheek. "Is that why you look so worried?" She ran a finger across his forehead. "See, I can trace those worry lines right here."

"Siv," he said softly, "I can't tell you. It's better you don't know. Everyone is fine."

"All right, everyone is fine. But Tore will testify?"

"*Ja.* He will testify." *And you better find Sorting, Herr Prosecutor or I'll bring the Devil down on you.*

Chapter 26

While Skele walked toward the heavy blue door of the old manor house, Sorting looked back up the gravel road to the main road and warily sought for a sign of any vehicles. He heard or saw nothing. No one was out, even though the long twilight was over and the sun was rising for the day. Sorting winced as Skele pounded on the door. He thought the sound was loud enough to alert the neighboring farmsteads. Instead, he heard only the sound of someone hurriedly padding down a hall. The door clicked and a bewildered young woman in hastily thrown-on robe and lace cap opened the door. She held a candle to Skele's face.

"*Ja?*" she asked.

"Need to see *Herr* Pilskog. Tell him Svart Hund is here to see him. He knows who I am." Skele put one of his big hands against the door and pushed, causing the woman to fall back.

The heavyset woman pushed back. "*Nei*, you must wait. Everyone is sleeping."

"I think not. Get him." Skele put his shoulder to the door and he was in, slapping a hand around the woman's mouth to mute her cry.

Sorting followed Skele in, then stopped. Skele held the woman against the wall. In the flickering candlelight, Sorting could see her face. As she looked at Sorting over Skele's hand, her terrified eyes widened in recognition. Sorting groaned inwardly.

"Let me talk to her," he said in a low voice to Skele. "You won't scream, will you, *Frøken?*"

The woman shook her head. A tear ran down her plump cheek and onto Skele's hand. Skele shook it away and let Sorting take over. Sorting grabbed her hand and led her away from the wall. It was dim in the hallway, but the lone candle held in the woman's shaking hand illuminated white paneled walls and doors leading off to rooms. Sorting guessed that the bedrooms were upstairs.

"Now, *Herr*—" Sorting looked at Skele—"Hund—is a friend of Professor Pilskog. There is no need to make alarm. He would be upset if he knew of your lack of hospitality. That right, Hund?"

"*Ja*, for sure."

From far-off upstairs a door opened and closed. Everyone froze as someone descended stairs in the back. A light came on. A tall man dressed in a flannel robe and slippers appeared, tightening his cloth belt across his ample stomach as he came down the hall.

"What the Devil? What are you doing here? Are you crazy?"

"Is that a way to greet an old comrade, Aage?" Skele said, taking charge. "We won't take up much of your time. Just a place to rest." He looked around the hall. "You and your servant the only ones here? Where is *Fru* Pilskog?"

Pilskog took a deep breath. "My wife is in Oslo."

"For what reason?"

"Family visit."Pilskog nodded at the woman. "*Fru* Norsby, you may go back to your room. There is no need to worry. We are not in danger. They are business acquaintances. I think they have been out celebrating and drank too much *aquavit.* " Pilskog emphasized the word acquaintances. "I will speak to you later."

He waited for her to leave the hallway and enter a door to what Sorting thought might be the kitchen. After the door clicked behind her, Pilskog motioned to a door on their left.

"Now, follow me."

"And the woman?" Sorting asked.

"A simple country girl. She knows her place."

Pilskog opened a heavy door and turning on a light instantly revealed a long room that displayed wealth and comfort. Set on the polished fir floor, a sofa and upholstered wingbacked chairs grouped around a large stone fireplace. By the tall window that faced the front of the house, covered with a blue velvet curtain, a round table displayed flowers. Paintings hung on the paneled walls. Sorting's unease grew. Rich bastard. Probably got off scot free.

Pilskog closed the door behind them. "I'd offer you coffee, but it's best that we speak alone. I can offer you some brandy—"

"Cut the shit," Skele said, taking off his gloves. "We need to talk."

Chapter 27

As soon as Pilskog closed the door, Sorting wondered what kind of hold Skele had over the arrogant bastard.

"What do you want?" Pilskog asked. "It's practically the middle of the night."

"Whatever I ask," Skele said. "And you know you'll do it. I've got the list."

Pilskog stood up. His face turned white. Then his focus turned to Sorting. "Who's this?" Pilskog said.

Sorting stepped closer. "Someone who is catching on fast," he answered. "We need a way south. Looks like you have the means to do it. Nice car. Now shut up."

The man shut up

Sorting watched Pilskog with suspicion as he directed them to sit by the unlit fire. The white paneled room was elegant, but it was also cold.

Pilskog poked around in the ashes in the fireplace, then put some paper and birch wood tinder together and lit them. The flame that took hold reflected gold on Pilskog's wire-rimmed glasses.

He's thinking he's still in control, Sorting thought.

Sorting was beginning to accept any attempt to reach Haugland would have to be delayed until they eluded the police. He studied Pilskog. He was tall with butter blonde hair and the aristocratic bearing of someone who had known privilege all his life. As much as Sorting despised anyone from the upper class, feeling them weak, he felt that there was some ruthlessness in Pilskog he should be wary of.

Pilskog said nothing. He crouched down in front of the fireplace and added some small logs. The flames leaped up and soon the room warmed up.

Skele put his hands out. "That's better. Now who else is here?"

"I told you. My wife is in Oslo. Visiting our daughter."

"When does she get back?"

"Not for a couple of weeks. She is preparing for our grandchild's baptism."

That wasn't enough for Skele. "Are you expecting any visitors? Workmen?"

"More precisely," Sorting interrupted, "when did you plan to join her?"

Pilskog's eyes opened wide. "I—"

Skele cut him off and smiled wryly at Sorting, exposing a gold tooth. He didn't smile back at Pilskog. "*Ja*, for sure you should tell us."

"I planned to go down next week." Pilskog cleared his throat like something was caught in it. "I don't expect any visitors today. Just myself and our housekeeper."

"Where exactly is she?" Sorting wondered if she had enough courage to bolt. "Does she have a room in this house?"

"There is a small bedroom off the kitchen. She sleeps there, but eats in the kitchen."

"Good." Skele pointed to one of the wingback chairs in front of the fire. "Now you sit."

Sorting looked at the clock on the wall. Pilskog was right. It was almost one in the morning. *No wonder I'm tired.* Yet, it had been only seven hours since they escaped. Sorting desperately wanted to lie down and sleep. But he didn't trust Pilskog. "Where do you have telephones in the house?"

"Why do you need to know?"

Sorting put his haversack on the other chair. "So you won't suddenly decide to call the police."

"I wouldn't do that," Pilskog sputtered.

"*Ja*, sure, you wouldn't." Sorting took two steps toward him. "The phones. Where are they?"

Pilskog turned to Skele for support, but got none. "There's one in this room and another in the kitchen."

"What about guns?" Sorting wasn't taking any chances. During the German occupation, Norwegian citizens were forbidden to have guns. Any guns dropped by parachute or sent by boat to the Resistance were taken back by the Norwegian government after the war. But firearms of all kinds were still out there.

Pilskog bristled, his shoulders pulled back in anger. Sorting almost laughed at his outrage.

Skele stepped in to smooth feathers. "Let's make a tour of the house, Aage, and take care of a few things for peace of mind. Then we need to rest here for a while. Make some plans. I promise you, your help will be rewarded. After all, what are business partners for?"

Pilskog swallowed. And Sorting was starting to get the picture of what this piece of shit did during the war. *Black market, colluding with the Germans in some way.* When Pilskog asked Skele what Sorting was in prison for, Sorting felt a thrill to see the man stare in horror when Skele answered and concluded with, "And he's with the Rinnan Gang."

Sorting would play on that.

Chapter 28

"Anna." Haugland's soft voice made her open her eyes.

"Jens?" Anna whispered. She pushed her blanket aside and half sat up in the bunk. "What is it?"

Haugland put a finger to his lips, then signed, Come with me.

Anna looked behind her. In the dim space, she could see Nils sleeping in the wooden box she had improvised for him as a bassinet. From the absence of sounds coming from it, he was deep asleep. Lisel slept not far from him. The rest of the cabin was quiet.

Haugland helped her to stand. Let's go up, he signed. Need to talk.

Up on deck, the crisp morning air hit Anna's face. A slight wind brushed back her hair. She sighed as she took in the breathtaking beauty of the *Trondheimsleia* defined by islands to the west and fjords stretching fingers into the land and mountains and *fjell* behind to the east. Here in May, the snow still lingered on one of the peaks. When she shivered, Haugland put his coat on her shoulders, then rubbed them. Anna leaned back into him. "Are we almost there?"

He folded her into his arms. He spoke in Norwegian. "Soon, but you're not going to Fjellstad."

"What?" She jerked out of his arms. "Why?"

"Let me explain." He nodded for her to go around to the back of the wheelhouse where they would be out of the wind.

Norwegian fishing boat wheelhouses were set at the back of the boat, the fish hold in front. As Anna made her way to the back, the *Kristine* gently dipped and rose over the cold, gray waves. She had to catch herself a couple times by the fish hold. As she passed the wheelhouse, Kjell and Helmer waved encouragement to her. They made her smile, but by the time she was settled on the small wooden bench behind them, she was angry. "Why?" she asked again, this time in English.

"There's been a change of plans," Haugland switched easily to English. "To protect you," Haugland reached for her hand, but she withdrew it.

Anna knew this was not the time to be petulant, but she had to stand firm. "Jens, I love you. I have agreed to all of this, but didn't you promise me just days ago you would tell me everything? Why am I going there?"

"Anna—"

Anna stood up and signed, Stop! Enough, slicing her hands through the air. "What is going on? Just tell me the truth." Anna almost said, *Or is lying all part of your years as an intelligence officer?*

"All right. Just before he met us, Kjell got word that a friend of ours saw Sorting in a place south of Trondheim. He could have been trying to catch the train to Oslo as he knows where we live, but he could have also changed his mind and be anywhere in Sor-Trondelag."

"Sorting." When Anna said his name out loud, she felt sick.

"We'll get him. The police are on it, though I suspect that the state prosecutor will not want word to get out to the public. It's an egregious breach in a trial already sensational."

Anna stepped away from him and folded her arms. Offshore, some white birds rose into the air and caught a spiraling current. *That's how I feel.* "So where am I going?"

"I'm taking you to a cabin south of Fjellstad. It's a place Tommy used during the war. There's a little lake nearby for fishing. It should be a pleasant time. Margit and eventually, Kitty, will help with the children, but Margit is well-versed in side arms and other weaponry. She will protect you."

"Hmm. This is not the place where I met you last spring?"

"No. That one is farther south." He smiled at her gently, a twinkle in his eye. Anna guessed at what he was thinking. She felt her face warm as she recalled memories of their reunion. Passion and heat in a cold, snowy world still languishing under the German thumb. She looked down and away to hide her grin. Nils had been conceived there.

Could she really be angry with him? To be honest, she felt a sense of relief she was not going to Fjellstad. Despite her finally being accepted by most of the villagers in the last months of the war, her time there had been miserable. After Jens was presumed dead, she was totally alone. She hadn't been in Fjellstad in over a year and didn't know how to face them again. "Are you going with us?"

"Yes, of course. When we land, transportation will be waiting for us. I'll get you situated, then we'll go with Tommy to the cabin."

"Where will you be after you leave us?"

"In Fjellstad. In plain sight."

"Oh, Jens. Must you?"

"I have some business to attend to." He opened and closed his hand encased in its leather half-glove as if to relieve some pain.

"Will you go alone to the trial?"

"*Ja*," Haugland said, switching to Norwegian. "But I really need you there. Someone will come and get you. One of Tommy's Milorg friends."

Anna couldn't tell if it was the wind hitting her face as the *Kristine* made a turn toward land or emotion, but tears rolled down her face. She did not resist when Jens took her in his arms.

Chapter 29

"Where is Tore, Mother? Where did they all go?"

Inga Haugland put down her cup of tea and studied her daughter Solveig for a long moment. *What should I tell her?*

"You were sleeping, dear. He had a call from Trondheim. His trial appearance date has been moved up, so they wanted him to come early. He needed to get his family settled."

The look on the young woman's face was blank for a second, then flushed as she turned way. Inga saw confusion.

"She—he's not coming back?"

"Oh, we'll see Tore soon enough." She motioned for Solveig to come closer to her. Outside the study's French doors, Inga heard her grandchildren playing. When Solvieg came alongside her, Inga took her hand and squeezed it. "I finished the dress for Tine. You should let her try it on."

"All right…" Solveig carefully removed her hand from Inga's tight grip and folded her arms. "Why did they go so suddenly?"

"Suddenly?"

"It was sudden, wasn't it? Isn't that odd?"

"I don't know, Solveig. This is a very important state trial. Apparently, there has been a lot of… arrangements. Made to accommodate everyone."

"Is Tore on his way to Trondheim?"

Inga stared at Solveig. *Why so many questions? How can I answer when I shouldn't? When I don't know the answer?* "I'm not sure."

Solveig went over to the French doors. Inga watched Solveig wave at Bjarne who was riding his tricycle. Lars had found it and restored it with new paint.

"Where is Tine?" Inga asked.

"By the garden wall. She's playing with her doll." Solveig became still, then suddenly stiffened. "Mother! I think someone is out there in the trees."

Inga got up with a start, then relaxed. It had to be one of Lars' friends. Solveig wouldn't know about them.

"It's all right. Our neighbor *Herr* Clausen is having some men check the stand for me. I may pull out some winter-damaged trees. They'll be around." Inga came over to the doors and stared through the window panes. She saw no one, but hoped that was their intent. Not to be seen. She put a hand on Solveig's shoulder. "Tore will call us when he's settled."

"Why didn't Anna—" Solveig seem to swallow Anna's name with distaste— "why didn't she and the children stay here?"

"I think Tore wanted them to find a permanent place to live. He wants to finish his studies at the university. And though he won't admit it, I think Tore needs rest. He only came out of surgery four weeks ago. A place of his own will be good."

Solveig shuddered, then fell still. It felt to Inga that her daughter had drawn away and not just in a physical sense.

"I think I'll go see the children," Solveig announced suddenly. "Maybe Tine can try on that dress now."

Chapter 30

Not long after Haugland spoke to Anna, the *Kristine* chugged into a small cove and weighed anchor. Except for a small, brick-red wooden building built on pilings and a rowboat tied up at a rickety dock, the rocky area looked deserted. Farther up a gravel road Haugland thought he saw a house painted a mustard color. Beyond it, forest and mountains.

"Are you sure someone's here?" Haugland asked Kjell as he stood in the door of the wheelhouse.

"*Ja*. Jan Karl Eidsvik is here. That's his rowboat."

"Who is he?"

"A fisherman and a *jøssing*. Worked in export until he got arrested near the end of the war."

"But he survived."

"*Ja*. Freed from Vollan Prison on the day of capitulation." Kjell cleared his throat. "He wasn't expecting us until tomorrow, but I'm sure he can take everyone up to his cabin as soon as possible. It's not far from the one you and Tommy used during the war. This one was his father's."

"Eidsvik. I didn't make the connection." *There's a lot I don't know.*

Unease pressed down on Haugland's shoulders. He hadn't realized how much a strain he was feeling coming back to the region. When he had returned with Kjell after liberation a year ago, he had received a warm greeting from the villagers. Everyone had been caught up with euphoria from being free of German soldiers and Norwegian collaborators. Then reality set in. Fjellstad had suffered. From what he was hearing, the village was still struggling after the loss of their fishing boats and several prominent citizens who had been shot by a firing squad in Trondheim. *Because of me.* Lately that knowledge lay as hard on him as the scars Rinnan put on his back.

He stepped out of the wheelhouse to join Anna and the rest of the travelers on deck.

Kjell signaled to Helmer to lower their dinghy. "We'll leave the ladies and children on board with Helmer," he said to Haugland. "You, me and Tommy will go up and see about transportation."

Once on land, the men walked up the rising road to the house they had seen earlier. As they approached, outbuildings and spring green fields came into view. A *fjording* pony neighed a warning. Soon the blue door of the house opened and a dog came out barking, its tail wagging.

"Kjell Arneson. You're early." A tall man wearing a vest and collarless shirt Jan Karl stepped out of the house, the sharp features on his tanned face softened as he extended his hand to Kjell.

"Change of plans, Jan Karl. I'll explain later."

Eidsvik turned his attention to Haugland and Tommy. "Good to see you again," he said to Tommy. "You've put on weight. Marriage must be good." Then he eyed Haugland

"This is Jens," Kjell said.

Eidsvik eyes widened. His face sober, he slowly shook Haugland's hand. Haugland wondered in what context he knew his cover name. He also wondered why Kjell had introduced him that way.

"*Vaer so snill*," Eidsvik said. "Come inside." He led them into a narrow hallway lined with bead board panels made of birch and into a *stue* with an ancient fireplace. A four legged wood stove poked its firebox out like a guard dog on the hearth. "Sit, sit," Eidsvik said indicating chairs by the window that looked out on the road. "I have coffee on the stove."

Kjell and Tommy sat down immediately, but Haugland took a chair farther out in the room. Out of old habit, he faced the door. He slung his knapsack on the chair's back.

"So what happened?" Eidsvik asked as he poured coffee for each of them.

"Thought it best not to bring the women and children to Fjellstad," Kjell answered. "Sorting escaped from Vollan last evening."

"Sorting?" Eidsvik nearly spilled coffee on his hands. "That bastard."

"*Ja.* He was seen a few hours ago heading for the coast. Until we know where he is going, they need to go to your cabin as soon as possible. Everyone arriving in Fjellstad in such numbers would draw attention."

"Then it will be done." Eidsvik looked at Haugland's hand encased in its half glove, then at Haugland. "You do not know me, but you saved my sister's son when he was *på skogen* two years ago. We do not forget such courage and sacrifice."

Which one? Haugland thought. In the spring of 1944, he saved two local boys, Petter Stagg and Karl Olavsen, when they fled to the mountains to avoid being forced into the AT and then sent to Germany. Thousands of young men all over Norway had gone into the woods. When these two showed up at his cabin, Haugland's cover had been nearly blown. "Karl?" Haugland asked.

"*Ja,* that's my nephew." Eidsvik smiled as he handed the steaming coffee to Haugland.

"He lives, thanks to you. And Renvik here, for passing him along the export line to Sweden."

"Our all for Norway," Tommy said as he raised his coffee cup. "And now, we must go to the mountains again."

"What do you have for transportation?" Haugland asked. Through the window, he watched the dog cross the one lane road and lie down next to a truck with a canvas back. It looked worn down. He wondered if the old truck ran at all. And there was the matter of fuel: it was still being rationed.

Eidsvik followed Haugland's line of sight. "That truck. The Germans confiscated it during the war, but returned it in better shape than when I had it." He made a spitting motion to the side. "German engineering. Bah."

Tommy turned to look at it. "You have fuel?"

"*Ja*. And if we need a second vehicle, I have an old Chevrolet car that still has a *knottgenerator*."

Running on wood, Haugland thought. "How long is the trip up there?"

"Should be able to get everyone settled before noon."

"All right," Haugland said. "Let's bring everyone ashore." Haugland turned Eidsvik. "And *takk* for your help in this."

"*Bare hyggelig*," Eidsvik answered.

Haugland wondered how much of a pleasure it would be if Eidsvik knew how really dangerous the situation was becoming.

Chapter 31

After a long winding drive, Haugland and his family arrived at Jan Karl Eidsvik's cabin high in the mountains. A log cabin with grass growing on its roof, it sat on a low rise with a pine forest behind it. Eidsvik pulled over on the rutted gravel road and parked his truck next to an old snow bank.

"This is it," he said. The truck growled and shuddered, then went silent as Eidsvik turned off the engine.

Haugland cupped his left ear. The noise in the truck's cab had made it hard to hear half the conversations in the last hour, but he understood Eidsvik this time. "When was the last snowfall?"

"About a week ago. It's melted away, but there are some big patches from winter. Not too bad when the sun is out."

"Let's get Lisel and the others," Haugland said to Anna who sat squeezed next to him. He helped Anna down.

"The place has a certain charm," Anna said as she bounced Nils on her shoulder.

"*Ja*, it does." Haugland put his arm around her and hugged her. "You and the kids will be fine here." *And safe.*

Haugland looked around. Below the gravel road that ran in front of the cabin, was a trail that ran through a rustic meadow to a small lake. Birch trees, made low by heavy winter snows, dotted the lake and surrounding hills, sprouting their new leaves of the coming summer. At the end of the road in front of him, buds were forming on the low-growing lingonberry bushes. Behind the cabin, another trail ran up to a ridge and the beyond. Here and there were small patches of snow.

Eidsvik joined Anna and Haugland. He pointed out a trail that went up to a ridge to a grove of trees. "It goes up higher to what I call wild *fjell*. I've seen reindeer up there." Eidsvik pointed out a small wood building with a grass roof. It was set away from the back of the cabin with a couple of birch trees growing next to it. "That's the outhouse."

"*Takk*," Haugland said. He liked this place for its security. There was only one neighbor and his cabin was a mile away. During the war, this was a forbidden region. No Norwegian could be here without a permit. That did not keep Eidsvik's place from being a hideout for Tommy and his Milorg group. During his assignment in Fjellstad, Haugland had come here once to see Tommy.

Tommy was first out of the back and helped Kjell get the rest of the party on the ground. Their few possessions followed. If Haugland hadn't felt the urgency, he would have enjoyed watching Lisel run ahead onto the porch and open the door to the cabin. Her excitement echoed as she explored the rooms. He wished he had her innocent resilience.

The men gathered all the suitcases and boxes they had brought with them and put them into the cabin. Haugland lit a fire in the stove. Then while Anna, the children and Margit unpacked and explored their small rooms, Haugland went back down to the truck with Tommy and Kjell. In the back, Haugland set his rucksack on one of the benches.

"Never thought I'd be using one of these again." Haugland pulled out the metal pieces to a Sten gun and grimly began to assemble it. In pieces, it looked like plumbing equipment, but he could put the submachine gun together in the dark. During the war, thousands of these semi-automatic rifles were dropped by parachute into Norway or delivered in boxes via the Shetland Bus. Haugland wanted to make sure it worked. He held the finished weapon and aimed it at the floor. It felt right.

"What else do you have?" Tommy asked.

"My old pistol. Ammunition for both." Haugland looked at Kjell. "When will Kitty come?"

"Ella can bring her up after we get to Fjellstad."

"All right." Haugland placed the lightweight weapon on his lap and after taking it apart, put it back in the knapsack. "Once I know things are in place here, I want you to take me out to the islands. It's time I went to see *Fru* Haraldsen and give her my respects."

"Really? Are you sure?"

"*Ja.*" Haugland leaned back against the canvas wall and pushed up his fisherman's cap. He knew Kjell would be upset, but he had to do it. The Haraldsens had suffered because of him. Sverre, his sister, Andrina Paal, and *Fru* Haraldsen were all who were left after Rinnan raided their island home before Christmas 1944. All the men in the family were shot the following month. Haugland had to go back.

"I have five days until I testify. The prosecutor has my deposition, so no need to show up in Trondheim until then. If Sorting is out looking for me—there is the question of why he was heading for the coast—why not lead the traitor around by his nose? Lay a trap if he comes to Fjellstad. As long as Anna and the children are safe."

"I hope the police find him before that," Tommy grumbled. "From what Sverre told Kjell, Sorting wasn't alone. It sounds like he had help. And I don't like that. Our country is still unsettled after five years of occupation. He seems bent on taking you out. Why else the notes?"

"Those notes. Something's not right about them."

"In what way?" Tommy was sitting up now.

"The last one. Kind of over the top. Melodramatic. Not like Sorting."

"I thought you said he did them. They are so cruel."

"Sorting is cruel, all right. Only he could come up with a way to send pliers to me, but the tone was different in the one I found with Nils. Sorting knows everything that happened to me in the Cloister. This one had to rely on a newspaper account."

"You still don't know how it got into the house?"

"*Nei.*"

"All the more you should be careful, Jens," Kjell said. "There are *quislings* everywhere who don't want to be found out for what they did during the war. Maybe you are a key to their exposure."

Haugland did not answer him. It had been on his mind. He wondered how trustworthy the ex-Milorg men Lars had assigned to the house were.

***

While the men discussed what they would do when they arrived in Fjellstad, Anna and Margit settled in. The cabin was built around the time of the Great War and thought tight, appeared to Anna to be well designed. There was a small *stue* with built-in seats around a small coffee table. A multi-paned window looked from there out onto the porch and the lake and meadow beyond. Next to the *stue*, a maple table and built-in hutch served as the dining area. The wood-burning cook stove in the kitchen would supply the heat if it got cold at night. The two small rooms down the narrow hall each contained one set of bunkbeds. Outside, down from the porch was the outhouse.

After they unpacked, Margit went outside. "To check out the back." While she was gone, Lisel sat by the window in the *stue* and played with her paper dolls cut out of an American magazine. Anna nursed Nils for what she'd hoped would be the last time for a while.

"Was there a dairy?" Anna asked when Margit finally joined her at the dining table. Anna put a light blanket over Nils as he nursed.

"Just up the hill. The pump's there. We should be fine here."

For a moment, Anna thought the woman was distracted. She wondered, *Why? Had Margit gone down to talk to Jens? Or was there something else?* While Anna smiled at Margit, she reminded herself that Margit had served with SOE Norway in Sweden during the war. The spare blonde woman was just a year older than Anna. Margit was here for a reason. *To protect us.*

"That's good to know." Anna grinned when Nils stopped nursing and batted his fist against her chest. He kicked the blanket with his feet.

"He's so busy. Is he always hungry like this?" Margit cocked her head.

Anna laughed. "He's much more settled now. Sometimes, he just wants to play, be comforted." She pulled the blanket away from Nils's face and said, "*Titt tei, titt tei,*" then flopped the blanket over his face again. He chortled when she quickly pulled the blanket away again.

"He's sweet."

Anna straightened up at Margit's solemn voice. "Do you want children, Margit?"

"Oh, *ja.* Tommy and I would like that very much. We had to wait due to Tommy's duties immediately after the war, but we've been trying for a couple of months now."

Anna lifted Nils up and burped him. "Sometimes it takes a while. My first husband and I didn't have Lisel right away. Boy or girl?"

"It doesn't matter. May I? Don't worry. I had many younger brothers and cousins growing up."

Anna laid a diaper on Margit's shoulder, then handed over Nils. She closed her nursing brassiere and adjusted her straps.

Lisel got up and came over to the table. "Mamma, can I go out on the porch with my dollies?"

"*Ja,* Lisel."

After Lisel left, the women were quiet for a moment, Margit patting Nils gently until he burped. Margit nodded after Lisel. "Do you ever think of Lisel's father?"

"Einar? *Ja.* I will always love him. And I must keep his story alive for Lisel—his wit, the things he cared about. I will tell her how we met in Amsterdam before the war and that it was love at first sight even though he was eight years older than me." Anna picked up a pile of diapers from a basket to fold. "I will tell her how with my father's help, Einar got me out of Germany to Norway before conditions under Hitler got worse."

"Such an amazing story, Anna," Margit said.

"*Takk.*" Anna swallowed. She smoothed out a diaper, folded it and put it on the table in front of her. "There are things I won't tell her until she is much older. Like I didn't know why he had become so distant. I didn't know he was in the Resistance until the day he was arrested. He was protecting us. I think what hurts the most when I think of him, is that I didn't really get a chance to tell him how proud I was of him for his illegal work."

Margit lay Nils on his back on her lap and dangled some keys in front of him. He reached up and gasped them with his pudgy fingers. "I'm sorry, Anna. I truly am. Just so awful." She paused. "I hope that you are happy with Tore."

Anna smiled faintly. "I am. It was *not* love at first sight. He was so different. It's hard to explain. Everyone thought he was a simple deaf-mute. The only way I could talk to him was with a pen and notebook. But I thought he was very nice and very kind."

"You never suspected he could hear or speak?"

"*Nei.* After Jens saved Lisel when she fell into the water, I went to thank him, but all he did was make motions and write his words down. I think he expected the worst of me. It was Lisel who drew him in. Her kitten got a fishing hook stuck in her lip. She asked him to help. He did, but he was still standoffish."

Margit shook her head. "He must have known something about you."

"He told me much later that he did. The Resistance had information on me. He felt sorry for Lisel. Only when the village sent him to gather wood for me for winter in exchange for my hay, did we begin to trust each other. Of course, I had no idea that Jens was in the Resistance, working with the British. I had no idea he had known Einar since he was a boy, either. I now know Jens was worried about being identified. Trust came first, then love."

"You call him Jens."

"I know that was his cover name, but that name remains in my heart."

Anna added that Einar was more serious and studious, while Jens was strong and passionate. "And Jens has a wry sense of humor."

"How did you know that before he ever spoke to you?"

"Only as I learned to understand his signing."

THE QUISLING FACTOR · 141

"You still do that? I saw you signing to each other at the Haugland home."

"We do. Lisel thought it was all a game. We continue it to please her." Anna laughed. "But then, it's also a very good way to talk without anyone knowing what we're saying." Anna stroked Nils's cheek. The baby turned his head and kicked his legs. Anna picked him up. "Oh, you're getting to be a big boy." Anna rubbed her nose against Nils' nose. "Still, Jens opened my eyes to the deaf world that he understands very well due to a beloved uncle. I have thought of continuing my learning and become a teacher for the deaf."

"Really? That's very interesting. You are incredibly lucky. Tore is a wonderful man. Tommy can't say enough about him."

"Who? Me or Tommy?" Haugland stuck his head through the door. Anna laughed, but she knew him so well. When he signed, Be strong, Anna knew he was telling her it was time for him to go.

Chapter 32

As the *Kristine* approached the fishing village of Fjellstad, the big sign of ARNESON OG SØNN on Kjell's warehouse rose above all the fishing boats lined up side by side along the bulkhead. Ella's *konditori* stood next to it. Haugland gazed up to the ridge behind the *konditori* where most of the villagers lived. To the right of the road going up was the Tourist Hotel. He wondered who managed it now. Its owner had been a secret member of the resistance group in the village. He had been exposed by Sorting and arrested by the Germans during the *razzia* before Christmas 1944. Shot along with several villagers in 1945.

Haugland remembered the first time he'd seen the village in the winter of 1944. He had arrived to begin his assignment to create a resistance cell of fishermen who would work with him and the Shetland Bus. Never had he felt so exposed, for once he was on shore, he would have to be silent while Kjell explained that his newly hired man could not speak or hear. Haugland was almost exposed when he started up to the ridge and did not heed the order of the Nazi sheriff, Fasting, to stop. He kept on walking until he was seized and beaten before Kjell intervened. Haugland knew that his action had frightened his new companion, but it had to be done. People must believe he was deaf. *Where are you now, Fasting? Vollan Prison?* Knowing the ex-sheriff had been arrested and tried last year didn't give Haugland much satisfaction.

As the boat came alongside the wharf, Haugland felt that nervous apprehension again. Wartime jitters did not vanish overnight, and for that he was glad. The events of the last forty-eight hours made it essential he stay alert and wary.

"Looks like you have a welcoming party," Helmer said as he prepared to toss the massive skein of rope over the posts. Down on the dock Ella Bjornson, and Doctor Grimstad waited. Farther back by the *konditori*, a small group of men and women stood and watched.

Haugland frowned. "I thought we were coming in quietly."

"We are."

"Is your cousin Petter here?"

"Don't see his boat. Still out fishing, I guess."

The *Kristine*'s motor began to sputter as Kjell eased the boat into its slip. While Helmer secured the bow of the boat, at the stern Haugland threw a tie over a post on the wharf and pulled the boat against it.

"Jens," Ella Bjornson said clasping her hands together as he climbed down next to her.

"*Fru* Bjornson."

"Oh, it's Ella to you, dear." She quickly signed, You look so well, Jens. I missed you.

Takk, he signed back. Ella was the only villager other than Kjell and his daughters who had made an effort to learn how to sign. It had always touched him. She embraced him with a fierce hug and then stood back. She looked behind him.

"Are Anna and the children coming?"

"There's been a change of plans, Ella," Kjell said as he handed a duffle bag and rucksack down to Haugland. "I'll tell you in the warehouse office. Where's Kitty?"

"She was at the *konditori*." Ella frowned for a moment, then brightened when Haugland signed, Anna and children are fine.

Ella patted his arm. He hoped that was all she needed to know for now.

Haugland shouldered his rucksack. He looked up the wharf. One of the

men had separated out from the group and started for the wharf. *Bugge Grande?* He hadn't seen the lanky fishermen since May of last year. During the war, he sometimes fished with Kjell, but he also had gone out with Sorting.

Haugland turned back to Ella. "Kitty can go up there today as planned. *Takk* for being here."

"Why aren't you wearing your sling?" A lean, gray-haired man came up to Haugland.

He grinned. "Hans." Holding his gloved hand against his chest, Haugland held out his right hand to the village's doctor.

"You're supposed to use the sling for several weeks. I have been reading up on this surgery."

"I was never a good patient, was I?"

"*Nei*. Impatient as ever. Hmph." Grimstad gave Haugland's good hand an extra shake. "Yet you look wonderful. I'm so very glad you have come back."

"*Takk.*"

"Jens, someone is waiting for you," Ella said.

Haugland looked up sharply. Standing by the door to Kjell's office was Kitty Arneson. In her arms she held a white cat with black spots.

"*Hei*, Kitty. You found Gubben," Haugland said as he came up to her.

"*Ja.*" Kitty tightened her grip on the cat. It was starting to squirm.

Where find cat? he signed. He was pleased she understood him and answered, "At the farmhouse. I've been feeding him all spring." She let the cat go. Gubben dashed back into the office. "He's a little wild."

Haugland smiled. "I can see. Lisel will be very happy. She has been so worried."

It had been a year since Haugland had seen Kitty. During that time, Kjell's seventeen-year-old daughter had grown from a plain teenager to someone on the verge of a blossoming beauty. *Duckling to swan,* Haugland thought. *What a change.* Kitty had had a crush on Haugland the whole time he was in Fjellstad. It had amused him then, but he re-alized later what it had meant to Kitty to have him as a part of her family. He was like a big brother. He could also sign with her. She had been a quick study.

Inside Kjell's office, everyone gathered by the wood burning stove where a pot of coffee percolated. Haugland continued to chat with Kitty.

"How are you?" Kitty asked. "Is your hand better?"

"*Ja*. It's better. Are you ready to go up to the *fjell*?"

"I'm all packed. I can't wait to see Lisel and the baby. Will you be going up?"

"*Nei*. I'm going out with your father to see old friends."

"Oh." Kitty blushed.

She still has a crush on me, Haugland thought. "I'll see you when I get back." Come little sister, Haugland signed. He opened his arms to her.

Her eyes lit up. J-E-N-S, she fingerspelled back and came into his arms.

He hugged her close, his gloved hand patting her shoulders. Across the table, Kjell mouthed, *Takk*.

The room filled with chatter as old wartime comrades became reacquainted and changes in the plan were explained. Haugland relaxed, though he wondered what the rest of the village thought in this post-war world.

His answer came not long after when someone knocked on the office door. A small group of fishermen waited outside.

"Is Jens here?" one of the men asked.

Haugland steeled himself and stepped out to greet them. "*Hei*, Sindre Moe," Haugland said to the speaker. "Still setting salmon net for herring?"

The group burst out into laughter. Some slapped Moe on his shoulders, others reached for Haugland. "We brought aquavit," one fisherman said. "Welcome."

Haugland was deeply moved, relieved that the trust he had built with the fishermen in Fjellstad over the seven months he'd lived here still remained. "*Vær så snill*. Come in."

***

After the truck left the cabin, Anna and Margit organized the food they had brought with them from the boat and started a pot of coffee on the stove. Anna laid out another pot for a stew she planned to make.

Since arriving back in Norway, Anna was acutely aware of how Norwegians were food starved for luxuries like coffee, meat, and baking ingredients as well as desperate for clothing. Anna hoped the extra boxes her family in Maryland had assembled would arrive in Fjellstad soon. Despite her anxiety about returning to the village, there were people there she wanted to help other than Kjell and Ella. Helmer Stagg was one. Marta, the cook at the Tourist Hotel, was another. During her time in Fjellstad, the woman occasionally watched Lisel. They had a tenuous, strained arrangement, but Anna's courage in standing up for Marta's daughter during the *razzia* had changed the villagers' opinion of Anna. Anna had saved Ingrid, but never told Jens what had happened to her when she and Ella were summoned to see Rinnan and a Gestapo officer at the Tourist Hotel. It was as bad as anyone in the village could have imagined. *My all for Norway.*

"You're rather pensive," Margit said.

"I'm sorry." Anna put down the potato she was peeling. "Just so much happening. I can't seem to get my bearings."

"Five days. It will be over soon. Then you and Tore can get on with your future."

Anna swiped her peeler across the potato. "I know. This has been an unexpected detour. I thought he would just go to Trondheim and testify. I never thought this might be dangerous. The war is over."

Anna must have struck a sober point with Margit. The woman was quiet for a moment, then said, "When we are able, I want to show you a pistol I have. I want to teach you how to use it. It will be a good thing to know."

"Do you think I need to?"

"Well, it will occupy our time here." Margit shrugged. She picked up a carrot and began scraping it with a knife. "Besides, I think women should know how to defend themselves. I was taught in Sweden along with the men, though I never had to use my weapon."

"What was that like? Being in Sweden during the war. Jens said you were with SOE Norway."

"We had to keep our heads low as the Swedish government did not officially approve of our presence there. I saw every kind of secret agent that came over from Norway. I was both their mother hen and sister."

"You told me last summer that you once saw Jens when he came over."

"I did. That was about two and half years ago."

"But you never saw him last year after Tommy smuggled him out. He was near death, I'm told."

Margit shook her head. "I didn't know about that until after the war. It was all very secret. Some of it still is. I don't know where they took him for treatment."

"So the war really isn't over."

Margit sighed and patted Anna's hand. "I'm afraid not. Not until justice is done.

Chapter 33

Lars Haugland couldn't get back to sleep after the phone call from Trondheim. Instead, he lay awake listening to Siv's soft breathing, the only source of calm in the bedroom. His mind raced over the events of the past six weeks that involved his brother Tore. Eventually, Siv woke up. After they had a quick breakfast, Siv took their son Tryge out to shop at the market. Lars promised to meet up with them later at their local *bakeri*.

Now as he sat at the kitchen table, reading the morning newspaper, his mind went back to the notes Tore had received. When had the first one come? A couple of weeks before he left for America. Since then, there were two more plus the startling one found inside their mother's house. Sorting had escaped, and was possibly heading down to Oslo, but so far no more notes. The prosecutor seemed to have no clue as to where the traitor was. Knowing that Sorting had some inside help disturbed Lars. It pointed to a larger conspiracy.

Lars rubbed his chin. By the clang of a trolley going by and the chatter of children coming through the open apartment window, the city of Oslo was awake. People were going about their day on a Friday morning. No sounds of jackboots on the cobblestones or commands barked in German. It was a normal day in the city, the way it had been before the war. Then why did he feel so uneasy?

The phone by the sofa rang. Lars answered, "*Hallo?*"

"Lars, this is Tommy Renvik."

"Tommy. Did everyone arrive all right?" Lars strained to listen. Tommy's voice sounded distant.

"*Ja*, we're here in Fjellstad, except for the women and children."

"I thought they would go up later."

"That's why I'm calling. Sorting was spotted on a coastal road south of Trondheim. We thought it wise to put in before Fjellstad and get the women up to the cabin earlier than planned. Margit is carrying a sidearm and will keep Anna and her children safe."

Lars gripped the receiver tight in his hand. "Sorting. Was he alone? I had a call early this morning from the prosecutor's office. Said they think the escape was an inside job."

"Sorting wasn't alone. He escaped with another inmate on trial for aiding the Germans. Listen, as soon as Sorting was found missing, officials at all bus depots and train stations were alerted. He can't get far."

"Does Sorting know he is in Fjellstad?"

"I don't think so. Authorities assumed Sorting would make a break for the Swedish border. This was unexpected."

"I still don't like this. All those notes. They were sent to my mother's house. That's why he left. What about Tore? What are you doing to protect my brother?"

"Tore will be well looked after. I've been in contact with my military friends. I've also gotten in touch with some former members of Milorg in this area. They are gathering and will be here in Fjellstad by early tomorrow morning at the latest. I'll have good security for him." Tommy cleared his throat. "If he would stay put. He wants to go out to the islands to see the surviving members of a family that worked with him."

"The Haraldsens." Lars sighed. "I don't think that's wise."

"Well, I rather he stayed in Fjellstad, but I can understand. He said that *Fru* Haraldsen was very kind to him every time he came to visit. He believes she never guessed he was more than a deaf fisherman. I'll be going out with him. Helmer Stagg, is coming."

For moment, Tommy's voice faded away. Lars asked him to repeat his last words. "Good," he said when Tommy finished. Lars paused. It was time for him to go out and meet Siv and Tryge at the *bakeri*, but unease was turning into action just as it had done during the occupation.

He was on the run, hiding from the Germans and Stapo. "I am coming up to Trondheim."

"Today?"

"*Ja*. I'll see if I can get on a military flight. I want to see the monster Rinnan at his trial. From there, I can work with my Milorg contacts and help the prosecutor's office make sure Tore's testimony happens. It's time to end this once and for all. Rinnan and his gang, all the *quislings* must be brought to justice

Chapter 34

Haugland stood at the apartment window above the *konditori* and looked down onto the Fjellstad waterfront. A year and half ago, he had stood in this very spot fingering a cyanide pill as he watched Kjell and other male members of the Fjellstad community being marched by German soldiers into the Arneson's warehouse. Haugland's signal to alert authorities in England that he had a group of American airmen in need of immediate export had been detected. Fortunately, after a tense few hours, the German officer in charge of the soldiers in the village, *Oberleutnant* Schiller, had the villagers released. For a while, they were safe. A few weeks later, Rinnan, along with SS troops, returned with lightning vengeance.

As Haugland looked at the surviving fishing boats tied up, he noticed farther out a lone boat with only its burned-out hull remaining. Kjell had told him that most of the waterfront had been cleaned up during the summer after war's end, but the remains of the fishing boat that belonged to the Stagg family was left as a reminder to what had happened to the village during the war.

They cared for me. Invited me in. This is what I gave them back. He rubbed his hand over the stump of his ring finger sticking out from the leather half glove. In his mind's eye he could see the boats on fire, the orange yellow flames and dark gray smoke pushing up against the falling snow. For a moment he studied the anchored boats, recalling the list of the boats that had been blown up for the village harboring an agent. And those left standing. Kjell and Helmer Stagg had been fingered, but even Kjell wasn't sure if the rest of the village knew what he and Haugland had been doing until after the war. Kjell told Haugland he thought the other boats set on fire were a warning. The Germans sent mixed messages as they needed whatever catch the fishermen could bring in. One thing, Bugge Grande's boat hadn't been touched. Haugland wondered about that again.

Haugland let the curtain drop. He owed the village much. The only way he could repay them was to testify against Rinnan and his cabal.

The door behind him opened. "Jens, it's time to go," Ella Bjornson said. "I'll take you up to the farmhouse, then head out for Eidvik's cabin with Kitty."

"All right. I should be walking up there, but Kjell wants to prepare for the trip out to the Haraldsons'. He thinks I forgot how to fish." He smiled, then turned back to the window. Ella must have caught the fall of his shoulders.

Ella came up to him. "Don't regret coming back. You are a part of our village. We are grateful for what you did for our *på skogen* boys while you were here, helping Kjell and the other fishermen during the fishing season. You saw how warmly you were welcomed. We do not forget." She looked down on the waterfront. "Funny thing, though, the only time I saw you in this room was the night Kjell and the others were rounded up. I didn't know how desperate you were at the time."

"If you knew, I would have failed you then. I never wanted the village to suffer. And yet, it happened anyway. Poor Rika, she never wanted it either."

Ella sighed. "Such a lovely girl. I hope you give Sorting what he deserves. Do you think the police will find him?"

"We're counting on it, but old resistance connections are on alert now."

"When he is found and convicted, then she will be truly at rest. We all will be at rest."

Haugland was quiet for a moment, then asked, "How many know I am testifying?"

"Only Kjell, myself and Helmer. And Dr. Grimstad. As you asked."

"And that Anna and I married?"

"Now that is known. People have been very curious."

"What do they think?" Haugland moved away from the window, then faced her. He counted on her to be direct.

Ella sighed. "Some were surprised. A few confused. But there were others who remember her courage. We women have not forgotten how she saved Ingrid from ruin with that German pig. Now that the village knows she hid Helmer and Kjell during the *razzia*, there are even more favorable opinions. It will just take time to accept that Anna was a *jøssing* all along. Whatever your wartime affair was with her is none of their business. Yet I do think everyone is glad for you being married and having a family. A happy ending to a very troubling time."

Haugland left it at that.

***

Out front, Kjell, Haugland and Kitty gathered beside Ella's old Buick.

Kjell put a bag of wood chips into the *knottgenerator* furnace on the car's back and closed the lid. "That should do," he said. "There are extra bags on the backseat." He turned to Kitty. "Be sure you dress warm. It will be cold at night."

"*Ja*, Pappa."

"I have some extras for Anna," Ella said. "Marta has some toys for the baby and Lisel. Everything is in the blue basket." She kissed Kjell on his cheek, then announced they should get going. "I want to get back before twilight."

Ella drove Haugland up to the farmhouse where Anna and Lisel once lived. Haugland had biked up and down this gravel road many times. On the right, the road flanked a wall of scree and rubble that dropped down to the beach below. A few fishing huts stuck out into the water. To the left, the hills were thick with pine forests and other evergreens, with the occasional openings for small farms.

They drove up the steep road to Anna's farm and came into the yard. It shocked him once again to see the upper part of the old farmhouse missing. Near the end of the war, a chimney fire took out the upper part of the old building. Gone was the roof and main floor that held the kitchen, bedrooms and *stue* with its long window that looked out on the fjord. Only part of the stone fireplace, a wall and few charred posts remained. The farmhouse had been in Einar Fromme's family for over a hundred years. By rights, his daughter Lisel would inherit it. Unfortunately, there was no money to repair it.

As they got out in front of the ancient barn unscathed by the fire, memory hit Haugland in waves as he recalled the first time he had come up here to take care of Lisel's kitten; bringing down wood for Anna's winter fuel—the village needed access to her hay field in exchange; how a tenuous friendship grew with Anna; and finally, the first time they had made love.

Ella stood beside him. "Jens, some of us in the village cleared most of the debris."

"Thank them for me. I think I'll go look around. You can head on down."

"You'll be all right?"

"*Ja.* I'll see you when we get back from the islands." He turned to Kitty. "Thanks for helping out. While you're gone, I'll make sure Gubben is watched."

Ella and Kitty got back into the car. Ella turned the car around, honked, and then chugged down the hill, leaving Haugland alone in the deserted barnyard.

After the car was out of sight, Haugland went into the barn. Here he had cleaned and sharpened Anna's saws and axes. The workshop was deserted now, the tools gone. He slapped his arms in the cold building. His breath came out in little puffs of cloud. He went back outside and took in the warmth of the day. Here on the edge of the barn door he first taught Lisel how to sign. Anna sat on the steps of the house across the yard. She had thought Lisel was bothering him, not realizing he had been genuinely touched by the little girl's attention. He didn't trust Anna then. He was curious why an American woman was accused of betraying her Norwegian husband. He knew more about her than he let on. Torn between revealing himself and helping Lisel who was an innocent child, the daughter of an old family friend, Haugland had banked his emotions down and played his role of deaf fisherman. *Then I fell in love with you.*

A seagull flew over the front of the house, its call a warning. It dropped down to the forest below, but not before revealing its black tips to Haugland. *Herring gull.* They used to swirl around Kjell's nets by the hundreds. He walked over to the farmhouse and climbed up a new set of steps onto the floor. Someone had laid an oiled canvas sheet over it. Here was the hallway that led into Anna's kitchen and the *stue* with its wonderful view of the fjord below. Now the view was open and raw, a warming breeze brushing his cheeks. He tested the canvas-covered floor and finding it solid, walked out to the edge of house.

The burnt remains of the porch lay below in some stacked order, but Anna's fruit trees were untouched and budding out. Farther down to the left, a hidden path through brambles led to his cabin where he lived and kept his illegal wireless transistor radio, his connection to England. To his right, he could make out Kjell's warehouse and fishing boats tied up. Still farther out the fjord's mouth opened to the *Trondheimslea* where he and Kjell would go to the skerries where the Haraldsens lived. He took it all in, then wiped the tears in his eyes.

This is what the war years did to me. Before he testified, he had to face *Fru* Haraldsen. What did she think of his charade? Kjell said that all the Haraldsen men willingly went to work with him in bringing in arms and agents via the Shetland Bus, but what about the women? What about *Fru* Haraldsen? Did she choose? His association with her family put them in mortal danger and eventually killed the majority of the men. He had to face Rinnan, but going to see her in hopes of hearing any words of forgiveness was as terrifying as seeing Rinnan.

The gull called again, joined in by others. *It found something.* Cocking his head to listen, Haugland focused on where the cabin was located in the woods and wondered if someone was down there. The cabin had been blown up by the SS troops once his identity had been discovered.

Three walls had survived, the beams of the roof fallen in. At war's end, he had panicked when he discovered the farmhouse burned down, thinking the villagers had taken their revenge on Anna and killed her, but smoke rising from the cabin gave him hope. He had found Anna there by the fire, waiting for him. He returned a fishhook to her, a symbol of their love and trust.

Now Haugland watched for any sign of smoke, but there was only the circling of the gulls. Still, there could be someone there. He headed to the back and jogged around the stone foundation where the door to the dairy remained locked. Anna had hidden Kjell and Helmer in a hidden cave there during the *razzia*, an act of courage that still amazed him. That took nerves. He jogged down to the path that went from the farmhouse to the cabin. The brambles were budding out, too. He wished he had brought a knife. Their thorns grabbed at his coat as he made his way through.

On the other side, the path opened into the clearing where the cabin sat. He quietly took out his pistol and stepped down. Still a jumbled mess, the beams on one side of the cabin sloped down to the ground, while on the other side beams rested on the wall by the fireplace, but no fire. No one was nearby as far he could tell, but the gulls were landing near the edge of the woods overlooking the road, squabbling among themselves. He went quietly so not to disturb them and looked out. Someone had thrown some garbage in a pile. That someone was on a bike, pedaling fast back to the village.

Chapter 35

Tommy sat at the curtained window of Ella's *konditori* and watched Haugland come down the hill to the waterfront. He looked grim, maybe in pain. When he came in, the little bell over the door rang. He joined Tommy immediately, but not before checking his surroundings even though the cafe was deserted. Ella had closed for the day.

"How was it?" he asked Haugland in English.

"Sadly, it'll take a lot of work to restore it. Still beautiful, though. Peaceful." Haugland paused. "There was someone down at the cabin. Saw him taking off on a bike. I forgot to ask Kjell if the owner, Magnuson, was working on it. Didn't look like him."

"Who would go out there?"

Haugland shrugged. "That's a good question. But then, I haven't lived here in a long time."

Tommy frowned. "Who knows the reason why you're here?"

"Kjell, Helmer, Ella." Haugland rested his gloved hand on the table. "No one else knows. Not sure my name is in the papers yet, but the prosecutor's office could want it confidential up to the time I testify."

"Maybe someone on Rinnan's defense team leaked it. Maybe why Sorting started sending you those nasty notes and escaped."

"I've wondered, but can't see the lawyers doing that, though."

Tommy sat back hard in his chair. "Damn it, I still worry about security for you. Anyone here in the village not happy about you being here?"

"I didn't hear any of that when they were drinking to my health in the warehouse. These fishermen are good people."

"Who was missing in that group of friends?"

"Petter Stagg is out. Think he's fishing with the Nass family, so another three there. Saw Bugge Grande earlier. Not sure he came in. Know there were a couple of deaths this past year. Didn't see anyone from the family who ran the *landhandel* during the war. Think the village booted out them out. They were in the Nasional Samling. Everyone who came to see me matches a boat in the harbor."

"What about the Tourist Hotel? Is the staff local?"

"I haven't been up there in a year." Haugland ran his fingers through his hair. He looked distantly out the window.

"You all right?"

"My hand hurts. I've been avoiding the pain pills. Makes my head cloudy."

"Maybe you should see Grimstad."

"I plan to. Just the scar tissue forming." He spread his fingers wide as far as he could with them in the glove and wiggled them. Then made a fist and opened the hand again. He smiled wryly at Tommy. "There was something else."

"What's that?"

"When I was up there, I had trouble hearing. Wind coming up from the fjord. Oh, I could hear the gulls all right, but not other sounds. My left ear was almost useless in that breeze."

"Would a hearing aid help?"

"Maybe. Still hoping that eardrum will close. I'm fine."

"Yeah, sure you are. Next time you wander off, you're not going alone. I called your brother, by the way. Let him know about Sorting. It's roughly eighteen hours since he escaped and we don't know where he is. I've called in some people from my Milorg group to augment security for you." He cleared his throat. "Lars says he's coming up. Will try to get an evening flight to Trondheim and work on the investigation into the jail break. He's going to see if he can get into the trial proceedings."

Haugland grinned. "My big brother. Did he say there were any more notes?"

"No."

"Good."

The *konditori's* bell rang again. Helmer stepped through the door. "*Hei*, Jens. Kjell's loading. Needs your help."

"I'll be right out." Haugland turned back to Tommy. He shifted in his chair. "I want to show you something before we leave." He placed a 4 x 6 inch black journal on the table. "This was my father's."

"The geology professor at Oslo University."

"Yes" Haugland opened it and flipped through a couple of pages, then stopped. "My father gave it to Starheim at the Viking Museum for safekeeping some time before he was arrested in September of 1940. Kept it hidden all these years. I just got it from Starheim a couple of days ago. " Haugland turned the small book around so Tommy could see the page. "Father lists the names of people at the university and industry that he was concerned about. Anything pop out at you?"

"Can I?" Tommy pulled the book toward him and read. "Hmm, names and notes."

Haugland leaned over, his arms resting on the table. "You had friends in the Norwegian police force that came to Oslo from Sweden to handle security after the capitulation."

"Yeah, but the 1st Airborne Division of the British Army was in charge the first couple of weeks in Oslo. Acted as a police and military force, helped supervise the surrender of the German forces in Norway."

"What about arresting war criminals?"

"They did that. " Tommy frowned. "What are you getting at, Tore?"

"I didn't return to Oslo until mid-June, so I wasn't around during the earlier days of liberation. The rector of the university last year was Adolf Hoel, an NS appointee. He was a geologist, well known for his polar explorations on Greenland and Svalbard. I don't know if he was arrested. He definitely was replaced." Haugland flipped to a page in the journal. "My father underline this name twice. Aske Pilskog. I remember him coming to my parents' home in the 30s, but I don't know what he did during the war."

"Pilskog. Funny, the name sounds familiar, but I don't remember why." Tommy quickly read the note next to the name. "Doesn't say he was in the NS. Your father's just suspicious."

Haugland leaned back. "*Ja*. But there is something going on. Like my father, Pilskog was a geologist. His specialty was in hard rock geology, mining. I wonder if he was associated with any of the mines the Germans took over."

Tommy tapped the page. "Did you see this little asterisk at the end of the note? It's faint, but it's there."

"I didn't."

"I wonder where it leads to." Tommy carefully searched through the journal pages until he came to the back. A pocket was glued to the end page. A faint asterisk star was penciled at the top. "Want to look?"

Haugland took the journal back. "Something inside." He pulled out a folded piece of yellowed notebook paper, its blue lines still visible after all the time. He gently opened it out. "It's a draft of some sort. Addressing the rector at the time, Didrik Seip. I remember him. It's—" Haugland stopped and looked up, his face strained.

"What is it?"

"My father is accusing Pilskog of intentionally fingering Jewish members on the faculty and at the teaching hospital."

"Is there a date?"

"September 10, 1940."

"When was your father arrested?"

"A couple of days later. My brothers and I had to run for it."

Tommy knew what happened next. Haugland got shot, hid at the Deaf School to recover, and then made it to the West Coast. There, Tommy met Haugland for the first time while commandeering a boat to Scotland.

Haugland looked out the window. "This Pilskog, I wonder if he had anything to do with my father's arrest."

"Want me to find out? I have contacts in a group dedicated to finding *quislings* who are in hiding." Tommy took back the journal and the note. "Why don't I copy down these names on the lists and give them to them? Did you ever show this to Lars?"

"Didn't have time."

"I'll see he gets the lists. In meantime, what time do we leave for the Haraldsen's?"

"In about an hour. That'll put us there around six." Haugland stood up. "I'd like it back when you're done."

"Of course. I'll be along shortly."

After Haugland left, Tommy watched him go down to the Arneson warehouse. A fisherman stopped to talk to him, then moved on. Haugland picked up a small crate and carried it down to the *Kristine*. The scene seemed like any other day, but Tommy rubbed his arms like a storm was forming. Maybe it was his apprehension on going out on a boat again. Or maybe there really was a storm coming.

Chapter 36

After forty minutes on the rough gravel road, Ella and Kitty came into sight of Eidsvik's cabin. First, Ella saw a pine forest on a hill to the left, then a meadow sloping away to the right. She looked for a wooden sign with the word, *Velkommen*, painted in blue. She found it leaning on its stake and pointing ahead around the corner. When Ella saw smoke coming out of a chimney, she knew she had arrived. Good, she thought, they are settled in after a day that began the night before. She pulled up in front of the cabin and turned off the motor. The *knottgenerator* on the back continued on. She would have to clear out the ash before she headed back to Fjellstad with new wood fuel.

"I see Lisel," Kitty Arneson said as she leaned over the dashboard. "She has really grown since the last time I saw her. She's six, isn't she?"

"*Ja*. I think her birthday was in February. It's sweet of you to help, dear," Ella said as she pulled up in front of the cabin. "*Fru* Haugland has a lot to handle."

Kitty laughed. "I'm happy to help. I can hardly wait to see the baby. And—I don't mind a few days away from school." Lisel stepped down off the porch and came alongside the driver's side. Ella turned off the car and rolled down the window. "Where is your mamma?" she asked the girl.

"Inside," Lisel jumped up and down when she saw Kitty. "*Hei.*"

Kitty got out of the passenger side. "*Hei*, Lisel." She opened the back door and took out two baskets. Soon the door to the cabin opened and Anna and Margit came out. Anna quickly introduced Margit to Ella who thought Tommy's wife a pretty, but mysterious young woman. *Very capable looking.* Ella wondered what exactly she did in Sweden during the war.

It didn't take long to get everything in the cabin. Ella had brought two glass bottles of milk which they put into the little root cellar in the cabin's floor, bread and pastries, and canned goods. She didn't explain the items were from her ration list. Ella's focus, however, was on baby Nils, awake in a drawer taken out from one of the built-ins in the bedrooms. He lay on his back moving limbs and licking his lips at the same time as he looked up at her. He burst into a smile and pumped his arms.

"Oh, he's precious, Anna." Ella touched one of his hands with a finger. He grabbed onto it. "His hair is almost translucent. I don't think he'll be dark like Jens."

"*Nei*. My grandmother said my hair was like this when I was his age."

"And how is your family in America?"

"Fine, *takk*. Lisel, why don't you show Kitty where she'll sleep," Anna said. "I need to talk to *Tante* Ella."

Ella smiled at being called "aunt." It was still hard to believe that this young mother had once been the most hated person in Fjellstad. All sorts of accusations had been thrown at her, yet Anna's courage when the SS troops overwhelmed the village and she had taken a young teenager's place for a forced dinner with Rinnan and his SD counterpart, had changed opinion of her overnight. *What courage, dear.*

"Oh, before I forget, Jens asked me to give this to you." Ella gave Anna the fishing hook. "He said that you would know what it meant."

Anna unwrapped the cloth and smiled. *Our symbol of love and trust.* "*Ja*, I do. I used to stick it into the post at the bottom of the road up to my house. This is how Jens knew I needed to see him. With the German soldiers occupying the village, I often overheard important things that I could relay to him."

After changing Nils' diaper and settling him down to nap, Anna joined Ella and Margit at the table. Over bowls of stew, the three women sat at the table and talked. Anna told Ella about their trip to Maryland, Jens' surgery and the tribute made to him by a group of fliers he had rescued in Fjellstad during the war seventeen months ago. It was hard sometimes for Ella to listen to stories about food and life moving on in America, yet at the same time it fascinated her with its almost Hollywood movie storyline of the rich America she had seen at the picture shows before the war.

Anna made it clear, though, that she had felt that her family would never totally understand what it was like for the civilian population of Norway to live under the German occupation and now struggle to get back on its feet. "They were very kind with their own war stories of loss and horror, but they are recovering quickly. It's much different here. I admire Norwegians so much."

"I have a friend who is emigrating to America," Margit said. "She's not alone."

Anna sighed. "For now, we stay."

Ella asked Margit about herself and learned a little bit more about her. She was no longer in intelligence—which was all she would say—but was hoping to get some sort of secretary work. "We are planning for a family."

Both Anna and Ella chimed in to say how nice that was to hear.

Through the multi-paned window, the sky to the west hinted at sunset, but there was still hours of light before twilight set. Margit excused herself and said she was going outside for a walk.

"Can we come?" Lisel asked from the hallway to the bedrooms.

"Of course you can," Margit said as she put on her coat. "Just bundle up. It's chilly."

After Margit left with Kitty and Lisel, Ella finally got a chance to speak with Anna on her own. She told Anna of her talk with Jens and his friendly reception with Fjellstad's fishermen.

"I'm glad," Anna said. She picked up the soup bowls and placed them in an old metal sink. "With the baby and adjustments to life immediately after the war, he has been restless, especially the last three months. He had planned to come back here, but not under these circumstances." Anna went on to tell Ella about the notes. "He and Tommy think it's Sorting sending them."

"Oh, dear." Ella shivered remembering her numerous encounters with Sorting at her *konditori*. Once she was told what a viper he was working his way through the fishing community for information, she was extremely careful around him. Sadly, her shop help, Bette, was not. Ella watched Anna put the plug in the sink and pour hot water from the stove over the bowls and silverware. She needed to tell her about what happened to the girl after the war.

"I don't think I really understood that Jens had other duties connected with his intelligence work," Anna said as she added soap to the water. "He's told me little about what he did before he came to Fjellstad."

Ella snorted. "Though Kjell was only in the export, there are things he's not telling me either. I think it has to do with them both working with the British."

"But Jens' also not telling me everything about Sorting, Rinnan and the trial. Is that a secret?"

Something fell outside and both women turned.

Ella watched Anna's face blanch. "I don't know how to answer that, dear. I just know that he loves you very much. Feels protective of you." Ella smoothed out the table cloth in front of her, "You said that Margit knows how to protect you. Is there anyone else who can watch out for you and the children? Not that I'm worried. I don't think Kjell would let Kitty come up here if he didn't think it was safe. It's only for a few days."

"Jens said *Herr* Eidsvik will come tomorrow and check on things. Said he was with Milorg during the war and has friends in the area." Anna came back and sat down at the table. "It's just the waiting. I feel like Jens is exposed. And I—I have my own nightmares about Sorting."

"You talked with Sorting in Fjellstad?" Ella was alarmed by this admission.

"*Nei*. Never. Never spoke to him *ever*." Anna swallowed. "But I know Sorting betrayed my husband Einar. I saw him and Rinnan in our village of Lillehavn. Twice. Then he came to Fjellstad. I was the one who warned Jens before I knew who Jens really was."

"And Kjell warned me." *Oh, how convoluted the German occupation made everything. No one trusting the other. Yet she trusted Jens.*

Anna sat back against her chair. "I wonder where Sorting would go if he couldn't go the way he wanted. I never took the road out of Fjellstad to Trondheim. How would Sorting know that Jens is here, not Oslo? Who does he know from his war days? Weren't they all arrested and now on trial in Trondheim?"

"It's just something we don't know. Unless..." Ella smoothed the tablecloth out again, though she didn't know why she kept doing it. Maybe because of her habit of cleaning off tables at the *konditori*. She cleared her throat. "I don't know if this could be something. I doubt Sorting knows. I had a village girl working at my place. Bette. She was always flirting with him to the point that I feared she'd give away some of our secrets. When the *razzia* hit us, it was discovered that Sorting had been sleeping with her. When the soldiers stormed her father's house, Sorting was brought out in handcuffs—I think to protect his cover. Bette was upstairs. Then the soldiers went in. When all the women were ordered to go to the church, Bette was missing. We assumed she had been raped."

Anna swallowed. "Where is she now?"

Ella smiled sadly. "Gone. She was shamed, shunned by everyone. Her father kicked her out of the house. I felt sorry for her, but it wouldn't do to have her continue to work at the *konditori*. Widow out on the road let her stay at her *pensionat* for a while. Then a couple of months later in early February, she came to see me. She—"

"—was pregnant."

"Exactly. Such a simple girl. Our village was destroyed and our livelihood ruined, but I just couldn't blame it all on her. So I helped her find a place to have the baby and eventually get a new identity."

"Does Kjell know?"

"*Ja*, he knows. But not where she is now."

Anna clasped her hands and put them on the table. "She kept the baby?"

"*Ja*, a little boy. Born in September 1945. He should be walking and talking now."

"Did she think Sorting was the father?"

"Most definitely. She said one of the soldiers tried to rape her, but they all were too drunk. She was so ashamed. I could barely get a straight sentence out her she was crying so much."

"She's not anywhere they say Sorting was spotted?"

"I'm afraid she is."

Chapter 37

Haugland stood at the bow of the *Kristine*, when he caught the first glimpse of the Haraldsen's island.

Their home is still there. His heart pounded. He had heard how SS troops swarmed the island, looking for contraband, explicitly coming for the Haraldsen patriarch, Sig Haraldsen. Sig and his sons had helped Haugland organize men in the local fishing community to meet the Shetland Bus. The black uniformed thugs beat Sig, killed their pets, and drowned their cow.

Haugland was surprised the German soldiers hadn't burned down everything besides the Haraldsen's fishing boats befor they left, taking Sig and all male members of Sig's family to Trondheim for torture and a firing squad. The gas pump on the dock looked operational and the *landhandel*, the Haraldsen's country store, was open for business. Stained dark brown with fiery red window trim, even at a distance Sig's home and business looked well-kept.

The two-story wood building stood on a barren rise with a few birch trees and a long, narrow field of grass for putting up hay. It suggested some degree of farming on the rocky island. As the *Kristine* came closer, Haugland started when he saw a familiar fishing boat tied to a worn dock. The *Marje*.

Haugland shouted back to Kjell. "You didn't tell me Sverre was going to be here."

"Eh?" Kjell stepped out of the wheelhouse while Helmer piloted.

Haugland yelled back again, "I didn't know Sverre would be here. Does he know I'm coming?"

Kjell joined Haugland at the bow. "I didn't say anything. Think that will be a problem?"

"*Nei.* No problem."

Kjell must have caught something in Haugland's tone. He put his gloved hands on the rail next to Haugland. "There are no regrets. *Fru* Haraldsen knew all along Sig was doing something with the Resistance. Only she didn't know the scale of the illegal work like the Bus, and she didn't know how deep you were involved. Sverre, of all people, understands."

Haugland nodded, but now as he thought of it, he wasn't so sure. From the beginning, Sverre had been skeptical, finally agreeing to join in at his father's urging.

"She's been asking about you. Been worried about you."

"Me?" The oppressive guilt Haugland felt since they left Fjellstad pushed down deeper on his chest and shoulders. "She's too kind," he muttered.

"She's a strong woman. She knows what she's lost, but will live for her remaining family. Her grandsons, Kolborg and Agnar, survived Falstad Concentration Camp."

For a moment they stood in silence. A slight breeze rippled the water as the *Kristine* lightly rocked through the water. Gulls began to follow them in hopes for something in the empty fish hold, their cries half-masked by the *tonka-tonka* of the *Kristine*'s engine.

"And Sig's daughter, Andrina Paal?" Haugland asked. She was an old love of Kjell's before he married Kristine Olavson.

Kjell draped his arms on the rail and clasped his hands. His face sagged. "Not well. I don't think she got over the loss of her husband at sea."

"I'm sorry, Kjell. I hope Andrina Paal will find peace." Haugland straightened up and put on a leather glove over his good hand.

Kjell sighed. He waved at the approaching dock. "The damned occupation is over, but every time I see a skinny child in worn shoes and holes in her woolen hose or a headline in the newspapers about some new mass grave found out in the forest, I want to throw a grappling hook at the ugly, ugly world. Damn Germans."

Haugland patted the rail next to Kjell, but didn't answer. Instead, he looked up at the blue sky dotted with wispy white clouds. The late afternoon was still bright, the long twilight hours to come. He breathed in the salt air, surprised how much he missed going out on the fishing boats. "You're getting married, *ja*? That's a good thing."

"How did you know that? We haven't announced."

Haugland laughed. "It's written all over your faces. I'm very happy for you."

As Helmer brought the *Kristine* into an open berth, Tommy gingerly made his way down to join them. Haugland thought Tommy looked seasick. Haugland went to the starboard bow and prepared to tie up. Kjell went to the stern.

Tommy made it to Haugland, grabbing onto the gunwale. "Who's here?" Tommy asked in English. He nodded at the two fishing boats tied up.

"I don't recognize the one with the Ålesund license," Haugland said, "but the other boat is the *Marje*. It belongs to Sverre Haraldsen."

"Is he the one who saw Sorting on the road?"

"Yes." Haugland checked to make sure the line was ready to toss.

"He's Sig's son? The only surviving son?"

"Yes."

"How did he get here so fast?"

Haugland shrugged. "I know his boat. It's fast. It's the one we used for the arms delivery."

"Do you trust him?"

Haugland straightened up. "Of course, I trust him. Why do you ask?"

"Just looking out for you. It wouldn't be the first time that someone blamed a member of Milorg or XU for what hell the Gestapo unleashed on their family or community. Or angry because the Resistance blew up a business and they lost their job." Tommy shook his head in disgust. "When was the last time you saw him?"

Haugland looked for Kjell down at the stern and nodded. In sync with Kjell, he threw the line around the piling and prepared to pull. "The night I got him exported out before they closed the city down." He stiffened, remembering that night. A resistance group had blown up the train at the Orkdal Mine. The German authorities shut Trondheim down and put up checkpoints. After Haugland had Sverre safely on his way to Sweden through a resistance "export" line, Haugland made it past the Gestapo and hid out at the Deaf School until arrangements were made for him to get out.

When Kjell gave him a sign, Haugland pulled on the line and winced. He forgot his healing left hand might object.

"Let me help," Tommy said. "You'll kill yourself." Together along with Kjell, they brought the *Kristine* in tight.

"Jens?" Kjell called.

Haugland looked up. He rubbed his hand.

"*Fru* Haraldsen is here."

So she was. Fru *Haraldsen*. Though from peasant stock she was as aristocratic as Haugland's own mother. He felt a pull of tenderness for her. She had always been kind to him. He wondered again about his charade as a deaf mute.

There was a man next to her who looked vaguely familiar. *Did I fish with him?* Haugland wondered. Sverre was nowhere in sight.

Once the *Kristine* was secured, Haugland and Kjell started up to the *landhandel*. *Fru* Haraldsen nodded at Haugland as he came up to the door. He noticed that she leaned on a cane. Her hair had turned completely white, still pulled back in a bun. She wore a black embroidered cloth scarf and long black dress. New lines etched her face, but her eyes were bright.

"Kjell," she said as he kissed her on both cheeks. "So good to see you. That is your new boat?"

Kjell's face flushed. "*Ja, ja.* Some very generous Americans are making things easy for us in Fjellstad. Helmer Stagg is my new partner. I'm sharing the *Kristine* with my neighbors until everyone is stable."

"Ah, the *Kristine*. She was a lovely woman, Kristine Olavson. You are thoughtful to name the boat after her." She turned to look at

Haugland. He had taken off his fisherman's cap and held it in his good hand. He felt as awkward as a schoolboy though he towered over her.

"Jens. I don't know your real name. May I call you that even though I think you no longer have your notebook or flash your fingers through the air?"

Haugland answered softly, "Jens is fine, *Fru* Haraldsen. *Tusen takk* for letting me come see you. I'm very grateful. I—"

"Shh." Leaning on her cane, *Fru* Haraldson reached up and touched a small scar near his left eye. She looked at his hand with its missing finger in its half-glove, then gently placed a wrinkled hand over it. "Dear boy. You have suffered. I have suffered." Her light blue eyes welled up. Her voice trembled. "You are forgiven."

Haugland fought back tears of his own when she opened her arms to him. In turn, he enveloped her in his arms. This was all he wanted from her. Forgiveness. Of all the people he had encountered during his dangerous mission to work with the Shetland Bus, the Haraldsen family had meant the most to him. Their destruction had haunted him ever since he had learned of their fate.

"Now," *Fru* Haraldsen said after a long moment, "you will come inside, have coffee and some *lefse*. Then we will talk." She wiped back tears. "You must forgive *me* for my state. You are most welcome here." She led the way in.

***

The country store was as Haugland remembered it, though less cluttered. The shelves still held foodstuffs, gear and repair materials for fishing boats. A few lanterns, ropes in neat loops and nets dangled from the beams treated with linseed oil. To the left where a stove burned peat—for it was chilly in the space—was the table in the bay window where many times Haugland had played cards with the Haraldsen men. Haugland recalled the night they had surprised him with a birthday cake. It wasn't his real birthday, only what was on his fake identify papers, but they didn't know that. Their complete acceptance of him had made it all the more hard for Haugland to come back.

Fru Haraldsen invited them to sit at the table while she fetched coffee from behind a heavy wood counter at the back. "Sit, sit, *Vær så snill.*"

"I'll do that, Mamma." In the doorway that led to stairs to the apartment above the store, stood a middle-age woman with fading reddish blonde hair. Like *Fru* Haraldsen, she wore a black dress. She wiped her hands on her striped apron and went behind the counter.

Andrina Paal. Haugland was shocked at the change in her. A once vibrant woman with a charming smile and musical laugh, she looked haggard and worn. *The war touched her like my sister.* When she brought a tray of coffee cups and an enamel coffee pot, Haugland thanked her. Andrina Paal gave him a soft smile as she put the tray on the table.

"Jens," she said.

"Why don't you join us?" Kjell asked. "Look, Helmer is coming in right now and a friend of ours, Tommy Renvik." He got up and pulled another chair over for her. There was a moment of scraping chairs as seating was rearranged around the table. Out of habit, Haugland sat on the outside for easy escape. After Tommy was introduced, Helmer placed a basket full of pastries on the table.

"Something from Ella," Kjell said. "She sends her love."

"Is Sverre here?" Haugland asked. "I see he has his boat back."

Fru Haraldsen and Andrina Paal looked at each other. "My brother is out on the other side of our island," Andrina Paal answered. "He is building a new shed out by the peat bog. His boat was returned by the Norwegian government a few months ago. It took that long after the Germans confiscated it."

Conversation was awkward at first. The women were not used to Haugland speaking, but with the real coffee he had brought and *lefse, krumkake,* and other pastries from Ella's capable hands, the conversation gradually relaxed. They asked Haugland about his postwar life, Anna, Lisel, the baby, and his health. And they were curious about how he knew how to sign like their nephew from Vikna, so he told them about his deaf uncle, Kristian Haugland. Haugland tried to get a sense of *Fru* Haraldsen's situation and the fate of the other widows, her daughters-in-law. Haugland learned that Finn Thorson, a cousin of Sig's and someone Haugland had fished with, was helping *Fru* Haraldsen run the marine repair side of the Haraldsen business. He lived on an island only minutes away. Finn's son was helping, too. Eventually, Finn joined them at the table. The conversation eased with talk of the future for the *landhandel* and Norway in general. Soon, there was laughter, but Haugland sensed an unspoken tension. Perhaps, forgiveness had come a little too quickly.

Chapter 38

Sorting paused on the back steps of Pilskog's house to light a cigarette, then stepped down onto the gravel path that went around the large home. In front of him was an orchard. Beyond the trees, green rolling fields abutted sharp forested mountains of pine. The *fjell* loomed to the south. The early evening was bright and clear, its cool air carrying the lowing of a cow. Sorting took a drag. Skele was right. Pilskog's house was a good place to hide. If only there weren't unexpected complications.

He patted the handgun strapped to his side. He had acquired it on the early morning's search for weapons. Pilskog seemed to be a little less high and mighty after Skele's announcement that Sorting was in Rinnan's Gang. And though Sorting could barely keep his eyes open, he followed Pilskog as they gathered up what arms there were in the house. Sorting ripped the cord to the phone in the hall out of the wall leaving only the phone in the study.

At three in the morning, Pilskog returned to his bedroom. Armed, Skele took over a room across the hall. Sorting preferred sleeping on the first floor. He didn't trust Pilskog and he wanted to keep an on eye on the kitchen where the housekeeper slept. Sorting was sure she was scared enough, but he wanted assurances that she wouldn't bolt. He took a *dyne* and slept on the sofa by the fire. When he woke at nine in the morning, he heard a radio. It crackled with news of the Rinnan trial, but nothing about the escape. Now, twenty-four hours after they had escaped from Vollan Prison, Sorting was anxious to plot their next move.

The back door opened and Skele came in.

"Where Pilskog?" Sorting asked.

"In the *stue*."

"He get the map we wanted?"

"*Ja.* We've been going over it. He's cooperating."

"Good. Anything new about the break on the radio?" Sorting asked.

"*Nei*, but I'm pretty sure they are out looking for us." Skele paused. "The trial certainly has grabbed people's attention. What did you do exactly?"

Sorting drew on his cigarette until the end glowed, then puffed out a cloud of smoke. He smiled. "Maybe you don't want to know." Sorting tapped the end of his cigarette and let the ash fall to the ground. "But that shouldn't put a dent in our friendship." He pointed his cigarette to where the road followed the line of Pilskog's farm. "You sure that's the only way south?"

"That's what Pilskog says. You still thinking of going after Haugland in Oslo?"

"Now that I'm out after a stinking year at Vollan, I think getting the hell out of here is more important. There are other ways to make his life miserable." Sorting paused. *Now why did I say that?*

"I thought you were worried that he's going to testify against you."

Sorting threw the cigarette on the ground and rubbed it out with his shoe. "What I'm worried about right now is where we're going next. I don't trust Pilskog and—that housekeeper is a problem. She knows me."

Chapter 39

At the Haraldsen home, the evening deepened—the sun still showing bright near the horizon—but the ache in Haugland's hand and back deepened, too. He had barely slept on the plane flight from Oslo to where Kjell met them. The long hours were beginning to catch up with him. When fish chowder and bread were brought to the table, he knew he could not leave. As they ate, the conversation finally turned to the most sensitive of topics: the *razzia,* its aftermath, and Rinnan. The subtle tension he had felt earlier deepened.

Kjell had told Haugland some of the story: that after Sig and his sons were executed in the forest near Falstad Concentration Camp, they were thrown into a common grave along with other luckless souls rounded up by the Gestapo. After the war, former members of the NS, the Norwegian Nazi party, were forced to dig up the graves. Sig and his sons were identified and their remains brought back to the island. They were buried up on the hill behind the *landhandel.* Haugland wondered if that was where Sverre really was.

Finn Thorsen wanted to know about the Rinnan trial in Trondheim.

Haugland looked at Tommy. He owed the family an honest answer, but told only what he knew so far, though it wasn't much more than what was in the newspapers. All of Rinnan's main gang members were in the docket. Haugland didn't mention that Sorting was on the loose.

"The bastards...." Sverre Haraldsen stood in the doorway, his tall frame blocking the light. The hate in his eyes made them look black. "I want justice... for my father and brothers... and for my cousins and friends. Why don't they just hang them like they did to traitors in France and Italy?"

Everyone looked at Haugland. He turned to face Sverre. "There will be justice, Sverre," Haugland answered firmly. "But we mustn't forget what kind of country we are and not what we might have become during those five years of occupation. If we don't, then what was the point of it all? Why did we resist?"

Sverre didn't look happy with Haugland's answer.

Kjell cleared his throat. "All of us here were affected by the *razzias* on our villages and homes. There isn't one of us who hasn't lost a family member to *razzias* or worse, the firing squad."

"What about my father?" Sverre balled his hands into fists. "My brothers?"

Haugland looked at *Fru* Haraldsen. "Do you want to hear this?"

"*Ja.*" Her voice was low, but steady.

"From what I learned later, your family and the Hitra men for the most part held up under torture. Which is remarkable because of the number of those involved in the August arms run that Helmer, Magnus, and Sverre took part in. I was arrested and taken to Rinnan's Cloister Christmas Eve. I didn't know about the scope of the *razzia* here, but guessed that something terrible had happened when Holger was brought in to break me. We were both beaten, but he never said a word about who I was. I never saw him after that. I had hoped he and the other men would only be sent to Falstad and remain there until the end of the war."

"Who betrayed us? Was it that A.C. Kjelstrup?"

Andrina Paal gasped, her hands on her mouth.

Sverre ignored her and came in closer. His face was full of anguish.

"Don't judge him too harshly, Sverre," Haugland said softly. "Your brother Holger was a brave man. So was your father. They and the others were able to withstand what was meted out, but not Kjelstrup. Let him rest."

"So Kjelstrup gave up things about our group," Sverre said bitterly, "that led to the *razzia* on my father's house and my brothers."

Haugland prepared to get up, but Sverre wouldn't let it go.

"And what did you do, Jens? What bargain did you make?"

Everyone froze, except Tommy. He jumped up to protect Haugland.

Haugland put out a hand to stay his friend. "I know what you're trying to say, Sverre," he said in a calm voice, "but I forgive you because of what you've lost." Haugland looked at *Fru* Haraldsen. "I loved your family, your fine husband and sons. If it had made any difference in the outcomes of their lives, I would have gladly given mine. There isn't a day that I don't think on it—that I am here and they're gone—but I can't let it ruin what time I have to do my duty. I have the rest of my life to think about it, however long that may be."

Haugland stood up. "*Fru* Haraldsen, if you would be so kind, it's been a long day. I'd like to retire to the boat for the night. I am sorry to have troubled you."

The old woman got up, her voice full of distress. She worked her way around the table. "Jens. *Vær så snill.* Don't go to your boat. I want you and Kjell to stay up in the annex. Much more comfortable. Finn will show you where it is. We can talk in the morning." She glowered at Sverre. "Drina, will you fill a pitcher with hot water for him? Finn, will you see candles are lit?"

Andrina Paal quickly filled the pitcher with water from a heavy boiler on the stove and gave it to Haugland. Her smile reflected shame and regret.

"Do you want me to go with you?" Tommy asked Haugland.

"*Nei,* stay here. I'll be fine. I know *Fru* Haraldsen will get you settled. *God natt.*" Haugland nodded to everyone, then left with Finn to go to the annex added onto the end of the store.

***

As soon as Haugland was out of the room, Kjell jumped up. "Now you've done it!" he spat at Sverre. "What the hell did you do that for? What were you thinking?"

Sverre shook his head. "I don't know. He was defending Kjelstrup. I don't understand."

"Well, you didn't think. How could you say that?" Kjell turned to *Fru* Haraldsen. "Forgive me for bringing such trouble to you this evening. I never thought I'd hear it from your son, my old friend."

Sverre choked back tears. "Why is he alive and my father and brothers gone? There will never be justice."

"Justice?" Kjell was disgusted. He pushed back on Sverre. "You forget that Jens stayed back in the city so he could get you safely on your way to Sweden. That is why *you* are alive. *He* nearly died." Kjell paused, gathering his words. "If you want to blame someone, blame me. I set your father up with Jens in the first place."

"Gentlemen, *vær så snill*" *Fru* Haraldsen put out her hands to separate Kjell and Sverre. "Let there be peace in this house. None of these accusations is doing us any good. What is done is done."

Kjell choked back his words. "I promise you, dearest lady, there will be justice." He looked at Tommy. "There will be justice."

"How?" Sverre asked.

Kjell took a deep breath. "We've haven't told you why Jens is back in Fjellstad. In just a few days, he's going to Trondheim to testify at the Rinnan trial. I must tell you, there is someone or a group of people who do not want him to do that. For the last of couple of months, he has been receiving threatening notes. Just last night, he and his family were forced to leave Oslo. They flew up by seaplane very early this morning. I met them out near Hitra and brought them to Fjellstad. Against my better judgement, Jens insisted that we come here immediately to see you—"

"—Oh, my God, Sorting on the road." Sverre's face turned white.

"*Ja*, Sorting. How could you forget?" Kjell turned to *Fru* Haraldsen." I don't think you know him, but one of Rinnan's men—Odd Sorting— escaped yesterday from Vollan Prison in Trondheim." He looked at Sverre. "I don't think Sorting has ever been out here, but he does know Fjellstad very well. And he has a personal vendetta against Jens."

"Oh." *Fru* Haraldsen put a hand over her mouth. "Does this man know Jens is here?"

"I don't think so. We just know that he was seen on the road down to Vinje. He could easily get down to Fjellstad. Or just flee. The police are out looking for him."

"You said his family came with him? Are they safe?" she asked.

"They are safe." Kjell looked back where Haugland and Finn had gone. "I think I'll retire. It has been a long day. We need to go back in the morning." He kissed *Fru* Haraldsen on both cheeks.

"*God natt*," he said, ignoring Sverre. He went past the counter and found a set of stairs leading up to a darkened hallway. Halfway up, Finn greeted him and handed a lit candle to him. "Jens is in the room on the far right."

Outside the polished pine wood door Kjell listened. The door was slightly ajar and he began to step into the room when he stopped in shock. To his far right at the foot of a built-in bunk bed, Jens was washing himself at a stand. He had stripped naked and had his back to Kjell. Kjell withdrew immediately back into the hall, but not before he had seen by candlelight what had been done to his young friend. Like the canals of Mars, Jens's back and buttocks were a mass of long and ugly raised scars that were still a dark rose color after seventeen months.

Tears in his eyes, Kjell pulled the door back to a crack, secure in knowing that Haugland probably hadn't heard him. He knew he had lost part of his hearing in his left ear. Unlike his other injuries, his hearing hadn't improved and the damage seemed permanent.

Kjell stood outside the door and waited for Jens to dress before going in. He didn't want to embarrass him. He waited for the sound of water splashing to stop and movement near the end of the bed. He prepared to go in again when Sverre came up the stairs. The fisherman didn't notice Kjell until he was almost up to the door.

"Is Jens in there?" he asked. "I want to see him."

"You can't," Kjell said. He turned his back to the door, still incensed with Sverre's behavior. "Wait until tomorrow when you've cooled off."

"I want to see him now," he replied. He brushed past Kjell and pushed open the door.

"Sverre!" Kjell hissed under his breath, but it was too late. Sverre went all the way into the room before he stopped. From where Kjell stood he could see Haugland had his back to Sverre. He was pulling on his woolen long johns. He had slipped them up to his hips and was about to slip into the top portion when he stopped and turned. Sverre just stared at him.

Kjell pulled out of sight.

"Sverre," he heard Jens say. "Close the door. I'd rather not let anyone see me."

Sverre closed the door. Kjell went down the hall and sat on a bench with his candlestick.

***

Inside, Sverre was so mortified by what he had said he couldn't move. What possessed him to blurt out his accusation? Of course, it was Jens who had helped get him out of Trondheim. Jens who had stayed behind, trapped in the city. Torture was such an ugly word, but he couldn't picture it. It was too painful to think of what happened to his own father and brothers. Now with the scars on Jens's back, he could plainly see.

Sverre stood still while Jens finished dressing, looking out the window at the last hush of twilight, ashamed to do anything else. He had seen the Swastika brand mark on Jens's hip. It and everything else was an obscenity. "I'm sorry, Jens. I don't know what got into me." He put his hands up to his temples.

"You always were the skeptic."

"At first. What we did, we did willingly. I just want justice for my family."

Sitting on the lower bunkbed, Jens awkwardly buttoned his wool shirt with his hands, then dried his hair with a towel. The room was unheated and cold.

"We're not unlike, you and I," Jens continued. "I lost a brother to Rinnan. He was one of the Ålesund boys caught trying to leave the country, then shot for Televåg. My deaf uncle was from that fishing village. He was rounded up and died with his neighbors in the Sachsenhausen Concentration Camp in Germany. I want justice too, but I can't condemn those who couldn't hold on. That's inhumane. I—" He threw the towel down on the floor in disgust. "Germany has lost, but now are we going to turn on each other?"

"*Nei.*" Sverre murmured.

"Good. If you think I'm soft on Kjelstrup, you're wrong. He made a mistake. But you or I could have made that mistake."

Sverre listened quietly. He wasn't sure if Jens would have made a mistake. He cleared his throat. "Do you think we'll ever find the person who compromised Kjelstrup?"

Jens answered carefully. "It was a negative agent, someone totally innocent, entrapped by Rinnan, something he was very good at."

"Your friend Tommy says that you are going to testify at his trial."

"*Ja.* In a few days." Jens settled down on the lower bunk and pulled back the down coverlet and a blanket laid out there. "Look, Sverre. Get some sleep. We'll talk some more in the morning."

Jens crawled under the coverlet and pulled the heavy wool blanket on top. "Keep the candle on for Kjell. And with that, he laid down and closed his eyes.

Sverre left, barely holding back tears in his shame.

184 · J.L OAKLEY

Chapter 40

With the coffeepot on the hotplate behind her counter and fresh baked pastries in the display case, Ella Bjornson was ready for the second round of customers to her *konditori*. The fishermen had come through hours before heading out to fish. Now it was time for the rest of the villagers to drop by. She also hoped that Kjell and Jens would be returning soon.

She wondered how it had gone yesterday. She had never met the Hararldsen family, but knew from Kjell that they had been an honest, God-fearing, and hardworking one. Their vicious destruction was a bitter memory from the war. Everyone in Fjellstad and throughout the islands in the *Trondhiemsleia* knew the story and shuddered. Many had wept. Yet, Jens had gone out to make amends. She couldn't imagine what he was going through. *How long can you carry unbending guilt for what you did to save the country we love?*

Standing at the window, she rubbed her shoulders to relieve an ache and thought about her goddaughter, Kitty Arneson. Since she could crawl, the girl had been in and out of this place. Having Kitty here to help out had been a blessing. Gone just twelve hours, Ella missed her chatter with customers in the seating area or helping out in the kitchen. Ella was teaching Kitty how to make some of the *konditori's* specialties.

Ella sighed. Kitty was not like her poor dead sister Rika, who had wanted to get far away from Fjellstad and make a life in the city of Trondheim. After going away to school to become a teacher, Kitty said she wanted to return here and stay. Ella was thrilled to see Kitty at eighteen, finally gaining confidence in what she wanted for herself.

The shop bell rang over the door.

"*God dag*, Per, Hanna," Ella greeted the elderly couple and went behind the display case to serve them. Once they were seated with their pastries and coffee, Ella stepped down into the small *landhandel* she ran alongside her *konditori* and busied herself around the shelves and window displays. In this part of the building, she sold canned goods, dry goods, and other supplies. Ella moved with practiced efficiency, but her mind was elsewhere.

She had come back from the *fjell* late last night and had made her sponges for the morning bake, then went to bed in her upstairs apartment. She hardly had time to get a good night's sleep. It had been a rewarding trip, though. Anna, her friend Margit, and the children were settled in nicely. They had firewood, food and proper clothing for whatever weather they might encounter. May was turning out to be mercurial with sunny days that lit up the skies for the long hours, but also with temperatures dipping down low at night. She had seen the snowbanks around the hills and Eidsvik's cabin. The road was clear, but that could change. Ella prayed that the weather would hold.

Ella adjusted a sign on the ledge in her shop's window. She looked up sharply at the sound of someone shouting on the wharf. At first, she thought it was Kjell's *Kristine* coming to its berth, but instead a small fishing boat come along in front and tied up. Two men got out. She immediately recognized the lanky form of Bugge Grande as he came running up the boards.

She took off her apron and went outside. Several men working on nets joined her.

"What is it?" Sindre, one of the fishermen asked Bugge.

"Found a body out on one of the skerries," Bugge said.

"Did you bring it in?" Ella eyed Bugge curiously.

"*Ja.* It's in the boat."

"Think someone should get *Doktor* Grimstad?" Sindre asked.

Ella turned to Sindre. "Why don't you call?" Grimstad was *statslege*—someone who kept track of illnesses and deaths for the county and could legally act as coroner. "But wait. Was the body in the water?"

"*Nei.* It was buried in the ground," Bugge answered. "Excuse me." He turned and started back down the wharf.

In the ground? Ella wondered what Bugge was doing out there. She also wondered if this was another secret from the war. She had her own secret buried in the church cemetery and feared it might be connected. Ella wrapped her sweater close around her and followed the small group down while Sindre went into the *konditori* to call the doctor. Besides Grimstad, Ella had the only other phone in the village.

Outside the Arneson warehouse, a bundle encased in a deteriorating tarp was lifted up and set out on the boards. Neatly sewn up with a fisherman's cotton line, it stank of earth and decay. Someone had opened the top up, exposing tufts of brown hair on a human head.

"Where was it exactly?" Ella asked.

"The first skerry just outside of the mouth of the fjord," Bugge said

Ella became very still, struggling to stay calm. Her heart pounded. *I mustn't let on.* "Put it in the warehouse. *Docktor* Grimstad can examine it there."

It took ten minutes for the doctor to arrive. By then, Ella had composed herself. During the war, the secret resistance committee of which she, Grimstad, the schoolmaster, and the mayor who was also the owner of the Tourist Hotel, were a part, had to deal with a dead German deserter. To avoid suspicion by the German troops stationed in Fjellstad, the young man was buried as a fisherman in the village cemetery.

Ella was pretty sure the body rotting on the warehouse floor was his killer, a Gestapo agent who had infiltrated the black market and escape line. This dead man had been disposed of by Helmer Stagg and Jens nearly twenty months ago. *What is buried is never hidden,* she thought.

Grimstad sat down on a low stool by the bundle and ripped its closure along its sewn line with a fishing knife. Ella put her sleeve over her nose and coughed as the air filled with dusty, dry rot. Bugge and the growing number of fishermen looked on as Grimstad pulled aside the cloth.

Inside, the body appeared brown and somewhat mummified, its eye sockets sunken. Some of its paper-like skin looked like something had nibbled on the face. *Or was it the time spent in two cycles of Norwegian winter?* The way the jaw and yellowed teeth jutted out showed someone in pain. As the cloth was pulled completely away from the man's chest, Ella could see a long tear and brown stain in what was left of a wool sweater and shirt.

"Looks like someone knifed him," Grimstad said. The doctor went through the motions of examining the corpse, but Ella knew that he knew exactly who this person was and who had buried him. It had been determined that he was a poacher who turned informer after he was arrested by a party of Germans looking for the *på skogen* boys from the village in the fall of 1944.

Was that only eighteen months ago? Ella folded her arms tight remembering how terrified she and the others on the committee were of the Germans finding out about this man and the German deserter.

Grimstad pulled on the sweater. It fell apart in his hands exposing, the wool shirt underneath. He put his hands carefully into the pocket, but found nothing.

"Any need to look further?" Bugge asked. "Do you have to report it?"

"Of course, I do," Grimstad answered. "You know that." Grimstad lowered the glasses on his nose to look at Bugge, then at Ella. "It's obviously an old burial from the war. I have to record everything." Grimstad stood up. "Let's see if a coffin can be made for him. I'll have to check on the death certificates for those lost during the war, but it's my opinion he is not from here. Possibly involved in something nefarious. Black market? Informer? I will, of course, check in with retired Milorg members for any accounts of missing operators."

"Milorg?" Bugge's face blanched.

Ella made note of that. "You can leave the body here for now, Hans. We'll build the coffin here," Ella said. "Kjell should be back soon." Ella looked out to the fjord's mouth and hoped it would be sooner rather than later.

Chapter 41

At the sound of vehicles coming down the Pilskog farm driveway, Sorting woke up. He jumped up from the couch where he had been sleeping in the study and crept to the window. Carefully, he pulled back one of the floor-length drapes. The two black cars marked "Politi" made him reach for his gun. Outside the study, he heard footsteps. Yanking open the hallway door, he grabbed the housekeeper and pulled her into the room.

"You know who I am?" Sorting asked as he pointed the gun at her.

She shook her head, her eyes avoiding his. "*Nei.*"

Sorting grabbed her jaw and forced her to look at him. "Liar."

"*Ja.*" Bette looked up in terror, her eyes wide. Little sweat beads gathered around her mouth.

"Good. And I won't tell who you are, *Fru* Norsby. Very curious why you're hiding here. So you know what to do when they come to the door?" Sorting grabbed her arm and put a finger to his lips. "Especially, if you value that kid with you. Oh, I know you have a little one." Sorting squeezed her arm tighter. "Got it?" When Bette's face went white and her body started to slump, Sorting knew she got his message.

Someone knocked out front. "Now go answer the door." Sorting pushed Bette out into the hall and then slipped behind the half-opened study door, his gun ready. *Where the hell are you, Skele? Where's Pilskog?*

"*God morgen,*" Sorting heard a man say in a raspy, but authoritative voice. "I'm *Inspektør* Knut Barness. Is *Herr Professor* Pilskog awake?"

"Right here, *inspektør,*" Pilskog answered. "How may I help you?" Pilskog came up to the study door and quietly closed it. Sorting leaned against the wide door to listen. All he heard were half-muffled words, but the gist of it was that the policemen were actively searching for two dangerous escapees from Vollan. Had Pilskog seen anything strange on the road?

Pilskog moved closer to the study's door. "*Nei*," he said clearly. "Quite quiet. *Fru* Norsby, you haven't seen anything unusual when you stepped out to get the eggs this morning?"

Bette must have just shook her head. She made no sound.

"See?" Pilskog answered. "If you like, you're welcome to check the sheds. It would give me peace of mind."

There was more muffled talk. Sorting heard the door close and then the crunch of shoes out on the gravel driveway. Once again, the the power of the powerful in society had been shown. Pilskog had standing and respect. If they only knew.

Sorting crept back to the long window, but didn't lift the drape. He could hear clear enough through the pane glass. Two men discussed what to do next. Since he never got a count of how many were in the cars, Sorting could only guess at the numbers, but more voices joined the men.

"I'll check the barn," a voice said. Another said he would check the other outbuildings. Footsteps crunched away around to the west side of the house. Sorting stayed put.

"What do you think?" the raspy voice Sorting recognized as the man called "*Inspektør*," asked.

"Pilskog? He's clean as far as records say. Kept his head down during the occupation. Worked as mine inspector and spokesman for a number of the mines around here. Guest professor of geology at the university in Trondheim."

"But the mines were under German control." The inspector coughed, then cleared his throat. "That makes uncomfortable politics for me. How did he *not* get on the hostage list in Trondheim in 1942? He had as much importance as the others arrested."

"I don't believe Pilskog arrived here until after that. The executions happened not long after the roundup."

The inspector's shoes scattered gravel as he turned sharply away from the window. When he spoke again, his voice was bitter. "There were dinner parties, socializing with the Germans. You could say that Pilskog was forced, but in my opinion, he's just one of many who took advantage of his station in society and simply got away with it while so many suffered." The inspector coughed and cleared his throat again. "Well, sergeant, I'll have you look further if need be. After we're done here, we need to check the next farm, but I'm having another team come in and continue the search beyond. Though Sorting and Skele were spotted on this road two days ago, they couldn't have gotten far on bicycles without being noticed. Damn, why the hell wasn't I informed? That note threw the whole department off."

Note? The note the jailer was supposed to mail from Stordahl? Someone saw me on the road and knew me? Sorting was not happy with this news, but there was little he could do about it. He wanted the men to leave.

A half hour passed. The inspector came back to the door one more time to talk to Pilskog. The housekeeper opened the door to him. Sorting couldn't hear what she said, but by now he was suspicious. *Where was she while they searched?* Once the inspector spoke to Pilskog, then left, Sorting knew he had to speak to her. Make sure the little mouse stayed cowered.

An image of *Fru* Norsby's plump body lying naked in the bed at her father's house in Fjellstad flashed before him. Her moans under him. Stupid country girl so infatuated with him that she gave in to his demands. She wasn't Freyda by any means, but she was the perfect cover. And fresh. He had made a night of it with her as he waited for the SD troops to arrive and the *razzia* on Fjellstad to begin.

That's why she was afraid of him.

Chapter 42

Lars Haugland didn't get a flight out of Oslo until very early the next morning. By then he was satisfied Anna and the children were safe in the mountain cabin and that Tore was on his way back from the Haraldsen's to Fjellstad. It was hard to believe that it was two days since Sorting and Skele had made their break. Lars planned to join in the hunt for them.

Lars arrived at Vaernes Airport north of Trondheim and was greeted by Axel Tafjord, a colleague who had been the head of Milorg in the Sor-Trondelag region during the war. "*Hei*, Axel," Lars said. "*Takk* for meeting me."

"Good flight?" Axel asked.

"The best the military can provide. Fairly smooth coming up."

Lars shifted his suitcase to his right hand and followed Axel through the low building that served as an airport terminal. Knowing that this pre-war civilian and military aerodrome north of Trondheim had been taken over by the Germans during the occupation chagrined him. A strategic German military airport during the war, the Luftwaffe sent out planes to patrol the coast, harass fishermen, and frustrate Allied efforts to move food and war materiel to Murmansk. The Shetland Bus had been a much desired target.

"Never been to this airport," Lars said. "Heard there were improvements."

"*Ja*. The bloody Luftwaffe wasted no time in putting in runways, hangers, and workshops. Had about a hundred buildings at one time. Finished the control tower over there."

"With Polish and Russian slave laborers?"

"*Nei*. Mostly civilians were employed." Axel shook his head. "We in Milorg kept an eye on it throughout the war, but security was tight.

The RAF took the facility over for a few months after capitulation, then turned it over to us. No civilian flights out of here now. It's all Royal Norwegian Air Force." Axel pointed to a small black car. "We're over there."

They loaded Lars's suitcase into the backseat of the car. Before getting in, Lars rested his arms on the passenger side roof. "Anything new about the search for Sorting and Skele?"

"That jailer who helped them get out—authorities found an envelope addressed to your brother in his locker. There's a note inside."

Lars pounded the car's roof with his fist and let loose a string of expletives. "The Devil you say. Have you seen it?"

"*Nei.* They are questioning the man now—trying to find out what he was going to do with it. Possibly mail it up in Selbu. Make the police think Sorting was headed for the Swedish border."

"What are the police doing?"

"I believe they are doing a house-to-house search down towards Vinje, but that coastal area is very rural. Just a few farms. Fishing villages to the west, very few roads going out to them. People mainly get around by boat. Sorting could be anywhere. Even up in the *fjell.*"

"What do you know about the other man with Sorting?"

"Gunnar Skele. Black marketer, poacher, informer. Worked both sides. He's charged on several counts, including murder."

"Fine company to run with. Two rats in a bag. Let's get out of here."

An hour later they were in Trondheim. Axel drove them straight to the expansive Torvet in the heart of the old medieval city. At its circular center the statue of Olav Tryggvason rose high on its tall pedestal.

Everything looks normal, Lars thought. People were out for market dressed in their spring coats and hats. Small stands crowded edges of the streets, their colorful awnings set up for the day. Children strolled with their parents. To the south, the blue-green roof of Nidaros Cathedral and its steeple loomed above trees flush with spring-green growth. Then his eyes caught a large crowd on the next street over. "What's going on there?"

"That's the Tinghus. The court inside is where the trial is going on."

Lars leaned over the dashboard for a better look. "I had no idea the trial drew so many people."

"Every day they gather along the street to see the bus that brings Rinnan and his gang to court. I'm always taken aback with the seven women who are standing trial with him."

Axel found a place to park, easy since there were few cars around. "You can leave your suitcase in the car, unless you need something out of it."

Lars patted his heavy jacket. "I have what I need right here."

Lars got out and stared at the tall building a block away from where they parked. "Is that the Mission Hotel? Is that where they keep the bastard?" An icy chill seized Lars.

"*Ja*. The old Gestapo headquarters. Rinnan's there when he's not in the courtroom," Axel took a satchel out of the backseat. "Now that's justice."

Lars swallowed, a sour taste in his mouth. "Tore was there."

Axel gave Lars a compassionate smile. "*Ja*, of course. We were shocked when we learned he had been arrested. Lost several of my friends in Milorg in the attempt to get him out of Trondheim. The rest of us had to scatter." Axel closed the back door, then paused. "Your brother is one of the bravest men I know. I can't imagine what it's costing him to face Rinnan again after what he went through."

"He's determined to do it, then move on. But right now we have to make sure that he *can* testify. There has to be more behind the notes he's been receiving. Something larger than Sorting wanting Tore out. That note found at Vollan Prison is disturbing. How can we find out more about the whereabouts of Sorting?"

Axel closed the front door. "I have a friend in the police department." Axel nodded to the street on the other side of the Torvet. "But first, let's go see if we can get into the trial. My contact is there on security duty."

Chapter 43

Buttoning up her sweater, Anna followed Margit Renvik down the stairs of Eidsvik's cabin and out onto the gravel road.

"Are you ready?" Margit asked.

Anna swallowed. "*Ja*. As best as I can be."

"Good. Here is the pistol."

"What is it?"

"It's a semi-automatic Walther PK38. It will suit our purpose. It's fairly light and easily hidden."

Anna took it in her hands. The snubbed-nosed gun felt cold. The whole idea of aiming it at someone with the intent to hurt or kill frightened her. She wasn't sure if she could do it.

Margit showed her parts of the gun. "This is the safety. When you are ready to shoot, you push it down. I'm going to keep it on." She went through the parts of the gun, how to slap in the magazine until it clicked. She finally had Anna hold the gun using both hands. "You lay your right finger above the trigger well until you are ready to shoot. For now, line up your sight through those notches." Margit adjusted Anna's fingers gripping the pistol. "Now your hands are right."

"Did you ever fire at anyone?"

"*Ja*. Fortunately, only in practice. But once I came very close when Gestapo operatives in Stockholm discovered one of our safe houses for our agents."

"What did you do?" Anna asked.

"Well, I'm really not allowed to say. But I was ready." Margit smiled at Anna. "I want you to be ready. So now use your left hand to push the safety down. Pull the slide back and let it slide forward."

Anna did as she was told.

"Good. See that pin come out? That's how you know there's a bullet in the chamber. See the stump across the road? Aim for that."

Anna swallowed. "Are you sure Kitty is with the children?"

"On an easy hike up the hill. The sling you put Nils in is very clever."

"It's something I saw in a magazine. Peasant women do it for their babies. It's easy to wrap the shawl around my shoulders and it keeps my hands free. Nils is still light enough for Kitty to carry him that way."

Anna squared her shoulders. "All right, I'm ready." Anna set her feet in the stance Margit had shown her and aimed the gun at the gray stump. She counted *one-two-three* in her head and pulled on the trigger. The sound of the gunshot ricocheted around the lake. She couldn't tell if she had hit anything.

"Do it again," Margit said. "Don't overthink. Just point and fire. You should also take a breath, let it out a bit and fire. You can grip harder if you're worried about the kick. Placing your hands correctly will help you."

"The kick did startle me." Anna fired and this time took out a twig growing out of the stump. Margit had her do it a few more times until Anna's hands felt tender. Anna lowered the gun and set the safety on as Margit had shown her,.

"Good," Margit said. The last thing Margit showed Anna was how to take out the magazine and put in new bullets. "You'll get used to it after awhile. Remember to keep the safety on and put the gun somewhere the kids can't get to it."

"You're scaring me, Margit. No one knows we're here. Is there something you're not telling me?"

"*Nei*, everything is fine. I just thought—" Margit flushed. "I'm sorry for worrying you. Just a couple of more days, then Jens will come and get you, right?"

Not soon enough, Anna thought.

***

The *Kristine* returned to Fjellstad around noon, Kjell piloting. While Helmer and Haugland secured the lines, Tommy brought up gear from the crew quarters. "Thanks, Tommy" Haugland said in English. "I'll keep most of my stuff on the boat, but we can sleep in the warehouse. Kjell has extra cots."

"I could use a nap. Spent most of the night on a bench outside your room watching your door."

"You didn't have to do that. Sverre is no danger to me. He's just troubled, that's all. Who can blame him?" Haugland sighed. "Sig Haraldsen was a rare man. I played a part in the old man's death. Sverre's reminded of what he's lost every day he wakes up."

"For that he should blame the Germans and bloody Rinnan, may he rot in Hell. Rinnan doesn't deserve a firing squad. They should do him the Viking way—throw him in a wolf pit and let them tear him apart. Long and painful." Tommy paused.

Ella Bjornsen stepped out of the office door to the warehouse.

"Huh. Looks like your welcoming committee is back. Something happen? *Fru* Bjornsen looks a bit worried."

Haugland thought she did look worried. "Tell Kjell I'm getting off now." With that he climbed over the bulwark and onto the wharf.

"*Hei*, Ella," he said in Norwegian. "Is everything all right? Is Anna OK?"

"She was fine when I left her. They are all settled in. You and Kjell need to come into the warehouse. We have a problem."

The "problem" was resting in a pine coffin set up on wooden horses. Haugland took one look, then closed up the top. He paused to breathe into his shirtsleeve to clear his nostrils of the smell.

Kjell frowned. Helmer looked sick.

"Who is this?" Tommy asked.

Haugland quickly explained.

"The Devil you say," Tommy said. "And how does this complicate things?"

"Depends on who knows about him," Haugland looked at Ella. "Who found him?"

Ella folded her arms. "Bugge Grande. He found it on a skerry out past the mouth of the fjord."

Haugland stepped away from the coffin. "Why would he be out there digging around?"

Kjell shrugged. "Good question. Bugge Grande doesn't have fishing rights out there."

Haugland looked at Ella. "Anyone in your secret committee put a cache of arms out there during the war?"

"*Nei.* Too dangerous."

"What about Sorting? He stayed in a cabin going out that way." Haugland also remembered that he kept a radio. "Who owns that skerry? Anyone back there now?"

"The Hillestad family owns it," Kjell answered, "but they don't live here. Family comes from Trondheim."

"Where were they during the war?"

"Børsa. Father worked at one of the mines." Kjell's voice was flat. "If you're wondering, Sorting showed up with a rental agreement to use the place. Seemed legit at the time. Later, I had my suspicions."

"What did Bugge say about being there?'

"Was going to have a picnic. Found the ground disturbed," Ella said. "Surprisingly, I believe him. However, he seemed unsettled when I mentioned contacting people we knew who were in Milorg during the war."

Chapter 44

A few hours after the body was sealed in a coffin and taken to the church up on the ridge, Haugland continued on down the road from the church to Doktor Grimstad's home where he also had his practice. Eighteen months after the *razzia,* the row of houses looked as forlorn as the last time Haugland had seen them in May of last year. Noticeably missing was Kjell's house, blown up by SD troops, its basement an open maw. He recalled going down into it with Kjell and discovering that Sorting had been there looking around for any evidence of their resistance work. Now, going down into any basement made Haugland break into a sweat. *The Cloister.*

Haugland hustled past the ruin and went onto Grimstad's home. When he knocked, Grimstad let him in and led him down to his private quarters.

"So, Jens, how have you been, really?" Hans Grimstad asked.

Haugland watched Grimstad look around before he closed the door to his study. When Haugland was here undercover, the village doctor was one of a handful who knew that Haugland was not the deaf fisherman he pretended to be. Haugland knew Grimstad always made sure his housekeeper was gone and his office closed for the day when he came here to talk about resistance matters. *Old habit of caution.*

"If you're asking how the surgery went, I think it went well." Since he knew his friend would be curious, Haugland gingerly took off his half glove and showed him his hand. In the mid-afternoon light, the hand showed no signs of swelling. A puckered, wandering red scar was forming on his palm.

Grimstad, his eyeglasses on his nose, examined Haugland's hand carefully. "Tender?"

"Aches sometimes, but it has only been a month. Just a couple more weeks in the glove and I'm done." Haugland gently slipped the glove back on. "I can close my hand and grab things. Just not quite strong enough in the holding-on-to-things department."

"Very interesting. I wonder if they do this surgery in Trondheim."

Haugland shrugged. "I was very fortunate. Johns Hopkins is one of the best orthopedic hospitals in the world."

"Maybe I could go and take some lectures there."

Haugland clapped Grimstad on his shoulder. "I hope you can."

"It'll be another hour before everyone arrives," Grimstad said. "I've made coffee." He invited Haugland to sit down on one of the over-stuffed chairs. Haugland had always enjoyed coming where he could enjoy looking at the doctor's books and his rock collection. Instead of sitting, he went over to the wall of bookshelves.

"You still collecting rocks?" Haugland asked.

Grimstad laughed. "*Ja.*" Joining Haugland, he picked up a small fossil next to one of the books. "That's my latest one. It's a trilobite found here in Norway."

Looks like my father's, Haugland thought. "My father was a geologist. Taught at Oslo University before the war."

"Really? Always thought you were well-educated. How is your father?"

"He died a few months into the occupation."

"Jens. I'm so sorry."

Haugland looked at the books for a particular one. "You still have that book with illustrations about birds?"

"*Ja, ja.*" Grimstad pulled out the heavy tome. "Beautiful paintings. Didn't know you liked birds,"

Haugland smiled softly. "I didn't let on back then, but my *Onkel* Kris is the artist." He flipped through the book until he found the page with a puffin. He tapped the full page colored painting with its tissue paper sheet over it. "He gave me this one."

"How wonderful. You still have it? I mean—"

"My mother keeps it for me." Haugland tenderly put it back on the shelf, using both hands. "My uncle was deaf."

"Really? Your uncle was deaf?"

"My cover wasn't far from the truth. That's why I can sign." Haugland paused. "My uncle was rounded up at Telavåg. Never came home." Haugland touched the spine of the book.

"Jens." Grimstad shook his head. "I don't know what to say."

For a moment they stood silent. *No words for unspeakable cruelty.*

Finally, Haugland spoke and asked if he could look at Grimstad's fossil.

"*Ja,* sure."

"Nice piece," Haugland said as he held the three-inch trilobite in his hands. "Didn't you once tell me you'd gone to lectures on geology over the years? Olso? Trondheim?"

"Did several times before the war. With the restricted travel during the occupation, only once in 1942."

"Did you ever hear the name of or attend a talk by Aage Pilskog?"

"Pilskog. Hmmm. It sounds familiar."

"He would have been lecturing in Oslo just before the war and in the early days of the occupation."

"Pilskog." Grimstad ran his fingers over a row of books on one of the shelves next to his rock specimens. He stopped and pulled out a book with a narrow spine. He handed the book over to Haugland.

The book had a tan cardboard cover with a glued-on label for the title: *Geology of Sor-Trondelag.* By Aage Pilskog.

"Is this who you think he might be?"

"*Ja.* Think so. Is there a photo inside?"

"Maybe."

Haugland flipped to the back. On the last page there was a short biography. Pilskog's photo was centered above it. "That's him. I met him once. Came to my parent's home." Haugland read through the biography. "Says that he is from Sør-Trondelag. Born near Løkken Verk."

"*Ja.* The pyrite mine."

"Do you know where he is now?"

Grimstad shrugged. "Hard to follow postwar news. I always thought he was up near there during the war. Some connection to all the mines, Thamshavn included. But where he is now, I have no idea."

Haugland frowned.

"Why the interest?"

"I think he betrayed my father."

Chapter 45

After Margit showed Anna how to fire a gun, Anna spent the rest of her morning taking their small assortment of clothes out of her suitcase and putting them away. As she put the folded items into the tight room's built-in drawers, Nils lay on the lower bunk next to her. His serious attention on trying to put a spoon into his mouth made her smile. Outside, through the multi-paned window next to the bunk beds, she could see Kitty and Lisel playing up in a clearing on the forested hill. Anna tested the window's latch and opened it to the sound of their laughter. It gave her temporary peace of mind, but she was glad they had brought warm clothes. Though sunny, the air was chilly. An old pile of snow glistened just inside the clearing.

Margit Renvik tapped on the room's door frame. "Anna?" She spoke in English.

"Yes?"

"When is *Herr* Eidsvik supposed to come up?"

"Sometime around noon. Why?"

"I got the radio to work, but not sure about the battery."

Anna closed the window. "What did you do when you needed batteries during the war?"

"Asked for more from England, but the shipping rates to Sweden were terrible." Margit laughed.

Anna smiled. "I don't know what Jens did when he needed replacements. I suspect the Shetland Bus brought him supplies." She put the last item into the drawer and shut it. "Jens kept his radio in a stump at his cabin."

"The SD didn't find it during the *razzia*?"

"It was already gone. I helped him ship it out of Fjellstad under German approval." Anna quickly told her about the German officer who

was in love with her, how she kept him at arm's length to gather information for Ella and her resistance committee.

"Anna, you continue to astound me."

"My all for Norway." Anna bit her lip and turned away.

Margit came over and hugged her. "I'm so sorry. I can't imagine
what it was like to be so alone."

"I do try to be positive, but some things I can't get out of my mind.
The Ice Front, the snubbing, everyone turning their backs when I came
into a room. Everyone thinking I was a traitor— or worse a German
whore." Anna looked over at Nils and grinned. His brow wrinkled in
concentration as he waved the spoon around his mouth. "All I could
think of was protecting Lisel." Anna looked out the window. Lisel and
Kitty were no longer in the clearing. "But we must go on, don't we?"

Margit squeezed Anna's arm and stepped away. "Yes. On that note,
I made more coffee."

***

They had just settled back in the *stue* when Anna heard the sound of
a truck coming up the road. "That should be *Herr* Eidviks now," Anna
said. She handed Nils to Margit and putting on her sweater, went out on
the porch. Seeing that it was Eidsvik, she waved to him as he pulled up
alongside the steps. He stopped and rolled down his window.

"*Fru* Haugland, *God morgen.*" When he opened the door, his dog
squeezed out and bounded up the steps to Anna.

"Well, *God morgen* to you," Anna said to the dog as it wagged its
feathery tail against her leg. 'You're friendly."

"Not always," Eidsvik said as he put a wooden box of eggs and a
bottle of milk on the porch. "He's usually more standoffish. Seems to
like you right off, *Fru* Haugland.

"Oh, *vær så snil*. Please call me Anna." Anna scratched the dog's
thick ruff above its collar.

"Anna. Then you must call me Jan Karl…" Eidsvik went around to
the back of his truck. "I brought something else." Lowering the gate, he
pulled out a pair of child-size skis made of wood. "For your Lisel. There

are adult skis under the cabin floor." Anna joined Eidsvik at the back, the dog bounding ahead of her. "Is it going to snow?"

"You never know up here. It's a tradition to ski on Easter. I did last month. Higher up behind the cabin there are still fields to ski in." He handed the skis to Anna, then pulled out ski poles. "I just thought it would keep Kitty and Lisel occupied. I assume your daughter knows how."

Anna smiled. "If she didn't, she would be a very odd Norwegian, wouldn't she? Lisel's father was a very good skier and taught her as soon as she could walk. Jens has been skiing with her."

"Good." Eiddsvik nodded at the bright sky dotted with clouds. "There is a storm front coming in, but it shouldn't arrive until a few more days. The fishermen are talking about it. It will bring rain, for sure. Maybe snow up here."

"Hopefully, we'll be gone by then. Have you heard from Jens or Kjell?"

"I had a phone call from Kjell this morning. They're back in Fjell-stad."

Anna wondered how that went. She hoped Jens found some peace from meeting with Fru Haraldsen. "Is there is any word about—Sorting?"

"*Nei.* But never you mind. I have folks working on it."

Margit came out on the porch. "*God morgen.*"

Eidsvik nodded back at her. "*Fru* Renvik. Did you get the radio working?"

"*Ja*".

"Good. Why don't you take the skis—Anna—into the house. I'll show you where the other skis are. I'll take the box. We'll get things put away, then we can chat."

Lisel appeared at the side of the cabin. "Are those skis really for me, Mamma?"

"Why don't you take the poles and see for yourself."

Chapter 46

After the police left, Sorting cautiously went in search of Pilskog and Skele. He found Pilskog alone in the dining room opposite the kitchen.

"Where is Skele?" Sorting asked.

"He stepped out. He's checking the back."

"And your housekeeper?"

"She's in the kitchen." Pilskog picked up his pipe from the sideboard next to him.

"And she didn't talk to the police?"

"*Nei.*" Pilskog struck a match and lit his pipe.

Sorting walked to the long dining table. "Where is *Fru* Norsby from?"

"East of here. She lost her husband during the last days of the occupation."

"Ah. Tragic. She has a child."

Pilskog cocked his head at Sorting, his eyes narrowed.

Sorting smiled. "I heard voices in the kitchen. A little one with the woman."

"*Ja.* A boy." Pilskog stubbed his match into an ash tray on a sideboard, then took a long draw on his pipe.

Still playing the country squire. Sorting's distain for Pilskog grew stronger. "She been with you long?"

"She does her work, stays to herself. I hope you'll respect that."

"Of course." Sorting picked up a hazelnut from a dish on the table and cracked it open with the metal nutcracker next to it. "How Christian of you."

Pilskog stiffened. "The war touched everyone, especially the women. It's the least I could do."

Sorting looked around the dining room with its white paneled walls, paintings, and the long oak table polished to a sheen. Adding to the room's elegance were exquisite white Hardanger lace runners on the side board and table, the kind Freyda loved to collect for her apartment. *The war didn't seem to have affected Pilskog.* "What exactly did you do during the occupation?"

"I spent part of my time in Oslo. Guest lecturer at the university."

"And here?"

"I did some work with the mines. I'm a geologist."

Sorting popped the nut into his mouth. "Nice place you got here."

"This was my family's home. The Germans occupied it for most of the war." Sorting felt Pilskog study his face. *Good.* The *Herr* Professor looked uneasy.

"Now tell me what you really did during the war. Where does 'Svart Hund' come in here? Why would you know Skele by a code name?"

Skele suddenly came through the swinging doors to the dining room. "Because of the nature of our work, isn't that right, Aage?" Skele clapped Sorting on his shoulder as he came around to the side of the table.

Pilskog choked out a cloud of smoke, then coughed a couple of times before gaining his composure.

"Pay him no mind, Odd," Skele continued. "I think the police visit has unsettled him."

"He should be unsettled. We need to go up into the *fjell* as soon as possible. I heard the police say they are going to continue their search southward through the valley. In the *fjell* we could work our way down that way."

"To where?"

"You know where, but first a safer place to lie low. Pilskog will come with us."

Pilskog gasped. "Absolutely not."

Skele straightened up. "He's got a point, Aage. You know this area well."

"I'd rather not. My wife and daughter are expecting me."

"You fucking idiot," Sorting shouted. He braced his hands on the table. "We're not here on some social call. I don't think you have much choice in the matter."

Pilskog's face turned white. His pipe trembled in his hand. He looked at Skele. "Why is he here? This is not what we agreed to."

"And what have you agreed to?" Sorting frowned at Skele.

"Nothing," Skele said. "Aage, you forget that Sorting and I are in this together. We go together."

Pilskog looked sick. He dropped his pipe in a bowl.

"You're right, Odd. We should get up into the *fjell*." Skele pointed to a collection of maps laid out on the table. "These are the maps I was talking about last night."

"They look like mining maps," Sorting said, still wary that Skele could be planning to ditch him.

Pilskog swallowed hard. "*Ja*. They show the best topography."

Sorting pulled out the top map. It showed the area around Sor-Trondelag, the fjords, and the islands of Hitra and Smola. "So going up into the *fjell* is possible?"

"*Ja*. There are some holiday cabins that have opened up since war's end," Pilskog answered in a nervous voice. "No more forbidden zone."

"Good," Sorting said. "How are the roads?"

"Gravel mostly, but passable. It can still freeze at night."

"Then we should make plans, right, Svart Hund?"

Skele glowered at Sorting, then let out a loud guffaw. "That's what I like about you, Sorting. A pragmatist and jokester."

Sorting didn't think it was so funny, but at least he felt they were on track. Skele waved for Pilskog to join them at the table and figure out where to go. For the next half hour, they did just that. When they were done, Pilskog asked if he could leave. He had something to attend to in the barn. "Sure," said Sorting, "but I think your partner should go with you."

Pilskog's face turned red. "I'm only going to check on the day's eggs."

"Isn't that something *Fru* Norsby does?"

"I—"

Sorting thought Pilskog had no answer.

Skele shrugged. "Let's take a stroll. Show me around the place. Where do you get the eggs?"

After the men left, Sorting crossed the hall and went through the kitchen's swinging doors. For a moment he thought the large working kitchen was deserted until he heard a noise on the other side of an oak table that dominated the center of the room. Curious, he went around to the other side. On the floor dressed in jersey shorts with suspenders and jersey shirt, a baby boy sat on the floor playing with a wooden horse. Sorting knew nothing about guessing a child's age, but thought he might be around a year old. When the baby looked up, he smiled at Sorting curiously and then held out his toy. When Sorting didn't take it, the baby went back to banging it on the wooden floor. *Where was the woman?*

"Geir!" Bette's voice came out in a gasp as she rushed past Sorting and scooped the baby up. She backed all the way to the sink, holding the baby tight in her arms. When Sorting advanced, she whispered, "Please don't hurt him." She began to tremble. "I'll do anything you want. But please."

Sorting came up to her. The baby turned to look at him, his dark blue eyes solemn. Sorting reached out and touched the boy's wispy light brown hair. Bette stiffened.

"Ah, I won't hurt him. He's a cute little fellow." He touched her cheek, pleased that she stood perfectly still. "You can do something for me while the others are out. Let's go back to the study."

Bette swallowed. "I—I don't want him to watch."

Sorting smiled. He grabbed her dress above her crotch and twisted it. "*Tusen takk* for the offer, but I want you to make a phone call."

"Phone call?"

"*Ja*. I have the number right here."

Sorting thought the look of relief on her face was comical, but he was beginning to admire her motherly fierceness. He wondered if Freyda would have been like that with their kids.

Chapter 47

The men came into *Doktor* Grimstad's study one by one, each respectfully removing their caps as they found a place to sit. Haugland counted six, including Tommy, who came in last.

"We're all here," Tommy said as he closed the door.

They were young— in their twenties and early thirties, Haugland figured. All once members of Milorg. One looked like an auto mechanic, another a farmer. Two men with their brown hair could have been electricians like Tommy before the war. The fifth smiled.

Haugland chuckled. "Petter Stagg. How are you?"

"Fine." Petter came forward and shook Haugland's good hand. "I thought I'd never see you again."

"An unexpected visit. What are you doing with this crew?"

"I'm here to help you. When Tommy asked..."

"Of course." Nineteen-year-old Petter was one of the two *på skogen* boys from Fjellstad that Haugland had rescued. Haugland had sent Petter to Tommy for training in Milorg. Haugland clapped Petter on his shoulder. "It shouldn't be too difficult an assignment. I'm not going anywhere." Haugland watched Grimstad step over to the bookcase. "We can talk later."

Grimstad called the group to order and briefed them on why they had beenthat hastily called together: the Rinnan trial. "The trial has been going on for a month. Court evidence to Rinnan's atrocities are sealing his fate, but not everyone welcomes their testimony." Grimstad turned to Tommy. "I'll let you explain what has been going on."

Everyone sat up at attention as Tommy joined Grimstad at the bookcase. "This is Jens. For our purposes, I will not say his real name. He is a key witness for the prosecution and you're here to protect him."

All heads in the room turned to Haugland. He nodded and then folding his arms, said nothing. He hoped Tommy would get this over as soon as possible.

Tommy went on to describe Sorting's escape, the previous threats against Haugland and last location of Sorting. Finally, Tommy said "Now, let's get to work."

After an hour, the meeting adjourned. Haugland was pleased that Tommy's plans to protect him included someone assigned to check on Anna and the children up at Eidsvik's cabin from time to time. Haugland wanted them safe. Since coming back from the Haraldsens, he had been unsettled. The old war jitters that had saved him more than once were kicking in.

Look below the surface. Who in the village might pose a threat?

The war had ended just a year ago, but the country was still in half-shadow in terms of returning to normalcy. Old scores were being settled outside the law. Secrets were being laid bare. Like the rotting body Bugge discovered.

As the room cleared out, the new men stayed back to chat with Haugland. One of them said, "We'll be around." Eventually, they left, leaving Tommy and Petter with Haugland and Grimstad.

"Is it true you saw someone up at your old cabin?" Petter asked Haugland.

"*Ja.* Do you know who goes up there now? The cabin is unstable."

Petter shook his head. "We did get permission from Kjell to have someone put up hay at the old farmhouse. The fields are still good. Unless kids from the village go up there, the cabin is pretty much deserted."

Haugland came over to Petter. "Magnuson owns the cabin. Doesn't he go up there? Before I came back into the village, I found some refuse out in front. It looked fairly recent."

"Magnuson is ill," Grimstad said. "I sent him to Trondheim for tests."

Haugland said he was sorry to hear that. "When was that?"

"A couple of days ago." Grimstad pushed a book back on his bookshelf. "Why?"

"I didn't pay attention at the time, but I think something was recently burned in that pile of refuse."

Haugland walked over to the window. Outside, two boys kicked a soccer ball back and forth down the dirt road. For a moment he was distracted, remembering his pre-war university days playing soccer. He had nearly blown his cover here in Fjellstad when Sorting caught him passing a ball to some village boys.

Tommy asked, "What are you going to do about the body, Hans? Are you really going to do a search of records? Haugland says you already know who he is, at least what he did." Haugland turned to listen to Grimstad's answer.

"*Nei*. That was for my neighbors' ears. They have no clue about this man." Grimstad paused and looked at Haugland. "I think, for now, we want to keep it that way. Our priority is to keep Jens safe until Sorting is caught."

"I appreciate that," Haugland said as he rejoined the men, "but news of the body's discovery won't stay in the village." He clenched and unclenched his bad hand. "We need to think about how to quash any further inquiry."

Grimstad frowned. "Why do you say that, Jens?"

"Finding the dead man could expose people higher up who wish to remain hidden. Those persons may have nothing to lose"

Chapter 48

Sorting led Bette into the study and closed the door. He pointed to the rotary phone on the sideboard. "Over there."

Her shoulders taut with fear, Bette obeyed him.

"Put the baby down. You can't phone with one hand."

Bette set Geir down on an Oriental rug. She adjusted her white maid's cap, then waited.

Sorting unrolled the strip of toilet paper with the information on Haugland. "I'm going to dial this number. When someone answers, you are going to ask if Tore Haugland is there. Say that you are an old friend from before the war."

"If they don't say, will that be all?"

"*Nei.* You will be persistent." Sorting dialed the number, hoping that the telephone connections from Pilskog's manor house were in working order. An operator came on and put the call through to Oslo. After a delay, he heard the phone ring. "Get ready to answer. Hold the phone so I can hear."

"*Hallo?*" A female voice came on.

Bette swallowed. "May I speak to *Herr* Tore Haugland. I—I'm an old friend of his from before the war."

"Tore?"

"*Ja.* I— we were in gymnasium together."

"Ah." There was a pause. "My brother is not here."

"He's gone out?" Bette asked. She glanced at Sorting. Her face was ashen.

"*Nei.*" The female voice paused again. "He's gone away."

"Away?"

"*Ja.*"

Sorting resisted grabbing the phone. "Ask where he is," he whispered.

"Oh, I had hoped to speak to him," Bette said. "Perhaps, I could write to him? So much to catch up."

A pause again. When the voice came on again, it sounded hoarse. "He's gone back to a village where he was during the war. That's all I know. No one is telling me, but I heard them talking. Up near Trondheim. I—"

"Solveig!" An older woman's voice came on. "Who are you talking to?" There was a tussle over the phone and the older voice came on. "Who is this?"

"An old university friend." At that point, Geir began to cry. "Oh, I must go. *Takk.*" Bette extended the phone to Sorting, then picked up her baby.

The only sound Sorting heard was the dead drone of the phone on the other end. "Damn!"

Soothing Geir who continued to fuss, Bette stepped away from Sorting. "May I go now?"

Sorting gripped the phone receiver. "*Nei.* You may not. You worked at the *konditori* in Fjellstad. Do you remember the phone number?"

Bette nodded.

"Good. I want you to call and ask for Bugge Grande."

Chapter 49

After being allowed entry into the expansive hall of the Tinghus that rose two stories above its stone floor, Lars Haugland was immediately struck by the number of people from the international press. There were not only reporters, but men with cameras shooting film for movie theater newsreels. On the far left and right, local policemen and military men guarded stairways trimmed with iron diamond-patterned grillwork. Lars looked up to the top floor where people moved back and forth behind windows with the same diamond pattern.

Axel Tafjord followed his gaze. "*Ja.* That's where we're going."

Upstairs, as they approached the doors to the Court of Appeals where the Rinnan trial was being held, Lars stopped and took a deep breath. He felt queasy at the thought of seeing the monster in person. Lars had to remind himself that this was what he had fought for during those five long years of occupation—to defeat the Germans and bring to justice the ones responsible for all the mayhem and cruelty. Last fall, Vidkun Quisling had been executed for his role as leader of the NS, but there was no one as despicable and vicious as Henry Oliver Rinnan. He didn't deserve this trial. He deserved a firing squad.

A soldier snapped to attention as Axel approached him. "Captain Tafjord, sir."

"Colbert," Axel answered and showed him a pass he attained a short while ago. "Who's on the stand?"

"One of Rinnan's women."

"Where's Rinnan?"

"In his seat. You can't miss him. Got a sneer on his face and the Number 1 pinned to his scrawny chest." Colbert nodded at Lars. "Who's your friend?"

"Lars Haugland. Milorg, Oslo. We just want to step in and see for ourselves."

"How is security?" Lars asked as Colbert opened the door.

"Tight."

But you missed someone. Sorting. Lars took another breath and entered the courtroom ahead of Axel.

Inside, Lars paused. He had only seen one photograph of this courtroom in the Oslo newspapers. Here under a high ceiling and lit by tall windows, the courtroom was laid out in efficient order. He stepped in farther, standing next to rows of chairs filled with reporters and the general public. When he looked to his right, he realized that the box of seats framed on each end by wire fencing held Rinnan and his gang.

Alex whispered over Lars's shoulder. "Those are the judges at the back wall seated at that curved desk under the coat of arms. Jury and prosecutor to your left."

Lars didn't hear him. He was vaguely aware of an attractive blonde woman on the witness stand being questioned by one of the prosecutors, but his eyes were on Henry Oliver Rinnan. Seated at the far end of the front row, it was hard to imagine that this man had been the cunning leader of a gang that terrorized *jøssings* and resistance workers for years. Compared to the others in the box, Rinnan was small. Narrow faced, his coarse dark hair was slicked back from his high forehead. He wore a tie and suit jacket with large lapels, but he looked lost in it. Yet as he leaned back and rested on his arm on his chair, occasionally brushing the tag on his chest with the Number 1, he exuded a relaxed confidence that he was in control. As if he was aware that Lars was staring at him, Rinnan turned in his direction and smiled—a slow smile that curled up like a half-Cheshire cat. It hit Lars like a punch to his already roiling stomach. *Bloody bastard. You killed my best friend. Had my brother Per shot. Left Tore for dead.*

Something inside Lars snapped. He lurched toward the defendants' box, but was pulled back by Axel. "Not now," Axel said. "He'll get his due."

"Then get me out of here," Lars growled. "I've seen enough." He shrugged off the policeman who rushed to prevent Lars from getting any closer to Rinnan. "I'm leaving. The Devil to them all."

Chapter 50

The first time the stranger called at the *bakeri*, Ella was there to answer the phone. She didn't recognize the man's voice on the other end of the line. He sounded educated, though, and polite, a local man by his Sør-Trondelag accent. After inquiring how her day was going, he asked her if he might speak to Bugge Grande. Ella didn't ask why. With the only phone with public access in the village, it was customary for Ella to take messages for people. Ella said that she would take a message to him. "May I take a number?"

"I'm afraid I can't do that," the voice said.

"Then call back in twenty minutes."

"*Tusen takk.*"

The second time the stranger rang, Bugge Grande was waiting. When Ella handed the phone to him after answering, he appeared confused that someone would call him. *Had someone died?* From the look on his face after he took up the phone and listened, Ella thought maybe someone had. His face turned from ruddy to white.

Not wishing to pry, Ella stepped down into the *konditori* and straightened cans on a shelf. She watched the half-curtained passage behind the counter where the phone was hung. All she could see of Bugge was his gesturing hand. Occasionally Ella heard his voice arguing. Once he poked his head out and looked around, then went back to speaking. Eventually, he put up the receiver and stepped out.

"Is everything all right, Bugge?" Ella asked.

"*Ja, ja,*" he answered. Bugge straighten up the straps on his overalls and came around the counter. As he stepped down into the *konditori*, he nodded to Ella, said "*Takk,*"and then left, the shop bell jingling behind him,

Ella folded her arms and watched him go out to the bulwark. He stood for what she thought a long time staring at the boats. He never turned when a gull strutting on the stone wall came toward him. When he finally left, Ella wondered what the phone call was about. What had shaken him? Her thoughts were interrupted by the arrival of Marthe and her daughter Ingrid from the Tourist Hotel.

***

Sorting put the phone receiver back on its cradle and turned to Pilskog. "See, that wasn't so hard, *Herr Professor*. You can go now."

"Is that all you want from me?" Pilskog asked. "Just to call that place?"

"For now." Sorting winked at Skele who was leaning against the sofa by the study's fireplace eating a piece of buttered toast. "You can go back to whatever you were doing." Sorting shook a finger at him. "But don't get clever and try something fancy. We don't want the police showing up here again."

Pilskog grimaced and said he understood.

"Good."

"What did you find out?" Skele asked Sorting after Pilskog left.

"Haugland's definitely there in Fjellstad. Bugge says he's staying down at the Arneson warehouse, which I know well."

"Is it easy to get to?"

"*Ja*, sure, from the water. But I could be spotted by any number of the fishermen. I'll have to think about it."

"Too bad."

"I did get an interesting tidbit. Found out Haugland's family is not with him."

"Is the family still in Oslo?"

Sorting laughed. "Closer. Bugge overheard someone speaking. Haugland's woman and kids are in a mountain cabin not far from here." Sorting looked out the window and laughed again. "Just the woman and the kids right up there in that *fjell* just south of us. Easy pickings."

"Humph. The old forbidden zone. Did you find out where it's located?"

"I got a description."

Skele wiped his hands on his pants and came away from the sofa. "Do you trust this fisherman? Can he get us a boat out of here?"

"He's got a boat for sure. Get the woman and kids as hostages first, then meet him south of here."

Skele looked skeptic. "How will you communicate that?

"Pilskog. He's going to be with us for a while."

"What kind of hold do you have over this fisherman, anyway?"

"Enough to get him to do what I ask. Like a lot of fishermen," Sorting went on, "near the end of the war, he could only to sell to German soldiers in the village. I crewed with him for a bit before that. Because he trusted me, I told him I worked with a secret resistance group helping those hiding from the Gestapo. We needed to keep an eye on who was holding back rations, who had extra quotas for fish in the region."

"And you passed it on. Clever." Skele stopped in front of a large oil painting on the wall. It was a country scene of a rustic farm with a woman tending her sheep. "Is that enough of a hold?"

"He's scared to death he'll be found out by the village. And he should be. We had other means to uncover Haugland's resistance cell, but the schoolmaster, and a few others were taken to Fjellstad and shot because of some of his findings." Sorting folded his arms. "Funny how things keep showing up from the war. He found a body out on one of the skerries. Someone murdered the man. Rumor is that it was someone caught poaching."

Skele cocked his head at Sorting. His eyes grew intense. "How long ago?"

Sorting shrugged. "He wasn't clear on it, but the village doctor was going to do some searching." Sorting stepped away from the window, then froze at the sight of a car stopping at the stone gate out on road. "We've got to find Pilskog. The police are back."

Chapter 51

Standing at his front door, Aage Pilskog steeled his shoulders before opening it. When he did, he once again faced *Inspektør* Barness. He was a sturdy man with ruffled dark hair and a no-nonsense look in his eyes. Pilskog guessed he was in his mid thrties and he had prayed that the police detective would come back to save him. Now he feared there would be bloodshed if he said anything wrong.

"*God aften,*" Barness said. "Sorry to trouble you again, *Herr* Professor, but I had a couple of questions to ask of you. May I come in?"

"*Ja,* sure." Pilskog stepped back to let him in. Another policeman followed close behind. Pilskog motioned for them to go into the study. As he closed the front door, he was startled by the number of men outside. Two wore military uniforms and berets. Standing off to the side, they were heavily armed with Sten guns.

"A very nice place you have here, *Herr* Professor," Barness said.

"*Takk.*" It was not lost on Pilskog that the detective would be impressed with the room, but what would he think of it now that many were struggling?

Barness answered Pilskog's unspoken question by acknowledging he had known the house had been occupied by German officers as a retreat. "Have you been back here long?"

"Just a few months," Pilskog answered carefully.

"And you are the only one here at the present?"

"My housekeeper, *Fru* Norsby, and her little boy are here." Pilskog swallowed. *You knew that.* He wondered what Barness was getting at. His heart began to pound. Barness lifted his chin in understanding. He walked up to one of the paintings and studied it with his hands behind his back. "Nice." Barness looked closer at something in the painting, then turned around back to Pilskog. "I want my men to search the house."

"Is there a reason why?"

"Just want to make sure you are not under duress. That you are safe." Barness came over. "The men who escaped are dangerous. They are Rinnan's men. They have nothing to lose." Barness leaned in. "We found two bicycles in your barn earlier. They escaped on bicycles."

"Really?" Pilskog felt the hair on the back of his neck rise. "My wife and I ride bicycles."

"But your wife is not here. Do I have your permission to search?" Before Pilskog could object, Barness, said, "*Takk*," and motioned for his assistant to gather the others for the search. Pilskog's mouth was still open in disbelief when the hallway began to fill with men.

"Stairs?" Barness asked.

"In the back."

"*Takk*," Barness said. He gestured politely with his hand. "And now, let us take a walk through the house. Is there a cellar?"

"*Ja*. We have to go through the kitchen."

Pilskog felt a slow rise of irritation. Barness was acting like *he* owned the house. But what could Pilskog say? Last second actions on his part he hoped would save him from disaster. He sensed, though, that Barness was a thorough investigator, which made Pilskog wonder what he did during the occupation. He couldn't see the man staying with the Trondheim police under German rule. Resistance? Training policeman in Sweden in preparation for capitulation? He smoothed down his hair to steady his nerves.

"Let's start in the hall," Barness was saying. When Pilskog didn't answer, Barness repeated his words.

"Uh. Sorry." Pilskog followed him out as a police officer stepped into the study. "They won't pull everything apart, will they?"

"*Nei*. You have my word on it."

The inspector paused in the hall. It gave Pilskog an opening. "You said Rinnan's men. Are they connected to the trial in Trondheim?"

Barness studied Pilskog in a way that made Pilskog's mouth go dry. "Odd Sorting is the one we want. He's wanted for the murder of a schoolteacher from Lillehavn and the attempted murder of an intelligence officer in XU during the war. This intelligence officer survived and is to testify against him."

"Oh, dear."

"Rinnan and his co-defendants are on trial now, but Sorting will get his due in court." Barness looked up sharply when someone called him from down the end of the hall. "Through the kitchen, I'm told. I'll be along shortly."

Barness pulled a notebook out of his uniform pocket. "So, you see why we are concerned. Sorting was seen on this road a couple of days ago. This agent has gone missing." He slipped out a pencil from the notebook's spine and turned to a page half-filled with scribbles. "Would you give me your telephone number? Please."

Pilskog complied, but his mind was on three policeman and a man with a military uniform going into the kitchen. It wasn't what was in the kitchen, but what was down in the cellar. Adding to his fear was the recent phone call to Fjellstad.

"I see you have a telephone in your study. Do you have another? Oh, what's this?" Barness cocked his head to look under the small telephone stand set against the wall a few feet away. He pulled out the end of a wire covered with a woven cloth binding. "Telephone trouble?"

"There was a buzzing sound on the line, so I took out the phone. I've made an appointment with the telephone company to come and have a look."

Barness stood up and let the line drop. "As you say. Must have been very loud." He nodded down toward the end of the hall. "Shall we? I'd like to see the cellar."

When they stepped into the kitchen, Bette was at the table peeling potatoes like everything was normal. Geir was in his wooden highchair mouthing a rye cracker. Barness greeted her with a polite "*God aften, Fru* Norsby," then proceeded to talk in a low voice to a police officer who was going through a cupboard. Pilskog kept his eyes on Bette. Only once did she look at him, her eyes darting to the inspector and back.

"Excellent," Barness said when he was done. "I see that Egan is ready to accompany us."

Pilskog wanted to ask who Eagan was, then realized he was the man in military uniform. He stood next to the opened door to the cellar, a Sten gun in his hands.

At the top of the stairs, Pilskog pulled the chain to a light bulb dangling from the ceiling and started down. Egan and three policemen pushed past him and stood at the bottom. Barness came behind Pilskog.

"You think someone is down here?" Pilskog asked, doing his best to keep his voice steady. "I would have heard something."

"Not necessarily. Just a precaution."

Pilskog made his way down, his shoes making a hollow clomping sound in the cold cellar. He pulled the chain to another light, illuminating a vast space with a furnace in the center of a concrete floor. Over by one of the stone walls, a pile of wood and a chute next to it showed how the wood was delivered to feed the furnace.

"Check that," Barness said, going around Pilskog. "Someone could have entered through the chute." The policemen spread out. After inspecting the chute, they moved on to a tall wood armoire set against the back wall. It was big enough to hide a person or more.

"Sir," Egan mouthed to Barness as he approached it carefully, his weapon pointed at the armoire's door. Pilskog stayed back, frozen in fear as the policemen made a half circle in front of it.

There was a pause, then Barness signaled for the nearest police officer to open the door. With Egan aiming, it was thrown open. It was nearly empty inside save for a broom and dustpan.

"What do you normally keep in here?" Barness asked, his voice irritated.

"What you see there. It's where my wife kept her golf clubs."

The policemen continued to search the cellar, stopping once to check a bookshelf full of boxes and crocks. Eventually, Barness signaled that they should go upstairs.

Back in the hallway, Barness opened the door to the back of the house and stepped down. The afternoon was still bright, but clouds were forming to the west. "Lovely day," Barness said. "I hope the weather will be as good for Constitution Day. Do you have plans, *Herr* Professor?"

Pilskog stayed in the doorway. "I plan to spend it in Oslo with my family." He watched a police officer study the ground around the kitchen steps. The man leaned down to pick up something with a handkerchief, smelled it, and then came over to Barness.

Barness took the handkerchief and opened it. "Ah. Do you smoke, *Herr* Professor?"

"I enjoy a pipe from time to time."

Barness smiled at him. "Very good. I think this will help."

To Pilskog's horror, Barness held a cigarette butt in his hand.

Chapter 52

From the pitch-dark space behind the wall, Sorting could hear the voices and the footsteps fade away for a final time. Behind him Skele stifled a sneeze with his hand.

"Use a bloody handkerchief," Sorting whispered. "We're not in the clear yet." He felt around until his hands hit the wall of shelves he had seen briefly before Pilskog closed the bookshelf door. Shelves filled with cans, boxes and wine bottles. Sorting looked upward. He heard floorboards creak. "I think they're back upstairs."

"Where? And how many?" Skele whispered back.

"We'll have to wait until Pilskog comes back." Sorting worked his way back to the door where a sliver of light came in from an edge. There was no way of peering into the cellar, but it gave hope that air was getting in. He didn't want to stay here much longer. It was worse than his cell at Vollan Prison.

The floorboards creaked again. Next to Sorting the ghostly shape of Skele looked up.

"Pilskog. You better come," Skele muttered.

"And you better be right about the bastard. You said that if anything happens to us, a letter would go out listing all of his secrets. Don't know how you'd do that, but I believe it."

Skele stifled a sneeze again. "*Ja, ja.* But now I'm worrying about that housekeeper. I don't trust her, either. What kind of hold do you have over her?"

"Oh, let's just say we got to be friends in that fishing village. Folks didn't take kindly to that after the *razzia.* That's why she changed her name."

They were silent for a bit. Sorting fingered the shelf next to him and touched the cool surface of a bottle. By feeling around, he discovered the shelf was full of bottles of similar size. He took one off the shelf and sniffed the top.

"What are you doing?" Skele whispered.

"Pilskog's got quite an inventory here. I smell aquavit."

Skele shifted in the dark. "Well, the Germans occupied the place for a few years."

Sorting felt around for something to open it. His fingers touched a string attached to a nail. Attached to the string was a bottle opener. "Why hide it?" Sorting gave the bottle opener a hard tug on the cap and it opened the bottle with a pop. He took a swig and choked. Though it was as fine a quality as the stash Rinnan kept at his hideouts, Sorting hadn't had any alcohol in a year. He liked the way it warmed his throat going all the way down. He took another swig, then swung the bottle out until it hit Skele on his arm. "Here. Enjoy yourself. I think we'll be here a while."

"*Takk*. Now tell me more about your conquest of *Fru* Norsby."

Sorting took back the bottle and slid down to the hard floor. "It was her stupid cow eyes. She was an easy mark…"

When Pilskog finally returned and pulled the bookcase away from the wall, Sorting was drunk. He was also beginning to wonder if his escapade with Bette had led to more than just a satisfactory night's fling. Who was her little boy's father? Him or the soldiers he had left behind with her?

Chapter 53

Anna stood on the cabin porch and watched twilight descend behind the forested hill to the west.

It's darker up here than down at sea level, she thought.

The tops of pines on the other side of the lake were like black serrated knife points against a fading baby-blue sky. Everything else was shrouded in a stunted light. Anna stepped to the rail and looked south. She could make out where the trees thinned, where the bare *fjell* and its low-growing birches and bushes began. The gravel road wandering toward it seemed like a creamy ribbon in the dim light. She pulled her sweater tighter. The air had a sharpness to it and she wondered if it would snow.

A year ago in April, there had been a heavy snowfall. Petter Stagg and some Milorg men had arrived at her farmhouse in Fjellstad on skis. They took her up to meet Jens in the mountains. For months she had believed Jens dead. The joy of seeing him alive restored some faith in her that the Germans would be defeated and life could return to normal. A tear rolled down Anna's cheek. *Not for me. Not for Jens.*

The screen door screeched behind her and Kitty stepped out. Anna wiped her cheek.

"Nils is asleep. Lisel's tucked in," Kitty said. "I think she'll be out for the night. She was very sleepy when I read to her."

"*Tusen takk*, Kitty. I appreciate your help so much."

"Oh, I love doing it. Nils is so adorable. Lisel is so much fun. I forgot she knew how to sign, but then of course, Jens."

Anna motioned for Kitty to join her. "*Ja*, Jens. Did you ever suspect he could hear?"

"*Nei*, never—though my Pappa knew. My sister Rika and I had to learn some signs so we could 'talk' to Jens." Kitty cleared her throat. "I think it's fun that Lisel, who is much better than I, can sign with me. And I love signing to Jens."

Kitty drew out the word 'love' in a way that made Anna smile. Jens had told her the eighteen year old had a crush on him the whole time he lived in Fjellstad. Kitty was trying to hide the fact she still had that infatuation.

"Well, it is a good thing to know," Anna said. "I'm thinking that I would like to learn more signs, maybe take a course at the University when we go back to Oslo." *When we go back to Oslo.*

Kitty went on like she hadn't heard. "Pappa said Jens has trouble hearing from what they did to him. Is he going to get better?"

"*Ja.* He is going to get better. It just takes time. I appreciate you asking."

Kitty blushed. "I—he's—"

"He's like a big brother, isn't he? And that's very nice. I know that he loves you."

"Oh."

"Kitty, are you all right?"

Kitty looked away then said in a quiet voice, "I'm sorry." She twisted her fingers. "I've been so worried for him—I know about Sorting escaping. And I feel so sad. Helpless. No one wants to say anything, but Rika was the one who got Jens captured by the Gestapo. It makes me weep every time I think of it." Kitty bit her lip. "Jens must hate me for it."

Anna took Kitty's hand. "Jens doesn't hate you. What happened to him does not reflect on you or your father. Rika was not the only one taken in by Rinnan. There is a woman from Smøla who was tricked by men like Sorting. Randi Rhue, I think is her name. She believed she was working with the Resistance, not informing on them. Rinnan's gang is pure evil." Anna took a handkerchief out of her apron pocket. "Here. A good cry is nothing to be ashamed of."

Kitty wiped a tear from her eye. "You are very kind to me."

"I trust you, Kitty. You're a lovely young woman. I know that your love will ensure the safety of my children."

Kitty laughed. "Maybe you think I'm just being silly."

"You are not silly. These are serious times with the trials going on all over the country. For us, we wait for justice in Trondheim. That includes justice for Rika. She will not have died in vain."

To Anna's surprise, Kitty flung her arms about her and gave her a long hug. "*Tusen takk,* for saying that. I miss her so much."

"Of course, you do. Always remember the happy times with her."

Kitty stepped back and wiped her nose. "Will Lisel be going into kindergarten this year?"

"*Ja.* Hard for me to believe. You'll be finishing your third year in gymnasium, *ja*? I heard that you want to be a teacher."

"I do. Just a year to go in school and I'll be at the university in Trondheim."

"I think you'll be a good teacher." Anna squeezed Kitty's hand.

"*Takk.*" Kitty squeezed Anna's hand back, then stretched. "I need to get ready for bed myself." She grinned. "First, a little trip around to the back."

"*God natt,*" Anna said. "See you in the morning." She watched Kitty leave for the outhouse in the back of the cabin. She would be going there soon. She turned back to look at the trees across the lake. The sky was dark, settled down for the short twilight. Somewhere off a night bird called. The screen door screeched again and Margit came out.

"*Hei,*" Anna said.

Margit leaned against the rail and folded her arms. "*Hei.* I've been wondering when you were going to bed. I've put more wood in the stove. We should be good for the night."

"*Takk,*" Anna peered toward the corner of the cabin to make sure Kitty was gone. "I didn't get a chance to ask you, but I saw you talking with Jan Karl before he left. Did he have anything to say about Jens other than what he told me?"

"Jens was due back from the Haraldsen's at noon. There was going to be some sort of meeting afterwards."

"And anything about Sorting?"

"*Nei.*"

Anna tried to read Margit's face. "You sure that is all?"

"Truly. That is all I know from Eidsvik."

Anna stepped down onto the first stair. "I can't stand all this waiting."

"I know. It will be over soon. Sorting will be caught. Jens will testify. What do you plan to do after the trial?"

"Jens and I plan to look for a place of our own in Oslo. He wants to look into going back to the university."

"And you?" Margit asked.

"When Nils is older, I might try to go to school."

"That's nice. I dream of that, too. Sometimes I feel like I'm striving to return to the life that I had before the war, but deep down I understand that can't happen. It's because of what I *know*. What the war and occupation taught me." Margit pushed back from the rail. "I can't share what I did in Sweden, but I hold countless stories of both bravery and depravity in my heart that can keep me up at night." She came over to Anna. "I have to lean on hope, just as I hoped that the war would be over during those five years of hell. I have to focus on the future and my determination to live fully."

At first, Anna didn't know how to answer, but she knew that Margit was telling a truth for both of them. "I'm leaning on hope, too."

Chapter 54

After meeting with the Milorg men, Haugland went down to Ella's apartment for a simple evening meal of salmon and potatoes which she had made for him, Kjell, and Tommy.

Takk, he signed to her as he sat down at her small dining room table. Like old times.

Værsågod, she signed back and smiled. "Now. Please help yourself. It's been a long day, *ja*? Kjell, you can start with the fish." She sat down and put her napkin in her lap, signaling it was time to eat.

The meal was mostly free of any talk about the events of the day. Instead, they talked about the good things happening in the village: a new roof for the school, the lumber for rebuilding the Stagg family home being delivered after Constitution Day. Haugland was also eager to hear more about Anna and the children. Ella had been so harried when Haugland returned to Fjellstad that there hadn't been much time for him to get more details about Anna.

"I think it's a very good arrangement, Jens," Ella said. "The place is comfortable and *Fru* Renvik very capable. Kitty is settling in nicely with Lisel and Nils."

"What about Anna?" Haugland felt guilty that he had to leave her up there.

Ella smiled. "Ah, I do love her. She's quite strong, you know. She was so brave—" Ella stopped and swallowed, then not finishing her sentence, she went on to say that Anna had things running smoothly when she left. She sends your love.

"How's my son? How's Nils?"

"Just precious. What a sweet little boy."

Haugland smiled at that. He knew she had lost her ten-year-old son in a boating accident years ago. "And Lisel?"

"Lisel has grown so much. Smart, very pretty. She reminds me of her father, Einar Fromme. He came here many times as a boy to visit with his grandfather, as you know."

Ella served coffee along with dessert of *lefse* and loganberry jam. The talk turned to what they would do about public interest in the poacher's body. Kjell was sure the newspapers could pick up its discovery and that could cause problems.

"Isn't Grimstad coming up with papers for him?" Tommy asked Haugland.

Haugland put his fork down. "That's the plan. But the police will want to make an inquiry, as they should." He absent-mindedly stroked his gloved hand. "Hopefully, I'll be out of here."

"If not," Tommy said, "I'll have you hidden away."

Haugland looked at the clock on the wall and was surprised that it said eight o'clock. No wonder he ached. He hadn't had a quiet night's rest since he flew out of Oslo three nights ago. He wiped his mouth on his napkin and stood up. "Ella, if you don't mind, I'd like to retire for the night. *Takk for maten.* For everything." He nodded at Tommy and Kjell. "I'll see you in the morning."

"You're not going anywhere without me." Tommy got up and thanked Ella. "*We'll* see you in the morning."

Outside the *konditori,* Haugland watched a fishing boat come in, birds trailing behind with raucous cries. The sun was just below the horizon and would go no farther. It put the hills at the mouth of the fjord into shadow. Pink clouds looking like fish scales gathered high up in the setting sky. Haugland folded his arms. The air had cooled to the point that Haugland wished he had his wool jacket.

Tommy joined him. "You're quiet, Scarlett. What's going on?"

"Not sure. Something feels off."

"I'd say everything feels off to me." Tommy studied Haugland. "You look beat. How's your hand?"

"I think it's gained the ability of predicting weather. Hurts like blazes."

"You might be right. I feel a change coming. The temperature feels like it's dropped. Why don't you go in now? I'll sleep on that old cot in the office."

Haugland sighed. "All right. Wish I knew how Anna is doing."

"Wasn't Eidsvik supposed to go there today? Kjell should be hearing from him soon enough."

"*Ja.*"

Inside the warehouse, Haugland took off his half glove and washed his face at the faucet. As he put the glove back on, he straightened up and leaned back to stare at the ancient rafters above him. Kjell had hung a net up there to dry. Haugland wondered if it was one of the ones he had patched.

He closed his eyes, fighting against the throbbing in his hand. Tommy was right. He was anxious. Haugland worried about Anna and he worried about his village friends and their struggle to recover from the war. He worried about his own frame of mind. *Do I have the strength to face Rinnan?*

Tommy was already settled down on his cot in Kjell's office when Haugland came in. "*God natt,*" Haugland said to him. "See you in the morning."

Tommy saluted him back. "I promise not to snore."

With the door closed, it was quiet in the back room of Kjell's office. Haugland had stayed here when he first arrived in Fjellstad two years ago. He eased down on the cot and laid his head on the musty pillow.

At first, he couldn't sleep, as thoughts and images rushed through his mind, one of which was facing his role of having brought such tragedy on all who had contact with him. The village had welcomed him back, yet he sensed an underlying resentment brewing. *Not safe here.* Eventually, he drifted off to sleep.

***

He dreamed of the cabin up on the hill where he had lived out of the sight of the village during his time here. Where he kept his wireless radio.

It was snowing. And he *was* on his W/T, sending a message to London. The signal made a dot-dot-dot pattern that drew something to the edge of his lantern light. Haugland looked up and saw red eyes glowing at him. The eyes blinked, then withdrew. Carefully, he took off his headset and reached for the Sten gun lying next to the stump where he stored his W/T. He stood up and backed away from the W/T. It continued to send signals without his hand on the key. When he tried to stop it, the signals continued. The red eyes came back, accompanied by two other sets of red eyes. The snow fell heavily. Haugland retreated to the side of the woodshed for protection. The signals continued, but all other sounds disappeared. Through the veil of falling snow, the eyes converged into a single red spotlight and advanced. Haugland stepped back and slammed into a concrete wall behind him. The signals sound hollowed—like dripping water in a laundry room. A door opened. It led down into a basement where something glowed. Haugland didn't want to go down, but the spotlight was cutting a red path toward him. Something told him that he had to go down. Something of value was down there.

The stairs creaked as he went down into the gloom. His heart pounded. He was in the Cloister. As he feared, at the bottom of the stairs a poster on a wall with a skeleton and its scythe greeted him. "*Velcommen til fest*"—Welcome to the party. His back stung in anticipation of the lash. The dripping water got loud, but the glow got brighter, too. He moved across the murky room toward it, then stopped. The glow hovered over a pile of rubbish. Beyond, huddling in the corner, was Anna. Her feet were bound. She raised her head, then signed, Be careful, love. The rubbish glowed, like it had been recently lit. It stunk of seaweed and treason.

I help you, he signed to Anna and took a step.

Suddenly, the skeleton peeled off from the poster and attacked Haugland with bony hands. Its unhinged jaw tried to bite him. Haugland fought back with all his strength and grabbed the skeleton by its bony neck. When he squeezed, the vertebrae fell apart like dominoes. He kept squeezing.

"Haugland!" a voice shouted in Norwegian, then in English. "For God's sake, let go. I don't want to hurt you."

Haugland gripped harder in a panic, then opened his eyes when something clamped around his right hand and twisted.

"Have you lost your mind? Look at me." It was Tommy.

"Tommy." Haugland let go of his hands around Tommy's neck and fell against the paneled wood wall. He clutched his bad hand in pain.

"Bloody hell. What's the matter with you?—" Tommy stopped, his face full of concern.

"Sorry," Haugland answered in English. "Just a nightmare. I get them from time to time." Haugland sat upright and rubbed his forehead.

"Enough to kill someone?"

"Not particularly. I was fighting that damn poster from the Cloister." He massaged his gloved hand and then swung his legs over the bed. He frowned when he saw marks on his friend's neck. "Honestly, it wasn't about you. And I am sorry. What time is it?"

"It's four in the morning. You slept pretty hard, then I heard you talking in your sleep. Almost shouting. You kept going on about a light and that refuse pile."

"Something's there." He didn't add that he thought Anna was in danger.

"You're talking about the cabin?"

"*Ja.*"

"Can it wait a few more hours?"

Haugland shook his head. "I don't think so."

Chapter 55

Haugland slipped out of the warehouse and looked at the early morning sky. It was brightening to the east, but to the west what light there was revealed low clouds. The fishing boats tied up nearby and farther out in the water bobbed gently, their rigging clanging against their masts.

"Don't like the looks of that," Tommy Renvik muttered as he came out and the closed door.

"Hopefully, the weather will hold until after we get back." Haugland swung his leg over his borrowed bicycle, one of several Kjell kept in the warehouse. He adjusted his knapsack over his wool sweater. "Sorry to drag you up there. I just want to check on that pile of rubbish. I was so focused on the person on the bike that I forgot that there were recent ashes. There was more than food in the pile."

Tommy pulled his bike up next to Haugland and straddled it. "Still can't figure out why someone would go up there."

"It's isolated, which is why I liked staying there in the past. I gather Magnuson hasn't bothered to fix it. Grimstad told me after the meeting that Magnuson has been ill for some time—he fears cancer—so it's stayed unrepaired all this time. A perfect place to hold secrets."

"The whole damn place is a minefield of secrets in my opinion."

"And some not of our own making." Haugland ran his fingers through his hair. The slight rise in the wind ruffled it more. The air felt cold and moist on his neck. He put on his fisherman's cap.

Tommy leaned over his handlebars. "What's the other reason you want to go up there?"

"I'm just curious. I didn't really get a chance to check around it the first time."

"You were mumbling about Anna. Was she in the dream?"

"*Ja*. Anna was in the dream. She was in the Cloister, tied up."

"Damn, Haugland. What do you think it means?"

"It's me wanting her and children to be safe while Sorting's still loose."

"Not to worry. One of my men should be up on the road to Eidvik's place by now," Tommy said. "And Margit is well-trained. She was not just a simple secretary during the war."

Haugland chuckled. "I thought you married her for her legs." He stepped on the pedal and took off. Tommy's laugh followed him.

As they rode past the *konditori* to head up to the ridge, Haugland noticed a light had turned on in Ella's apartment. He wondered if she was up earlier with Kitty gone. The girl had lived with her ever since the Germans blew up the Arneson home.

"Do you think we should wake Kjell?" Tommy nodded back at the *Kristine* tied up by the warehouse.

"*Nei*. Let him sleep. He's got a lot on his mind."

The ride out to the cabin seemed longer than Haugland remembered, but he hadn't forgotten the view as the partially graveled road wound along the fjord edge. To his left rose stands of pine and birch that marched back to the top of the steep hill, hiding the precious pastureland beyond. To his right, the land dropped down to a scree of boulders and rocks before it met the fjord's waters. Occasionally, a fish hut on stilts stuck out over the water. As the road was a dead end, few villagers came out this way. Eventually Haugland spotted the lone mailbox marking the dirt driveway that went up to Anna's ruined farmhouse. Here is where she would stick the fishhook into its post to let him know she had something important to tell him.

"That the way to the cabin?" Tommy asked.

"*Nei*. Just a few more feet and you'll see a trail."

Tommy went ahead and stopped. "Someone's here." He pointed to a bicycle half-hidden in the grass that lined the trail.

Haugland joined him. He motioned to a spot ahead of the trail and motioned to hide their bicycles there.

"Which way up?" Tommy whispered after he laid his bicycle in the grass. He took out his pistol and checked his clip.

"A little farther up, there's another trail. You can get to the side of cabin from there." Haugland put his bicycle down and walked down past the trail to the cabin.

"You're not going up that way?" Tommy sputtered.

"*Nei*. I'll go up the farmhouse road and slip down. You check that way. I'll go this way, Right now, we don't know who is up there. It could just be kids."

"At this hour?"

Haugland shrugged. "You never know."

"Or some monster from your dream. I don't like it."

Haugland motioned that he carried his semi-automatic pistol, too. "Meet you on the other side."

As soon as Tommy was out of sight, Haugland jogged up the tree-lined driveway, slowing down where the pines opened up. From there he saw the fruit trees planted below the ruined farmhouse. Haugland cocked his head to listen to any sound, frustrated that he had to rely on the hearing just in his right ear.

He surveyed the scene carefully. It would be a while before the sun cleared the hills and *fjell* to the east, so the light was dim. But he could see clearly. He looked at the house and froze. The ancient door to the dairy in the stone foundation was open. He was certain it was locked when he was up here a couple of days ago.

Who was at the farmhouse? Someone pilfering it? Times were hard, but stealing from a neighbor would be a terrible infraction. He watched for any sign of movement around the door and saw none. Caution, however, told him to wait. Tommy would be getting close to the cabin by now. If Haugland didn't show up, he'd find his way up here.

On Haugland's right, the field ran alongside the edge of the pine and birch forest until it came to a jumble of brambles. A narrow path led down to the cabin. He was torn about going up to the dairy or starting down. He decided to go up.

At the dairy door, Haugland listened carefully. Drawing his pistol, he slowly pushed the door open. It was dark in the cellar. He had come down here once with Anna—was that nineteen months ago? He was with her when she discovered the secret cave hidden in the back of the dairy. That finding had saved Kjell and Helmer while German soldiers searched the house during the *razzia*. But now, the chill of the cellar stirred in Haugland claustrophobic memories of the basement in Rinnan's Cloister. Without a flashlight, he could not make out anything other than long-discarded tins and wooden boxes used for butter and cheesemaking next to him. Satisfied that no one was inside, he came out. Shaking off his unease, he turned toward the brambles. Whoever had come up here must have felt safe leaving his bicycle down on the road. Haugland hoped Tommy would approach the cabin with caution.

He listened for any movement above him, but heard nothing. He left the door open and started down.

The wind had picked up, bringing with it stinging bits of frozen moisture. By the time he reached the brambles, he felt sure they were in for sleet or hail. He took a deep breath and stepped onto the path.

The brown brambles were thick and woody, their thorns catching Haugland's sweater as he passed through. Holding his pistol high in the air, he pulled back, then when freed, went forward.

The shortcut to the cabin began to descend down toward the pines around the back of the cabin. He stopped and listened. Somewhere ahead, a bird flitted in the underbrush, making sharp chirping sounds, but he couldn't tell where exactly it called from. The bird continued on, then suddenly stopped. Haugland stood dead still, searching for the reason. Again nothing. *My ear is playing tricks on me.* He took a step out of the brambles and onto ground covered with pine cones and needles. He heard the click too late. Something cold and metallic touched the side of his head.

"Stay where you are," a familiar voice said. "Put your hands up and drop your gun."

Haugland carefully raised his hands. "You don't want to do this. I'm not alone."

He heard the man shift on his feet. The gun shook in the man's hands. *Be careful with that.* Haugland surmised the man wasn't sure how to use a firearm which made him dangerous. Haugland didn't want to die by the pistol going off accidentally.

"I said put your gun down," the man repeated. He pushed the barrel of the gun against Haugland's skull.

"All right, but if I drop it, it could go off. Hit you in the leg. I'll need to bend down to lay it on the ground. Slowly, of course."

The man eased up on the gun's pressure. He sounded less confident when he told Haugland to do it.

"I'm going to step away," Haugland said. Holding his pistol high, he moved out from the gun's threat and began to crouch down. He laid his pistol down, then gathering all the strength he could muster, he kicked his left leg out at the man's shin. Haugland's foot hit the man's tall rubber boots hard enough to make him wobble, then fall and roll into the pines. It also caused the man's gun to go off. Pine needles rained down on Haugland as he charged the man struggling to get back on his feet.

"Sindre Moe," Haugland shouted as he slammed him into a pine tree. "What were you thinking?"

The fisherman answered by swinging his gun into Haugland's face. Haugland struggled to take the gun away from him, his left hand in its half glove barely able to hold on. Sindre fought back, head bumping Haugland in his face. It was enough to push Haugland back. The fisherman twisted away from Haugland and fired his gun. The shot was wild, but it skimmed along the arm of Haugland's sweater.

"Sindre!" Haugland leaped at Sindre and pulled him down onto the ground. Straddling him, he tore the gun out of fisherman's hand and threw it away. Sindre fought back, trying to scratch Haugland's face. Haugland grabbed Sindre's wrists and forced his arms to the ground. "Stay still. I don't want to hurt you."

Sindre spat at him. That action hurt Haugland more than the stinging in his arm. This was a man he had fished with, played cards with during his time undercover. Someone he trusted. Believing Haugland deaf, Sindre had always treated him with respect. Always patient when he wrote down his words in his notebook or signed, even if he didn't understand what Haugland was saying.

Haugland pushed harder on Sindre's wrists. "Stay still."

Sindre continued to twist and turn, trying to throw Haugland off. "Stop it, Sindre. Enough."

"Do what he says or I'll blow your head off," Tommy barked. "Now."

Sindre stopped struggling. To Haugland's surprise, he began to cry softly. Haugland eased off him and got up. "Sit up, Sindre."

Sindre sat up and drew his knees to his chest. He avoided looking at Haugland, but Tommy must have scared him. Sindre's eyes were wide, growing wider when Tommy said in English to Haugland, "You're hurt."

Haugland looked down on his sweater. Blood bled through the knit sleeve and made a dark trail. "I'll be all right," he answered back in English.

Haugland was pretty sure Sindre didn't speak English, so their conversation made him look even more nervous. He looked back and forth as they talked.

"What do you want to do with him?" Tommy continued in English. He kept his gun on the fisherman.

"I'd like to talk to him. Don't think anything dangerous has been going on here."

"So you say." Keeping his gun trained on Sindre, Tommy picked up the loose pistol. He looked up at the sky. "We don't have much time. Weather's coming."

Sindre finally glanced up at Haugland. Tears still rolled down his cheeks. He looked so miserable that Haugland felt sorry for him.

Haugland sighed and folded his arms. Blood came away on his half glove.

"I'm sorry, Jens."

"I see you are," Haugland answered in Norwegian. "Because you got caught." He wiped his hand on his pants.

"I panicked."

"I can see that, too. Where did you get the gun? It's a Luger."

"Some German left it behind."

Haugland shook his head. "This is not like you, Sindre. Not the man I got to know during my time here. How long have you been taking things out of the cellar? When did you become a thief?"

Sindre swallowed. "Things have been hard. Fishing is hard. I thought it was OK to take what was there. Our village suffered because of her treachery."

Haugland leaned toward him. "Are you talking about Anna? Are you talking about my wife?"

"She was seeing that German officer, Schiller. She—"

"She's an American. After the *razzia*, she was giving information to Ella and what remained of the committee."

"I didn't know."

"Nobody knew. Only Ella. It was always dangerous for Anna to walk such a narrow line with the German troops stationed in the village. Especially with Schiller's interest in her." Haugland was angry now and on the brink of changing his mind about being easy on Sindre. "What were you burning in the fire down by the cabin?"

"Papers. Just papers."

"What kind of papers?" For a moment Haugland thought he might have accidently left something under the cabin's floorboards before he left Fjellstad in late October, 1944—before his arrest in December, two months later.

"Just stuff from the cellar."

"What else?"

"There were a few things that survived the fire. Dishes, tools from the barn, a baby crib. I sold them at a market in Trondheim." Sindre looked at Haugland. "What are you going to do to me?"

"I should turn you over to the sheriff. Stealing from innocent people is a bad thing no matter how hard the times. When the house is restored, it will belong to my step-daughter, Lisel. With her father, Einar Fromme gone, by the law of the *oder,* she is the rightful heir to the property."

"My wife's father-in-law was shot because someone talked."

"I know. But it was not Anna."

Something icy hit Haugland on his cheek.

"We better go," Tommy said, speaking in Norwegian again. "I don't relish a ride back in a hail storm. Grimstad should look at your arm." He waved his pistol at Sindre.

Haugland turned to Sindre. He was up on his knees. His hands were clenched together as in prayer. "What is so interesting about the cabin?" Haugland asked.

Sindre looked surprised. He shrugged. "I guess I wondered how you did it all those months. And had a radio there. No one guessed you could hear."

"You treated me as a decent human being in a time when there was such cruelty. That is why I am surprised by you. This thievery is not the action of the good man I knew." Haugland looked at Tommy. "Maybe I should tell his wife."

"*Nei.* Not Ragnhild. She'll kill me."

"That's exactly the point," Haugland said as he picked up his pistol. "I will, however, tell Ella Bjornson and Doktor Grimstad. They will decide what to do. In the meantime, I want you to show me what you brought down to the cabin, if anything. Show me any papers you haven't destroyed. I want a list of what you sold. I..." Haugland's words were cut off as hail the size of ball bearings rattled down through the pines and clattered onto the forest floor. Together, all three of them ran to the safety of the cabin.

Chapter 56

"About time you got us," Sorting spat when Pilskog finally let them out. "What took you so long?" He put up a hand aching from the cold to shield his eyes from the glare coming from a lone lightbulb hanging in front of him. When he turned back to look into what he thought was a cave, he saw a small room packed floor to ceiling and on shelves with wood boxes, bottles of wine and aquavit, and canned delicacies. Its walls were stone.

German hoard, Sorting thought. *Keeping what the* Wehrmacht *left behind*. He put his fingers to his forehead to quiet the headache growing there.

"I had to make sure they were gone," Pilskog said as he pushed the bookcase back in place with Skele's help. "The inspector is suspicious. He came back because earlier he saw those bikes in the barn. After we went upstairs, he took another look around the house, the barn, even sent his men to look for bike treads on the driveway and out on the road."

"Did he say anything?"

"*Nei*. He thanked me for my time and left."

"You better hope," Skele pushed past Pilskog and started for the stairs. "Where's *Fru* Norsby?"

"She went to bed hours before. She was quite shaken."

"Did *she* say anything?" Sorting asked Pilskog as they went around the big furnace. The chill of the cellar made his breath come out in clouds.

"Not when I was there."

"But you weren't there. You came down here with the inspector. I heard you talking."

"She was in the kitchen when we went back. Just as I left her."

"That's not enough." At the stairs, Sorting paused. He was not only chilled to the bone, but unsteady on his feet. Between him and Skele, they had drunk the whole bottle of *aquavit* or was it two? He realized that he shouldn't show any sign of weakness around Pilskog. He still didn't trust him.

"What time is it?" Sorting asked.

"It's past one in the morning."

"What?" Sorting raised his fist at Pilskog. "You bastard."

"Please. Come upstairs. I have *lapkaus* and coffee." Pilskog waved Sorting forward, then gasped when there was shouting upstairs.

Skele. Sorting brushed past Pilskog and stumbled through the cellar door into the kitchen.

"What's going on?"

"The bitch is gone. She's not in her room." Skele pointed to the opened door to Bette's room.

"The Devil." Sorting turned on Pilskog as he came into the kitchen and grabbed him by the shirt collar. He shook Pilskog hard. "Where is she? You send her after the police?"

"*Nei, nei*" Cowering, Pilskog crossed his hands in front of his face. "I said goodnight to her hours ago. I thought *Fru* Norsby and her son were asleep."

Skele paced around the kitchen table and pushed through the swinging kitchen door. "Hall's dark," he said and came back in. "We've got to get her."

"What we need to do is get out of here. Now." Sorting shoved Pilskog against the wall. "When did the police leave?"

"A-about six hours ago."

"And you didn't get us out then?" Skele rushed across the room and pinned Pilskog on his other side. "I told you what I'd do if you crossed us. Your precious wife and daughter will get it. Everyone will know your whole sordid business."

"Wait, wait. It wasn't safe to bring you up. I think the police put a couple of officers out on the road."

"How would you know?" Sorting took the pressure off Pilskog's shoulder.

"Because I've been watching from the study. All night. I thought I saw a small light leave about a half-hour ago, but I still didn't think it safe until now."

Now Sorting was alarmed. *Would Bette have gone out to them? And when?* He let go of Pilskog and went to the back door. When he opened it, a blast of cold, moist air hit him hard enough to sober him up. He fumbled for a light switch and turned it on. To his shock, the steps were covered with snow. He turned back to Pilskog. "When did this happen?"

"Not too long ago."

Sorting looked closer at the steps. He could make out faint footsteps. Beyond the light, a lone snowflake drifted down, then another and another. Sorting thought the footsteps went out toward the barn. "She went out this way. She couldn't have gone far. Not with the kid."

"I'll go get her," As Skele stepped away from Pilskog, he pulled a gun out of his pants belt and pointed it briefly at him.

Pilskog swallowed hard. "*Vær så snill*. Please. I didn't know she was gone."

"Don't waste time on him." Sorting shook with rage. "Where do you keep your flashlights?"

Pilskog waved his hand at a drawer near the sink. Sorting found a large one along with a knife. He gave them to Skele. "Go get her, but be careful."

After Skele tore out into the dark, Sorting grabbed Pilskog and forced him down on a chair at the kitchen table.

"Now," Sorting said. "This car you have. It's filled up?"

"*Ja, ja.* I got gas the other day." Pilskog clasped his hands together and put them under his chin. "You're not going to hurt her?"

"Why would we hurt her?"

Pilskog didn't seem to listen. "She's just scared. She's a mother. She wants to protect her little boy."

"Taking off in the snow like that?" Sorting paused, remembering his suspicion about the kid's parentage. "How come you care so much?" Sorting didn't wait for an answer. "Norsby isn't her real name. Did you know that?"

Pilskog's eyes widened. He frowned like he was thinking through something. Finally, he said. "*Ja*, I knew. My wife and I both knew." He looked at Sorting. "There was a *razzia* in Fjellstad and she was assaulted. I think you gather where I am going. The war was hard on the women."

Geir, Sorting thought. He caught himself. For some women it wasn't so hard. There were seven of them on trial right now along with Rinnan. They helped the Rinnan gang run smoothly. They did it willingly—with enthusiasm.

Sorting changed the subject. "Those maps you showed us. There's more than one way to get up into the *fjell*?"

"*Ja*. I showed you."

"Your car has chains?"

Pilskog nodded that it did.

Sorting got up. "We'll need extra clothes. Sweaters, coats. Gloves. Whatever you have. And I bet you have the best."

Pilskog started to sputter when they heard a scream from outside. A second one followed, but was squashed. That sound reminded Sorting of the time he accidentally stepped on a mouse at his grandfather's *seter*. Just a squeak, but one of dying agony. Sorting ran to the door and threw it open.

The snow was drifting down steadily, yet Sorting could see two figures coming toward him. One figure was pulling, while the other one seemed slumped over. When Skele got to the steps, Sorting realized he had Bette under his arm. She seemed dazed.

"Where did you find her?"

"Up on the road. She must have thought the police were still up there." Skele half-dragged, half-lifted her up the stairs and continued through in the kitchen to her bedroom where he threw her on the floor. I'm going to teach her a lesson." He undid his belt.

"Wait. Where's the kid?" Sorting realized that the baby wasn't with her.

Skele waved his hand out toward the open kitchen door. "Out there." He turned back to Bette who was struggling to her feet. She got to her knees when Skele gave her a vicious kick in her side that sent her head banging against the corner of the metal bedframe. For the second time, Sorting heard a sound that brought an unwelcome memory: the body of Einar Fromme down in the Cloister; Sorting standing over him with a sledge hammer in his hands. Bette's head made the same sickening sound as when Sorting mashed the dead man's limbs.s

"Oh, my God," Pilskog cried as he jumped up from the table. "What have you done?"

"Shut up." Skele jabbed her slumped body with his shoe, but she didn't move. Around her head, blood began to appear.

"Leave her, Skele," Sorting shouted. He turned to Pilskog. "If you value your life, you will go out and bring back the baby. Then we will load the car and go. Do you hear me?"

Pilskog's face had turned white. Sorting barely heard him answer, "If I help you get out of here, will you let me go?"

Sorting thought that was unlikely. The only thing that would get them out of this mess was to find Haugland's woman and kids and take them hostage.

Chapter 57

Lying in bed, Lars sensed someone at the bedroom door before he heard a voice. He silently sat up in the dark. For a moment he was disoriented, then remembered he was in the apartment of Axel Tafjord, his host. He relaxed as Axel whispered, "Lars, are you awake?"

"I am now. What time is it?"

"Sorry, it's five."

"What's wrong?"

Axel knocked, then came in. "You're wanted down at the police station."

"Why? What's going on?"

"The police inspector didn't say, but stressed it was important. I'll meet you out in the hall when you are dressed."

Ten minutes later, Lars and Axel stepped out of Axel's apartment and onto the city streets. The cold air jarred the last bit of sleepiness out of Lars. In the early morning light, the sidewalk glistened with what Lars first thought was frost. Then a snowflake brushed his cheek.

"How do they know I'm here?" Lars followed Axel to his car and joined in as he scraped frost off the car's windshield.

"My friend Colbert. We could walk, but we should hustle." Axel did a final scrape on the windshield and got into the car.

The streets were deserted, ghostly with a sheet of white. As they passed through the street toward the Torget, Lars noticed a lone light on the top floor of one of the apartment buildings. A year ago, it would have been dark, covered by a blackout curtain. Such was freedom.

They parked close to the police headquarters and walked in. A policeman greeted them in the lobby. "*Herr* Haugland?" the man asked.

Lars acknowledged him with a nod.

"This way, sir."

They were led into a sparsely furnished office. Two stacks of paper files threatening to fall over were set on a table behind an oak desk. Behind the desk, the curtain on the window was shut tight. Somewhere far off, a radiator clanged as the heat came on.

A door opened to their left and a man stepped out. Lars noticed the insignia on man's uniform collar and guessed he was the police officer who had summoned him. Though he filled out his uniform, it was not from bulk. Lars wondered if he boxed.

"*God morgen,*" the police officer said. "*Takk* for coming in so quickly. I'm *Inspektør* Knut Barness of the Trondheim police. Please sit, though we won't be long." He gestured at the chairs in front of his desk, then went behind it. He took off his round eyeglasses and cleaned them with a handkerchief as he sat down. "You must forgive the state of my office. I have not been in it for the past forty-eight hours."

Lars was wondering when Barness would get to the point. He hadn't been summoned from bed—and he felt summoned—to be played with. Lars nodded at the stack of files. "Bureaucracy seems to have returned to pre-war normal."

Barness chuckled. "*Ja. Ja.* But that is not why you are here." Barness leaned in over his desk. "You are the brother of Tore Haugland. Do you know where he is? We have found Sorting."

"Where? Did you catch him?"

"*Nei—*"

"—Why not? Sorting has been threatening my brother for months. Trying to stop his testimony at Rinnan's trial. It's unacceptable Sorting broke out of Vollan Prison."

"I agree. Please, *Herr* Haugland."

Lars wanted to say, "Colonel Haugland to you," but let it go. They were wasting time here.

"I can understand your anger and your impatience," Barness said. "But I must be careful. Sorting's holed up at an estate farm south of here—out near the coast. He is not alone. A man by the name of Gunnar Skele is with him and he is a murderer in his own right."

"If he's holed up, how do you know it's Sorting?"

"Because of the bravery of the housekeeper there. She was able to slip a note to one of my officers while we were searching the house." Barness went on to tell Lars how they had first approached the manor house in the initial search of the area, discovering the two bicycles and other details Barness wouldn't reveal. "I grew suspicious so I returned a few hours later with some police and military backup."

"Military backup?"

"*Ja.* Some contacts I know from the local Milorg group—disbanded, of course. Axel is one of them."

"Who owns the place?"

"A man named Pilskog. He's—"

"Pilskog. Aage Pilskog?" Lars looked up and frowned.

"*Ja.* You know him?"

"Enough not to trust him. The Resistance in Oslo for years was trying to connect him to a couple of incidents at the University before it was shut down by *Reichcommissirat* Terboven."

"Interesting," Barness looked straight at Lars. "My colleagues say he managed a couple of the mines in the Orkdal area. I don't think he ever got a reprimand for working with the Germans." Barness searched around for a pen and wrote a note on a piece of paper. "I'm putting together an armed unit to capture Sorting and bring him in. I would like you to join us. It's short notice, I understand, but we can't wait. The snow is picking up south of here. It could become difficult to get around."

"How long will it take to get there?"

"Forty-minutes. I left a couple of men behind to scout for possible ways to go in. I'm hoping that there won't be a hostage situation."

"Pilskog?"

"Possibly, but I'm more worried about that brave young woman. She has a baby. Those men are vicious. They will do anything to get away."

Chapter 58

By the time Haugland made it safely into the tumble-down cabin with Tommy and Sindre Moe behind him, his temper was short and his arm throbbing. Sindre didn't make him feel any better. The fisherman spilled out every grievance he had been forced to endure during and after the occupation. Sindre paused. "Kjell Arneson got a new boat," he mumbled.

"Why don't you just stop right there, Sindre," Haugland said in a loud voice over the rush of hail hitting the grass roof. With his compromised hearing, it had been difficult to follow the fisherman's lament. "There's no excuse for breaking into the farmhouse. You know it hasn't been easy for everyone. Remember, the SD soldiers blew up Kjell's boat *and* his house. He has been living with Helmer. Now he sleeps on the boat or in his office." Haugland stepped closer. "And you know he has offered his new boat to help everyone get in their catch."

Sindre bowed his head as he sat on the remains of Haugland's old bed. "I know. I know." Sindre paused, then looked up at Haugland. "I'm sorry for shooting at you." He nodded at the bloody line on Haugland's sweater sleeve. "Don't you need to see Grimstad?"

"Not until you tell me what is going in Fjellstad." Haugland found a chair that still had four legs and sat down. He rubbed his wrist to ease the pain in his hand, but it made the wound in his arm ache.

Sindre noticed that. "I remember when you came back at war's end last year, folks said you got hurt. Gestapo messed you up."

"*Ja*. Messed up is a good explanation."

"You were a good fisherman, Jens." Sindre was mumbling again.

Haugland didn't want to let on that he was having trouble hearing. He did hear the compliment and smiled. "And I enjoyed going out on the *Otta* with Kjell. I admire all of you, the fishermen of Fjellstad and

Hitra. You work extremely hard. Under harsh German rules, you had to contend with so many restrictions under the pain of death only to have the Germans take most of your catch. Trying to recover from five years of that I know has not been easy."

"*Ja.*"

"So what is going on? Is the village divided?"

"What do you mean divided?"

Haugland leaned over. "All of those who were with he *Nasional Samling* party—Fasting, the hotel manager, the lady that ran the *landshandel* up on the ridge—they are gone from Fjellstad and punished. Are there still hard feelings? Are there some people others don't trust?"

Sindre looked down. "There have been rumors." He clasped his hands together in thought, then cleared his throat. "That body Bugge brought in. What do you know about it?"

Haugland looked at Tommy. "He was someone no good. A poacher turned informer with the Gestapo."

"Who killed him? Did you do it?"

"*Nei.* I did help bury him."

Sindre's mouth dropped open. "Why was it kept secret?"

"You know why. If the Germans stationed in the village had found out, there would have been consequences as bad as the *razzia*. What are people talking about it?"

Sindre chewed his lip, but said nothing.

All this time, Tommy had been standing with his arms folded. Now he came over to Sindre. "What about Bugge Grande?"

"What about him?" Sindre answered slowly.

"Has he been up here? Is there any reason for him to snoop around?"

Sindre looked like he didn't know how to answer. Haugland thought he was afraid of Tommy. "He might have been up here," Sindre answered.

"Looking for what?" Haugland asked.

Sindre shrugged. "Maybe what you left behind."

Haugland waved his good hand at the log rafters leaning down from the back wall to the smashed floorboards. It made the cabin look like a bivouac shelter. "Not much here. Maybe a tin cup. But maybe you took that already."

Sindre's face flushed.

You're ashamed, Haugland thought. *Good.* "What's the rumor?"

Sindre swallowed. "Bugge might have done something to cause the *razzia*."

"Do you believe that?"

"I don't know what to believe. He did fish with that Sorting fellow. That *quisling*."

"Rinnan's man," Haugland said, his voice bitter. "Sorting is on trial for what he did here and in other villages." He looked at Tommy and wished he knew how to sign. He would ask him if he had the same thought—Would Sorting try to contact Bugge for help? Did Sorting have some hold over the fisherman? The big question was how would Sorting do that?

"Anything else, Sindre?"

Sindre paused. "Bugge's boat didn't get blown up during the *razzia*."

Haugland had wondered about that, too. Only certain people's boats were targeted, such as the Stagg family's and Kjell's *Otta*.

"The hail is letting up," Tommy said. "Let's go back to the village. I could do with some coffee. And you need to have Grimstad check your arm."

Sindre started to get up. "What about me?"

Haugland got right into Sindre's face. "You're going to keep quiet about what we talked about here. I'll decide whether to report you or not. We'll deal with Bugge." With that, Haugland turned and headed for the door.

Chapter 59

Siv Haugland eased her heavy body to the edge of the bed and took a deep breath. She didn't remember being so cumbersome when she was pregnant with Tryge. But that was eight years ago. The five years' separation from Lars during the occupation had ended all intimacy.

Siv smiled at his picture by the bed. Smiled at the memories of longings fulfilled and the great passionate joy of being together in bed again. Such nightly and sometimes daytime passion stirred her even now and made her blush.

She rubbed a hand over her belly and took another breath as a small contraction came on. The baby had been kicking all night long. She had forgotten what the last months of a pregnancy would be like. *Was this normal?* She wasn't due until mid-June. *Oh, Lars do call when you can.*

"Mamma?" Tryge came to door. He was holding a toy pinto horse that Tore had brought back from America. A cowboy sat astride it.

"*Hei. God morgen.* Are you ready for breakfast?"

"Uh-huh. I made it for you."

Siv blew her son a kiss. "What a sweet boy you are." She shifted her weight when another contraction pulled at her. "Oh."

"Mamma?" Tryge rushed over to her and took her arm.

"I'm all right. Just have to get up." Siv gave him a reassuring smile, though she wasn't so reassured herself. "Did you make coffee?"

"*Ja.* And I made toast."

"Now that sounds delicious." She took his hand and let him pull her up off the bed.

In the kitchen, she had just settled onto a chair when the phone rang. "Tryge, be a good boy and answer for me." She ran her hand over her belly and held it there. The doctor told her at the last visit that baby had moved down into position. All was well.

Siv closed her eyes and imagined holding the newborn in her arms. Lars hoped for a girl. Siv had told him she didn't care one way or the other. She wanted a healthy baby, the starting point of their renewed life as a family. When the baby moved, Siv said out loud, "I know little one, but please wait for your Pappa."

"Mamma. It's *Bestemor* Inga."

Inga? What does my formidable mother-in-law want?

"Do you think you could write a message, Tryge? I can call later. She'll understand."

Tryge held out the phone and shook his head. "*Nei*, Mamma. She asked for Pappa, but I told her he was gone. She says it's very, very important she talk to you."

Siv groaned. "All right. I'm coming." She struggled to her feet and lumbered over to phone stand in the *stue*. By the time she took the phone from Tryge, she hurt all over. "*Hallo?*"

"Oh, Siv, how are you? Is it true Lars is gone?" Inga's voice was full of concern.

"*Ja*, Inga. Lars is not here. He'll be away for a few days." Siv sucked in a breath as a pain rolled through her.

"Oh, dear. I hate for you being alone."

"I'll manage."

"Well, if you need anything, don't hesitate, please call me. I'll come right over, but first is there any way you can get a message to Lars? It's extremely important."

"He did leave a number for me to call in case I needed him. What is it?"

"It's Solveig. A woman called the house yesterday. Solveig said she was someone Tore knew from before the war. I don't know where Tore went with Anna and the children, but I know it had to do with the trial. I assume the prosecutor wanted him to be safe."

"Did this woman want to know where he was?"

"*Ja*. That's what I'm afraid of. Solveig told her that he had gone north, maybe back to that village where he was during the war. I don't know how she knew." Inga's voice was unusually worried-sounding.

"Do you have any idea who this person on the phone was?"

"*Nei*. But I think Lars should know. Would you please call him?"

"*Ja*. I can do that." Siv braced herself on the phone stand as another wave of pain went through her.

"*Tusen takk*. Now take care and give my grandson a big hug. He has such nice manners. You have done so well, Siv. I love you very much."

"I love you, too, Inga. I promise to call right now."

After her mother-in-law hung up, Siv rested for just a moment, wondering about the urgency of calling Lars. She was beginning to think she should call him for another reason. The baby was coming early. She turned to look at Tryge playing with his horse and cowboy on the kitchen table. Almost eight years old, he had grown up during the occupation. Getting back with Lars also meant Tryge had to get reacquainted with his father. Lars's identity had to be a secret all those years. She sighed, then pulling a slip of paper out of the stand's drawer, she lifted the phone to call.

The phone rang and rang. There was no way to leave a message. Siv decided she would call again in an hour. But before she put the receiver down, a terrible pain seized her and her water broke.

Chapter 60

Anna looked out the large paned window and watched the snow falling outside. In a few short hours, it had come down so steadily that the road in front of the cabin was totally covered. She could not tell where it started and ended. The rolling land around the lake and behind the cabin was hidden underneath white hummocks. Only the tall pines to the west remembered their true form, but they too were burdened with the heft of the snow. The dull mid-morning light was obscured by the curtain of snow.

"Mamma," Lisel said. "We're ready to go." Lisel came over to the *stue* with skis in hand. She was dressed in a coat, heavy sweater, and wool pants. A white wool cap was on her head. Kitty came with her.

"Where do you plan to go, Kitty?" Anna asked.

"I thought we'd go up behind the grove above us. We found another cabin there the other day. We can shelter there, if need be."

Anna came over and tugged on Lisel's knapsack. "What do you have in it? Hope you have your scarf and extra socks."

"*Ja*. Kitty has the hot chocolate and *leftse*. I have extra gloves, too."

"Very good." Anna nodded at Kitty. "You shouldn't stay out too long. You can always go out again later."

"We'll be careful. And we'll have fun, won't we, Lisel?"

Lisel said that she could hardly wait.

After they left, Margit put more wood into the stove, then joined Anna on the padded seats by the window to visit and read. Nils was asleep in the back, so Anna finally had time to read the book she had brought from America: *Captain from Castille*.

It was quiet in the cabin. Candles and a lone lantern lit the space. Outside, the snow kept coming down like a curtain of falling feathers.

Neither woman spoke. Margit eventually dozed off. Anna kept reading, but after a time she worried about the kids and decided she'd go back to her room and see if they were up on the hill. They should be coming back in. As she got up, she noticed headlights out on the snow-buried road. As the heavy black car took shape in the falling snow, it seemed to be struggling and eventually, it stopped short of the cabin. There was movement in the car. A door opened and a stocky man with blonde hair stepped out. He quickly put on a wool cap, then looked over the hood of the car toward the cabin. Anna gasped and pulled back in horror.

"Oh, God," she said and grasped Margit's arm. "Oh, God. It's Odd Sorting."

Margit was instantly awake and pulled Anna down on the seat. She blew out the closest candles.

"The children." Anna's breath came out in gasps. She lowered herself to the floor and started to crawl across it. "I'm going to check to see if they are in the back."

"Good." Margit lowered herself down to the floor. She took out a Sten gun from low drawer. "Do what is best."

Doing what was best was getting Kitty and her children as far away as possible. Once Anna got to the short hallway to the rooms, she stood up and ran.

Nils was still sleeping in the drawer. Anna ran to the window and carefully opened it. To her relief Kitty and Lisel were just coming down on their skis. She frantically waved her hands at them. Kitty stopped, looking a bit bewildered.

Stop! Danger! Anna signed. Be careful.

Anna's heart pounded. She could barely think straight, but she knew that if Sorting and whoever was with him got into the cabin, all would be lost. Nils, Lisel and Kitty would be lost. Knowing Sorting's history with Bette, he could rape Kitty and Margit. *And me.*

She looked at Nils sleeping in the drawer and made a harde decision. She carefully lifted him from the drawer and slipped him into the wool bunting Inga Haugland had knitted for him. Back at the window, she motioned for Kitty to come down. Stay, she signed to Lisel.

Lisel stayed. Kitty glided down to the window.

Be silent, Anna signed. Danger.

Kitty nodded. Anna handed Nils to her. Then gave her the sling. "I'm coming out. Just give me a moment," Anna whispered. She found a low stool under one of the bunks and standing on it started to climb over the window sill when she remembered her pistol. She climbed down, got the pistol from its hiding place and started out again. Out in the front of cabin, she thought she heard a car door slam and some racket on the porch. It made Anna get onto the snow faster.

She took back Nils who was starting to stir. "Put on the sling under your coat, Kitty. Quickly."

"What is going on?"

Anna tried hard not to show terror, but Kitty must have read her face. "Don't alarm Lisel, but it's Sorting," she whispered. She started to breathe in short gasps again. *Calm, stay calm.*

While she held Nils in one hand and the pistol in the other, she watched Kitty secure the sling. Then pulling the bunting's hood around Nils, Anna put him in it. Kitty tightened the sling and buttoned the coat. Only a bit of Nils's wool hood showed.

"Do you know what I'm asking?"

"*Ja.* Go to the village. Get help. But I hate leaving you here alone." Kitty's breath came out in little clouds.

Anna sniffed back a tear. "I'm not completely alone. Right now, you are my only hope for my children's safety, Kitty. That is all I care about. Go back up the hill and find your way down the way Ella brought you. Get away from here as fast as you can. I think it should take you an hour on skis to get to Fjellstad. If you get lost, find a cabin. It's all right to break in and warm yourself. It is the courtesy of the mountain." She patted Kitty's cheek already pink from the cold. "*Tusen takk.* No matter what happens, I will be eternally grateful."

Out front they could hear voices. Margit was talking to someone in a loud voice. Anna kissed the top of Nils's head. Go, Anna signed to Kitty.

Kitty turned her skis around and climbed back up to Lisel. The teenager leaned over and said something to Lisel. Lisel looked at Anna. The look on her face nearly broke Anna's resolve.

I love you, Anna signed. Go find Pappa Jens. With that she shooed them away.

Anna watched Kitty stab her poles into the snow and sign to Lisel. Together, they disappeared into the pines and veil of falling snow.

For a moment, Anna stood flat against the cabin wall, her arms spread out. She was outside with no coat and wore only her shoes. Snowflakes were sticking in her hair and on her shoulders. She wasn't sure if she could climb back in the window. She looked at the automatic pistol in her hand and decided to go around on the south side of the cabin. Margit's voice grew louder as Anna came close to the porch.

"I'm telling you, I advise you not to come in. There is a case of measles in the cabin. We have quarantined ourselves."

"Are there children in the cabin?"

"*Nei.* Only my husband."

Anna crept closer. The area on the south side of the cabin was higher than the north side, so that Anna was almost level with the porch when she came to the edge. Out on the snow, she could make out Sorting and a man in a long coat and a fedora hat in a standoff with Margit in the ambient light.

"We're only inquiring," Sorting said. "We are looking for a woman and her children. My sister. I was told they may have come up here and when I saw lights, I thought—"

"—There is no one here like that. I'm not asking you to move on. I'm telling you."

Anna carefully looked in Margit's direction.

Margit was on the porch. She raised her weapon in Sorting's direction. Sorting put his hands up and backed off. The other man next to

Sorting looked anxious and started to step away, when a voice bellowed out from the north side of the porch.

"Don't believe her, Sorting. I found some ski tracks on this side. One's small enough for a kid."

In an instant, Sorting fired at Margit. The bullet missed her, splintering the log wall of the cabin. Margit swiftly fired at the new threat and knocked him off the porch, then fired back at Sorting. The stuttering shots from Margit's firearm hit the toe of the man in the fedora and blew up the snow around him. He yelped, lost his balance and fell. Her second round sent Sorting scrambling for cover. Margit backed up toward the cabin door. To Anna's horror, the first man Margit had shot, rose up and fired at her.

Grunting, Margit went down, but she still held on to her weapon. Rolling up, she fired back. The man aimed his pistol and hit Margit in the shoulder. In an instant it was over. Sorting bounded onto the porch and put his pistol to Margit's head. He ripped the gun away from her. Margit tried to rise, but he kicked her back.

"Fucking bitch," Sorting's companion growled. "Who the Devil is she?" The man struggled to get up on the porch. He was holding his side.

"She'll tell us." Sorting kicked her in her side. Margit screamed. "Not so tough." Sorting pulled her head up by her hair. "First, where is Haugland's woman?"

Margit responded by spitting in his face. Sorting slapped her down.

Anna pulled away from the edge and closed her eyes. *How long has it been since Kitty and my babies got away? Probably only minutes.* At least, the men would be in no shape to go after them. Lisel and Nils would be safe. They would be rescued. But what about Margit? When Margit screamed again, Anna knew that she had to stop Sorting and the other man from hurting her more. She didn't know how Sorting had found their hiding place. *But they want* me *so they can get to Jens.* She hid her pistol in the back of her pants and stepped out.

Chapter 61

As soon as Haugland and Tommy were back in the village, they split up. Tommy took

Sindre with him. Haugland rode his bike through the slush over to Grimstad's. The weather had changed from hailstorm to a light fall of snow.

It was too early for patients. After Haugland rang the bell at the front door a couple of times, Grimstad himself answered. "Jens? Is something wrong?"

Haugland pointed to the bloody line on his sweater.

Grimstad shook his head. "You've been here only forty-eight hours and look what trouble you've gotten into. What happened?"

"I surprised Sindre up by my old cabin. He shot me."

"Sindre Moe?" Grimstad quickly closed the door behind Haugland and started down the hall to his study. "Sindre did this? What in the Devil is going on?"

"He's been stealing from the Fromme farm." As they walked, Haugland quickly told him what happened.

Grimstad opened the door to his study. "Has he lost his mind?"

"I shouldn't have come back. The village is unsettled."

"What do you mean? You are welcomed here."

"Not just about me. Anna, too. People are still trying to grapple with the five- year occupation. They are not feeling secure. I only remind them of that."

Grimstad invited Haugland in and shut the door. "That's no excuse to break into the Fromme place—your place. I can't imagine Sindre with gun."

"Fortunately, his aim was off."

"It could have been worse. The fool needs a good talking to. And you—stop blaming yourself. With the *Wehrmacht* stationed here, something was bound to go wrong with or without your presence."

Grimstad went to the long window and drew the curtains closed. "Why don't you to take off your sweater?"

Haugland hesitated. He thought about what taking his sweater off meant. *His back.* Grimstad had never seen it before. He closed his eyes.

"Jens?"

Haugland sat down on the wood chair by Grimstad's desk. "Sorry. It's just a nick, I think." He slowly took off the sweater. He wore a long-sleeved knit undershirt underneath. When he looked at his left arm, the blood had soaked through the sleeve. He looked at Grimstad, someone he had trusted during his assignment here. He took a deep breath, then took the undershirt off. In the cool office, the skin on his muscular chest and arms broke out in goosebumps.

Grimstad said nothing as he examined the gash on Haugland's bare arm. He went to his medical kit behind Haugland and again said nothing as he passed. When he came back there was a sympathetic smile on his lips. Though Grimstad's eyes betrayed pity, he made no comment other than to say, "Well, you won't need stitches. I'll clean up the wound and bandage your arm. That's about all the medical supplies I have on hand. This will sting."

Whatever Grimstad put on the gash did sting. Haugland looked at the bookcase while the doctor worked silently.

"There," Grimstad said when he was done. "You are all set."

Haugland put on his undershirt, pulling the sleeve gingerly over his half glove and the thick gauze bandage on his arm.

"Where is Sindre now?" Grimstad asked.

Haugland finished dressing. "Tommy is taking him to Kjell. I think it's up to your town committee to decide if you want to prosecute him."

"We'll definitely see to that." Grimstad came back and pulled a chair over to Haugland. He frowned as he sat down. "I thought you were getting protection. Where were those Milorg men?"

"Tommy was with me."

"You should have two on you. I'm shocked by what Sindre did."

"It could be a coincidence," Haugland answered.

"Coincidence or not, we can't have anything more happen to you. Sindre is—Sindre. What if it was Sorting and whoever is running with him? Our whole village's future depends on your testimony, Jens. It will bring the justice we deserve."

Haugland smiled gently at Grimstad. "I'll do my best, Hans." Haugland rolled his shoulders to loosen them up and immediately regretted it. He touched his bandaged arm and winced. "Won't you have patients soon?"

"*Nei*. At least another hour. But I could tell you were about to say something," Grimstad said.

Haugland grinned. "There was something Sindre said about Bugge Grande. He said that some were wary of him because he worked with Sorting. And that his boat was not blown up like so many others."

"That's true about his boat," Grimstad said. He looked thoughtful, then sighed. "I've heard the rumors, too."

"Do you think there is any way Sorting could have contacted him?"

"That would be unlikely. Sorting would be recognized."

"And if he tried to call?"

"Ella knows Sorting's voice. And she is as shrewd as any."

Haugland chuckled. "*Ja*, she is. Ella Bjornson is a natural leader and nothing gets past her."

"What do you think we should do, Jens?" Grimstad asked.

Haugland got up. "Ella told me Bugge was acting odd when the body was brought in. And to be honest, based on that, I thought it might be him who was up at the cabin the day I saw someone ride off on a bike. Bugge could have been searching around there, too."

Grimstad stood up. "I hate to be a pessimist, but is there any chance Bugge might not want you to testify? Let's say that Bugge could have informed on any of our village leaders that led to the *razzia*. Even if it was a matter of him accidently saying too much to Sorting. Is it possible your testimony might implicate Bugge? Something Bugge might think would get him into trouble?"

"The only thing I worried about was when Sorting was fishing with Bugge and Kjell and I had to meet the Shetland Bus for that large arms delivery to Trondheim. I fixed Bugge's fuel gauge so he ran out of fuel." Haugland shook his head. "Kjell got really mad at me because at the time all he could think about was that Bugge would lose his gas ration. Then I told him my suspicions about Sorting getting close to my radio operations. Sorting could not go out on Bugge's boat the same time we left."

Grimstad started to pace the room. "Any chance Bugge knows about that? Could he be angry with you if he knew?"

Haugland put a hand on Grimstad's shoulder to stop him. "Possibly. He was missing from the fishermen who greeted me when we first arrived from Oslo. On the other hand, with all the trials going on for quislings, he could be feeling vulnerable if the rumors are true. I'll have Helmer keep an eye out for Bugge just in case. Better a villager than Tommy's Milorg friends. They would draw attention."

"I think that is a very good idea. From now on, don't go alone, Jens."

"I won't. *Takk* for dressing the wound. I'll go out the back door."

Chapter 62

Lars Haugland lay on a snowy rise and through binoculars watched Barness put his men in place around the Pilskog farm's perimeter. "It looks like he knows what he's doing," Lars said to Axel Tafjord lying next to him. "What did he do during the war?"

"He trained men in the police camps in Sweden, but Knut was a police officer in Trondheim before the war, so he rejoined the force after liberation."

Lars adjusted the focus on his binoculars, concentrating on the driveway that led to the front of the manor house. "When was he in Sweden? Didn't the NS try to Nazify the police?"

"Oh, Knut resisted. Fled to Sweden in 1942 after the Chief of Police, Erling Østerberg, was arrested for being the main leader in the resistance against the NS. Østerberg has been back in charge since he was released from a centration camp last year."

"A *jøssing*." Lars wiped some snowflakes off the lens and refocused on the house. "That's odd. I only see one light on in the house. It's nearly nine in the morning."

"Can't worry about that now. Lars, they're ramming the front door."

"Time to go." Lars slipped in the snow as he scrambled to his feet. He hefted his Sten gun and with Axel, ran down the rise and across the snowy ground to the house.

There was shouting inside, but no gun fire. By the time Lars and Axel stepped into the manor house's long, dim hallway, Barness and his men appeared to have moved quickly throughout the house judging by the sound of boots above them and the men charging in and out of the first-floor rooms.

At the end of the hallway, an open door on the left splashed light on the opposite wall. Hearing a commotion coming from there, Lars moved forward with Axel close behind him.

Barness stepped out and motioned for him to join him. Lars lowered his weapon and entered a large kitchen filled with men. All eyes were on a group on the other side of the kitchen hammering on the hinges to a door.

"Is the bastard in there?" Lars asked as he followed Barness into a kitchen. Lars was appalled at their incaution. Sorting could be armed.

"*Nei*. We're looking for Pilskog and the housekeeper now."

"Are you telling me Sorting is gone?"

Barness looked pained when he said, "*Ja*. Some of my men found car tracks leaving the property by the barn. We believe Sorting and Skele are in it. They did not go out the driveway."

"The Devil take him," Lars spat. He felt like pounding walls, throwing dishes on the floor. "Your men never saw them leave?"

"*Nei*."

Lars began to shake.

Axel put a hand on Lars's shoulder to calm him. "Who's here from District 21?" he asked Barness. Lars knew he was referring to a disbanded Milorg group.

"Hans Pedersen." Barness nodded at the tall blonde man in a beret and uniform standing at the door holding a pistol.

Across the kitchen, the group had managed to lift the door off its hinges and set it against the wall. Pedersen and two others armed with guns rushed into the room, shouting. Barness and Lars followed.

At first, all Lars saw was an empty bedroom and the disappointment on Pedersen's face. Then he noticed a rag rug scrunched up by the metal bedframe. Pedersen noticed it, too. "Sir," Pedersen said to Barness. "Blood."

Lars joined Barness at the bed. A floral *dyne* covered it. A stuffed bear lay on the pillow. Then Lars looked down and, crouching, examined the bedpost. He found blood and a couple of brown hair strands clotted against the footing. Blood pooled on the floor. "Sorting really is a bastard."

"Keep looking," Barness said to Pedersen. "She could still be a hostage. Find Pilskog. And the baby. Find the baby. Surely…" Barness's voice trailed off.

"I'm going into the basement," Pedersen said. "Axel, want to join me?"

Lars followed the group down into the cold basement as lights were pulled on. The small armed group made a sweep of it, then came back to the stairs. By now, Lars was frustrated. And worried. *Did Sorting know where Tore was?* After all, he had lived in Fjellstad for several months. *Would he go there next?*

Barness came down and joined them. "Nothing?"

"*Ja,*" Pedersen said. He patted his gloved hands together; his breath came out in clouds.

Barness looked thoughtfully at Lars. "I have one more possibility. Please come with me." He stepped down onto the concrete floor and walked around to the back of the furnace. He crouched down in front of a large bookshelf full of goods. He studied its left side. "I didn't notice this before, but see these lines? They swing out. I think this shelving is a door."

Lars's heart began to pound. He lowered his voice. "Sorting's in there?"

"He could have been when we searched the second time. The housekeeper didn't mention this in her note." Barness motioned for everyone to get ready to fire, then with Lars's help, he tugged on the bookshelf. To their surprise, the heavy piece gave away easily. As the overhead light bulb brightened the space, they found the body of Bette crumpled on the floor. Her hair was matted with blood and one of her shoes was missing.

"*Herregud,*" Barness said, his voice croaking.

Lars wasn't thinking about God when he stooped down and felt for her pulse.

"Is she alive?" Barness asked.

"Barely. I feel a weak pulse."

Barness began to shout orders. Someone brought the *dyne* from Bette's bed and gently wrapped her in it before she was taken upstairs. "Find that baby." Barness implored.

Lars stood up and followed the men upstairs.

Chapter 63

Anna's heart pounded as she stepped out from the side of Eidsvik's cabin. For a brief moment, she knew she was crazy to do this, but reality had sunk in. She would have to take her chances because her situation was just as desperate outside the cabin as with Sorting. She had no coat, no boots, and no skis and poles to simply skate away. Most of all, she couldn't leave Margit. She pulled her hip-length sweater over the gun and came to the porch's side right in front of Sorting.

"What the Devil," Sorting jumped away from Margit. He pointed his gun at Anna. He looked confused at first as if he didn't recognize her. Then he said, "Anna Fromme. You are here after all."

Anna swallowed. She raised her hands up. "Vær så snill. Please don't hurt my friend any further. I want to help her."

"Your friend?" the wounded man behind Sorting said as he came over holding his side. "Who's the bitch that shot me?"

Anna wanted to shout at him that Margit had been in the Resistance and was a better man than he would ever be, but Anna knew that she should be very cautious. What if she totally miscalculated her value to Sorting? She didn't dare upset him. By interacting with Sorting and the despicable man with him she hoped it would give Kitty more time to get help. She hoped it came soon. Anna sensed this other man could be more dangerous than Sorting.

Anna came around to the front porch stairs. The third man she had seen fallen was on his feet and complaining.

Sorting turned to Anna and waved his gun at her. "You. Come up here."

Anna lowered her hands to hold onto the railing for the steps were slippery with wet snow. She kept her eye on Sorting and the other man who was glaring at her, but mostly she was looking at Margit.

Margit lay on her side with her eyes closed. Snowflakes drifted by her and mottled her hair and sweater, but failed to cover the blood stain on her front. At first, Anna thought she was gone, then saw her eyelids flutter.

Sorting grabbed Anna by the sleeve. "Anyone else inside?"

"Nei."

"Where's her husband?" the stranger besides Sorting asked. He appraised her from head to toe.

"There are no adults in cabin other than the two of us." Anna worked to keep her voice calm.

"Right. You better not be lying." Sorting jerked his thumb up. "Pilskog get up here and find the kids."

"My foot. It's bleeding."

"I don't give a damn about your foot. Get up here."

"I'll send him in, just in case," Sorting said to the other man as he picked up Margit's Sten gun. "Who knows? The little girl might be armed. How's your side, Gunnar?"

The big hairy brute took a bloody hand away from his wound and pointed a finger at Anna. "I'll have her look at it."

Sorting shrugged. "Wait until Pilskog comes back out."

Pilskog struggled up the steps, leaving bloody footprints in the snow. Sorting pushed him to the door. "Bring them out. You should be looking for a little girl and a baby. They could be hiding."

Anna listened to the conversation in horror. Sorting would know about Lisel having lived in Fjellstad, but how did he know about Nils? Did that mean he knew where Jens was? More than ever, she was glad she had made the dangerous decision to get Kitty and the children as far away as possible.

"May I help her?" she asked Sorting.

"Help yourself. I'm not sure it's going to make any difference."

As the cold seeped into Anna's hands, she knelt down next to Margit. She gently brushed a clump of bloody hair away from her face. "Margit?" Anna felt for a pulse and found a weak, but steady one. Then she looked down at the blood stain on her sweater. Anna cautiously unbuttoned the lower half of the cardigan exposing a bloody knit shirt. When she pulled it up, Margit moaned.

Anna's experience with anything medical, other than scrapes and bumps on Lisel and changing the post-operation bandages on Jen's hand, were nil. Yet, she knew instinctively that the neat hole in Margit's lower side was serious when she checked Margit's back. There was no exit wound. The bleeding, at least, seemed to have stopped. Anna looked at Margit's shoulder next and found that a bullet had gone through.

"That's enough," Sorting said. He waved Anna up on her feet.

"Let me at least get her inside out of the cold."

"I say, let the bitch stay where she is," the other man said. "Keep your bloody hands off her."

"Skele," Sorting said. "That's no way to talk to a lady." He started to say something else when Pilskog came to the door.

"The kids are gone. I looked everywhere."

"What?" Sorting pulled Anna to him. "Where are they?"

"They're gone. Far from here."

"The Devil," Skele said. "I saw tracks by the steps. I say they are hiding." Skele frowned at Sorting. "I thought there was a baby. A six-year-old kid can't manage that."

"Nei, she can't." Sorting studied Anna and Margit on the snowy porch floor. "She said her husband was here. Who would that be?"

Anna said nothing. She would let them believe what they wanted.

Pilskog limped out onto the porch. Anna could see that his left shoe was soaked with blood, but this Pilskog confused her. He didn't seem to be with them.

Sorting and Skele talked between themselves, Skele sometimes getting heated as he gestured at Anna. Finally, Sorting said, "Everyone inside." Sorting waved his gun at Anna.

"*Vær så snill*," Anna said as she rubbed her arms. "You have to bring her inside, too." She didn't like begging but she had to get Margit out of the cold.

Sorting grudgingly agreed. He ordered Pilskog to pick Margit up. She cried out when he did that, then went limp in his arms. Anna reached out to support her head and, following Sorting, they carried Margit into the cabin.

Anna hoped that they could lay Margit down on one of the benches so she would be close to the stove, but Sorting asked Pilskog where the bedrooms were. Pilskog nodded to the back. Sorting started for them. In the narrow hallway, the door to Anna's room and window were open. Anna knew that he would get a picture of how the children got away. "Where is your daughter and your baby?"

"I told you. They got away."

"They're not alone." Sorting rubbed his chin. "I'm not sure how you did it, but I don't think a man would leave two women behind." He studied her. "What mother puts her baby out in the cold? You're lying to me. They're hiding close by."

Anna hoped they were not. "I assure you I am—" Sorting slapped her hard on the cheek making her fall back into Pilskog. Before she could recover, Sorting pushed her into the tiny room next to her room.

"Put them in there," Sorting told Pilskog.

Pilskog was gentle when he laid Margit on the bed. Sorting waved him out and slammed the door.

With that Sorting stomped away leaving Anna to wonder if she had done the right thing.

Chapter 64

Haugland was back at Kjell's warehouse not long after he left Grimstad's office. The snow had continued to fall, heavy enough to cover the road and dust the ruins of the blown-up houses along the way and the few homes under reconstruction. By the time he reached Kjell's office door, snowflakes covered Haugland's fisherman's cap.

"*Hei.* Jens." Helmer Stagg said when Haugland opened the door. "I was just coming up to get you."

"Well, I'm here. Where is Sindre?" Haugland wiped his boots on the doorstep.

"Kjell is with him in the warehouse right now. Kjell brought in Kaare Stua."

"I remember him. He was a leader in the fishermen's association when I was here."

"He still is. He's also our mayor."

Haugland took off his cap and slapped it against his thigh. From the warehouse he could hear Kjell's voice rise and fall. The door to the warehouse opened and Tommy came out. Sindre's whiney voice hung in the cold air before Tommy closed the door.

"How's the arm?" he asked Haugland in Norwegian.

"I'll survive."

Tommy shook his head. "Be honest. How did Sindre manage to surprise you? Could you hear him?"

"*Nei.*"

"Bloody hell."

The door to the warehouse opened again. Kjell came out with Stua and Sindre and to Haugland's surprise, Ella Bjornson. She was still wearing her apron under a heavy coat.

"What's the plan? Haugland asked Kjell.

Kaare Stua answered. He was a wiry man with gray hair and a neatly trimmed beard "Sindre Moe is going to be fined. I'm giving him hard labor which means he's going to have to help in the cleanup and rebuilding of the homes."

Sindre looked up at the sound of his name and quickly glanced at Haugland.

"In the meantime, he'll be confined to his house." Stua took Sindre by the arm and went toward the door.

"Just remind him that we can still tell his wife," Haugland said.

Sindre flinched as he went out the door.

After they left, Haugland asked Ella if she knew what was going on.

Ella shook her head in dismay. "*Ja.* Your friend told us everything. I am so sorry, Jens, that you got hurt. I don't understand Sindre at all." She put a hand on Haugland's good arm. "Is everything going to be OK?"

Haugland assured her that he would be fine.

"Good." Ella paused. "Now we must ensure that there are no further threats to impede your testimony in Trondheim. Just a few more days and then it will be done. There is something, though, that has been worrying me." Ella went on to tell Haugland about the odd phone call that had come in the day before. "A man called asking for Bugge. He would not let me take a phone number. Instead, he said he would call back later."

"And did he?"

Ella crossed her arms. "*Ja.* Bugge talked with him for a bit. When he hung up, he looked unsettled."

"Do you know who this man was?"

Ella shook her head. "I have no idea. He did sound cultured, educated."

Tommy frowned. "Someone looking for you, Tore?"

"It does sound strange." Haugland turned to Ella. "Hans Grimstad was wondering if Sorting had some way to reach Bugge. Maybe Sorting forced someone to call Bugge."

Ella looked shocked. "Oh, dear. If that is true, Bugge could have said anything to this stranger."

Haugland started to fold his arms, but his wounded arm ached, so he put his hands into his pants pockets. "Where is Bugge, by the way?"

"I saw him on his boat," Helmer replied. "He looked like he was going somewhere."

"He's going out in this weather?" Haugland wondered why. "Let's keep an eye on him."

"I've got that,' Tommy said. "One of my Milorg buddies knows boats, so he's working on Kjell's and keeping an eye out for any movement. This is a new reason to distrust Bugge."

Tommy jabbed Haugland on his good shoulder. "In the meantime, you will stay here. And we will watch. When this is over, you will go to Trondheim and testify. Then home." Tommy patted his stomach. "I'm hungry. Is it possible to get breakfast around here?"

Ella said she had just the thing. "I have to go back to work, but I'll send Helmer back with some treats."

Kjell cooked some eggs and potatoes on his stove in the office. The smell of food made Haugland's stomach growl. He glanced at the clock on the wall before sitting down at the table. It read sixty-thirty. Had he been up for only a few hours? It felt like twenty.

Helmer arrive with a basket of cinnamon rolls. He set the rolls on the table and sat down opposite Haugland and Tommy.

"Anything going on at the *bakeri*?" Haugland asked Helmer. He speared a piece of potato with his fork and held it over his plate.

"Well, there's the weather. Most are choosing not to go fishing today. Big swells out there. Someone said the weather was worse up on the *fjell*." Helmer took a roll out of the basket. "And, of course, they are talking about the body that was brought in yesterday."

"Did you say anything about it?"

"*Ja.* I said *Doktor* Grimstad thought it was someone who apparently drowned last year during the occupation. No paperwork, so Grimstad was working on identifying the man. That seemed to satisfy most of the curious, but I'm sure the rumors will continue."

Haugland took a couple more bites of his potatoes and eggs. His thoughts turned to the snow still coming down. It was ironic that exactly a year ago on this day he was on the hunt for Rinnan and Sorting with members of Axel's Milorg group. Rinnan had been stopped by such a May blizzard near the Swedish border. *It was worse up in the* fjell. Helmer's words about the present storm chilled him. He hoped that Eidsvik could get up there to check on Anna and the kids.

After breakfast, Haugland and Tommy helped Kjell organize his gear for the approaching fishing season. It eventually became too cold, so they came back in. They spent another half hour in the office strategizing over the real coffee Haugland had brought back from America.

Finally, Kjell got up. "I'm getting cabin fever. Let's go up to the Tourist Hotel. I know Marthe Larsen will want to see you, Jens. She has a special place in her heart for you and Anna. I hope you have pictures of Lisel and Nils."

Haugland grabbed his coat off his bed and followed Kjell and Tommy outside. The snow had let up, but flakes still drifted on a bitter wind. He looked back to the end of the wharf where the *Kristine* was tied up. Beyond, he could see a light in Bugge Grande's boat. He was going nowhere.

At the top of ridge, the men stopped. Coming down toward them was a truck at high speed. When its lights hit them, it slid and stopped. One of the doors opened and Kitty Arneson got out.

"Pappa!" she called out. "Help me."

When Haugland heard the weak cry of his son, Nils, he knew the morning's nightmare had come true.

Chapter 65

After securing the shutters on the back of the cabin, Sorting stomped back in and slammed the door. He didn't like what he saw: Skele was leaning against the padded seating by the window. He looked pale. Pilskog sat at the dining table examining his wounded foot. He had removed his shoe and sock, exposing bloody toes.

"Is the bitch who shot me dead yet?" Skele growled.

"Don't know." Sorting opened the small wood-burning stove and checked the fire. It was going strong, but he would have to get wood soon.

Skele loosened his coat. Taking a deep breath, he lifted up his bloody sweater to look at his wounds. "Still wonder who she is. Never saw a woman shoot like that."

Sorting wondered, too. He hadn't expected any sort of security. This place was supposed to be a secret. Bugge's limited knowledge had come by accident—an overheard conversation—but nothing about someone like this Margit. Sorting had underestimated Haugland. Of course, he would have protection for his wife and children. But a woman? There had to be a man somewhere.

Sorting turned his attention to Skele. "How does it look?" He could see two wounds: a gash in Skele's side and a jagged bullet hole just below the ribs.

"Too numb to tell." Skele pulled his sweater down. "Where's the Haugland woman now?

Pilskog looked up sharply. "Haugland?"

Sorting turned to Pilskog. "*Ja*. Do you know the name?"

"I know of a family in Oslo named Haugland."

Sorting rubbed his chin. "You continue to surprise me, professor. You seem to know everyone. Do you know a Tore Haugland?"

Pilskog answered carefully, "*Ja*. Tore Haugland was the youngest son of a colleague of mine at the University. I only met him once or twice. He—" Pilskog's eyes grew wide. "This is his wife? And the missing children are his?"

Sorting laughed.

"What do you have to do with him?"

Sorting signaled for Pilskog to stop. "You are asking too many questions." Sorting tested a copper kettle on the stove and discovered it half-full. He went into the kitchen and found a wood bucket filled with water in the dry sink. He poured the hot water in the kettle into a ceramic bowl and brought it over to Pilskog. "Clean your foot. Then help me with Skele here. I'm going to get the woman."

Sorting went down the hall. Before going into the locked room, he did a quick search of the other room with bunks. He found baby clothes and the pungent smell of a cloth diaper in a bucket full of water. In the drawers, he found clothes and underwear. He lifted up a bra with unfamiliar snaps on it. He put it to his nose and smelled it. It had lavender scent to it and something he couldn't put a finger on. He searched around the bed and *dyne*. Under the bunk, he discovered a radio. He picked it up. Feeling that his search was done, he took it out into the hall and placed it on the floor. At the door to the room he had shoved Anna into, he listened, then unlocked it.

Anna Haugland was sitting on the edge of the bunk holding the hand of the wounded woman. When she looked up at him, for a moment he saw fear, then anger crept into her face. God, she was beautiful. All the time he had watched her in Fjellstad, he had wanted her. Had dreamed of bedding her. Now he had her—Haugland's woman. He would teach Haugland for what happened to Freyda. "Get up," he said to her.

Anna lay the woman's hand on her chest and pulled the *dyne* up to her chin. "She needs help. Please allow me to clean the wounds."

"She's a dead woman. I have a different task for you."

"She is not dead."

Sorting was taken aback that she would dare talk back to him. At the same time, he liked the prospect of a cat and mouse game. "If you say so. Get up."

Anna got up. She buttoned up her sweater over her light jersey up to her neck.

"I want you to look at my friend's wounds." He motioned for her to move. As she passed him, he touched her curly blonde hair. Anna stiffened slightly, but kept moving into the warmth of the living space.

"I don't know anything about wounds," she said to Sorting, "but there is a first aid kit in the kitchen. I'll need hot water and something to clean the wounds." She swallowed, then went over to Skele.

Anna helped Skele out of his coat, but made him take off his shirt and sweater on his own. She worked quietly using a kitchen towel to clean his wounds. When she pressed on the worst wound, he groaned. To complete the cleaning process, she took a small bottle of alcohol out of the first aid kit. He swore when she applied it. She had Pilskog go to the closet in the hallway and bring back a flannel sheet. From it, she tore up some strips to make pads for the bullet wounds and a couple of long pieces to bind them. Skele leaned into her and nuzzled her ear. Anna pushed him away.

"Cut it out or I won't help you. You shouldn't be moving around, anyway. I, at least, know that. A bullet is still in you. For all I know, you could be torn up inside."

When Anna was done, she told Skele to lie down on the cushions and rest. Then she looked at Sorting. "Should I help the other man?"

Sorting shook his head. "*Nei.* Pilskog can help himself to the first aid kit. Go, professor. There's a stool in the kitchen. Better yet, see if you can find something to cook up." He motioned Anna over to the dining table and sat her down on a chair beside him. "Now tell me where your children are." He took her hand.

"I told you, they are gone."

"Your infant can't be far. I suspect you'll have to feed him soon."

Anna slipped her hand away. "You know so little, *Herr* Sorting. They are long gone. Help will be coming soon."

"We'll see about that." Sorting didn't want to let her know that he knew what she said was true. When he had gone around to the back to secure the shutters, he had seen ski tracks outside the window. He had followed them up to a grove of pines and found a second, smaller pair. He turned away from Anna and looked out the front window. It was gray outside. The snow was still coming down.

"I don't know how you did it, but what kind of mother sends her baby out into those conditions?"

"A mother who loves her children and will do anything to protect them. I know who you are, *Herr* Sorting—Rinnan's man. Do you think I would let my children be near you, especially my daughter? You killed her father."

Sorting half-smiled. "And when did you think I was with Rinnan?"

"I saw you with him in Lillehavn. You were talking with my husband, Einar, at the schoolhouse."

This revelation shook Sorting. He had always assumed she had no knowledge of his efforts to work his way into the Resistance group in that area near Bergen. Cat and mouse. Sorting didn't like being the mouse. This woman had more steel in her than he imagined.

Sorting leaned toward her. "One more time. How did your children get away, as you say? And who is this woman Margit?"

Anna seemed to consider his questions carefully. Finally, she said, "Margit was in the Resistance. And since you do not believe women are capable of defending themselves or the people you love, you will never find my children."

Sorting wanted to slap her, but oddly, he refrained. Instead, he decided to hit her where it would hurt the most: the truth about her first husband, Einar Fromme.

"Did you ever wonder how your husband died?"

Anna turned pale and silent.

Good. He had her. "He died, that is true, but not by my hand." Sorting studied her, surprised that no one had told her the truth. "He killed himself."

Anna shrunk away from Sorting. She took a deep breath. "Then I truly know how brave Einar was by not give anything away to hurt others in his group." She swallowed. "I never knew he was in Milorg." She paused. "I was told he was buried at sea."

Sorting wasn't expecting such a calm answer, so he hit back harder. "Not in a coffin," he sneered. "In a box. I chopped him up because he wouldn't fit in. What do you think about that?"

Anna's look of horror was short-lived. Screaming and weeping at the same time, she leaped up from her chair and attacked Sorting, raking her fingernails across his cheeks. She grabbed his ears and pulled until Sorting overpowered her.

"You!" He raised his hand to strike her this time, only to be stopped by Pilskog.

"Don't you need her?" Pilskog asked as he pulled back on Sorting's wrist.

Sorting pushed Pilskog's hand away. He trembled with rage, but as he looked at Anna with her hands up in protection, the ugly image of what had happened to Fromme after he was found dead in the Cloister—what Rinnan had made him do—overpowered him. The poisonous Cloister would always haunt him just as it must haunt the man Sorting wanted to destroy for surviving it—Tore Haugland.

"Take what you need and go to your room. Get out of my sight."

Chapter 66

As Kitty Arneson rushed across the snowy road toward him, Haugland's first thought was that he had imagined Nils's cry. That it wasn't real.

"Tell me everything isn't as bad I think it is," Haugland said as Kitty came up to him shivering and out of breath. "Where are the children?"

"Nils is here with me." The teenager unbuttoned her coat, exposing the baby wrapped in the sling she wore. Nils began to fuss, then cry as she unwrapped him.

"Where is Lisel?" Haugland looked beyond her, wondering if Anna and Margit were with them. Something had gone terribly wrong.

"Lisel is in the truck." Kitty burst into tears. "I didn't want to leave them, but Anna made me go."

"What happened?"

Kitty gulped. "Sorting and some else showed up at the cabin."

"Sorting? At the cabin? Bloody hell," Tommy spat.

"Where are Anna and Margit now?" Haugland asked Kitty, trying to stay calm. As soon as Haugland had his son in his arms, he put Nils under his own coat. The baby's heartbeat calmed his.

"I don't know. Lisel and I were outside playing on our skis," Kitty went on between tears. "Anna gave me Nils and said get as far away as we could, then head home." Kitty burst into tears again and went into Kjell's opened arms. "I was so scared," she wept. "I heard gunshots. Oh, Pappa."

Haugland exchanged looks with Tommy. Gunfire surely meant Margit was involved. Both women were in danger, but Haugland felt sick with worry for Anna.

The driver's side of the truck opened. One of the Milorg men who had been at the meeting at Grimstad's stepped down. Before closing the door, the young man helped Lisel down.

"Pappa Jens!" she called as she staggered to Haugland. He pulled her to his side and hugged her one-handed. She looked cold and exhausted.

"Where did you find them, Christian?" Tommy asked the Milorg man.

"Right on the road where I was waiting. They skied right to me when they saw the truck."

Haugland leaned down and kissed Lisel's cold cheek. He felt like his world had just been blown apart. He was glad when Kjell said, "Let's get everyone out of this wind and cold."

Kjell nodded at the Tourist Hotel overlooking the ridge a short distance away. "Marthe Larsen and her daughter can help with the children. Helmer, could you let Ella know?"

Christian came forward. "I'll drive him down and then round up the rest of our group. We'll meet you back up here, Tommy."

"Would you go get the doctor first?" Haugland asked. "Just to check them out."

"Good plan," Tommy said. "You do that, Christian. Then gather our men together. We need to move quickly."

Holding Lisel's hand, Haugland carried Nils through the back door of the hotel's kitchen. Though he had worked at the hotel as part of his cover during his time in Fjellstad, Haugland found little comfort when he came into the familiar kitchen with a howling Nils and a cold and exhausted Lisel. Only the presence of Marthe Larsen, the head cook, tempered his anxiety. Haugland could not shake off the feeling of being out of control and helpless.

"Let me take him," Marthe said. "You sit. Oh, he needs a change."

Haugland sat down hard on the nearest chair. Tommy and Kjell came in and stood beside him.

The cook gave orders to one of the kitchen girls to bring cocoa for Lisel and Kitty. When her daughter Ingrid came into the room, Marta sent her off to a neighbor's house where the wife had just had a baby and would have cloth diapers to share. "Ask if we can borrow a bottle. Don't forget your coat." Marthe tapped Nils on his mouth and let him suck on one of her fingers. "Now, tell me what is going on?" she said as she bounced him.

Kjell put a hand on Haugland's shoulder. "Marthe, we can't explain everything all at once, but we need your help with the children. They've been out in the cold for hours."

"Where is their mother? Anna wasn't here when you came, Jens."

Haugland looked up. "There's been trouble. Odd Sorting escaped from Vollan Prison."

Over the cook's gasp, Haugland beckoned for Kitty to come to him. "This brave young woman saved my children. Came all the way down on her skis to warn us. Anna—she's up in the *fjell* where I thought they would be safe."

Haugland choked on his words. He rubbed his forehead, close to breaking down. His arm hurt, his hand hurt, but most of all, the dread of Anna being in extreme danger hurt like a sword piercing his heart. Yet for right now, he had to push his fear aside and focus on what to do next.

***

Things moved quickly after Grimstad arrived. While he examined Nils and Lisel in the small tool room off the kitchen, Haugland and Tommy's men gathered in the hotel's sitting room to plan the rescue of the women. Everyone felt the urgency to leave immediately, but with the storm, they needed to know the weather conditions up on the *fjell* and the situation around the cabin.

Haugland turned to Christian. "Did Kitty say how many were with Sorting? Sverre Haraldsen said he saw another man with him."

"*Nei,*" Christian answered. "She heard only the one male voice and, I suppose, the voice of Margit Renvik. Kitty said that *Fru* Haugland had climbed out the bedroom window to give her Nils."

Haugland cringed at the thought of Anna outside in the cold. "How do you think Sorting got past you?"

"I swear no one came up that road."

"Is there another way, Helmer?"

Helmer shrugged his shoulders. "Could be. There is a road—more like a track—that connects from the east side of the mountains to a road that travels on the spine of the *fjell*. It's not maintained, but a local person would know it."

"What are the conditions up there, Christian? Can your truck make it?" Kjell asked.

"I can get up there, but skis once up on top might be more efficient. There is certainly a good layer of snow for skiing. Plus the snowfall a couple of weeks ago."

Haugland rubbed his wounded arm. "Who are your best skiers, Tommy?"

"I'd say they all are."

"Good. One final thing. Does anyone know where the main road comes out?"

"About ten miles south." Helmer said. "Comes out near a village. Get me a piece of paper and I'll draw you a map. The third route is a road that travels on the spine of the *fjell*. It drops down to a valley south of it."

"Then let's move. Gather our equipment and go." Haugland studied the ex-Milorg men gathered in the sitting room and hoped they had not lost their skills so hard-won during the war. Haugland didn't think he had lost his. Despite the wound in his arm and his healing hand, physically he was in very good shape.

"Hans," he said to *Doktor* Grimstad. "Could you see that the district police are notified? Perhaps a road block could be set up on the other—"

All heads turned as the French doors opened. To Haugland's surprise his brother Lars stepped in, followed by a police officer.

"I think the police are already here," Tommy said.

Chapter 67

Back in the bedroom, Anna tended to Margit. With the shutters over the window, the room was dark, lit only by a candle next to the bunk bed. As Anna sat on the side of the bunk cleaning the wound on Margit's side, Margit opened her eyes.

"Anna," she said in a hoarse voice. "I'm sorry. I didn't see the other man."

"Shh. Kitty got away with the children. That's all that matters."

Margit weakly grabbed Anna's wrist. "Did the men take away all the guns?"

"Not mine. I've hidden it under the bed."

"Good." Margit closed her eyes briefly, then opened them again when Anna put a dressing on the wound. "Where are the men now?"

"Out in the *stue*." Anna told her how she had cleaned the wounds of a man named Skele. "He's the man who surprised you. I think he might be more dangerous than Sorting. He is definitely not happy about you shooting him."

"The other man?"

"I don't know. I think he's a hostage. You hit him in his foot." Anna sat up. "While you were out, I cleaned your shoulder wound and put a bandage on it." Anna swallowed. "Your side, of course, is more serious. The bleeding has stopped, but do you think you could manage to sit up a little bit so I can wrap it tight?"

"I think so." Margit took Anna's hand, groaning as Anna pulled her up into a sitting position.

"I tore up some flannel sheets for the men," Anna said as she wrapped a wide strip around Margit's waist. "There, that should do, I think." She helped Margit lie back down. She pulled down her sweater and put the *dyne* back in place. "Now rest."

Anna heard footsteps coming down the narrow hallway. She braced herself for more abuse from Sorting. She had been shaken by what he said about Einar's death, but she sensed that he was testing her resolve. Anna had no idea what he intended to do next.

Someone knocked on the door, then cautiously opened it. It wasn't Sorting.

"*Fru* Haugland," the man said. "How is the other woman?"

Anna leaped up from the bunk and pushed back on the carved wood door. "Who are you?"

"I'm not a friend of Sorting," he said. "I'm Aage Pilskog. Like you, I'm a hostage."

When Anna asked him how, a hurried explanation spilled out: of how Sorting took over his home, how the police had arrived and forced them to flee. "Please tell me that your friend is still alive," Pilskog said.

"*Ja,* but she needs a doctor; she needs a hospital." Anna cracked the door open.

Pilskog looked behind him. "You must be very careful. That man Skele was abusive to my housekeeper. I think he killed her."

Anna gasped. All she could muster to say was, "That's terrible," but she was frightened to the core. "Is her baby all right?"

"He's—"Pilskog looked behind him again like the Devil was on his tail. "I have to go, but I think Skele is crazy." Pilskog shut the door before Anna could tell him that he should be careful, too. Sorting was vicious as well. Hadn't Jens told her so?

Anna rested her head against the door, waiting for Pilskog's footsteps to fade away. When he was gone, she turned to Margit. "Did you hear that?"

Margit was out cold, her head turned to the side on the pillow.

"Margit," Anna said in a panic. She felt for a pulse and found one, steady though weak. Anna brushed back the hair on Margit's forehead and was relieved that her brow was warm and sweaty. God protect us, she thought. She stiffened when she heard more footsteps in the hall.

***

Sorting came into the cabin and dropped a load of firewood by the stove. Snowflakes clung to his knit cap. He scowled when Pilskog came out of the hallway to the bedrooms. "What the Devil do you think you are doing?"

"I-I was looking for more linens in the closet."

Sure you were. "Did you cut up the carrots and potatoes like I told you to?"

Pilskog nodded at the pot by the dry sink. "*Ja.* They are ready."

"Good." As Sorting loaded the stove, he looked over at Skele who seemed asleep. Another worry. Why did things continue to go wrong? What had started out as a reasonable plan had turned into a nightmare. He was beginning to think that he should take the car and leave them all. Well, not all. He'd take Anna Fromme—he still thought of her by that name—for insurance. First, he needed something to eat.

Sorting straightened up. "Find an onion. There must be butter some-where. What's that in the floor?"

Pilskog leaned down and pulled on a metal ring lying flat in square groove in the pine floor. It opened the top to a root cellar. Milk and butter were on a shelf. Sorting instructed him to brown the vegetables and then add water. "I'm going to get the woman."

At the door to the bedroom, Sorting stopped to listen. He heard noth-ing. He opened the door and smiled when Anna started.

"Get up. I need you in the kitchen."

Anna pulled the *dyne* up to the wounded woman's chin and smoothed it down, ignoring him. The defiant move enraged Sorting. "I said, get up."

Anna patted the woman's hand, then got up. Her steady look made him furious. He would be the cat this time. He motioned her out into the hallway. As she passed him, he grabbed her and forced her against the wall. He pressed his body against her, one hand on her neck, the other touching one of her breasts. To his surprise, it felt hard. When he squeezed it, a wetness came into his hand.

Anna turned her face away. He ran his hand down her side and over to the top of her wool pants. He slipped a hand inside. She twisted away. He took the hand out and pressing his groin into hers, he forced her mouth to his. She struggled, making him want her more. He put his hand back on her breast as he kissed her mouth and neck. He caressed her hair, that curly blonde he had always wanted to crush in his hands.

Anna got a hand loose and began to pound his shoulder. It angered him. Sorting eyed the other room. Holding onto her, Sorting began to move her along the wall to the door. She spit at him which made him laugh. She twisted and struggled, stamping his feet and trying to knee him, but he got her to the door and turned her around so her back was against him. His arms held her tight as he penguin-walked her to one of the bunk beds. He threw her on it, then falling on her, pinned her arms above her head with one hand.

"There," he said. "Where's your hero now?" He kissed her mouth, fondled one of her breasts. Fully clothed, he moved on top of her as she continued to struggle, then stopped when he realized that she was look-ing around for some escape. Sorting grabbed her mouth. "Hey, look at me."

Anna's blue eyes widened. Her lips trembled. Yet Sorting saw something that took him by surprise—defiance. In a low voice, she said, "He will find you. And he will testify. Hurting me and all the threaten-ing notes in the world will not stop him."

Sorting slapped her face hard. "You'll never see your children again."

"And you will never know your son. Unless you already killed him and his mother."

Sorting jerked back giving Anna a chance to push hard on him. He hit his head on the underside of the top bunk. Before he could right himself, Anna reached for a metal alarm clock ticking on the table next to the bunk. She hit him twice in his face and pulled out from under him. Before he knew it, she had jumped up and fled out the door.

Chapter 68

Inga Haugland closed the outside French doors and locked them. She paused and wondered if the Milorg men were still up in the woods behind her house. *Should I take them coffee?*

The weather in Oslo had suddenly turned chilly. Frost covered the brick patio. Some of her flowers looked nipped. *Was it only few days ago that spring was here and my whole family gathered to celebrate Tore's return from America?* With ice tea, no less.

She had not heard from Lars since Tore left three days ago. Her short call to her daughter-in-law, Siv, gave no further information except that Lars would be gone for a few days. The mysteriousness of his absence only increased her concern for her youngest son, Tore. Had he gone back to the fishing village where he was during the war? She hoped Siv was able to relay her message to Lars about the strange phone call.

"Mother, have you seen Ole?" Solveig stood in the door of the study. She was wearing a long black dress and shawl.

"Ole? Our neighbor Ole Bode?"

"*Nei.* My Ole." Solveig went over to the French doors. She wrung her hands. "I have to find him. He needs to hide." She started to open the doors.

"Solveig, dear. Wait. Ole is not here. He's gone, remember?" Inga's heart sank as she realized that her daughter was having one of her episodes. It was best to play along.

"He was just here. The boats are coming. The Germans are going to take him away." Solveig's voice broke.

Inga gently put her arm around Solveig's shoulders. "Ole's safe now. He's with God. But your children are here." Inga gave her a squeeze and kissed her on her cheek. "You must think of Tine and Bjarne. Shall we go find them?"

For a moment, Solveig complied, letting Inga lead her out of the study, but once in the hall, she became agitated again. She shrugged Inga's arm away. Her voice began low then turned into a wail. "I tried to hide Ole when the Germans started rounding up the men, but he wouldn't hear of it after the Germans shot some of them. He said he was not a coward. I tried to keep my babies close, but the Germans took them away."

"Solveig, you'll make yourself sick." Inga tried to brush her daughter's hair off her clammy forehead, but Solveig twisted away.

"Don't." Tears rolled down Solveig's pale cheeks until they hung on her slim jaw and dropped. She made no attempt to wipe them.

Inga stepped away. *How can I ever comfort my daughter?*

Solveig moved down the hallway toward to the dining room, then stopped in front of a gold-framed painting on the wall. It was Inga's deaf brother's painting of Telavåg. She had found it in storage in Oslo a couple of months ago. She watched with trepidation to see how Solveig would react.

"What do you think, Solveig?" Inga asked as she carefully approached her daughter. "Didn't *Onkel* Kris capture it so well?"

Solveig nodded. "*Ja*. I see my house." She cocked her head as she studied the painting. "The island looks so barren."

"*Ja, ja*. And windy, too." Inga came a little closer.

Solveig's eyes softened. "Tore used to come down to see us and *Onkel* Kris. Once, he went out on the boat with Ole."

"I remember that."

"Tore was so patient with *Onkel* Kris. I never learned to sign. I just let *Tante* Sophie tell me what he meant." Solveig stepped closer to the oil painting. "I was so happy there. Then the Germans came and took the men to Sachsenhausen." Solveig sniffed. "We lost everything."

"I know, dear." Inga paused. "I'm so sorry." She didn't add how much it hurt that she had lost her brilliant, talented brother at that terrible camp too, but Solveig was too lost in her own grief to hear that.

Inga changed the subject. "Did you know that the government plans to restore Telavåg? Isn't that wonderful? Would you go back? *Tante* Sophie has decided that she will." As soon as Inga said that, she regretted it.

Solveig stiffened. "*Ja*, I heard about that, but I don't think I can." She touched the painting, moving her finger around one of the houses on the barren hill above the bay. She smiled wistfully, then tears came on again and she wept quietly. Suddenly, Solveig's eyes narrowed. "Why did Tore marry that German bitch? How can he forgive any of them after what they did to him? What they did to our family?"

Inga didn't know how to answer that when it was a Norwegian, Henry Oliver Rinnan, who had tortured Tore. Solveig had slipped away again into her own world where she was beyond reason and understanding. If only the laughter of her children, Bjarne and Tine, playing in the *stue* around the corner would give Solveig some future direction for everyone's sake.

Chapter 69

In Pilskog's manor house, Lars joined the rush to find Geir. Still shaken by discovering Bette in the basement, and the massive collection of luxury goods, he followed the group of police and military men charging upstairs to the main bedrooms on the second floor. Lars stepped into the first one on his right, a large bedroom full of expensive furniture and rugs. A fine brocade *dyne* covered the large bed. *Who did this Pilskog think he was?*

While the other men swept the room, Lars opened a door to what he thought might be a bathroom and instead discovered a closet full of luxury women's clothing. He pulled on a string to a light bulb hanging from the low ceiling. Dresses, coats, and furs hung from racks on both sides. Shoes were displayed on racks. Hat boxes, and baskets peeked out from under long glittering gowns. As he walked down to the end of the long closet, pushing back on the clothing to check underneath, his disgust grew for this display of privilege when the rest of the country was on rations.

In the very back, he discovered a large laundry basket piled up with blankets. Carefully, he unwrapped the top blanket. To his shock, he had discovered the missing baby.

"Found him!" Lars pulled the blanket further away from Geir's face. A teething ring was taped to his mouth. In a panic, Lars checked to see if the baby was still breathing. He lifted the baby out and held him in his arms as other men joined him in the tight space.

Geir stirred slightly but remained asleep. Lars sniffed the baby's mouth.

"Is he alive?" a policeman asked.

"*Ja.* But I think he's been drugged. Whiskey or sleeping draught, maybe?" Lars carried Geir out to the bed and laid him down on it. On inspection, Lars found him changed and in clean clothes, as if someone cared.

Inspektør Barness joined him. "*Prise Gud*," when he saw the baby. "I was extremely worried."

Lars shook his head. "I'm still not comprehending all this. Why such cruelty on his mother's part and some sort of care for him? They could have just killed him. It makes no sense."

"Maybe Pilskog had something to do with it. In any case, we get him and his mother to the doctor in the next village. We're loading her now into our police van."

"And from there?"

"The hospital in Trondheim is sending down an ambulance as soon as possible, but I'm afraid this weather is going to make that difficult. I hope that the local doctor can help her."

Lars picked up the sleeping Geir and gently removed the tape that held the teething ring The baby moved his head and fluttered his eyes, but didn't cry. He remained in a deep sleep. Lars held Geir against his chest. For a brief moment, he thought of Siv and their baby due next month. He had forgotten how small a baby could be. How helpless Geir was. *Who would do this to a baby?* His treatment infuriated Lars.

Downstairs in the hallway Lars joined Axel and Barness. They watched as Bette and her baby were carried out on a stretcher to the police van. Once the doors were closed and the van on its way, they stepped into the study near the front door.

"Sir," a policeman said to Barness. "Thought you might like to see this. I found some notes with numbers scribbled on it. They look recent."

Barness looked them over and handed the notes back. "Why don't you call one? See who answers." The policeman dialed up the operator and after a few moments, the call went through.

"*Hallo?*" a woman on the other end answered.

When the police officer asked her to identify herself, she said, "Ella Bjornson. This is my *bakeri*."

"Where?"

"Fjellstad. Do you wish to make an order?"

"*Nei. Takk.*" The police officer hung up.

"Who was that?" Lars had been curious about the phone numbers, too.

"Apparently, it's the phone number of a *bakeri* in Fjellstad," the man said. "A woman named Bjornson answered."

"Fjellstad? Why would Sorting call Fjellstad?" Lars frowned. The name Bjornson sounded familiar. "Could I see the other phone number?"

The police officer handed the second note to Lars.

As the phone numbers wavered before Lars's eyes, a sinking dread filled him. "What the Devil. How the hell did this number show up here?" Lars felt like he had been hit in his stomach.

"What is it?" Barness asked.

"It's my parent's phone number in Oslo." Lars stepped away from Barness. "With your permission, may I take a car and some of Axel's men and go to Fjellstad immediately? My brother is in danger."

Barness wasted no time in answering. "As soon as we are done here, I'll call for more reinforcements, then we will all to Fjellstad."

Lars didn't wait for any follow up. He was out the door and gathering Axel's men.

***

Two hours later, Lars Haugland arrived in Fjellstad with Knut Barness, Axel, and a group of armed men. It was only by chance that they met someone from Tommy's Milorg group on the road, who directed them to the hotel. It had taken them longer than anticipated to plow through the snow to the village. The snow had covered the back-country road, creating drifts that obliterated the edges of ditches or downed branches. Yet still they drove on in the murky daylight and sometimes near-zero visibility, fueled by the knowledge that someone had leaked the location of where Tore Haugland hid.

It was a relief to Lars, as he stepped into the sitting room of the Fjellstad Tourist Hotel, to see his brother sitting next to Tommy Renvik, surrounded by serious looking young men.

"*Hei,* Tore."

"What are you doing here?"

"You're in danger. I'm here to ensure your safety, brother. This is *Inspectør* Barness of the Trondheim police and Axel Tafjord from the Sor-Trondelag Milorg group. We've been on Sorting's trail. We think he spoke to someone here in the village about your whereabouts. What is going on here?"

"You're too late. He didn't strike at me. He has Anna and Margit Renvik."

Chapter 70

Anna ran blindly down the short hallway and straight into Skele. He grabbed her by the arm and pulled her against his bloody sweater.

"Where are you going, *lille jente*?" Skele laughed and rocked her back and forth.

"Let her go," Sorting said as he burst out of the hallway. He held a hand next to his eye.

"Ah, Odd. Did you lose her?"

"I said, let her go."

Locked in Skele's arms, Anna dared to look at Sorting, unsure of what he would do now. A bright red gash had appeared on the side of his eye where she had struck him with the alarm clock. He was fuming, but then turned his glare on Skele. *Am I his prize?* She turned away, trying her best to stay strong, though she felt like she would buckle and fall to the ground. Sorting had already humiliated her. She was not about to give Skele the same satisfaction. Still, she felt shaky when he released her.

"Just getting to know her," Skele said.

"Well, forget it." Sorting motioned for Anna to go into the kitchen. "See that those carrots and potatoes get cooked. You got anything else you've started for the day?"

Sorting's request was nonsensical to Anna after his violent attack, but it gave her a chance to compose herself. "Only *smørbord*. There is bread and cheese in the cupboard."

"Make more coffee," Sorting ordered. When Anna passed him, she felt a hand brush her shoulder. She twisted away and joined Pilskog in the tight space of the kitchen.

"Did he hurt you?" Pilskog whispered.

"Sorting is a brute, but I hit him hard," she whispered back as she reached for the coffee grinder.

"But the children are truly away?"

"*Ja.*" Anna glanced at the clock. It had been almost two hours. A lifetime. She prayed for Kitty, asking for strength and courage for her and Lisel to get safely to Fjellstad.

"What are you talking about?" Skele barked. Favoring his side, he shuffled back to the dining room table and sat down in a heap. Anna glanced over at him, worried that she had miscalculated the extent of his injuries. When he had held her, she could feel him trembling, yet he was able to move around. He was still dangerous.

Pilskog answered, "Nothing. She was showing me where things were."

Sorting joined Skele and for several minutes they talked in low voices. Anna couldn't make out what they were saying. When she was sure they were preoccupied, she looked for something that she could use as a defense if Sorting should attack her again. She found another potato peeler and hid it in a pants pocket, then went back to grinding the coffee. Anna dared not draw any more attention to herself. She kept her head down and got the coffee pot boiling and the carrots and potatoes browned in butter in a pan on the stove. Outside the kitchen window, the snow continued to fall making everything feel closed in and dark, even though it was almost noon. The hood and roof of the car in the road lay under a white mantle.

Anna avoided looking Sorting's way, but once she did glance over to the table and found Sorting staring at her. His expression was puzzled—as if he was trying to figure out what she meant about Bette and Geir. What did she know? Anna also noticed that Skele was not looking so well. His color was pale as he leaned against the chair back. It made Anna anxious to check on Margit.

Anna and Pilskog remained confined to the kitchen. Pilskog invited her to sit on the stool, an offer she accepted. She noticed that he limped when he walked. She wonder how his toe was doing, but didn't dare say anything.

As time passed, Anna faced a new pressure. It had been several hours since she last nursed Nils. Her breasts were painfully hard and warm. With the men in the cabin, she had to find a way to discreetly express her milk. Or she could just suffer, but she didn't want to get sick with milk fever. She had to do something. Finally, she stepped to the edge of the kitchen and asked Sorting if she could check on Margit and then be allowed to go out to the outhouse.

Skele chuckled. "You gotta watch her, Sorting. She'll clock you again." Skele started to say something else, but ended up coughing and holding onto his side. He closed his eyes and winced.

Good, thought Anna. One less man to worry about. She waited for Sorting's answer.

"All right," he said. He got up and pulled a gun out of his coat hanging on his chair. *Margit's gun.* He waved it at Anna to move. Anna grabbed a jar of water by the sink and took it with her.

Down in the bedroom, Margit appeared asleep, but she opened her eyes when Anna sat down next to her.

"Water," Margit said when she saw the jar.

Anna helped her sit up and drink it. Margit sipped, then laid back down on her pillow. She smiled. "Quite the pickle we're in, aren't we?" Margit's voice was weak.

Anna wasn't sure if Sorting heard what Margit said, but answered in a low voice. "Depends on who is in the brine. That man you shot is in pretty bad shape."

"Be careful."

Anna smoothed down Margit's hair and pulled the *dyne* back up to her shoulders. "I will."

"Stop chitchatting," Sorting said. He leaned against the door frame, his gun pointed at her.

Anna got up. She hoped she didn't look scared. "I'm ready to go. I'll need my coat." She had a crazy thought that this would a good time to grab the gun under the bed and shoot Sorting, but he was armed and too close. He could shoot her and Margit before she even touched the gun. Delay and survival were all Anna cared about.

Out on the porch, the world looked like a Christmas postcard, but it was anything but. The lanterns and candlelight in the cabin splashing through the window added to the snow's eerie glow. All they needed was a Christmas *nisset*. Her own lantern led the way down the steps around to the back of the cabin. The snow was several inches deep, but not hard. Behind her, she could hear Sorting huffing as he followed. It made the hair on the back of Anna's neck rise.

Inside the outhouse, Anna set her lantern on the bench next to the toilet seat and closed the door. After relieving herself, she opened her coat and set about expressing her milk. The chill of the outhouse gave her goose bumps as she pressed down on her breast. Everything was so tender, but once one side was soft, she worked on the other. She longed for Nils tugging on her, his smile infectious as his hands held her breast whenever he stopped. She longed for Jens to find her, but she had put her hope and faith in an eighteen-year-old girl to accomplish that. There was no guarantee for success. For now, Anna was on her own, with only her wits to save her.

"What's taking so long?" Sorting said. He was standing next to the door. Anna feared he might swing the door open or see her through one of the slats. Not even when he assaulted her, did she feel so vulnerable.

"I'm almost done." Anna decided she had better stop. She put her clothes in place and buttoned up her coat. When she stepped out, she held her head high, though she shook from the cold.

The snowfall had decreased slightly, lifting the foggy curtain that went with it. Anna could now see the trunks of the pines and birch on the other side of the road and a bit of the lake. She silently followed Sorting down to the side of the cabin, nearly bumping into him when he stopped.

Sorting turned and faced her. He pointed his gun at her. "You're going to tell me everything you know about this Geir. Did Pilskog say something?"

Anna felt for the potato peeler in her pocket to give her resolve. She wished they would go back in, but there it was. She had a hold over Sorting. "He said that Skele hurt his housekeeper, but I never met Pilskog until now. I learned about your little boy from Ella Bjornson in Fjellstad just a few days ago."

"My little boy? How do you know that?"

"From what his mother, Bette Norsby, told Ella." Anna stepped away from Sorting. She felt emboldened to tell Sorting everything, but she kept it simple. "All I know is that after the baby was born under her new name, Bette was placed in the Pilskog home. But again, I never knew this until a few days ago."

Sorting looked away. "Hmph."

"Did you see the little boy?"

Sorting frowned. "The hell with you."

"You didn't harm him, did you?"

"Shut up." Sorting waved the gun at her.

Anna started to shake, but couldn't stop talking. "For all your evil, I can't imagine that you would do that. Somewhere in you there is a man who is not so cruel."

Sorting stared at her and snorted. He chewed his lip. "I didn't hurt the baby." He pulled on Anna's coat sleeve. "Move."

They stepped down around to the front of the cabin. Anna noticed a man on skis near the lake. *Jens?* Then she remembered Eidsvik said he would come up and check on them. She wasn't sure if it was him, but it was somebody. For a moment the man hesitated, then skied closer to the road. That movement caught Sorting's eye.

Sorting raised his gun and fired. The skier skated away. Sorting fired again. This time the man yelped and went down in a heap. Abandoning Anna, Sorting slipped and slid across the snowy road and hid behind the car. To Anna's relief, when she finally got to the porch for a better view, the skier was up on his skis and madly skating away into the fog.

Sorting waited for a few more moments, leaning across the hood of the car with his gun aimed toward the lake fast disappearing behind the mist. Eventually, he made his way back to Anna, swearing angrily. "Who was that?"

"I think," Anna said with a bit of joy in her voice, "Milorg has found you. And they will never let go."

Book 3

Norway let us sing!

Let all our voices ring

For our liberty, our laws,

Our mother-wit, still as it was

For justice and its cause.

~Odd Nasen

Chapter 71

Outside, at the back of the Tourist Hotel, Tore Haugland and his brother, Lars, watched Axel's men load two idling trucks with skiing gear and weapons.

"Ready to do this?" Lars asked as he buttoned up his coat.

"*Ja,*" Haugland nodded.

"With your hand?"

"*Ja.* Stronger every day. Ski poles will be no problem." Haugland looked up at the sky. Its gray ceiling had lifted, increasing visibility. Only a few scattered snowflakes drifted down.

He prayed that similar conditions would be up on the *fjell.*

Only a few minutes before, it was agreed Lars Haugland, along with Axel and his Milorg group, would join Haugland and Tommy in the search for the women on the *fjell. Inspektør* Barness and his police officers would stay back in Fjellstad and interview Bugge Grande for what he knew about Sorting's whereabouts. By now, Lars had told Haugland about the discovery of the phone numbers at the Pilskog farm. The news spurred Haugland's need to leave immediately to rescue Anna and Margit.

"Sorting," Haugland spat. "The bastard has to be the mysterious caller to the *konditori* who wanted to speak to Bugge. How in the hell did Sorting get these numbers?" Haugland ran his fingers through his hair. "Who at the house knew where I was?"

"Only my men, Polson and Øyen, knew you were coming back here. Mamma didn't know. Who's this Bugge?" Lars asked.

"A local fisherman who sometimes hired Sorting. Somehow, Sorting got to Bugge Grande." Haugland took a deep breath and let out a gush of air. "Let's move. I don't want to waste another minute." He pulled a wool stocking cap over his ears and put on his wool coat.

"Jens," a woman's voice said behind him. It was Marthe Larson. She stood in the kitchen's back door, jiggling Nils in one arm and holding onto Lisel's hand. "I thought you might like to say good-bye. I'm going to put them both down for naps."

Haugland kissed a sleepy Nils on his forehead, then picked up Lisel and held her in his arms. "I won't be long, Lisel," Haugland said. "We're going to go get your Momma. *Tante* Marthe and Ingrid will look after you."

Lisel rested her head on his shoulder and hugged Haugland hard. "I love you, Pappa Jens."

"I love you, too." Lisel felt so light, but his responsibility for her lay heavy on him. Standing below him by a truck with its motor running, Lars gave Haugland a soft smile in understanding.

"I have to go." Haugland gave her a big hug, kissed her cheek, and put her down. "Be a good girl." He signed, Be good.

Lisel signed back, I be good, then giggled.

Marthe Larson took Lisel's hand and led her inside. As soon as the door shut, Haugland joined Lars by the truck. He gently put on a mitten over his healing hand. He wore a glove on the other. "We need to go. Where is Barness?"

"Right here," Barness said. "I thought we'd see you off."

"*Takk.*" What had happened at the Pilskog farm deeply troubled Haugland. Poor Bette. She was only a young woman desperate for affection. She often flirted with him. Thinking Haugland deaf, she left notes for him whenever he came into the *konditori*. Haugland was repelled by what Sorting did to her. And frightened for Anna.

Tommy joined them. "Axel just gave the signal. I'm driving. You and Lars will go with me. Helmer, Petter, and Kjell are going with Axel."

"How many men do we have?"

"Twenty. We might get more." Tommy started for the driver's side of the truck. Behind them, men with Sten guns and side arms climbed into the canvased-covered back. "There are skis for you, Tore."

Lars opened the cab door and got in. When Haugland joined him, Lars asked if there were any escape routes Sorting might use.

"Helmer drew us a map. There is a road that goes along on the top of the *fjell*. It drops down to a valley south of it and meets up with a county road to the coast." Haugland closed the door and waited for the trucks to move.

Tommy rolled down his window and adjusted his side mirror.

Suddenly, there was a commotion on the road that came up from the waterfront.

"What the Devil?" Haugland opened his door and looked behind him. A group of villagers were moving quickly on the snowy road. Petter and Tommy's Milorg man assigned to watch Bugge's boat led the way. Then Haugland saw Bugge being tightly held between two fishermen. With them was Mayor Stua. From the bruises on Bugge's face, it looked like he had been roughed up. Haugland stepped down from the truck and went out to meet the group. Tommy got out and joined him.

"What's going on?" Haugland asked, though he guessed what might be going on. Bugge had been found out.

"Some unfinished business from the *razzia*," Mayor Stua said.

Petter pointed to Bugge Grande. "He was caught trying to go out on his boat." He grabbed Bugge by his coat sleeve and yanked him forward. Bugge looked terrified. He tried to twist away. Two fishermen seized him and marched him up to Haugland.

"Is it true about Bugge and that agent provocateur Sorting?" one of the fishermen asked. He was an older man, with grizzled gray hair and an unshaved face reddened by the cold.

"*Ja*," Haugland answered. "Bugge's guilty of working with him when times were tough, not knowing who Sorting was. That can be forgiven. But it went beyond that, didn't it, Bugge? Like forging your catch numbers. Cheating on your ration cards." Haugland shrugged. "Sorting had some hold over you which led you to give him information that fingered people in the village when the *razzia* hit." Haugland's voice rose as he added, "And now Sorting has my wife."

"*Nei. Nei.*" Bugge put his hands up in protest. "It was never my intent. I never thought—" The growing crowd of men and women surged in around him. One of the fishermen slapped Bugge hard on the back of his head. Others tried to pull him away from Petter.

"Stop!" Kjell yelled as he joined Haugland. "This is not us."

"*Quisling*," a woman shouted at Bugge.

The crowd moved in, forcing Haugland, Tommy, Kjell, Petter, and the mayor into a tight circle protecting Bugge.

"We want justice," another shouted. "Justice, justice." The chant took off, increasing in volume on the frigid air as new voices joined in.

Inspektør Barness ended the escalating crisis when he fired off his weapon. The crowd backed away when they saw his uniform and the police officers.

"There will be no village justice here," Barness said in loud voice. "You should be ashamed. This man will get his day in court. I'm arresting him right now." He nodded to his men to take Bugge. "If you want justice, you will join us in the search for Sorting."

Haugland thought that was grand speechmaking on Barness's part, but he was touched when several said they would join in on the hunt.

"For you, Jens," the grizzled fisherman said. "We haven't forgotten how you made us strong."

Chapter 72

As soon as Sorting felt it was safe to move from behind the car, he ran back to the cabin, waving his gun at Anna. "Get inside." He slipped a couple of times on the stairs, but was behind her as they stumbled into the cabin.

"What the Devil is going on?" Skele shouted as he forced himself up, bracing his hands on the table for support. As he did so, he began to cough.

"We've been spotted." Sorting pushed Anna. "Get over there by Pilskog."

"Who has seen us?" Skele worked his way around the table.

"I'm not sure." Sorting scratched the blonde stubble on his face. He stared at Anna. "Maybe someone's husband. Maybe someone local. I think I got him."

Anna stood next to Pilskog. Sorting thought she jumped when he asked her, "That's right, isn't it? Your kids are near, after all."

Anna hesitated, then said, "I told you there were no men with us. Just us, and a very brave girl took it upon herself to get my children as far away from you as possible."

"I don't believe you."

Anna choked on her next words. "She should be in Fjellstad by now."

"And if not?"

"The skier you shot at is someone who has been keeping an eye on us. He is an ex-leader of a Milorg unit in this area. He will sound the alarm."

Skele swore and threw his metal coffee mug onto the floor, its contents splashing the wall. Sorting watched it bounce over toward him. Skele hopped in front of the table. "Could anything else go wrong on this fucking escape to nowhere? What's the next big plan?" Skele limped away from the table and pointed his finger at Anna. "Kill her. Kill the bitch that shot me and kill Pilskog. I'm sick of looking at him. We need to get out of here."

Skele continued his barrage of words, but Sorting knew better. He needed Anna for his own purposes and Pilskog, as irritating as he was, knew the area. They needed them both. His gun pointed at Pilskog and Anna, Sorting walked over to Skele. He picked up Margit's Sten gun at the end of the table and handed it to Skele. "Here. Get over by the window. If you see movement out there, let me know. I'll get us ready to move."

Sorting came back to Anna and Pilskog. "Are there any other cabins are up here?"

Pilskog stepped in front of Anna in a protective move which amused Sorting. "Except for some simple shelters, there is nothing. It's all dwarf birches and bushes. No cabins."

Sorting lowered his gun. "At your place, you pointed out a fjord south of here. What's down there?"

"When you come down off the *fjell,* you first come to a small village. It's about five miles to the fjord from there."

Sorting turned to Skele. "We can take a boat from there."

"To where?"

"To anywhere we want. Pilskog here can help us with that. Isn't that right?" Pilskog gave him a sullen nod, but Sorting was more interested in the woman's response. Though she said nothing, Anna's eyes burned with hatred.

Good, Sorting thought. He expected nothing less. He touched the gash by his eye and made a note to watch her more carefully. "Now get that food you were talking about. We don't have time to eat. We've got to go."

It took no more than fifteen minutes to get everything together. With Skele watching the outside from the cabin's window, Sorting had Anna and Pilskog gather food and blankets and put them on the table.

"Do you have a rucksack?" Sorting asked Anna.

"*Ja*. It's in my room."

"Show me. You could put the food in that. Skele, watch the professor." Sorting waved his gun at Anna and motioned her to head down the hall. She stiffened as she passed in front of him, but avoided looking at him.

When they got to the end of the short hall where he attacked her, Anna paused. She pointed to the room. "It's on top of the dresser."

"Get it," Sorting said. Anna came out with a weathered leather rucksack. Sorting took it from her, his gun aimed at her. "Now let's take a look at your friend."

Anna hesitated. Her eyes grew fearful. "Just let her be. She can't hurt you."

"She put a good size hole in *my* friend. And I don't want her around talking her head off."

"She won't. Just let her go in peace."

Sorting cocked his head at Anna. "You think she's dying?"

"She's worse off than that man Skele. *Ja*, she's dying."

Sorting studied her. "All right, go see her. Then we go." He watched her go into the room and kneel down next to the woman. Anna spoke to her in a low voice, then eventually pulled the *dyne* up to her chin and got up. There were tears in Anna's eyes when she passed him.

Moments later they were loading Pilskog's car. While Pilskog cleared the snow off the windshield and back window, Sorting had Anna sit in the back seat where he tied her ankles and hands together. "Just so you don't get ideas."

Once Anna was secured, Sorting checked around the car and walked across the road. It had stopped snowing and visibility had improved. The icy fog had lifted, exposing the lower trunks of the pines and birch behind the lake. Sorting looked toward the woods, feeling more confident now and believing he had scared off the skier. Stepping down into the snow-covered field below the road, he found some blood drops that trailed off down to the woods. Good, Sorting thought. Now we can go.

Sorting helped Skele into his seat and closed the door. "Get in the back," he yelled to Pilskog. When Pilskog was in, Sorting tied his hands and feet, then went over the driver's side. He looked back at the cabin. Was Anna Fromme right? Help would be coming soon? Sorting didn't like the odds. Better to leave things settled. He jiggled the car keys in his hands, then made a decision. He slipped and dashed up the steps and into the cabin. He located the lantern by the window and lit it. Stepping into the middle of the room, Sorting took a deep breath and threw the lantern onto the floor. It exploded into flames and caught the rug on fire.

Sorting ignored Anna's screams for Margit when he got back to the car. Ignored her pounding the back of his seat with her tied hands. He turned the key to the ignition. For one heart-stopping moment, it didn't turn over. When it finally went, the car lurched forward and they were gone, leaving the cabin on fire.

Chapter 73

The truck crawled its way up to the top of the snowy *fjell*. Haugland remarked to Lars how different the area was when he was in Fjellstad two years ago. "I don't think the Germans ever maintained this road during the occupation, being in the forbidden zone, but the *fjell* certainly was useful in the winter for the Resistance groups."

Tommy peered over the steering wheel as he drove. "The *Wehrmacht* wasn't up here much in the summer either. That's why it was safe for me to keep a Milorg group here during the last year of the war. Lazy bastards."

Haugland looked out on the snowy scene. *This is going too slow.* He tapped his fingers on the window.

Lars caught the movement. "We'll get Anna. Both of them."

"I don't think we can wait. When we get to the top, Tommy, stop the truck. This is taking too long."

Tommy shifted gears as the truck slipped in the snow. "What are you thinking?"

"I want to go ahead on skis. We'll go three times as fast as this." He nodded at Axel's truck in front of them. "Axel would agree."

"If you go, I'm going with you. That's what we are here for." Tommy's voice was firm.

The trucks reached the summit of the *fjell*. Tommy drove the truck along the ridgeline of the mountain for a quarter mile, then put the brakes on.

"Lars, will you take over?" Tommy asked.

Haugland didn't wait to hear Lars's answer. He was out of the cab and dashing around to the canvased-covered back of the truck. Tommy's group sat there, armed and ready to go. As soon as he caught up with Haugland, Tommy told his men what was happening. He lowered the gate and the men got down. Haugland took the skis Tommy handed him and strapped them on. Haugland slung his Sten gun over his shoulder and skied to the front of the truck. He saluted Lars behind the steering wheel as he passed.

"Our all for Norway," Tommy shouted. "Let's get the bastards."

With Haugland and Tommy in front, the group took off and passed Axel's truck. When Haugland looked back, it had stopped and Axel's men were getting out. Haugland stabbed his poles into the snow and increased his speed.

The weather had changed dramatically since they left Fjellstad. The snow storm had stopped and the icy fog that had troubled them on the way up had lifted. Here the thick forest that flanked the *fjell* below gave way to scrub birch and bushes hidden under the rolling hills covered with snow. Occasionally, there were clumps of dark green pine trees standing like sentinels.

Haugland thought they were making good time, but sensing that they were getting close, he signaled for Tommy to stop.

"There is a small grove above the cabin," Haugland said. "What if you send Petter and some of your men up behind the cabin?"

"Show me." Tommy took out a worn, detailed SOE map of the region from his rucksack and opened it. Haugland pointed out the location of the cabin marked with black ink

Tommy studied it. "I can send two teams up behind it—one can go down south of the cabin and the other stay on the north side." He turned to his Milorg men. "Petter, you'll take three with you and set up on the south side. You, Kåre, you'll go with the others and set up on the north side." He tapped the map. "Haugland and I will approach the cabin from the west."

Axel's group caught up. Haugland looked for Kjell and guessed he was driving the truck for Axel. He was probably not the best skier. He recognized a couple of the fishermen from the village. Axel and several of his men joined Haugland and Tommy. The rest joined the teams led by Kåre and Petter.

"How close are we?" Axel asked.

"From the map, about a mile," Haugland answered. He stepped away from the group. There was an acrid smell on the light breeze. *From where?* It increased his anxiety. "Let's move."

The men took off, and on signal Petter and Kåre led their teams up into the hills that followed the road on its east side. Haugland, Tommy, Axel and members of his group skied forward. About a half mile in, a strange orange glow appeared in the sky. The acrid smell was stronger and was definitely smoke filled with—*creosote? Was the cabin on fire?*

"Bloody hell," Tommy said. "Do you see that?"

Haugland charged off without answering. Tommy followed suit and caught up with him. Axel and his men followed them. As they came around the corner of the hill, Haugland came to a full stop and gasped in horror.

"Anna!" he cried out, forgetting that there could be danger from gun fire. "Sorting. You sick bastard," he choked out. His hand and back began to hurt, like they were on fire, too. Every indignity he had suffered under Rinnan and Sorting flashed before him, but this was the worst.

The front of the cabin was engulfed in flames, swirling tongues of orange and yellow coming out through the roof. The windows had blown out, one of the sills collapsing onto the porch. Sparks rose up against the gray sky or drifted across the road. Haugland frantically looked for a way to get in.

Tommy glided up next to him, his usually ruddy face white. "God, are they inside?" he asked Haugland in English.

"Can't tell. The front looks gone, but they could be in the bedrooms in the back." Haugland pushed away and cautiously skied up closer. He noticed the faint rectangular patch in the snow where a vehicle had been parked. He skied closer, careful of the sparks raining down and leaving punctures in the snow. Whatever was here had left heading south, a swerving track showing its struggle to get going. He counted four sets of footprints. Sorting, Pilskog, and this Skele made three. Anna and Margit made five. That could mean that someone was dead.

His heart pounding, Haugland turned his skis around and on the other side of the road, dropped down to take them off. When he stood up, he noticed the outhouse behind the cabin. It was far enough away to not be affected by the heat or sparks from the fire. Leading up to it on the left side of the cabin was a series of footprints and drag marks in the snow. Tommy took off his skis and together, they cautiously followed the tracks. Out on the road, Axel and his men arrived.

The heat from the fire was intense. They held their arms in front of their faces and made it to the back of the cabin where Haugland found a mix of prints, one set small enough for Lisel. The tracks led to the still intact bedroom windows. Flames reflected on the glass as the fire spread to the back. Haugland looked in. The room where Anna and the children had been sleeping was empty. Tommy stood on his toes to look into the others room. Flames in the hallway lit the room and revealed a disheveled bed and —blood.

"Jesus Christ," Tommy said. "Is this Margit's room?"

At that point, the door to the outhouse swung out. Haugland swung around "*Herregud.*" A tousled Eidsvik stepped out and lowered his pistol. "I never thought I'd be so happy to see you," he said. When he stepped out, he slipped. He grabbed onto the door and swung out like he was on a swing. Haugland and Tommy scrambled to help him. Up close, Haugland could see he was bleeding heavily on his shoulder. Haugland swallowed. Lying behind Eidsvik was a blanketed bundle laid across the wooden bench of the one-hole outhouse.

"I didn't know what to do," Eidsvik said. "When my cabin was set on fire, once they were out of sight, I was able to get inside to the back rooms. I—"

Tommy yelled out. "Is it Margit? Is she alive?"

Eidsvik collapsed onto the snow. "*Ja. Ja.* She is alive. This was the only shelter around to keep her safe."

"Where's Anna?" Haugland already knew the answer, but he asked anyway.

"They took her." Eidsvik sighed, then collasped.

Chapter 74

Kjell brought the heavy truck to a stop and turned off the ignition. Draping his hands over the steering wheel, he stared at the scene in front of him. The smoke seen from a half-mile away had instilled terrible fears, but the chaos of Eidsvik's ruined cabin and armed men milling around only increased them.

Axel Tafjord rushed up to him. "Thank God you got here."

Kjell rolled his window down. "What in the hell is going on? Where are Anna and Margit? Did they get out?"

"*Ja*, Margit got out of the fire thanks to Eidsvik, but Skele seriously wounded her. Eidsvik is hurt, too."

"And Anna?"

"Sorting has her."

"The Devil take his soul if he hasn't already." Kjell pounded his hands on the steering wheel, before he got down from the truck. He slammed his door shut. He shook with anger and fear. "Is Tommy going with Margit?"

"*Nei*," Haugland said as he skied over. "He's going with me to get the bastard."

Kjell thought Haugland looked tired as he leaned on his ski poles. Dark whiskers shadowed his jaw. What more could he take? "Are you leaving now?"

"*Ja*. Eidsvik thinks we are forty minutes behind them at the most. We plan to make up time up on skis." Haugland opened and closed his left hand a couple of times as he talked.

"What can I do?" Kjell hunched his shoulders in the cold air. His eyes began to water from the acrid smoke of the fire.

Axel put a hand on Kjell's shoulder. "Well, since you offered. I know you just arrived, but we need to get Margit Renvik and Eidsvik to *Doktor* Grimstad immediately. Will you turn around and take them to Fjellstad? Petter Stagg will go with you so he can help Kare Pederson look after Margit in the back. Pederson from my Milorg group is trained in medicine."

"All right. What about the truck Lars is driving?"

"It's coming up now. We'll use it to transport our men and weapons." Axel waved to a group of men on the side of the road. Kjell was astonished to see them pick up a bundle lying on what appeared to be a door. *Margit?* With Tommy rushing alongside, they went around to the back of Kjell's truck and loaded it. Eidsvik came next. He waved to Kjell and limped over. He motioned that he was going to get into the cab.

Kjell blew his breath out in sharp clouds. Tears formed in his eyes as he stood next to Haugland. Things were happening so fast and he was worried about Haugland. When he faced Sorting, this time it would be a fight to the death.

"What is Sorting thinking?" Kjell said. "He can't believe he'll get away this time. Barness said he would alert the local police in the valley where the *fjell* road comes out."

"He's desperate. That makes him more dangerous than ever. Eidsvik said that the other man with him—pretty sure that's Skele—looked ill. Can't be much help."

Kjell watched Axel wave Lars's truck forward. It roared past Kjell on the lake side of the road and parked just past the smoldering ruins of the cabin. Immediately, men on skis started to assemble on the other side of it. Lars got out and joined them.

"Give the kids a kiss for me," Haugland said to Kjell. "Tell Lisel I'm bringing her momma home. And as soon as you see Kitty, treat her like the heroine she is. Anna and I will always be grateful—no matter what happens." Haugland turned away.

"Jens." Kjell turned him back. "You will come home with Anna. You will testify and make the quislings pay."

My all for Norway, Haugland signed.

The last thing Kjell saw of Haugland as he turned the truck around was him digging his poles into the snow and taking off at a fast clip with his brother Lars and Tommy. The truck's gears ground as he put it in gear and then he was off to Fjellstad with his precious cargo, Margit, Petter, and Kare in the back and Eidsvik at his side.

Chapter 75

"Damn car." Sorting pounded the dashboard as if that would make the car move forward. After slogging through deep snow up on the *fjell* for nearly an hour, as they finally descended down the *fjell*'s southern flank, the car reached its limit. It gave one last shudder and a popping sound, then stopped. He tried the ignition again, but the motor wouldn't turn over. After several more tries, he gave up.

Sorting opened the car door and got out swearing. All around him was a forest of pine and birch draped in white. In front of him, the road dropped down to the valley. The snow had stopped, but an icy fog weaved in and out of the land below, obscuring its features. He could see that the trees had thinned out, hinting at the possibility of farmhouses or cabins. He thought he glimpsed a building painted in a mustard color. Occasionally, he could see clear patches of a graveled road. Little good that did them. They were miles from their destination on the coast. He hugged his arms and rubbed them to warm up. The heater in the car hadn't worked well.

A sinking feeling overcame Sorting. The possibility of escape was shrinking by the hour.

Skele rolled down his window on the passenger side. "Did you check the engine?"

"I don't think it's worth it." Sorting opened the passenger door on Skele's side and untied Pilskog. "Get out of the car."

Reluctantly, the man got out. He limped to the front of the car. Sorting wondered if the wound in Pilskog's toe had worsened.

What a pathetic group of captors and captives we are. Sorting recalled how they had taken hostages from the Cloister when he and Rinnan were trying to get into Sweden last year. Their male hostage, Caperson, had been severely beaten and branded, yet when they sent him out for wood, he got away wearing minimal clothing. He alerted the Resistance in the area. That led to Sorting's capture with Rinnan and others. Sorting wasn't about to repeat that.

Pilskog and Sorting got the hood up. Nothing appeared wrong. Sorting jiggled some of the lines. They seemed good. Sorting closed the hood. "Get in the driver's seat. You try it," Sorting ordered Pilskog.

Pilskog got in and turned on the ignition. The only sound it made was a click. Pilskog frowned. He tried a second time, but it wouldn't start. Sorting had him get out.

"That's it." Sorting swore. Whatever was wrong with the car, Sorting knew they weren't going any farther with it.

"Now what?" Skele growled.

"We'll have to find another car. Thought I saw a possible farmhouse down the hill." Sorting nodded at Anna. "We'll use her to get in if someone is home. We'll get someone to look at your wound."

Sorting went around to Anna's side of the car. Since they left the cabin, after her initial outburst, she had been quiet. Whenever he spoke to her, she said nothing and looked away. He pulled open the door and untied her feet and hands. "Get out. We're taking a walk."

Anna adjusted the scarf at her neck and buttoned up her coat, then got out. Sorting waved for her to move forward, then helped Skele out of the car. "Grab what you can. Then we're going to push the car into that ditch by the snowbank."

"You can't do that," Pilskog protested. "This is an expensive, new car."

"And you'll do what about it?" Sorting took out his gun and pointed it at Pilskog. Pilskog did what he was told.

They left the car in the snowbank and took off. Thinking the rucksack would slow Anna down, he made her wear it. Margit's Sten gun was hidden in a canvas bag hanging on Sorting's shoulder. They were half-way down when Sorting noticed that Skele was having trouble walking.

"Let me see your wound." He opened Skele's coat. "You're bleeding." Sorting lifted up the sweater. The makeshift bandage and wrap was soaked with blood.

Skele took a big breath. "The bitch got me good. I don't feel so hot."

"I warned you that you shouldn't move around," Anna said, speaking for the first time.

Skele shook his finger at Anna. "But in the end, she got roasted like a pork roast."

Anna turned white and started forward.

"Not so fast," Sorting grabbed her rucksack and pulled her back. "You stay alongside me. Pilskog, come here and help Skele."

The patch of mustard color Sorting spotted earlier came into view. It was a two-story farmhouse with outbuildings. Set in an open space on a hill, the fog hid part of it, while a pine forest surrounded it on three sides. Budding birch trees guarded an access road in. He didn't see any human activity nor livestock, but they could be inside. The important thing was that it was isolated. By the time they reached the road into the farmyard, Sorting had a plan. Hiding his gun, he took Anna by her arm and led the way in.

***

Anna adjusted the rucksack on her back and with trepidation walked toward the farmhouse with Sorting by her side. Behind them, Pilskog held up Skele as they followed. Skele was looking worse at every step, often slipping in the icy snow. Sorting told Anna how to present themselves: to say that Skele had been injured in a car accident and that they were seeking help for him. Anna was relieved that, so far, they hadn't seen anyone outside the farmhouse. Maybe the owners were away or the farm was abandoned like so many after the war. Relief turned to fear when two people stepped out of an outbuilding. One was a man, the other a young boy.

"*God aften,*" Sorting said as he raised his hand.

The farmer looked up sharply, his arms holding a load of wood. He wore a black wool coat and red watch cap. "*God aften*," he answered cautiously.

"Can you help us? My wife and I had an automobile accident up on the *fjell*. Our friend has been injured." Sorting waved Pilskog and Skele forward.

The farmer looked skeptical as if he was wondering what stupid city folk were doing up there in this weather.

Anna wanted to scream "Run!" but she didn't want to make things worse.

"Go get Bestemor," the man told the boy. "Tell your grandmother to get her medical kit ready." He studied Sorting, then Skele and Anna. "*Fru—*"

"—Mossing," Sorting blurted out. "Can you help us?"

"*Ja. Ja.* We'll go to the kitchen. My wife is the area's midwife." He waved his hand to the east side of the house. "My name is Per Undset. And yours?"

"Odd Mossing." Sorting explained that they had been staying at his friend's cabin—he nodded at Pilskog—when they got caught in the spring storm coming down.

Anna thought Sorting spun his story so easily. No wonder Bette was taken in.

As they walked, Anna could see that the farmer was an older man who walked with a trick knee and slight stoop, but everything else about him was hardy. She wondered how he fared during the war. The farmhouse's paint was peeling; the red-colored outbuildings with white trim were in need of paint as well. The barnyard was clean and tidy, however. She looked for animals, nearly missing Sorting asking if Undset had a car. The farmer said that he did. It was in the barn.

The farmer waved his hand at a blue door. "Here we are." He tapped the door with his load of wood.

A thin, middle-aged woman with her gray hair pulled back in a bun answered. She raised her dark eyebrows when she saw Anna and Sorting. "Per?" She wiped her hands on her apron.

Undset turned to Skele. "This man needs your help."

"*Fru* Undset," Sorting said politely. "We'd be most grateful."

They were led into a warm, paneled kitchen, painted white. Across the room stood a large kitchen hutch painted with rosemaling designs of flowers and leaves. It held two rows of plates facing out. Colorful rag rugs covered the plank floor. After the freezing walk down from the *fjell*, Anna felt like she had arrived home. The kitchen smelled of cardamom and a rich stew which enhanced her feeling of comfort. It also made Anna's stomach growl. It had been hours since she had breakfast. Yet, she was fully aware that things could go terribly wrong here.

Undset put his load of wood into a bin by the cookstove, then invited them to sit at the stout oak table on the other side of the room. Sorting nodded to Pilskog to help Skele get seated.

Sorting pulled out a chair for Anna. She tried to think of a way to warn Undset, but when the boy Anna had seen earlier came into the room and put a leather satchel on the table, she knew that warning them right now could be dangerous. He couldn't be any older than ten years. *Where were his parents?* She was aware that Sorting could also be curious about who else was on the farm.

"*Takk,*" Anna said to Sorting to keep up the charade. Keeping her coat on, she carefully looked around the room for some escape. The boy had come into the kitchen over by the hutch. The door appeared to open into a hallway on the left side of the room. She hoped it led to the front door of the house. As Skele and Pilskog were seated at the table, she sensed a rising tension in the room. Sorting remained standing, with the cloth bag holding the Sten gun slung across his back.

"Would you like some stew?" Undset asked Anna.

His offer surprised her, but she welcomed it. Behind her, Sorting cleared his throat. Was that his note of disapproval? She didn't care.

"What is your name?" Anna asked the boy.

"Erik," he said shyly. Erik walked over to the hutch. He was a dark-haired boy, thin from the war. He wore a knitted sweater and a pair of knickers that looked too big on him. His shoes were scuffed and worn.

Anna's heart went out to Erik. "That's a nice name." Anna looked across the table where Pilskog sat diagonally across from her. Undset was at the stove. *Fru* Undset had pulled out a chair next to Skele. As she helped him take off his coat, Anna's heart began to pound. Anna was sure the woman would know the wound was made from a bullet. Quietly, Anna slipped her hand into her trousers' pocket. The potato peeler was still there.

Undset brought over a bowl of stew and placed it in front of Anna. "It's reindeer," he said.

Anna thanked him and watched him go back to the stove. Something about his demeanor suggested to her that Undset wasn't buying Sorting's story. He was too quiet. She was torn about taking advantage of the hot food offered her when she should be paying attention to Sorting and Skele. *But I need to be strong. Sorting killed Margit. He could kill this innocent family. I could be the only one to stop that.* She decided that she should eat. On the first bite of the meat in the stew, she knew she had made the right decision. As she ate, she listened to *Fru* Undset's comments on Skele's injury.

"You're bleeding badly," *Fru* Undset said. "What happened in the car crash?"

Sorting answered for Skele. "We spun out into a ditch. A tree branch pierced the passenger side of the car and came into his side."

"*Ah,*" *Fru* Undset said. "Well, we have to take off your sweater. Can you lift your arms?"

Skele shook his head no.

"Then I'm afraid I'll have to cut it off." She nodded to her grandson to get scissors out of the hutch.

Undset brought a bowl of stew to Pilskog who thanked him profusely. Pilskog dug in, then paused to look up at Anna. He rolled his eyes at Undset who had gone back to the stove.

"Erik," Undset said, "could you go get a blanket from the front room?"

Sorting moved away from behind Anna. She saw his frown.

Fru Undset cut the sweater off Skele and began to unwrap the bandage. Skele groaned. Undset had his back to them at the stove, fixing another bowl of stew, Anna assumed. Sorting stood rigid, his hand near his coat pocket.

"How is the hot water coming along, Per?" *Fru* Undset asked. "The bandage is nearly off." The woman paused, then looked up sharp first at Skele, then at Sorting. "Oh," she said. "Who are you people? This man has been shot."

Undset turned. He held a gun in his hand, but Sorting was quicker. He pulled out his pistol and shot Undset. *Fru* Undset screamed. Undset went down in a heap, his gun going off. The bullet hit the ceiling, then ricocheted into the table in front of Pilskog. Pilskog scrambled back and tipped his chair over. He fell to the floor with a loud crash, his bowl of stew splattering along with him and breaking into shards.

Skele grabbed *Fru* Undset and put a hand over her mouth to keep her from screaming again. Pilskog got up and tried to run to the hallway door, but Sorting fired at him, hitting the door trim. Splinters struck Pilskog's cheek. He stopped. Defeated, he came back to the table and sat down.

"Get the kid," Sorting yelled at Anna. "No funny business or I'll have Skele break this woman's neck."

Anna wondered if Skele could really do that in his diminished state. She decided that he could. She got up and started for the door when Erik ran in. His eyes were wide with horror.

"Bestefar," Erik cried when he saw Undset on the floor.

Fru Undset muffled something behind Skele's hand and shook her head violently. She finally got loose. "Run, Erik!" The boy froze.

"I wouldn't do that, kid." Sorting pointed his gun at *Fru* Undset's head. "You come over here."

"Let the boy come to me," Anna said. Her voice was hard, but softened when she told Erik to come by her. The boy hesitated, then came over when she opened her arms. His blue eyes were wide. "You're not a bad lady, are you?" His voice trembled.

"*Nei*. I am not." Anna looked directly at Sorting. "Definitely not."

"I'm not either," Pilskog said. "These people—"

"Shut up. You're a piece of shit, Pilskog," Skele said. He still had his hand clamped over *Fru* Undset's mouth, but by the way his arms were shaking, Anna wasn't sure how long that could last.

"Everyone stay where you are *Fru* Undset, you will treat my friend." Sorting kept his gun pointed at her as he made his way to the stove where Undset laid.

Anna rose up slightly from her chair to see how badly Undset had been wounded. Erik strained to look, too. She patted Erik's shoulder when he began to shake with fear.

Undset was curled up with his back to them. Sorting reached down and picked up the gun that lay next to his knees. He pushed down on the man's side with his boot and rolled him over face up. Undset's head lolled in Anna's direction, his eyes wide open. That's when she could see he had been shot in the head. Not seeing any movement, Anna feared he was dead.

Anna was standing up by now. She whispered to Erik, "Does that door lead to the front of the house?"

"*Ja*," he whispered. "The forest is just below."

Fru Undset took out supplies from her medical bag and began to clean Skele's wound.

"Can you fix my friend?" Sorting asked.

The midwife's blue eyes swelled with tears and hate. "Your friend can't be fixed."

"You better try."

Once Skele was cleaned up and a fresh bandage wrapped around the wound, Sorting asked if the farmhouse had a cellar. When Fru Undset, didn't answer, he pointed his gun at Erik and Anna.

"It's over there," the woman said. All Anna saw was a blank wall on the right side of the hutch. A large, framed picture of Jesus praying in the garden hung on it. "Erik, show them how it works." *Fru* Undset slumped in her chair, a hand over her eyes. Tears rolled down underneath it.

Erik went over to the wall and pushed on it. It bounced back, revealing an entrance to the cellar below.

"Clever," Sorting said. "Now everyone is going to go down into the cellar while I get the car. *Fru* Undset is going to show me where in the barn."

Sorting yanked her out of her chair. "Stand here."

Sorting gave his gun to Skele. "Keep it on her." He picked up the rucksack and took out the lengths of rope he had used to bind Pilskog and Anna earlier. Anna held her breath in fear he would find something else. He ordered Pilskog over to him. Once his hands were bound, Sorting took off his glasses and stepped on them. "So you don't get any more ideas. Get over by that door." Next, he tied the boy's hands and pushed him toward Pilskog.

Finally, he motioned for Anna to put her hands together. "One more time." Sorting wrapped the rope around her hands and tightened it before he put a knot on it with great flourish.

Anna tried not to wince, but holding her head high, asked him, "What do you think you will gain? You are alone. Soon you will be outnumbered."

Sorting scoffed at her. "Oh, he'll come for you. I'm sure of that. But—he'll never get you. He'll never see you again."

Anna shrank back in fear he would strike her.

Sorting laughed. "Get over there." He slipped the bag off his shoulder and pulled out the Sten gun. *Fru* Undset gasped when he threw away the bag and pointed the weapon at Anna. "Skele, watch the woman. Shoot her if she tries something. We're going to the cellar."

Anna looked at Pilskog who had turned as white as the painted walls. As she walked toward him with Sorting prodding her with his firearm, she realized she was also weak with fear.

Sorting is going to kill us all. When she got up to the open door, she pulled Erik into her arms. He was shaking all over. "Come with me. We'll go down together."

"Is he a Nazi? I don't want to die." Erik whispered in a hoarse voice.

"You go first," Sorting ordered Pilskog. "Then the boy."

Pilskog started down, limping as he went. Anna wondered how well he could see things without his glasses.

Erik was next on the stairs. "Now you go down," Sorting told Anna.

Anna took a deep breath. *Jens, was this how it was when you went down into the Cloister?* He had once told her the terrible details: how he was taken out of Mission Hotel, the Gestapo headquarters in Trondheim, and driven blindfolded to Rinnan's Cloister. She did not need to know what happened next. She had seen it on his back and hand. *But, Einar, dear Einar. He had died in the Cloister. Killed himself, then was chopped up because he couldn't fit in a box.*

Anna could barely breathe. The chill of the cellar felt like entering icy fjord water. She supported her way down each step by placing her bound hands on the wall and leaning into the cold stones.

When they got to the bottom of the stairs in the freezing space, Sorting lined them up against the wall. He waved the Sten gun at them.

Lisel, Nils. Jens, Anna thought before she closed her eyes and waited for the final blow.

Chapter 76

Haugland stood at the edge of the forested hill that looked down on the farmhouse. He saw no cover except from the pine forest he stood in and a barn and some outbuildings if they could reach them. There appeared to be only forest to the south and east of the farmhouse but it was hard to tell how thick it was with the drifting fog. Somewhere farther down the *fjell* road he knew it met up with another road that led out to a fjord. If Sorting had Anna in the farmhouse, the bastard could fire at anyone coming down from the hill.

Tommy stabbed his poles in the snow. "See any tracks?" he asked Haugland in English.

Haugland turned his binoculars back on the snowy *fjell* road. "Looks like they entered from the main road on foot and cut over to the house." He sharpened the binocular's focus.

Tommy put a gloved hand to his mouth and coughed. "From the way they abandoned the car, they weren't prepared for breaking down. When I get the bastards, I'm going to kill them all." He blinked like something was in his eyes and turned away from Haugland.

Haugland understood his friend's rage and sorrow. He breathed some warmth onto his aching hand, then resumed studying the farmhouse. He saw nothing moving outside the building that looked like a gingerbread house with its scalloped eaves. "Smoke's coming out of the chimney so someone is there." *But where was Anna?* Not much of a believer, he prayed hard.

Axel arrived and skied up beside Haugland and Tommy. "*Hei.* We're all here now."

Haugland shook Axel's hand. "Good. We got here faster than I thought we would. We can't be too far behind them now." Haugland nodded at the farmhouse. "I'm pretty sure Sorting is in there or somewhere on the grounds."

Axel pulled off his watch cap and scratched an ear. "Did you see the blood drops all the way down the road to here? Someone is hurt bad." He put his cap back on.

"I saw that, too. The front seat of the car has blood on it. Eidsvik said that Skele looked ill." Haugland put a hand on Tommy's shoulder. "Maybe Margit got him."

The three men discussed how to approach the farmhouse and its outbuildings. Axel took out his binoculars and focused on the barn. "I see two sets of tracks going in," Axel grunted. "Strange. I see only one set going back into the house."

Haugland studied the barn. One set of prints coming out wasn't a good sign.

"I'll send my men out in teams again," Axel suggested, "one to the left of the farm, the other to below the farmhouse. The front of the house faces south."

"All right." Haugland decided that he would come in from the road using the birch trees at the entrance to the farm road as cover. Tommy, Helmer Stagg, and the rest of Tommy's men would go with him. A couple of men from Axel's team would provide cover for them.

"I want Sorting alive in case he has concealed Anna," Haugland said, "but once she is safe, I don't care. He can't get away this time for what he has done."

Tommy frowned. "What about Skele and the other man, that Pilskog?"

Haugland adjusted the Sten gun's strap on his shoulder. "Skele is as dangerous as Sorting. If you have to, take him out. Do it, but make sure Pilskog is safe. The justice courts may want to speak to him, if they haven't already. I need to talk to him about my father."

"Let's coordinate, then," Axel said.

Haugland synchronized his watch with Tommy and Axel. They agreed on the time they would enter the barn and house together. When they were done, Haugland stepped out onto the *fjell* road and pushed off on his skis.

The entrance to the farm was partially hidden by the birch trees lining it. Haugland and the small group with him made their way in, keeping to the right side of the snowy lane. When they reached the edge of the farmhouse, Haugland signaled for them to stop. The men removed their skis. Tommy motioned his men to cover the door on both sides. Once they were in place, Haugland checked his watch. When the minute hand reached the agreed time, Tommy tore open the door and entered. From the opposite side of the house there was shouting as Axel and his team entered from the front of the house. His Sten gun pointed, Haugland entered the kitchen behind Tommy. To his surprise, there was no resistance. Instead, he stumbled upon a horrific scene. Over by the wood cook stove, a man lay on the floor in a pool of blood.

"Dead," Tommy said after checking for a pulse.

Haugland moved toward a large kitchen table. Plates of left-over food and tipped-over coffee cups told that there had been people eating here. At the table's edge, Haugland discovered another body on the other side. A big man lay on his back, his eyes wide open and his bloody hands clawing at his neck in death. Haugland lowered his weapon and stepped around the table, avoiding a pair of crushed eyeglasses on the floor.

"Who's that?" Helmer asked Haugland.

"Don't know. Skele? Pilskog has blonde hair." Haugland slung his Sten gun on his back. He knelt down by the body to study the cause of death while Christian from Tommy's Milorg group, covered a door next to the hutch. Overhead, men from Alex's team tramped through what rooms might be up there. Again, no gun fire, no resistance. Haugland's anxiety increased. *Where's Anna?*

He pulled open the bloody collar to the dead man's shirt and leaned back in surprise. Sticking out of the man's throat was a potato peeler. The man had been stabbed several times, the final blow deep into his neck.

Axel entered the kitchen. "What happened here?" he asked Haugland.

Haugland got up and wiped his hands on his pants. "We're trying to figure that out." He let out a rush of air. "Still haven't found Anna."

"It's all clear upstairs and out front in the *stue*," Axel said. "And that is Skele. *Inspektør* Barness showed me his picture at police headquarters in Trondheim. Who is the other man?"

Haugland shrugged. "He must be the owner of the farm."

"Haugland," Tommy said. "There's a door to the right of the hutch." Tommy started toward it. Haugland stepped over Skele and joined him.

Slightly ajar, the wood paneling revealed a crack in the wall. While Tommy pointed his gun, Haugland opened the crack with his good hand. When the door was fully opened, it revealed wooden stairs going down.

For a moment, Haugland paused, as the real and imagined terror of the Cloister suddenly seized him. He knew it would take all his strength to make the first step. His mouth went dry. His breathing became short. His back began to burn along every whip mark laid down by Rinnan and his thugs. The swastika branded onto his hip throbbed. This is what he had dreaded the most ever since they fled Oslo three days ago: Sorting finally winning, taking what was the most precious to Haugland— Anna. Like in the nightmare he had in Kjell's warehouse, Haugland would have to go down into this damn cellar to see what Sorting had done.

Haugland stepped down.

"Be careful," Tommy whispered.

Haugland signed that he would be careful, not caring if Tommy understood him. He unslung the Sten gun, relying on instinct and training and fearing the worst.

The basement was bitter cold, but there was a light of some sort coming in from—basement windows? They revealed in the dim light the heavy stones of the cellar walls and a dirt floor. Somewhere, farther back there appeared to be light from a light fixture. Haugland cocked his head to listen for any movement, but only heard Tommy moving behind him. He tightened his grip on his Sten gun, moving stealthily at each step down, trying to keep the wood steps from creaking. He prepared for a firefight. As he cleared the last overhang from the floor beams above, however, it was apparent that there was no trap laid for them. Except for a stack of boxes and some old furniture, the space was nearly empty. Then he saw the figure curled up against the wall. Haugland gasped when he saw the blonde hair.

"Anna!" Haugland called out, then realized the figure was that of a man. *Pilskog?*

"Careful," Tommy said as he joined Haugland. He and Helmer immediately began a sweep of the cellar while Haugland approached the figure.

Haugland gently pushed on the man with a boot. Pilskog moaned and opened his eyes.

"Where's Anna?" Haugland shouted. "Where's my wife?

"She's gone," Pilskog said in a weak voice. "She got away."

Chapter 77

Anna kept her eyes shut anticipating Sorting shooting her, then opened them in surprise when he told her instead to sit down. Sorting gave her a little push. Her hands bound, she pulled Erik to her and together they sat down on the dirt floor.

"Now you, Pilskog." Sorting waved his Sten gun at him. "Take this rope and tie their feet." Sorting threw lengths of rope at him. Pilskog complied, but Anna thought him quiet.

"Pull them tight," Sorting ordered. He smirked when the man had trouble tying when his own hands were tied.

When Pilskog was done, he stood up. He held the last piece of rope in his hands.

"Now get against the wall with them." He poked Pilskog with the barrel of his weapon.

Erik began to whimper. "I want Bestemor. I want Bestemor."

'You're scaring the boy," Pilskog said. "Why don't you let him be with his grandmother?"

"Why don't you shut up?"

Pilskog stepped back for just a moment, then flung the piece of rope in Storing's face. Sorting staggered back as Pilskog reached for the gun's long barrel. The two men fought over it, but Sorting finally managed to twist it out of Pilskog's grip. Sorting hit him in the face with the gun's metal stock and then shot Pilskog several times when he hit the floor. Pilskog curled up in a heap and went limp.

Anna flung her arms around Erik and hugged him hard. "Stop!" she shouted. "Haven't you done enough?"

Sorting turned on her. "Get against the wall."

"I am against the wall. You have me. That's what you want. Just stop hurting people."

Sorting glared at her. "Why should I?"

Anna rocked Erik to sooth him. "I know what this is all about. It's about that woman—Freyda. Jens told me about her."

"What did he say?" He kept a distance from her as if he was aware that if Pilskog could attack him, so could she.

"He said you loved her. And that Rinnan or one of his men killed her." Anna sat up erect against the cold wall. "You want to hurt Jens by hurting me, but you don't have to hurt this boy and his family any farther. Think of Geir."

"Why don't you think about your own children? I can kill you right now."

Anna began to tremble. *Was it the cold or her recklessness?* Her voice cracked when she spoke again. 'My children are with their father. You will never, never, reach them."

Over in the corner, Pilskog moaned.

"Ah, fuck it." Sorting kicked Anna in her side, doubling her over in pain. He turned and ran back up the stairs. The door in the wall shut hard, putting the cellar into a deeper gloom than it was already.

"*Fru* Mossing, wake up," Erik said as he wiggled out of her arms. Anna gasped when he pushed on her.

"I'm sorry," Erik said. He looked up at the ceiling. They both listened for sounds over their heads. There were only voices. No gunfire.

"It's all right," Anna said breathlessly. "We'll be all right. Where is your grandfather's car? Is it in the barn?"

"*Ja.* They'll have to find the keys first."

Anna looked over at Pilskog. He lay still. He appeared unconscious. "We haven't much time." She tried to work her hands out of the rope, but Sorting had made Pilskog cross her hands over her wrists before tying them. She wondered if Erik could help untie her hands, but his hands were tied like hers. Then she remembered the potato peeler in her pants pockets. With her feet bound, she struggled to her knees. She told Erik to reach into the pocket and take out the peeler.

"Now," she said once he had it in his hands, "start sawing on my ropes."

For the next couple of minutes, Erik worked on the top strand of the cotton rope until it began to fray. Anna twisted and yanked her hands apart and the rope gave way. "Good boy." She stopped to listen for any sounds upstairs and heard nothing. "Why don't you cut the rope on your feet while I get mine free?"

She quickly worked to untie the rope that bound her own feet, occasionally stopping to blow warmth on her fingers, but soon she had her feet untied. She finished undoing the rope on Erik's feet and hands, then staggered up holding the peeler like a weapon. She used the wall for support, a hand on her tender and aching side.

"Is he gone?" Erik asked.

"I think so. You said he needed the keys to the car. Where would that be?"

"In the barn."

"I'm sure your grandmother is with him. We have to move quickly. You said there is a way down to the road? Is there another farm down there?"

"*Ja.*"

"Good. You can run there for help. First, we have to get out of here."

Erik opened and closed his mouth. "Bestemor doesn't want me to go down there."

"You'll have to get help somewhere. Do your best." Anna limped over to Pilskog. He had opened his eyes, his bound hands against his stomach. Anna held her side and leaned over. She could see he was hit several times, but she couldn't tell how badly by the thick coat he was wearing. He had never taken it off upstairs. "I promise we'll send someone back for you."

Pilskog's eyes moved. He nodded, but he seemed to have lost his voice. He slumped further against the wall and closed his eyes.

Anna took Erik's hand. "We have to be very quiet when we go up the stairs. Can you do that?"

Erik whispered that he could.

"The wounded man could still be at the table with a gun. We need to find something we can throw at him. If we can knock him down..."

"Bestemor keeps her clay pots down here. We could throw them." Erik pointed to a stack of small spots with dead flowers from last summer still in them.

"Those will do. Let's some."

"I can bring rope, too. Are we going to tie him up?"

Anna nodded yes, but she had no intention of doing that. Skele needed to be down and out. She put a finger to her lips. "Now, let's go.

"I have another idea," Erik whispered. "You can knock on the door. I used to tease my friends all the time. When they answered, I pushed as hard as I could and they would get knocked over."

"That doesn't sound very nice."

"It's funny. Sometimes, they weren't there and I fell through."

Anna thought about it. It might work. She had asked Jens once if he had ever been in a tight spot. He told her that the simplest things could be used to defend yourself. Anna held a small pot in her right hand, the potato peeler in her left hand. The pot still had dirt in it. At least, she could throw that in Skele's face.

At the top of the stairs, Anna stopped and listened. Faint light came through edges of the door, so she had an idea where it was located. She heard no voices. Skele had to be alone. Her heart pounded hard. At the last minute, she told Erik to stay on the left side of the door. She didn't say that Skele could fire through the wall door.

Anna took a deep breath and knocked. For a moment there was silence, then she heard a chair scrape and a slight shuffling as someone came forward. She watched the crack in the wall where the door was. A shadow crossed it. When the wall clicked and went ajar, Anna said, "Now!" She and Erik pushed back as hard as they could. Just as Erik predicted, the door in the wall swung wide open. Their weight against it knocked Skele to the ground.

Off-balance, Anna tumbled through the door nearly tripping over Skele. He was struggling to get upright, but could only manage to crawl toward the hutch. Erik came in behind her and threw one of the clay pots at Skele. It hit Skele in his forehead and knocked him down on his back. Another throw laid him flat.

"Run!" Anna said to Erik.

"But I have rope."

"*Nei*, you must run and get help. You must save your grandmother." A cold fierceness overtook Anna. She did not want Erik to see what she was about to do. Skele rolled over and tried to grab Erik as he hopped past. Anna knocedk Skele down with her own pot. The dirt blinded him.

"Bitch," he snarled as he frantically tried to brush the dirt away. "I'll get you."

"*Nei*. Never again." Anna dropped down on him, and with two hands, plunged the potato peeler into his neck. Before he could react, she pulled it out and stabbed the bloody peeler into him again. The tool went deep into his throat, splashing blood back on her hands and sweater. Skele's eyes grew wide. He clutched the potato peeler and gurgled something at her. She stabbed him again in the neck with a shard from the pot. "For Margit and Bette." Skele didn't answer, only with blood that pulsed over his hands.

Anna staggered to her feet. She felt weak and sick to her stomach. The only thing she had ever killed in her life were chickens at the farm. Then she would say a prayer of thankfulness for the poor things providing food for them. There would be no prayers for Skele. She looked at the chaotic scene in the kitchen and grabbing the rucksack and her coat, she ran out of the room and down the hall to what she hoped would be safety.

Chapter 78

After everyone was secured in the cellar and Skele made comfortable, Sorting ordered *Fru* Undset to take him to the car. "Where are the keys?"

"In the barn."

Sorting thought that unusual, but then there were signs all around the farm that things were not quite right. Maybe they didn't live here during the war. It made him wonder what Per Undset did during the German occupation.

Fru Undset stepped away from him, avoiding her husband's body by the stove. She hadn't cried since he took her grandson and the others down into the cellar. Something about her stoicism made Sorting wary. She still wore her apron stained with blood from tending to Skele. She slipped into clogs and put on her wool coat and scarf.

Outside, the air was sharp and cold. Tendrils of fog floated around the trees on the hills. As they crunched their way across the snow to the weathered red barn, Sorting thought of his uncle's farm up near Levanger. His family was poor, but at the farm Sorting spent many happy summers helping with chores and playing in the forest. During one of the summers when he was in his late teens, he met Rolf Rinnan, Henry Oliver Rinnan's brother. *Look where that took me.* After the Germans invaded, every man had to register for work. They could get in trouble if they refused. Sorting found it more rewarding to work with Rinnan. Sorting had always been in it for the money.

"We go in this way," *Fru* Undset said, pointing at a door to the left of the large barn door.

"What kind of car do you have?"

"It's a sedan."

"That will do." Sorting figured that he could get Skele and Anna in it. There was still a chance they could get to that fishing village. On second thought, maybe Skele was becoming a liability. Haugland's woman might be all he needed.

He kept the Sten gun pointed at the farmwife as she opened the door. When he stepped into the barn, the familiar scent of dry hay hit him, but it was stale, devoid of any fresh animal smell. It felt empty and cold, with lumber stacked against the heavy hewn posts that supported the roof beams high above. He followed the woman toward them. In the dim light Sorting could see a car with a sloping back covered in canvas.

"Take off the cover." He waved the gun at her.

She went to the driver's side and yanked the heavy cover off. She left it in a pile on the ancient plank floor and stepped back.

The car was an old model with bug-eye lights. It looked well-cared for. Sorting wondered if it was used at all during the war. Gas was not available for the average person. This car had no *knottgenerator* on it. Once again, his instinct for caution was triggered. "Where are the keys?"

"Over on the post."

"Get them."

Fru Undset sighed. She walked over and took a set of keys off a nail stuck in the post. She brought them back and put them in Sorting's hand. She looked straight at him. "Are you going to try it?"

"Is something wrong?"

"*Nei*. It runs. My Per takes—took—good care of it."

Sorting looked at her closely. "Go sit by the post where I can watch you."

Fru Undset bit her lip. She looked thoughtful for a moment, then complied. She walked over to the post. Next to it was a stack of two-by-four boards.

She turned around and faced him. Sorting couldn't tell if she was boiling with hate, but he recognized that same strain of toughness in her that his grandmother had. Country folk were strong, enterprising people. He waited until she was sitting on the ground, then got into the car. He laid the gun on the passenger's side and slipped in the key. The car's motor growled, but didn't start up. Sorting glanced at her. *Fru* Undset got up and made a turning motion with her hands. Sorting tried a couple more times and finally the engine roared to life. It sounded many times better than Pilskog's new car.

Sorting, absorbed, looked back at the woman. It was too late. She ran at the car toward him with one of the boards. She jammed it under the door's handle, than ran off into the gloom beyond the stalls.

"Bitch. Damn you!" Sorting threw his weight against the door, but it didn't budge. "The Devil take you!" He slammed against the door a couple of times, but it wouldn't open. Rubbing his shoulder, he grabbed his weapon and crawled across the passenger's seat. When he finally stumbled out and followed the direction she had gone, she had disappeared. *She must be going back to the farmhouse to get her grandson and the others.*

Sorting hurried back to the car and discovered for the first time that one of the tires on the passenger side of the car was flat. The car could run, but it was useless until he could get the tire fixed. Or not. He could still drive it down to the main road. The snow could ease the way.

Despite the cold, Sorting broke out in a sweat. He had little time to get away. His only option now was to leave Skele and take Haugland's woman. He left the car running and ran back to the front of the barn and out. As he ran across the snow, he thought he heard someone cry out in the house. Upon entering the kitchen, he found the door to the cellar open. On the other side of the kitchen table, Skele lay dead on the floor in a spreading pool of blood, his jaw open. Something stuck out of his throat. *Skele, you stupid bastard, how did you let this happen?*

Sorting tore down the stairs, swearing as he went. He raged when he found Haugland's woman and the boy gone. He ignored Pilskog. He hadn't moved since Sorting shot him.

Sorting raced back upstairs two steps at a time. He glanced at Skele, then looked beyond his body. A set of bloody footprints led to the hallway door. *Did Haugland's woman do this to Skele?* Sorting looked for the rucksack full of food, but it was gone.

So this is how it goes. Sorting went back by the kitchen window, ready to return to the barn to get the car. Something up on the hill caught his attention. A figure on skis moved among the pines. Then another.

Impossible. Sorting panicked. He never trusted the bitch's assurance that she and Margit were alone. That man he shot—she said he had been with Milorg—had he alerted a search party that fast? Sorting had no time to waste. He grabbed a small loaf of rye bread and cheese from the hutch. He stuffed the food inside his coat, then picking up the Sten gun ran to the front of the house.

Outside, he saw two sets of footprints in the snow. The smaller one had to belong to the boy. The other, Anna's. The boy's prints could be heading to the road. Instinct told him to follow the boy, but he was raging now. Haugland's woman had tricked him from the beginning. He stepped off the snowy stairs and, tracking her steps, faded into the foggy woods.

Chapter 79

"Anna's gone," Haugland shouted to Lars and Axel as he came back up into the kitchen. "She got away. We've got to move fast." He tried to keep fear out of his voice. "Did you find Sorting?"

Axel stood with Lars by the body of the farmer. A tablecloth had been laid over him. "*Nei.* But my other team found this man's wife hiding in the barn. According to her, we just missed him. Sorting must have come back here, then left. Maybe he saw us before we moved into position. He left their car in the barn running. He—"

Haugland didn't wait to hear him finish. Shouldering his Sten gun, he dashed out to the front of the house, following footprints stained with what was probably Skele's blood. When he got outside, Haugland paused to study the two sets of tracks that led down to the forest. A smaller set went off to the right, but they were too small to be Anna's. The other set had to be hers and Sorting. *Did she really get away?* By the length of the bigger footprints, that person moved fast.

He buttoned up his coat. Snowflakes the size of nail heads were drifting lazily down from the low gray sky. The air felt moist with anticipation of further bad weather. He cocked his head. Far off a raven called, but that's all he could hear. A gentle breeze building up along with the snow, misdirected sounds coming at him. He stepped down into the snow. He had no choice but to go.

"You weren't planning on doing this alone, were you?" Tommy said in English as he burst through the door.

"Apparently not." Haugland gave him a half-smile, though he didn't feel like smiling.

"We'll get him. I don't know what happened in the kitchen, but I think Anna fought back."

"With a potato peeler."

"Never underestimate a woman."

Haugland agreed. He couldn't imagine the hell she had been going through, but she had persevered. He was immensely proud of her.

Tommy nodded at the tracks. "Which way?"

"Over there." Haugland pointed to the left.

"Just my thinking. Axel said that *Fru* Undset's grandson was also in the house. He was forced down into the cellar with Anna and Pilskog. Those tracks must be the boy's over there."

The door opened and Helmer and two other men came out. They were heavily armed. "We're coming with you, Jens," Helmer said.

"Then let's move."

***

As soon as Anna was among the trees, she looked back at the house. She craned her head just in time to see Sorting come out of the barn and stride quickly toward the house.

Oh, God, she thought. She turned and ran down through the trees, knocking snow off their boughs as she went. The hill became increasingly steep as it sloped down. Struggling to keep her footing in the snow, she grabbed onto the prickly branches of the pines and spruce to slow her speed. All at once the trees thinned out, giving way to clump of birch trees. Their white trunks and new leaves just budding looked stark against the evergreens on the left and right of the stand. A dark rocky outcrop appeared beyond them. When Anna came out on the outcrop, she could see below her more pines and conifers. Sticking up further out was the snow-covered roof of another farmhouse. Was this the house the boy Erik worried about?

Anna came back from the edge and took off the rucksack. For the first time since she put it in the rucksack, she took out the pistol. She wondered if she could really use it. Adrenaline and fear had made her drive the potato peeler into Skele. A gun was different. It required a cold steadiness. She checked the magazine as Margit had taught her. It was fully loaded. Making sure the safety was on, she put the gun into her coat pocket. Before she set the rucksack back on her shoulders, she took out pieces of cheese and rye bread and stuffed them into her mouth.

I must keep moving. So far, she had been careless, knocking snow off the branches as she ran, making deep footprints in the snow. She was leaving a trail for Sorting to follow easily. She looked to the right of the outcrop and saw a clean snowy trail that led down into the woods to another rocky level. *What if?*

She carefully set out on the snow-covered pathway that led down to the rocks. When she reached them, without turning around, she stepped back into her bootsteps until she was on the rocky outcrop again. This time, she continued to back up until she reached the left side of the outcrop. Here, a clump of thick spruce trees met the edge of the rock and the birch trees. Doubling over, she took a deep breath and slipped between them, careful not to disturb the snow on their low branches. Winding around the trees, she came out onto a snow-covered depression that seemed to lead down toward the farmhouse. She sensed it was once a well-used road, now overgrown.

Eventually, Anna was on the lower end of the woods. Coming to the edge of a clearing, she realized that she had come onto the pasture of the farmhouse she had seen earlier. Small and tight in acreage, it reminded her of her own farm in Fjellstad. Just enough land to get by. There was something odd about this place, though. Shutters hung from their hinges. The door was ajar. A haunted feeling of some past tragedy pervaded it. The only good thing about the farm was the road that led away from it. It promised access to the main road and the village Pilskog had told her about in one of their whispered conversations.

She started to step out from the trees when caution told her to look back up to the outcrop. Standing there, looking down on the farmhouse, was Odd Sorting. His blonde hair fluttered in the breeze before he put his knit cap back on. Anna eased back into the woods just before he turned his head in her direction. He held onto the shoulder strap of his Sten gun, staring her way a long time. Anna held her breath as she stepped back. She was relieved when he turned away and seemed to study the tracks she made. He started to follow them when he ran back up into the birch woods and started firing. There was an intense exchange of gunfire before he reappeared and charged down the path by the outcrop. After that, she lost sight of him. For the first time since her capture, Anna began to feel hope. Either Eidsvik was alive and had gone for help or Kitty had safely delivered Lisel and Nils to Fjellstad and help had arrived.

Chapter 80

Haugland moved quickly through the forest, Tommy right behind him. Despite the lingering fog that hovered around the lower trunks of the trees, Haugland found it easy to follow Anna's panicked tracks. Sorting's pursuit alarmed him. Sorting's tracks were deliberate, focused. How many minutes were there between Haugland's arrival and Anna's escape? He worried that Sorting would find her before he did.

Sometimes they paused to listen, then moved forward in measured steps with their weapons pointing the way. Helmer and the other Milorg men spread out through the descending forest. Haugland noticed that Axel had joined him with three more men. Haugland nodded at him, then continued down. When the pines thinned out, revealing a large stand of birch in front of them, Haugland slowed down and planned his next move. Even with his diminished hearing, Haugland was aware that the forest had become deathly still. He quietly moved behind a birch tree and made his profile narrow before moving to the next tree. His training in Scotland came back in a rush.

Haugland waved his hand at Tommy and pointed to where he would go next. At the last minute, Helmer joined them. Together, the three of them advanced. The birches thinned out and opened up. Too late, Haugland saw a figure running toward them. *Sorting!* The man opened fire, taking down one of Axel's men. Everyone returned fire, but Sorting took cover behind one of the trees. He fired back, bullets from his gun splintering off bark and low branches. Despite overwhelming odds, it seemed that Sorting might be able to hold them back. Then, as quickly as he appeared, Sorting vanished down a snowy trail. Haugland burst out of the trees and down onto a large rocky outcrop. He looked for Sorting below, but he was gone, safe into the thick woods and fog below.

Haugland pulled back in case Sorting started firing again. Tommy and Axel joined him by the birch trees. "How's your man?" Haugland asked Axel.

"Not too bad. I think he can make his way back to the farmhouse. Where did the bastard go?"

"There's a farm down there." Haugland said. "How many men do we have now?"

For a minute, the men discussed the best way to approach. Axel was willing to take some of his men down the trail. They talked about another team going back up into the woods and approaching the farm from the way the boy had gone. That was when Haugland noticed the tracks that seemed to be coming out from the spruce trees to the left. Curious, he went over to the trees, keeping a low profile. He pushed away the branches and saw the footsteps had turned around and led out into the woods beyond.

Anna. He smiled and turned back to Tommy. "Anna went this way."

Instantly, teams formed. Tommy, Helmer, and two of Tommy's Milorg men would go with Haugland and search for Anna. Axel left immediately, leading a team down the trail. As planned, another team left to look for a way down closer to the road.

"Sorting can't get far," the leader said. "He's outnumbered."

"Good luck," Haugland said, as he went through the curtain of spruce.

***

Anna waited for the gunfire to cease before she moved again. She wondered what Margit or Jens would do next. The farmhouse, despite its haunted appearance, beckoned as a place of shelter, but she decided not to risk it and expose her position to Sorting. Instead, she stepped back into the trees. She crept along the edge of the woods, weaving in and out until she came upon a narrow break in the wall of trees. Here the snow had blown in and covered a dip in the ground. Anna decided to wait here. She could see anyone entering the farmyard from two angles. In addition to the farmhouse, two small buildings offered cover for anyone attempting to thwart the storming of the house. From where she was, she could give warning to friendly forces. She found a log to sit down on, took off the rucksack and pulled out the gun from her coat pocket and waited.

She had barely settled when Sorting burst out of the foggy woods and ran across the field to the closest shed. He waited there with his gun, watching the entrance to the forest trail.

He doesn't know there is another way here.

Anna got up to watch him more closely. With his back to her, Sorting was at such an angle that he didn't see a group of men creep to the edge of the abandoned road on his upper right.

Jens! Anna's heart filled with joy at seeing him. He was so close, yet if he were to move out, he could give himself away. Taking a deep breath, she stepped out of the trees, hoping he would see her.

Danger, she signed. And pointed. Danger!

Haugland must have caught her movement and disappeared into the cover of the trees. Anna crept back into the dip and hid behind a spruce tree, relieved that Sorting hadn't seen her. He was too occupied anyway.

Moving out into the field, Axel and three of his men ran low. Sorting opened fire on them. Axel and his men dove to the ground and began firing back from lying positions in the snow. To her right, Anna heard men racing through the woods. Someone in the group fired at Sorting. Sorting turned in that dirction, fired into the trees, and then ran to the shed closest to the house. As Axel raced after him, Anna watched Sorting fire from his new position and hit one of Axel's men. He went down, rolling in the snow until he stopped on his back. He lay still, his arms flung out. Horrified, Anna shrank deeper under the boughs of the spruce tree.

Out of nowhere, Haugland appeared twenty-five feet away from her. With him were Tommy and Helmer and two other men. He looked for her. When he didn't see her, she poked her head out. The relief on his face nearly broke her heart, but he came no further. He nodded in the direction of Sorting where there was a lull in the fighting.

He took the mitten off his left hand and tucked it under his armpit. No talking, he signed. You all right?

Ja.

True?

Anna nodded that she was all right. L-I-S-E-L? N-I-L-S? she finger-spelled.

Fine. Safe. You did good. You brave. *Tusen takk* for saving children.

M-A-R-G-I-T. Anna didn't have a name sign for Sorting, so she signed, Monster killed her.

Hauglad shook his head and smiled. Not dead. She alive. E-I-D-S-V-I-K got her out. But—hurt bad.

Thank God. Anna sank back, trying not to weep. She knew it was from the strain of the past three days, but couldn't she just hold out a bit longer? What must Jens think? She looked up at him. He was smiling at her, his gray eyes full of love and—respect.

I love you, he signed.

They both turned their heads as gunfire resumed. Axel and his men had made it to the first shed. Sorting was firing back, but more meas-ured.

I go, Haugland signed. Stay here. He blew her a kiss and slipped back into the woods. The group headed through the trees behind her. To get closer to the farmhouse, Anna assumed.

The last image Anna had of him was that blown kiss and him stand-ing there so tall and unbeaten, his dark hair sticking out from his watch cap. Her body ached for him.

Will I ever see him again?

Chapter 81

Sorting pulled back from the edge of the weathered shed and took the expended magazine out of the Sten gun. He was glad he searched the cabin and located the Margit woman's small stash of ammunition under the window seat. In the stash were two full magazines for the weapon. He put the old magazine in his coat pocket and replenished the gun with a new one with what ammunition there was left.

He had little time to think about where the new gunfire had come from. The man with the beret leading the group from the forest was an experienced commander. Former Milorg, most likely. He and his group had made it to the first shed. Sorting could hold them off for a bit longer, maybe take out another man, but odds were against that. *Maybe I can make it to the house, use that as cover and head out the back.*

He also wondered where Haugland's woman was. He had followed her footprints down to the next rocky outcrop. They did not go beyond that. Or at least he hadn't seen anything. When he saw movement up in the trees, he had rushed back up and opened fire. After that, he got away as quick as possible. *So where are you?*

Sorting peered around the corner. Someone shot back at him, nicking the edge of the shed above him. Splinters got snagged in his knit cap. He stepped out and fired at a man starting to head toward him. The man yelped and dove back to the shed. Heavy fire broke out, forcing Sorting back against the shed's wall. He turned to his left, calculating the distance he needed to run to the building. He jumped out and fired in the direction of the shed. He waited for the volley of bullets coming back at him to stop, then ran for the door of the farmhouse. Shots spit around him, kicking up snow and dirt. One shot broke out a window, sending shards of glass out onto the snow and back inside. Sorting just made it through the door when he heard the sounds of guns and men charging. He forced the broken door back into the door frame and locked it. He turned around and gasped. *What the fuck?*

He should have known that something was wrong about the place with its broken fences, worn sheds, and shutters handing off their hinges. At one time it must have been some place—judging by the peeling wallpaper, the overturned furniture in the kitchen, and the smashed paintings out in the hallway floor—the word "QUISLING," painted in bold red letters on the walls and cabinets, spoke volumes. It was too dangerous to linger here, but as he hurried down to what he hoped would be an escape route to the outside, Sorting spotted a shattered framed photograph of a young man dressed in the uniform of the *Hird*, the military wing of the *Nasional Samling*. Sorting kicked it away, shattering it more.

Halfway down the hall, Sorting noticed a door ajar in an entryway to his right. He paused to look. The door opened up to a stairway going up to the next level, but he had no time to spare. The banging on the back door behind him spurred him to move. He hurried to the end of the hall, glancing into rooms on either side of it as he passed. They were equally trashed, but no sign of Anna. He opened the front door and came face to face with Tore Haugland and two others running toward him.

***

Haugland raced through the thick forest of spruce and pine until he was parallel to the derelict farmhouse. The sounds of gunfire continued as Axel advanced to the sheds on Haugland's right.

"Did you see the bastard?" Tommy asked, catching up with him.

"No," Haugland said in English, then switched to Norwegian when Helmer joined them. "But I think he's going to make a run to the house."

"I saw him change out his ammunition," Helmer said. "Do you think he's getting low?"

Haugland checked his own ammunition. He frowned. He didn't have much left. "I wouldn't be surprised if someone helped him escape from Vollan, I doubt he was given anything more than a handgun."

"I think he has Margit's Sten gun," Tommy said sourly. He spit into the snow.

"Let's take it back." Haugland took off again through the trees when there was a lull in the gunfire. *Sorting's up to something,* he thought.

Haugland reached the edge of house opposite him. It looked as derelict as the back. Some of the windows were broken, but most telling was the peeling portico that rose over the steps to the front door. Someone had gone abroad to bring back such a design. Not typical of a Norwegian farmhouse and useless with the amount of snow in the region. Above the portico supported by simple columns was a railed-in porch. One of its sections was gone.

"That place is truly haunted," Helmer said as he shook his head. "I've never seen a troll before, but I bet a troll could live there. This place stinks just like one."

Haugland clapped Helmer on his shoulder. "You've never seen a troll because you're a fisherman and you spend all your time on the sea. You've most likely seen a Draugen."

Helmer grinned, "*Ja, ja.*"

Haugland nodded at Tommy as he came alongside him. His friend was already focused on storming the front door and cutting off Sorting's escape. "How are you doing, Helmer?" Haugland asked. "It's been a grisly business."

"I'm fine. I—"

The men turned their heads when a sudden burst of firepower exploded. "Sorting's running for it," Haugland shouted. With that, he jumped out of the trees and sprinted across the snowy ground that in some places had turned hard as ice crystals.

The three men were soon running in unison, coming around to the front porch with their weapons ready. There was shouting and pounding at the back of the house when, to Haugland's surprise, the front door was flung open. Though taken off guard, Sorting aimed and fired at Haugland. He missed, but it caused Haugland to lose his footing on the icy snow.

"Jens!" Helmer shouted and jumped in front of Haugland. Sorting's stuttering gun hit Helmer several times in his chest. The fisherman crumpled forward, blood blooming on his front.

"Bloody bastard," Tommy shouted. He had never stopped running toward Sorting. He leaped over Helmer as Haugland was scrambling to his feet and shot Sorting. "That's for Margit," he yelled.

Sorting stumbled back into the house. Tommy kept firing as he came and nicked Sorting on his earlobe. For a split second, Sorting seemed disoriented.

"Tommy, watch out," Haugland shouted. Too late, Sorting recovered and fired back at Tommy. Tommy cried out and spun around. He landed hard on the porch, his head hitting the floor boards.

The sounds of shouting and banging at the back door grew louder and new voices were coming around on the side of the house. When Sorting turned, Haugland fired at him, but the Sten gun jammed. Haugland dropped it and lunging through the door at Sorting, grabbed Sorting's weapon on the barrel. They fought over it, slamming against the walls of the entryway, pushing and grunting as Haugland tried to twist it out of Sorting's hands. Plaster fell from the rotten walls on their heads and shoulders as they banged their way into a room that might have been a *stue*. Stuffed chairs lay on their sides. A bookcase had been pulled from the wall. Their breaths came out in little puffs in the unheated space.

"You bastard, Sorting. You threatened my family. You kidnapped my wife."

"The notes got to you, *ja*?"

"You'll pay for it. For everything you've done, you'll pay. You killed my friends." Haugland, struggling to take control of the weapon with his weakening hand, twisted it and jabbed the weapon's metal butt hard into Sorting's shoulder. Sorting let go of his hold with a yowl. He pushed back on Haugland, and took off holding his side. Haugland aimed, but Sorting was gone.

At the back of the house, men broke through the door. Out on the portico, there was a commotion. *Good. Help had arrived.* Haugland slung the Sten gun over his shoulder and went in search of Sorting.

Chapter 82

Sorting dashed out of the room, going back into the same hallway that had led him to the front door. Now with the sound of the back door crashing in, Sorting had no choice but to go back to the hidden stairway to the upper floor. Attic or not, it was his only hope to stave off his capture as long as he could. He dashed back to the entryway and was in the stairwell just as voices came into the hall. He closed the door and started up, treading as softly as he could manage. His heart was pounding, and for that matter, his side was pounding where he had been hit. He put his hand on it. His fingers came away bloody.

Shit.

At the top of the stairs, Sorting stopped to catch his breath. He felt slightly dizzy. When he leaned against the wall, the pistol stuck in his coat pocket jabbed his leg. He took it out. At least he had that.

He could hear voices and footsteps beneath him, but so far, he had not been discovered. That wouldn't last long. He stared at the wall in front of him. Made of uneven wood panels with a simple arched opening it could offer some advantage point. When he looked through, he saw in the dim light, another arched opening in a wall about halfway down. *Was the attic divided in sections?* The attic was as neglected as the rest of the house, some wood crates and a trunk left long ago to the elements. A peep hole in the roof had let in snow near one of the crates.

Sorting put a hand on the wound in his lower side. Blood glistened through the threads of his wool coat in little pools of dark red.

What a stupid place to die. Sorting never thought much of that throughout the war. He had always been protected by Rinnan, though in the end he had begun to distrust him. Rinnan blamed Sorting for Haugland supposedly dying without giving away the location of an incoming Shetland Bus. Probably the reason why Rinnan had beaten

Freyda for trying to leave Rinnan Banden. *You wanted to teach me a lesson.* Sorting began to fear Rinnan after that.

Sorting thought of Freyda. *The one person in the world I truly loved.* Sorting hated Rinnan for killing her and Haugland for telling him of her murder.

The door at the bottom of the stairs creaked open. Sorting crept through the first opening and set up behind a large barrel. He would be ready for whoever came through first.

* * *

The first person Haugland met in the hall was Axel as he came in from the back. Behind him were four other men.

"Where is he?" Axel asked.

Haugland lowered the gun. "He came out here. Helmer—he's been shot. I think he's dead. Tommy—" Haugland couldn't finish.

"I'll find out," Axel said. He signaled for two men to search the rooms going down the hallway. "Is there an attic?"

"There has to be."

"Check the kitchen."

While Axel headed to the front, Haugland turned back toward the kitchen. As he passed a room with a small entryway, he noticed a door in the wall.

Haugland took a deep, silent breath, then opened the door.

The stairwell was dark, but above him he detected some light source. Haugland could make out some sort of paneled wall. As he carefully started up the stairs, his boot slipped on something thick and wet. Blood. So Tommy did get him. Haugland strained to listen for movement. A lone whistling sound came from somewhere. A hole in the roof? Was the attic empty? His hearing was betraying him again. At the top of the stairs, he carefully stepped up on the thick boards of the attic floor, his Sten gun aimed.

He got only a few feet to the side of an opening in the wall, when Sorting fired at him. Haugland fired back through the doorway and pulled back. Sorting returned fire. Haugland counted to three and moved quickly to the other side of the opening for a better view. He caught Sorting diving into the next room.

"Sorting, you can't go anywhere. Give it up."

Sorting answered with his gun. Haugland and Sorting exchanged fire back and forth until Haugland ran out of ammunition. He threw down the Sten gun. While he got out his pistol, Sorting moved deeper into the attic.

Haugland dashed through the opening and came into a space cluttered with boxes and barrels. He had enough light to see that at the other end there was yet another opening. Had Sorting gone there? Haugland hid behind one of the barrels. "Despite your notes and threats, I'm going to testify, Sorting. I'm going to wipe the whole gang out. That includes you."

"You have a lovely woman. I enjoyed her." Sorting shouted back.

Haugland ignored the taunt. "She outsmarted you. Our children are safe."

"Her friend is dead. Why would anyone think a woman could be a bodyguard?"

"Margit is alive. She was rescued before the cabin burned down. That's another crime to add the list. Attempted murder."

Sorting didn't answer. Haugland thought he heard Sorting moving again. Haugland prepared to move forward, too. He dashed to the far end of the room, using another barrel flush against the wall to cover him.

"How did you know where Anna was? Did Bugge tell you? He's arrested, you know. He'll talk."

"I bet he will. Coward." Sorting's voice grew distant.

"How did you get that note into my infant's hand? Who put it there?"

"Don't know what you're talking about."

Haugland cocked his head, but all he heard was the wind whistling through the peep hole in the roof. *What was Sorting doing?* Haugland looked down on the floor. There were blood drops.

Haugland took a chance and poked his head around the opening. There was another wall beyond this one, creating a nearly empty space in between. Haugland saw no signs of Sorting. He listened again and heard faint movement on the other side of the far wall. Behind him, he thought men were coming up the stairs. *Time to go.*

He took a big breath and ran through the door way to the other side of the room. Sorting opened fire from the next section of the attic. A bullet whistled by Haugland's head. Another hit something metal behind him and clanged as it ricocheted into a wall. Haugland went flat against the wall. He put a hand over his left ear. The loud sounds of gunfire hurt it. He waited for another round of firing. He strained to listen.

Did he hear something click? Was Sorting out of ammunition?

Haugland waited one more beat and then, firing, burst into the room. Again Sorting had slipped away, this time into an opening that was bright with light and freezing cold. Haugland ran low toward the opening and discovered that he too, was out of bullets. He slowed down. Through the opening, Haugland could see another opening. Its missing door brought in a cold wind and shouts of men below. For a second, Haugland worried Sorting could get away, then remembered Axel would be there. *Helmer. Tommy.* The thought of his friends made him angry.

"Give it up, Sorting," Haugland shouted. "There is nowhere to go."

"Why should I? Why make it easy?" Sorting leaped through the opening and attacked Haugland, smashing his right fist into Haugland's jaw. Sorting's left fist came in too low and hit Haugland in his shoulder. Haugland recovered and threw a punch back. They fought hard and viciously, hitting and wrestling in the narrow space stacked with chairs in its corners. Sometimes they made contact. Sometimes they missed as they tired. Haugland knew he was at a disadvantage with his weak hand. It couldn't take it for long. Sorting was bleeding. Haugland was bleeding. He finally tripped Sorting and knocked him down on his back. Sorting felt around and threw a piece of wood at Haugland. When

Haugland put up his hands to deflect it, Sorting scrambled up and grabbed Haugland on his coat. They both tumbled outside onto the roof of the portico Haugland had seen earlier.

Haugland had no time to assess the danger he was in. The snow-covered porch was icy and a large section of railing was missing. They each tried to shove the other toward it, but every time one of them slipped. They finally broke away. It gave Sorting time to grab a baluster from the broken railing and bring it down directly at Haugland's hand. He cried out in pain, lowering his guard for a moment. Sorting hit him again on his forearm. Haugland slipped and fell down. He was vaguely aware of people shouting down below. Of Sorting raising the carved baluster over his head when Sorting stopped in mid-action. Blood spurted out from his neck. He grabbed his throat, staring down at the person who had shot him from below. He swayed, choked on his blood and fell through the gap. Haugland heard the thud on the snow below. Holding his forearm, he crawled to the edge of the porch. There beyond the group in front of the farmhouse, Anna stood trembling with both hands on a pistol. Her face screwed up in tears as she collapsed to her knees in the snow. Haugland felt faint. He closed his eyes, but opened them when someone put a hand on his shoulder.

"It's over, brother," Lars said.

***

When Haugland came down with Lars, Axel and others were gathered around the body of Sorting. Someone was pressing down on the wound in his neck, but it pulsed red blood into the snow. Another Milorg man tended to Helmer. He gently folded his arms over his chest and closed his eyes. Haugland went around them and looked for Anna.

Anna was in the back with an extra coat around her. She had compose herself, but her face was drawn in anguish. He walked quickly toward her. Opening his arms, Anna ran into them.

For a long moment they said nothing. Haugland gently rocked her, murmuring his love and comfort. She trembled in his arms. Finally, she stirred her head against his chest and spoke. "Oh, Jens. I didn't know what to do. He was going to kill you."

Haugland answered that it was most likely. "Brave, brave Anna. It couldn't have been an easy thing to do."

Anna laid a fist on his chest. "*Nei.* I could have killed you instead. I don't want to ever see a gun again." She looked up at him. "Poor Helmer. Is he dead?"

"*Ja.*' Haugland released her, feeling choked up inside. "He was a true friend. A *jøssing*, like the rest of the Stagg family." Haugland turned back to the house, holding his forearm in pain. He was relieved to see Tommy sitting on a broken chair not far from the porch. He had a bandage around his head.

"Let's go back." Haugland took Anna's hand.

They walked back to where Helmer lay. Haugland crouched down beside Helmer and touched his bloodstained coat sleeve. "Tusen takk, friend, for all you did for me when I was in Fjellstad. I won't forget. I'll make sure the village knows what a jøssing you are. I'll help your family in any way I can." He patted Helmer's shoulder, then struggling, stood up. The exertion of the fight was finally getting to him. He gave a rueful smile to Anna.

Axel put a hand on Haugland's shoulder. "I don't think he suffered. One of the bullets went right through the heart.

Haugland called out to Tommy. "How are you doing? I thought he got you good."

"The bullet hit my shoulder holster. I'm bruised. My head is killing me, too."

"Thank God it's nothing more serious."

"Tore." Lars motioned him to come over to where Sorting lay. "It's Sorting."

Haugland started over. Anna pulled on his coat sleeve. "Is he still alive?" she asked. "I want to see him."

"It's not pretty."

"I don't care. I want to see the man who brought so much misery on me, Einar, and you."

Together, they walked across the stirred-up, blood-stained snow.

Haugland looked down at Sorting's broken body lying in the snow. Blood was coming out of his mouth.

"Wounds fatal," Lars said. "Can't stop the bleeding. No trial for him." He avoided looking at Anna, looking instead at Haugland. "Does she want to see this?"

Anna nodded that she did.

Sorting lay on his back, his eyes staring up at the dull gray sky. His face had turned white and chalky. His bloody hands lay limp in the snow beside him. When Haugland got down next to Sorting, though, his head turned toward him. He opened and shut his mouth, each time a gurgled noise coming from his mouth.

"Can't help you, Sorting," Haugland said. "Looks like you'll get away with murder, but I assure you, I will tell everything I know about you at the trial. Put it on record for eternity. When Rinnan and his gang go down, you'll be there in spirit." Haugland looked up at the sky. To his surprise, a weak sun was appearing above the trees to the west.

"G-eir." Sorting managed to spit out the name along with a volume of blood.

"Who's Geir?" Haugland looked up at Lars.

"Bette, the shop girl's boy," Anna answered. She got down next to Haugland.

Sorting's eyes widened when he saw her. "Freyda—" He fixed his eyes on Anna. Then slowly, the light went out of his eyes. His head rolled to the side and lay still.

Haugland didn't think anyone felt sorry for Sorting, but as he and Anna got up, there was an audible sense of grief. A numbing exhaustion set in around the gathering.

"Let's take Helmer back to Fjellstad," Haugland said. "Get the kids and go to Trondheim so I can testify." He pulled Anna to him and stepped away. "I want the war to be over and never do this again."

Chapter 83

Up in the wheelhouse of a hired fishing boat, Lars kept watch over Helmer's body carefully wrapped in a piece of sailcloth. Sorting's body had been sent back with Axel, to be delivered to the police in Trondheim. Tommy went with Axel, anxious to learn of Margit's condition. There had been no word about Margit since they left Eidsvik's cabin for Fjellstad. The plan was for Grimstad to examine her, then send her to the hospital in the city. Tommy didn't know whether she was dead or alive. Pilskog, still clinging to life, went with them.

Sitting next to the fishing boat's owner, Arne Orkdalsen, Lars smoked his pipe. He wished he could sleep, too. He had been up since five o'clock in the morning and had not stopped since leaving Trondheim with Axel and *Inspektør* Barness. It had taken several hours to arrange transportation for the various parties and to secure help for *Fru* Undset and her grandson. It was decided that he, along with his brother and Anna would return to Fjellstad by boat.

Now nine at night, as Lars looked out over the fish hold to the choppy gray sea at the boat's bow, he saw the sun had finally come out. Settling near the horizon for the night, it spread a golden warmth over the water and on the islands touched by snow. Normally, he would enjoy the sight as he rarely was at sea, but the day had been a bitter pill. He was fast learning that liberation didn't always bring peace. The war crime trials going on around the country could bring justice, but not necessarily resolution. It was going to take some time before Norway would feel normal again.

Lars worried about Tore, who would testify at the Rinnan trial in two days. Would he find resolution? *And what about me? I promise you, Siv, things will be different.*

Lars turned to Orkdalsen, a slight man grizzled and hardened by a lifetime of fishing. He stood at his wheel, his watery blue eyes on the water as the boat Tonk-a-tonked along. "How much longer to Fjellstad?" Lars asked.

"We should be there in thirty minutes. The fjord's mouth is just ahead. It'll cut down on the wind once we're in."

There was movement out on the deck as Tore came up from the crew's quarters. As he pulled together his coat against the wind, Lars thought his brother looked tired. His face was bruised and he walked stiffly.

Lars waved to him, inviting him in.

"How is Anna?" Lars asked Tore once he was inside the wheelhouse.

Tore slid the door shut. "She's sick. She needs Nils, but I want Grimstad to see her right away. She's running a fever." Tore looked out the wheelhouse window. "She's also exhausted, emotionally and physically."

"We'll get her to Fjellstad well enough," Orkdalsen said.

"*Takk*," Tore said.

The boat entered the fjord and smoothed out as it moved in less troubled waters. Birds swirled overhead in the endless twilight. Orkdalsen studied Lars and Tore. Finally, he asked, "What happened at the Undset farm?"

"Do you know the family?"

"*Ja*. We all know the family. One member in particular." Orkdalsen made a spitting motion to the side.

Lars explained to him how Odd Sorting, one of Rinnan's men, had escaped from Vollan Prison in Trondheim three days ago and what had ensued.

"Is he the one who murdered Per Undset?"

"*Ja*. And this *jøssing*—" Lars nodded at the wrapped body. "—Helmer Stagg of Fjellstad."

Orkdalsen pursed his lips. "I knew the Stagg family. The schoolmaster." He cleared his throat. "Per Undset and his wife were good people. I am sorry to hear about Per. Is *Fru* Undset all right?"

Lars said that she was.

The man shook his head. "That this should befallen him after all they went through."

Haugland sat down on a stool. "What's their story? What do you mean by one member in particular? When the local police arrived at the farmhouse, there seemed to be a universal disdain. Who owns that place?"

"A nasty piece of business named Dag Kalberg. They should burn the house down. There are things he did that are unforgiveable."

"What did he do?" Lars asked.

"He ran the local branch of *Nasional Samling* during the occupation. He had his hands in everything: policing, the issuing of passes, licences, even took over the harvest. He was just sentenced to ten years at hard labor, but that won't make up for what he did to our community or to his son-in-law, Kasper Undset. Totally corrupted the young man."

"Kasper Undset. Is he the one in the photo wearing the Hird uniform?"

"*Ja.* After he married Bodil Karlberg, Kasper joined the NS. When the occupation began, Dag encouraged Kasper to sign up for the Hird. We were all disheartened when Kasper did that. He changed. Became cruel. He lorded it over our community for quite a while, parading around in his uniform." Orkdalsen grew quiet as he steered through a series of rocky skerries.

Orkdalsen resumed talking. "Kasper fingered his own parents in resistance work. They spent two years in the Falstad Concentration Camp doing forced labor. Everyone cheered when Kasper was killed up on the Swedish border last year."

Lars looked up sharply. "Is Erik Kasper's son?"

"*Ja.* The Undsets have full custody of him now. Erik's mother was arrested along with Dag Kalberg and his wife on Liberation Day."

Lars rubbed his forehead. "Poor kid. What will happen now?"

"Now that Per is gone, we'll see after him and *Fru* Undset. What else can we do?"

As Fjellstad came into view, Tore announced he would go down and get Anna ready to come up. "I wish there was some way to warn everyone that we are coming with Helmer. It will be a shock to everyone, especially Kjell who just went into business with him."

Lars put his pipe down. "Do you need help, Tore?"

"*Nei*. When we dock, you might ask someone to go get the kids at the hotel. Another to summon Grimstad."

"Be sure you look after yourself, brother."

"I will."

After Tore stepped out of the wheelhouse, Lars watched him work his way around the fish hold to the bow and go down behind the scuttle. Two more days, Lars thought. Get a good night's sleep, then travel to Trondheim for the trial. It was the one last obstacle for his brother before he could truly be free.

***

Anna was awake when Haugland came down into the crew's quarters.

How you? he signed.

Sick, she signed back.

"Do you need to go up and get some fresh air?"

Nei, she signed. She sat up, putting a hand on her breasts. "Oh."

Haugland reached over and felt her forehead. "You're burning up."

"I know. That's what I was afraid of."

"Sweetheart." Haugland sat down next to her. Where Sindre's bullet had grazed him, the arm was still tender. When she leaned into his shoulder, he tried not to flinch. Sorting's attack only made his whole arm and hand throb. He gingerly put his arm around her and let her settle into him.

"Are we almost there?" Anna asked in English.

"We'll be docking soon. Do you think you can get up the ladder?"

"Uh-huh."

"We'll send someone to send for the kids. I'm sure Ella will let you stay in her apartment. More private than the hotel. I want Grimstad to see you right away."

For a time, neither of them said a word. He was full of emotion thinking he had nearly lost her and their kids. He worried he would betray that fear. At the same time, her courage and resourcefulness reminded him how strong she was. She had saved herself, and the children under extraordinary circumstances. He knew she was suffering for it right now, not only due to the strain of the last few days, but because no matter how heinous Sorting was, killing him was against all moral human instinct. His death and Skele's would haunt her for a long time.

Haugland squeezed Anna's shoulder and kissed her head. She had saved him, too.

Haugland looked at her left hand. Her thumb was heavily bruised. He wonder if it was from not holding the gun properly when she fired it. He gently lifted up her hand and supported it in his palm. "Does it hurt?"

Anna sighed. "No. Oh, Jens. I'm sorry to be such a bother."

"Bother? You're not a bother. God, I would have been devastated if I had lost you. I never wanted you to get hurt.'"

Anna withdrew her hand. She pushed a strand of hair off his forehead. "I know and I understand why you wanted me up there." She looked away. "Poor Helmer." A tear ran down her cheek.

"I know. He insisted he had to come. He wanted to help find you."

Anna leaned back against him. Haugland rocked her for a moment and thought she was falling asleep when she suddenly lifted her head and asked, "Who knew where I was?"

"We think it was Bugge Grande. Sorting somehow managed to contact him."

"But how did Bugge know?"

Haugland had no answer. An uneasy idea was forming in his head. Sorting had said, "I don't know what you are talking about," when

Haugland asked him how he got the note into his parents' home. *What exactly did that mean?*

Chapter 84

Anna stood at the bulwark of Orkdalsen's boat and watched a large crowd surge forward on Kjell's wharf as the boat made its way to a berth behind Kjell's *Kristine*. She held onto Haugland's arm, feeling weak and feverish.

"How did they know we were coming?" She hadn't expected to return to Fjellstad under these circumstances. She worried that the villagers would judge her once more.

Haugland put an arm around her shoulder. "I don't know. The hamlet below the Undset farm didn't have a *landhandler* or a post office. Word of mouth, village telegraph?" Haugland pulled Anna close. "I see *Doktor* Grimstad and Ella. I'll get you down right away."

The boat came to rest alongside the wharf. The crowd, bundled up for the cold, moved close, murmuring and reaching their hands out to Haugland and Anna. Their faces reflected sorrow and concern. Anna felt uneasy until she saw Petter Stagg plow his way through the crowd. He climbed on board to help Haugland secure the lines.

Once the boat was tied up, Petter came over to Haugland. "Where is he?" Petter's voice was thick and trembling.

"In the wheelhouse." Haugland put a hand on Petter's shoulder. "I'm so sorry. He was a good man and friend."

Petter acknowledged his condolences with sorrowful eyes, then looked at Anna. "I'm happy to see you, *Fru* Haugland. We were afraid and shamed for what you've had to endure. Are you all right?"

Anna nodded that she was OK. She reached out and took Petter's hand, saying, "I can't believe he's gone," when she suddenly felt faint. His face began to shimmer before her. She turned her head beyond him to the crowd below. She thought she saw Kjell coming through. Behind him, Kitty stood by the office door holding Nils in her arms. Lisel was beside her. They moved in jerky movements as the crowd parted. *Like the Red Sea.* Anna turned back to Haugland. A-N-N-A. Did he say that or sign it? She felt herself slipping away from his strong arms and finally into darkness.

When Anna came to, she was lying in a bed, dressed only in a simple shift under a *dyne.* Hot water bottles wrapped in linen kitchen towels were pressed against her breasts. She put a hand to her head and rubbed it. *Where am I?*

The room was dim, the curtains were pulled shut. Yet from where she lay, she could make out some framed pictures on the walls and a dresser. A vanity reflected back into the room where she saw Haugland asleep in a cushioned armchair. He was slumped over. His good hand rested on his cheek. Anna thought he looked miserable. She wondered how long he had been sitting there.

Under the *dyne,* she ran her hands down her body. She ached everywhere in her body. When she touched her breasts, they felt warm under the cotton shift. She pushed down on one. Though not hard, she winced. She took a big breath and carefully scooted up so her head rested against the headboard. The movement woke up Haugland.

"Anna?" He sat up. "You're awake. Do you need anything?"

"Maybe some water. Where are the children?"

"In the next room. Ella has made a space for them." Haugland went over to the dresser and turned on a small lamp. He poured a glass of water from a pitcher and brought it to her. Anna noticed how stiffly he moved. It was not just from sleeping crooked in the armchair. He had had a hard day, too.

Haugland sat down next to her and gave her the glass. "How are you feeling?"

"Tired, but not so feverish." She took a long sip of the water, then gave the glass back to him. "How long have I been out?"

"From the sounds coming up from below, Ella is about to open for the day. About ten hours."

"So long? I don't remember a thing."

"Grimstad gave you something for the fever and for you to sleep."

"Did I faint?" Anna adjusted the pillows behind her and picked up one of the hot water bottles and put it on her chest.

"*Ja*. I have never seen fishwives so worked up." Haugland gave her a hint of smile. "I think it was a hard awakening for their men to see who really runs the village. Before I knew it, Ella and several women on the wharf had their men get you off the boat and up here. Grimstad and Ella took care of the rest. The good news is that you have no breast infection." Haugland patted her hand. "The women have been keeping vigil for you downstairs ever since."

Anna felt the sudden surge of tears. "Why? They should be doing that for Helmer."

"They are. A vigil for him at the church *and* here for you because of your courage."

"Oh," Anna said in a small voice. "I didn't really do anything."

"But you did. You demonstrated things these villagers hold dear: your fierce love for our children at all costs and for defending the village. You brought the village's worst nightmare to an end."

"Sorting?"

Haugland nodded, yes.

Anna sighed. "It's not something to celebrate. I killed a man. Two men."

"You used your wits. You kept yourself safe. You saved our children." Haugland took one of her hands and squeezed it. "You also saved an innocent boy. Erik. People are talking about that, too. I am so proud of you."

Anna cradled the hot water bottle, letting its heat seep into her. She lowered it when Haugland leaned over and kissed her on her lips.

"Jens." She put a hand around his neck and returned the kiss. She kissed him deeply. Suddenly, more than ever, she wanted him. He must have been thinking the same thing. When she fumbled with his knicker's belt, he pulled on her shift.

"Are you sure?" he asked.

Anna didn't answer. She sat up and tore at his clothes. Soon the bed was creaking as they fell into each other, into the comfort and communication they knew so well. When they were satisfied, they lay in each other's arms on the pillows. They were hot and sweaty, but for the first time since having rescued herself, Anna felt safe again.

She traced a line down his solid chest to his navel. He jerked and smiled at her touch. He had rolled onto the wall side of the bed. She noticed for the first time, in addition to the bruises on his face and on his left forearm above his half glove, the gash on his upper arm. "Did Sorting shoot you?"

"*Nei*. That was Sindre Moe's doing." He went on explain what was going on in the village before he left to find her, including his trip out to the Haraldsens and Bugge Grande's betrayal.

Anna wiped his wet, dark hair off his forehead. "Poor Jens. Not the return you had hoped for."

Haugland stayed silent.

I love you, Anna signed. Forever. She didn't mind when he entered her and started the lovemaking all over again until they were finally spent. They rested and dozed.

"Mamma?"

Anna sat up suddenly. Haugland scooted up against the headboard. They stared at the closed door.

"Lisel?" She looked around for her shift. "Where are my clothes?" she whispered to Haugland.

"Ella took your dirty clothes to wash and gathered clean ones for you. They are on the dresser with your underthings."

"Mamma? Are you still sick?"

"I'm all right. Just a minute, Munchin." Anna sat on the edge of the bed, half giggling, half wondering if she could stand up.

"We're coming, Lisel," Haugland said. He scooted over and got up. "Let me get them." Anna watched him walk over. Despite the terrible scars on his back and buttocks, he looked strong and fit. His bare feet padded on the wood floor when he came back with the clothes and the pitcher of water. He grinned when she admired him full on.

He handed her a linen towel. "Take your time. I'll get dressed first and see to Lisel and Nils, then get some breakfast for us. We don't want to start a scandal, *Fru* Haugland."

Anna laughed, then turned serious. "Margit. Have you heard anything about Margit?"

"I know she went into surgery last night. I'll find out more. Tommy's with her in Trondheim."

"And Pilskog?"

"I don't know."

Anna slipped on her brassiere. "When will we go to the city?"

"As soon as you think you are able to travel. I do need to be in Trondheim tonight so I can be ready to testify tomorrow. But you can come later, if need be."

"*Nei.* I'll come with you." She pulled a sweater over her head. "What about Helmer?"

"They've made a coffin for him. He's lying in at the church. They are planning a memorial for him, but I don't know how soon."

"I want to go say goodbye to him."

"All right. Shall I let Lisel and Nils inn?"

Anna signed that she was ready.

Haugland signed back, Good. "Oh, I do have good news."

Anna cocked her head at him as she never thought she would hear those words again.

"Lars got a call from Trondheim. He has a baby girl. Siv and baby are doing well."

Chapter 85

When Kjell stepped into the church, he saw Petter Stagg and his mother. Standing next to them were Helmer's mother, Greta Stagg, and the female members of Helmer Stagg's extended family gathered in vigil in front of the church altar. The woman were dressed in black. Lighted candles illuminated their faces drawn in sorrow as they stood at Helmer's open pine coffin. The solemn sight made Kjell cry. Five men in the Stagg family, including Ola Stagg the schoolmaster and the grandfather of Petter and Helmer, and their fathers had been executed along with the Haraldsens in retaliation for the blowing up of the Jorstad Bridge a year and a half ago. Now the women had lost another male family member. *It's almost too much to bear.*

"*Hei,*" he said when they waved him up. He kissed Greta Stagg on both cheeks. He took her hand.

"*Takk,* for coming," Greta said. She guided him to the front of the coffin. "He looks peaceful, *ja?*"

Kjell looked down on Helmer and said that he did seem at peace. In death, Helmer looked asleep, his eyes closed; arms crossed in front of him. Someone had cleaned his fingernails, usually dirty from working on the *Kristine* and her fishing equipment. He wore his best dark Sunday suit. Kjell put a hand on Helmer's arm and patted it. He had so many words he wanted to say to Helmer, but he kept choking up.

All our plans for the Kristine. *What will I do now?*

Helmer had been so hopeful about his future. Only last week, Helmer talked about how he would celebrate his thirtieth birthday on St. Hans Day in the summer solstice.

Helmer. His one regret was that he had been so suspicious of Anna that he doubted her loyalty even when she risked her life to first hide them and eventually get them out of Fjellstad eighteen months ago.

Kjell tapped the edge of the coffin. *That's why you insisted on going on the chase to rescue her.* Kjell swallowed hard. He blinked at the sunlight coming through the simple, stained-glass windows. "When will Pastor Helvig say words? I don't like leaving you, Greta."

"This evening. But you must go, Kjell," Greta said. "Helmer would insist. Our village is on trial, too. You must help Jens."

The family gathered around Kjell and for a while, they shared memories and stories about Helmer that brought tears of laughter and sorrow. Finally, they broke off when at the back of the church, the floor boards creaked.

Haugland came in and stood behind the last row of pews.

"Kjell?"

Kjell waved him forward. "Is it time?"

"Two-thirty sharp. The cars are loaded."

Haugland came up to the coffin and kissed Greta Stagg's hand. "I am so sorry. He was a good man. I owe him my life."

Greta put a work-hardened hand on Haugland's brow where there was a large bruise and smoothed his brow down on both sides. "My son was proud that you trusted him to work with you during the war. It makes the whole family proud. He was a *jøssing*. Now you must do one more thing for us— testify and tell the truth." She took his healing hand and ran a thumb over the stub of his missing finger. "I know it will be hard facing that monster Rinnan, but I know you can do it." Greta kissed him on his cheek.

Kjell could tell Haugland was embarrassed, but Haugland accepted her words gracefully. Haugland gave her a soft smile, then looked down at Helmer. Haugland touched Helmer's shoulder. "Good-bye, Helmer. *God fiske*." There were tears in his eyes when he stepped back.

Greta acknowledged Haugland with a bow, then turned to Kjell. "Will you go now?"

"*Ja*. The snow is melting. We should be in Trondheim by early evening. Don't want the roads to freeze up again."

"And Anna. How is she feeling?" Greta asked Haugland.

All heads turned when the church door opened and Anna came in holding Nils. Lisel hung on her arm. "May I come up? I couldn't leave without saying good-bye. I want to light a candle for Helmer."

Kjell watched Greta lose all of her composure. Sobbing, she opened her arms to Anna and took her and children in her arms. "My beautiful girl," she said. "Of course, you can."

Kjell exchanged looks with Haugland. They would have to wait a little longer. This was woman's work.

Together with Greta, Anna and Lisel lit a candle and put it into the sand of the candle box. Then, standing by Helmer's coffin, Anna talked with the rest of the Stagg family. Nils was passed around; Lisel was complimented on her borrowed coat.

At last, Haugland said, "I'm afraid we must go." He looked at Kjell for support.

"Of course," Greta said. She shooed them off with her hands.

Kjell sighed. "Why don't you and Anna go ahead, Jens? I'll be out in a moment."

"We'll wait by the door." Haugland took Nils from Anna and started down the aisle.

For a long moment, Kjell stood by Helmer's coffin, saying nothing. It would be the last time he would see Helmer. As soon as the ground warmed up, they would dig his grave and bury him. Finally, Kjell cleared his throat. "Good-bye, dear friend." That was all that Kjell could say without breaking down. He gave Greta one last kiss, shook hands with Petter and then left.

Outside the church, Kjell was surprised to see so many from the village gathered around the two cars loaded for the trip to Trondheim. A double line of villagers went down the thawing lane blotched with patches of snow. It passed the burned-out houses and those under construction and out to the main road. Some held Norwegian flags and waved them when Haugland came out behind Kjell.

"It's a nice turnout for Helmer," Haugland commented. "I didn't know the memorial was starting now. They began showing up as soon as we parked the cars."

Kjell put his arm up to block out the sun breaking through the afternoon clouds. "I don't think it's for Helmer. I think this is for you. And Anna."

When Haugland looked confused, Kjell said, "Come."

Haugland took Anna by her arm and followed Kjell down the steps to Ella's car. The crowd immediately surged in close, avoiding the *knottgenerator* chugging away on the back of the vehicle.

Mayor Stua came around Ella's car. "Jens, this a sad day for all of us, but in remembering our friend Helmer, we wanted you to know that we have not forgotten you and what you have come north for."

Stua handed Haugland an envelope. "We have collected money for you to use while in Trondheim. The day after the trial tomorrow is Constitution Day. We hope it will be a day of rest and celebration." He cleared his throat. "We also hope you will come back someday."

The crowd murmured its agreement and best wishes for his testimony.

Marthe the cook and her daughter waved for Anna to come over. She held a worn leather suitcase in her hand. "And for you, these are clothes to replace the ones you lost in the fire."

Seeing that Haugland and Anna were overwhelmed and speechless, Kjell stepped in and thanked everyone for them. "Everything will work out all right."

Chapter 86

Haugland and Anna arrived in Trondheim around six in that evening after a long drive on country roads half-covered with melting ice and snow. They spent the night at the home of Thomas and Bea Nissen, old friends of Kjell. Their home was set up high on a hill above Trondheim with a view that looked out over the city, the Trondheim Fjord and the mountains around it. Haugland thought it looked like the snow had come and gone. Spring had come to the gardens. The budding fruit trees glowed under a mid-May sun still high in the sky. A comfortable place, the Nissen home was large enough to accommodate everyone from both cars.

Haugland had been here a year ago, on the day the Germans capitulated in Norway. Amid the jubilation, there had also been sorrow. Kjell discovered that his daughter, Rika, had killed herself after finding out she had been unintentionally working with Rinnan. That unwitting involvement led to the *razzias* on the Haraldsens, Fjellstad, and Haugland's capture. On a beautiful May 8th day, Haugland had come to the Nissen home seeking Kjell and found him sitting distraught by her coffin.

There will always be ghosts from the war, he thought, yet it was hard to think that way when children were present. Nils's cooing and making bubbles and Lisel's laughter as he helped put them to bed made Haugland think there might be hope after all. *I just have to get through the trial.* Increasingly, he felt tense and edgy.

At eight the next morning, Tommy showed up to take Haugland and Lars into the city. The day had started off with a drizzle. As Tommy scraped his feet at the front door, Haugland asked him in English about Margit. "How is she doing?"

"She survived the surgery and is awake."

"That's great news, isn't it? How long will she be in the hospital?"

Tommy moved stiffly as he came inside the doorway. Haugland remembered how he had been struck by one of Sorting's bullets on his holster. *Probably heavily bruised there.*

Tommy swallowed. "She will be there for some time. It turns out she was a few weeks pregnant. We lost the baby."

"Jesus, Tommy." Haugland clapped a hand on Tommy's shoulder. "I don't know what to say. "Jesus, Tommy." Haugland clapped a hand on Tommy's shoulder. "I don't know what to say. Did the bullet cause it?"

"*Nei.* The doctor said it was more likely the trauma and loss of blood." Tommy looked downcast. "We really want children. I don't know if it will be possible now."

Haugland stepped away. "If it's any comfort, Anna had a miscarriage before we met. We have Nils. Margit is healthy and Trondheim has a good hospital and good doctors. It might take time, but she will heal." Haugland rubbed the stump on his hand. "I feel guilty about this."

"Why? It's not your fault."

"It feels that way. On one hand, if Margit hadn't stopped Skele, Anna and the children would be dead. I'm sure of it. On the other hand, Margit took the brunt of it. I'm sorry about the cost to both of you."

Tommy sighed. "She did what she was trained to do. I just never expected this in peacetime."

"Then let's put an end to this. I have an appointment with the prosecutor. I testify this afternoon."

"Are you ready?"

Haugland said he was, but in reality, he wasn't so sure. His heart pounded as he thought of facing Rinnan. *Will it be like my nightmares of late?*

He reached into his coat pocket and touched his father's trilobite. He had found the fossil only this morning in the suitcase he had brought from Oslo. He rubbed his fingers over its ridges. When Lars joined them, Haugland said, "Let's go."

***

They arrived at the *Tinghus* a half hour later. After Tommy parked the car, Lars got out and headed toward the back entrance of the court-house where uniformed armed guards stood. In addition to the military guards, local policemen wearing raincoats against the wet, nippy air stood off to the side by the brick wall. They were armed, too. Lars had seen the crowds in front of the building when he came with Axel to observe the trial—*Was that just three days ago?* The streets were full of energy and intrigue. Here in the back, it was serious and orderly. Lars had been told this was where Rinnan would be let out of a small bus, handcuffed and led into the courthouse under guard. Lars looked back at his brother. Tore seemed quiet.

Axel and Tommy went down the concrete steps to the door first. One of the military guards saluted Axel when he gave him a card. The soldier looked it over, checked a list, and gave it back. "You can go in, sir."

The men were led to a room down the hall from the back where a policeman and two officers of the court waited outside a door. A man with round wire glasses and a trim suit came through and greeted them. He held his hand out to Tore. *Ola Borstad.* He had been in security in the Trondheim area during the war and had pushed for Haugland to tes-tify against Rinnan and his gang.

"Tore Haugland, it is good to see you again. You are looking well. This is...?"

"My brother, Lars Haugland, of Milorg District 13 and my friend Tommy Renvik, SOE Norway, now with the Royal Armed Forces."

"Welcome, gentlemen. I am Ola Borstad with the prosecutor's of-fice." Borstad turned to Tore. "I appreciate you coming in early. I'll make sure that you are comfortable." He motioned for him to enter the room.

"I'll wait out here," Tommy said.

Not waiting for an objection, Lars said, "I'm coming in." Lars fol-lowed Tore into a small, windowless room. He noticed that right away one of the court officers held a camera. The other court officer shut the door.

"If you don't mind, *Herr* Haugland," Borstad said, "would you please remove your clothes so we can document your injuries? You can place them on the chair here."

"All right," Haugland said as he removed his suit jacket and began to unbutton his shirt. He smiled wanly at Lars. "You don't have to stay."

"Is this necessary?" Lars asked Borstad. "This can't be part of his testimony."

"But it is. We've had a statement from your brother for months, but we never got any physical evidence that we need to introduce into the record. It's a bit late, but as soon as the photographs are processed, I'll do just that." He turned to Tore. "Now when you are ready, I'll have you stand in front of the sheet we've hung." The prosecutor nodded at Lars. "That will be all for now. You can wait outside."

"I'm not leaving." Lars stepped to the side and folded his arms. He felt helpless and angry at the same time as he considered this to be Tore's final humiliation: When the photos were made public, his brother would be exposed to the world.

Undressed, Haugland stepped in front of the sheet, his back to Lars. Though he had seen Tore's back a couple of times, Lars hadn't seen his brother fully undressed. It pained him to see the scars again. *How much did his brother suffer to earn such terrible wounds?* Lars had never seen the swastika brand on Tore's hip. He put a fist to his mouth to keep the bile down. The policemen looked ill and left the room. The other men looked shocked. Or was it pity?

"We won't show your face, *Herr* Haugland. Just the damage to your back and hand. We have the medical records from the hospital in Sweden where you were first treated." He nodded to the photographer who seemed to have composed himself enough to prepare the flash on his camera. His hands shook for a brief moment, then he stepped up.

The session, to Lars's relief, was over quicker than he expected. Borstad thanked Tore and, ordering the others join to him, left the room.

Soon Lars and Tore were alone. Neither of them spoke while Tore dressed. When he was done, Tore put his hand brace back on.

"Now what?" Lars asked.

"I go on the stand at one o'clock." Tore smiled gently. "Then we can go home to Oslo. You get to see that new daughter of yours."

Chapter 87

Up at the Nissen's home, Anna walked out into the garden with Ella. Around noon, the drizzling rain had stopped and the sun had come out. The temperature was warm enough to wear a light sweater over her borrowed clothing of dress, shoes, and stockings that replaced what she had lost in the cabin fire.

From where she stood, Anna could look down into the town. She sought out the blue-green roof of the Nidaros Cathedral and from there where the *Tinghus* was located. Though she had come here to rest after her ordeal with Sorting and Skele, she still felt apprehensive. Her children were safe, Jens was safe, but for her there was no relief. The violence of the past couple of days had left its mark.

Ella cocked her head at Anna. "How are you doing, dear?"

Anna fought to keep tears from her eyes. *How can I explain my thoughts?* She kept going back to Einar and Jens. They were the two men she loved. Each man had been treated brutally by Sorting. *Einar chopped into pieces. Jens beaten and branded.*

She finally told Jens last night how Sorting had taunted her about Einar. Jens took the news bitterly, then said he was relieved she knew. He had known all along, but didn't want to hurt her. Now he would be free to talk about it at the trial.

"I'm feeling much stronger. Nils takes to me gently as if he knows something was wrong." She put a hand on her forehead and rubbed it. "But...I keep seeing things that go over and over in my head. Sometimes I dream it and wake to find that it really happened. I'm beginning to understand how difficult it has been for Jens with his struggles. He has nightmares, too."

Ella put her arms around Anna's shoulders. "You're exhausted, but I know you are strong just as you were strong when we had to eat with that pig of a German officer and Rinnan during the *razzia*."

Anna stepped away. "I know I am, but this is different. I had to kill to save myself." A vision of her fighting Skele and plunging the potato peeler into his throat jumped out at her. She shivered. "I wonder what to do now. I was hopeful when we returned from America. We had a future here. Now that seems impossible." Anna continued along the edge of the garden. Ella followed. Someone had put out heavy wood lawn chairs, but they were too wet to sit on.

"There is always hope," Ella said. "We can't erase what happened to us, but we must go on for ourselves, our families, and our country."

Anna paused to watch boat traffic out in the fjord. She thought she saw where the huge German U-boat pens were located and pondered what that had looked like during the war with the submarines going out on the water. "What if Jens's testimony comes to nothing? He has risked his life to give it."

Ella answered, her voice strong, "Rinnan and his gang are on trial, not Jens. His testimony matters. Jens will be speaking not only for himself, but for the people of Fjellstad, the Haraldsens, and for Einar. Jens will be speaking for all those *jøssings* executed by the Gestapo for working with the British and our resistance groups. And those who were killed as hostages. You will see."

Anna put her trembling fingers on her lips. "I hope so. I love him so much. You don't know how much this is costing him."

"Then we will help him bear it."

Chapter 88

As he stood with Ola Borstad in the spare anteroom that led into the courtroom, Haugland pulled the sleeve of his borrowed suit jacket over his half-glove and clenched his hand.

"We will be calling you soon, *Herr* Haugland," Borstad said, "unless there is some unforeseen procedure." Borstad cleared his throat. "This is your first time giving testimony in court, correct?"

"*Ja.*" Haugland was taller than Borstad, yet he felt he was shrinking as he realized that giving testimony was going to be painful. But he had promised he would do this. *For all of those who were lost working with me. And for those who survived.*

"You will be questioned by Rinnan's team of lawyers. This is not some German charade posing as a trial as we saw during the occupation, but a true Norwegian trial. The defendants, no matter how heinous the actions they are accused of, have a right to counsel. The cross-examinations could be—difficult for you, I'm sure. But I will do my best to help you."

Difficult? Haugland leaned toward the door and thought he heard murmurings in the courtroom. Had a recess been declared? Some outburst from the defendants' stand?

The murmurings grew louder in his head with the imagined voices of the dead, then silenced, leaving only the sound of dripping water. Haugland took a deep breath and let it out with a loud gush of air. He knew what he would say about the men and women who worked with him—Sig Haraldsen and his sons, Kjell and Helmer, the schoolteacher Stagg, Ella Bjornsen, Hans Grimstad and the other members of Fjellstad's secret resistance committee; Pastor Solheim of the Deaf Church in Trondheim, his cut out. He knew what he would say about how he ran his line and coordinated with the Shetland Bus for its deliveries.

Haugland would tell the court of the bravery and resourcefulness of the ordinary people of Sor-Trondelag. He wondered, though, if Rinnan's defense lawyer would know of any mistakes he made. Would Rinnan's lawyers try to discredit him? Would they know about his love affair with Anna? Did that harm his operation?

The sound of dripping water buzzed in his head. He would also have to tell about what happened to him in the Cloister. *Can I get it straight?* He remembered the night he had been brought blindfolded to the house on Jonsvannsveien 46 by Rinnan's men. As soon as someone removed the blindfold, Haugland was pushed along the hallway. As he passed an opened room, he saw instruments of torture mounted over a mantel-piece. A door opened. Down below, the cellar with its poster of the skeleton welcoming him to the party, the wine caskets, and the blood on the wood plank floor would be his hell on earth.

Suddenly, Haugland felt as if he were hovering above that floor as someone, something guided him to an open door, then slammed it down on his hand—

The door to the courtroom suddenly opened, causing Haugland to flinch. An officer of the court came out. "*Herr* Haugland, we are ready for your testimony. *Vær så snill.* Come this way."

Haugland took another deep breath and entered the courtroom. Just as Lars had described it to him, the courtroom had a high ceiling and was well lit with tall windows. The only thing his brother had not men-tioned were the huge lights set up for filming the trial. Haugland followed the court officer around the right side of the curved bench where the judges presided. He was shocked by the number of people in the courtroom. On the far side of the room, the gallery was crowded with people. Haugland counted five rows, including newspaper report-ers who worked at small tables in the front of the bar. Lawyers for the prosecution were on his right. Lawyers for Rinnan and the twenty-six other defendants from *Rinnan Banden* with him were on the left. Both parties sat at long tables, their papers and thick folders stacked in front of them. The witness stand, a plain wooden podium, stood in the middle of the room. It seemed to taunt Haugland. Though it faced the judges, it was directly parallel to where Rinnan sat in the defendant's box.

Borstad stepped away from the prosecutor's table and motioned for Haugland to go step up into the witness stand. "*Herr* Haugland, *vær så snill,* if you would please."

Haugland's face prickled as he walked to the stand. The air pressure in the room seemed to drop, like a storm was coming. An image of him sitting on the stool in the Cloister, battered and bleeding, flashed before him. *The nightmare.* He was relieved that there was no stool. He would stand during his testimony. Still, his heart pounded as he took his place.

He did not look at Rinnan. Instead he turned to look back into the gallery. Anna was just coming in with Lars. When she saw him, she signed, You strong. Speak for *jøssings*. Bring R-I-N-N-A-N down. I love you. She smiled, then sat down next to Tommy.

Haugland did not sign back. As if her signing had opened a spotlight on them, he saw who was in the gallery. Not only Grimstad, Ella, Kjell, and other friends from Fjellstad, but *Fru* Haraldsen, Sverre Haraldsen, and Pastor Solheim. Sitting next to Solheim was Conrad Bonnevie-Svendsen. They craned their necks to see him and nodded when they spotted him. Haugland felt their strength pour into him. He was ready.

Haugland was sworn in by a court officer.

"Now, *Herr* Haugland," Borstad said, "could you tell the court your name, where you were born, and your work during the occupation."

"My name is Tore Kristian Haugland. I was born in Bergen in 1920. I was an intelligence officer in the Resistance. I worked with SIS and XU. Later, I ran a line that served SOE-Norway in England and our Home Forces via the Shetland Bus."

"You began working in the Trondheim and Sor-Trondelag area in the spring of 1944. Have you met Henry Oliver Rinnan?' Borstad moved around the room as he talked.

"*Ja.*"

"Can you identify him?"

Haugland turned and looked at Rinnan. The little man wore a military-type jacket with double pockets and lounged in his chair like he was bored. He straightened up when Haugland pointed a finger at him. "That is Rinnan—defendant Number One. He's the one who destroyed my line and murdered those who worked with me." With that, Haugland's testimony began.

For the next five hours, Haugland stood at the stand. After an hour, someone offered him a stool. By then, the fear of sitting on a stool that had stalked him for a year lessened. He was grateful to sit as aches and pains from his fight with Sorting two days earlier had set in. He was stiff all over. His hand throbbed and his back seared him with agony. Not long after he was given the stool, the leading judge called for a short recess.

After the court reconvened, Haugland resumed his testimony as the team of prosecutors led him through the events that led up to the *razzia* on Fjellstad, the island home of the Haraldsens, and finally his arrest. They asked about how he ran his line of fishermen working the Shetland Bus. In that instant, he stated that some of the survivors of the *razzia* were in the room. The courtroom buzzed.

Finally, the questioning led to how Rinnan was able to infiltrate his group. "Odd Sorting," Haugland answered. "He was Rinnan's man." He went on to tell how Sorting worked his way into the fishing community of Fjellstad and, more importantly, drew the daughter of Hauglands's contact in Fjellstad into Rinnan's negative campaign. As Haugland promised Sorting, he made sure the traitor's name was written into the court documents.

"And this led to your exposure and arrest?" one of the prosecutors asked.

"*Ja.*" Haugland looked at Rinnan. The man had folded his arms. A sneer spread across his face as he looked down. He looked so small. The male and female members of his gang beside him and in the back row seemed like giants compared to him. *How could someone who started out as a car salesman and truck driver become the face of evil in Norway?* Haugland had listened in disbelief when Alex Tafjord told him just this morning that Rinnan was married. Though his wife was estranged from him, Rinnan's family lived not far from the Cloister. Rinnan had children, one a year and a half old. Haugland turned away, feeling sick to his stomach.

"May I address the court?" one of Rinnan's lawyers asked. "I'd like to question *Herr* Haugland on Sorting's connection to Rinnan."

When defense was granted permission, the man rose up at the table. He was a thin-faced, bald-headed man in his 50s in a suit that looked too big for him. Haugland could sympathize. Everyone had lost weight during the occupation. Even lawyers.

"*Herr* Haugland, we appreciate the courage it took for you to come here to testify, but I would like to ask you about this Odd Sorting."

Haugland nodded at the lawyer, wondering where this was leading.

"It's my understanding that you did not come in contact with the defendant, *Herr* Rinnan, until the morning of December 24, 1944."

"That is correct." *Mission Hotel*, Haugland thought. *My first beatings.*

"Then, may I ask how you connect Rinnan to Sorting in Fjellstad?" The lawyer looked down on his papers. "Sorting arrived in the spring of 1944. Rinnan was not in Fjellstad at that time."

Haugland worked to keep his voice calm. "I saw Sorting from time to time in the village working around the boats, in the *konditori*. I was alerted to his connection to Rinnan in August 1944 just before the Shetland Bus was set to resume. Someone saw Sorting with Rinnan some nine months earlier. On two occasions."

"Where was that?"

"Lillehavn. Rinnan was using the *deknavn* Olaf Whist. Through my Fjellstad resistance contact, Kjell Arneson, the local committee was warned to be wary of Sorting. They soon cut him out."

"Ah, the Milorg unit destroyed in that region. We know Rinnan was involved in that. But this hearsay was good enough to connect Sorting?"

Haugland replied that it was not hearsay.

The lawyer tapped his pile of folders with his pencil. "Didn't you recently have an encounter with Odd Sorting?"

Haugland flushed. "I'm sorry. I didn't quite hear that."

The lawyer repeated the question.

"I did. What does this have to do with Rinnan?"

A judge rapped down his gavel and told Haugland to be respectful and answer the question.

Haugland took a slow breath in and out, then stood up. He put aside the stool. This exchange was more like an interrogation. More like his nightmare.

"Do you need a moment?" the lawyer asked as he shuffled his papers.

"*Nei*, I will tell you," Haugland said, his voice rising. "Sorting was to be tried here along with the other members of Rinnan's gang, but he escaped. I and others pursued him into the *fjell*. That was the end of that."

"I wonder if it would help my client if Sorting was present today."

Haugland stared at the lawyer. He started to shake with rage. "*Nei*. Sorting was with Rinnan from the beginning. Rinnan was fully aware of Sorting's operation to uncover the Resistance in Fjellstad and in particular, to discover me. In the process he destroyed many families. I was gone when Rinnan led the *razzia* on Fjellstad, but Sorting was there." Haugland swallowed. "Sorting was present at my—my interrogation in the Cloister."

The lawyer started to pose another question when counsel for the prosecution objected. "I think *Herr* Haugland has answered your questions sufficiently."

The lead judge agreed and the lawyer sat down. Haugland remained standing.

At this point, Haugland would have liked another recess, but the prosecution was determined to go on. For the next hour and a half, Borstad led Haugland through his experiences at the Mission Hotel and eventually the Cloister.

Haugland remained standing most of the time, though sometimes when he answered Borstad's questions, his hand and back burned so much with pain that he had to sit down. Things grew worse when Borstad finally asked about Haugland's treatment in the Cloister. Haugland thought that he was prepared to answer, but he had to stop several times.

"Could you point out which instruments of torture from the Cloister were used during your interrogation?" Borstad asked.

The crowded courtroom became so quiet that Haugland thought everyone there could hear his heart thumping in his chest when he pointed to the whips and *totenschläger*. Haugland's mouth went dry. A glass of water was brought to him before he continued.

Bostad picked up the *totenschläger*. "Could you tell us how this was used?" Borstad shook it in his hand.

Haugland swallowed hard. "You put your hand through the strap and have at it."

"What does it do?"

Haugland knew Borstad was attempting to show the viciousness of the torture instrument, but it only increased his anxiety. Finally, Haugland answered. "There are little hooks and barbs on the neck. When it hits flesh, it catches hold and rips gashes on the body."

"And this was used on you by Rinnan and his men?"

"*Ja.*"

"*Tusen takk, Herr* Haugland." Borstad faced the judges. "I wish to enter into evidence these photographs taken of *Herr* Haugland this morning," He turned to Haugland and gave him a sympathetic nod of encouragement. "In exhibit Number 4, you will see the full extent of the injuries to his back. Number 5 is more heinous showing the levels of cruelty to which Rinnan and his men stooped." Haugland knew it was a photograph of the brand on his hip.

Haugland felt his stomach surge, but did not flinch. He stared Rinnan down. The little man had shown little interest up to this point, but seemed surprised that the prosecutors knew so much about what went on in the Cloister. Rinnan stared back.

Haugland told the truth, while thinking of all those who lost their lives and those trying to reclaim their lives and move on. He spoke, above all, of the courage of ordinary people in the fishing villages and settlements in the islands and Sor-Trondelag that Haugland had grown to love and admire. Ordinary people who risked everything to resist the German occupiers and the *quislings* who worked with them. They were the true *jøssings*.

Eventually, the court thanked Haugland for his testimony and excused him. As Haugland stepped down, he gave Rinnan one last look. He couldn't physically reach Rinnan and beat him like he had a year ago, but Haugland was satisfied that his testimony would help seal Rinnan's fate.

As the court officer closed the door to the courtroom behind him, Haugland stood alone in the anteroom shaking. A great weight lifted from his shoulders, but as tears streamed down his face, he felt violently ill and threw up in the wastepaper basket near the far door.

My all for Norway.

Chapter 89

The morning after Haugland's testimony, those who had come to support him met for breakfast at the Trondheim *Hjemmet for Døve*, the Home for the Deaf. When the Gestapo was searching for him in the winter of 1944, the head pastor, Harald Solheim, hid Haugland at the school while they worked on a way to get him out of the locked-down city. Now, as Haugland arrived with Anna and the children and stepped into the school's large institutional kitchen, memories of that stressful time flooded him. When the German SS stormed the building, Haugland had hidden in the kitchen's dumbwaiter, guarded by a teenage girl from the school.

Fru Andersson, the school's housekeeper, greeted him with open arms. Solheim, hearing voices in the kitchen, invited Haugland and Anna into the dining room. When Haugland entered, everyone rose up from the table. Standing around the table, festooned with miniature Norwegian flags were Ella, Kjell, *Doktor* Grimstad, Tommy, Conrad Bonnevie-Svendsen, and the Haraldsens. The first to greet him was *Fru* Haraldsen.

"Happy Constitution Day, Jens," she said as she beckoned for him to come to her.

Haugland had been deeply moved that Sverre Haraldsen and his mother had come all the way from their island to be at the trial. After the confrontation with Sverre at the Haraldsens just days ago, Haugland wasn't sure if anything between them could be mended. *Another cost of the war.*

He folded *Fru* Haraldsen into his arms, accepting her hug with gratitude, trying hard not to let his emotions overcome him. His five hours on the witness stand had been physically draining and emotionally exhausting. Being in the same room with Rinnan had made him ill. He was at a tipping point of totally breaking down. He cared so much for Sig Haraldsen and his family. The loss of Sig and his fine sons would haunt him the rest of his life. *Fru* Haraldsen's warmth soothed him. He felt for sure she had truly forgiven him.

Fru Haraldsen clapped her hands when she saw Nils and asked to hold him. Soon she was talking to Anna and Ella. With the women engaged, Conrad Bonnevie-Svendsen and Solheim came over.

"Well done, Tore," Conrad said. "Your father would be so proud of you. I am. I know that wasn't an easy thing to stand near Rinnan and testify."

"*Takk*," Haugland said.

"And how are you doing?"

Haugland shrugged. He looked over at Anna as she sat down at the table by Lars with Lisel. Ella had taken to bouncing Nils in her arms. "Time will tell, but I never thought that I would have to return to wartime skills to save Anna. Or see such cruelty in postwar Norway. People suffered because of what Sorting and Skele did." Haugland nodded at Tommy who sat that the table looking distracted. "Tommy won't stay long. He needs to get back to the hospital to be with his wife."

"Sorting and Skele's actions were unconscionable."

"Worse than that. When I was fighting Sorting, my anger was at him for threatening my family and taking Anna. But really, it was also for *Fru* Haraldsen and her family. Sorting destroyed them. The villagers of Fjellstad are recovering from their losses, too." Haugland went on. "The press calls these trials the Legal Purge, but I don't think everyone will be held accountable for the hatred the Nazi war machine brought to Norway. Some welcomed them. Some benefited from them. Sorting will never pay for what he did." He rubbed the stub on his left hand. "Who will ask years from now, what did you do during the occupation? Not everyone is a hero."

"Rinnan and his gang will be held accountable. And God will judge, if not the courts."

Haugland's voice started to choke up. "I know you have faith for goodness and justice, Conrad, for you have sustained me all these long years, but will that bring solace to those like my sister Solveig and *Fru* Haraldsen's daughter, Adrina Paal? They are suffering from mental anguish caused by the Gestapo *razzias* on Televåg and the Haraldsen home. They have silent wounds you cannot see. Where is their justice?"

Conrad put a hand on Haugland's shoulder. "*Ja*, I have faith. In you, your family. Everyone. I will pray that you will continue to heal physically and spiritually. God bless you, Tore." Conrad leaned in. "And get that hearing aid."

Haugland harrumphed.

Conrad stepped back. "When will you be returning to Olso?"

"I'm not going yet. I have some business to attend to with the prosecutor's office. Anna and the children are leaving on the train for Oslo this afternoon after the parade. I expect them to be in Oslo this evening. Lars is going to Oslo with them as well. He has been away from his wife, son, and new baby too long."

Conrad said he planned to return to Oslo, but not for a few days as he too had business to attend to, including preaching at the deaf church on Sunday.

"You're welcome to stay here at the school tonight," Solheim said. "You can have your old room back."

Haugland signed, *Tusen takk*.

The door to the kitchen opened wide and the food, simple that it was, was brought to the table. Everyone gathered, bent their heads for grace and then sat down. They would celebrate Constitution Day.

A few hours later, Haugland was at the train station with Anna and the children. For the first time since liberation a year ago, Anna had walked with Lisel in the Children's Parade, a traditional way of celebrating Constitution Day in Norway. Haugland walked with them holding Nils in his arms. The people of Trondheim laughed and sang. Many wore traditional clothing and waved flags. Both banned during the occupation. Only blocks away, Rinnan and his gang languished in their cells. The trial would resume on Monday.

Now in the train station waiting room, similarly garlanded with flags, Haugland and Anna said good-bye to Kjell and Ella.

"The road to Fjellstad should be good," Kjell said. "Except on the mountains to the east on the Swedish border, I'm told the snow has completely gone away."

"Good." Haugland felt sad about them leaving. He wasn't sure if he would see Kjell and Ella for a long while. In Fjellstad, Kjell would have to face the loss of Helmer and the impact on his recovering fishing business. There was also the rebuild of Kjell's house. Haugland wished he could help him with that.

"You take care of yourself, Anna," Ella said. "And those sweet children of yours."

"*Takk*," Anna said. "Give our love to Kitty. We'll be forever in her debt. Will she continue to work for you?"

Ella said she would. She squeezed Anna's hand. "Write to me, *vær så snill.*"

"When you set the date for your wedding, Ella," Haugland said, "I'll come up. I promise. Maybe I'll give you away."

Ella laughed and patted his arm. "Oh, Jens."

They made small talk for a while, then Kjell said it was time to go.

After Kjell and Ella said their final good-byes to Anna and Lisel, Haugland followed them out to their car in front of the station. Outside, the sun was shining in a blue sky. A warm breeze brought in the sharp smells of the fjord's water and rustled the new leaves on the trees nearby.

As Kjell opened the car door, he turned to Haugland. He put a hand on Haugland's shoulder, his eyes tearing up. "I don't think I have ever told you, but you are like a son to me. If I don't see you again, I hope that you will remember us. It's time the war was over."

"Kjell...How could I not remember you?" Haugland took his friend's hand. "Let it be over. Here's to the future. I *will* come to your wedding."

Kjell gave Haugland a hug. "*Tusen takk*, my courageous friend. I hope you will find peace in our renewed country."

Haugland waved them off and started back into the station when a car pulled up and Lars got out carrying a suitcase.

"Tore, sorry to be late, but Axel and I stopped off at the hospital to see Bette Norsby."

"How is she?"

"She's out of her coma and awake. She may have trouble with one of her eyes, but otherwise she can move her arms and legs."

"Where is her little boy?"

"In the nursery not far from her."

"Did you see Margit?"

"*Ja*. Tommy's with her. She walked down the hall this morning." Lars turned to wave at Axel as he drove off. "I think Tommy plans to take her back to Olso sometime next week."

Haugland patted his coat on his chest. He had reclaimed his father's journal when he returned to Fjellstad. He never had the time to show it to Lars. "Have you heard anything about Pilskog? Is he at the same hospital?"

"*Ja*. He's in rough shape, but *Inspektor* Barness was questioning him when I was there. He's an odd duck. According to Barness, *Fru* Norsby said that he had always been kind to her."

"Anna said the same thing. Pilskog stopped Sorting from killing her. Saved the kid." Haugland frowned. "That doesn't absolve him for his crimes, like the hoarding and benefitting from working with the Germans running the mines." Haugland took the journal out of his inner coat pocket. "I never showed you this, but Starheim gave it to me at the Viking museum a couple of days before we fled from Oslo. It's a journal Pappa gave to him for safekeeping just before he was arrested.

Pappa was keeping a list of people he was worried about at Oslo University. Names and notes. Pilskog is on the list." He handed it to Lars. "In the back there is a pocket that holds a folded piece of notebook paper. It's a letter Pappa was drafting to the rector at the time. He is accusing Pilskog of intentionally fingering Jewish members on the faculty and at the teaching hospital."

Lars swore. "Does it ever end?"

"After I see you off with Anna and the kids, I'm going over to talk to him. I think they will let me." Haugland looked at his watch. "On that note, it's time to leave. Who's picking you up in Oslo?"

"No one. I'm taking the trolley home. My mother-in-law will be there. She's finally accepted the fact that I didn't divorce her daughter at the beginning of the occupation for another woman, but to protect her. Siv says she's quite taken with our daughter. We don't have a name yet. She's offering suggestions. Loudly."

"You spoke to Siv?"

"Just a while ago. I finally got through to the hospital. It was Barness who first let me know Siv was at the hospital with the baby in the first place when we got back to Fjellstad. It caught me off guard."

They walked into the waiting room. "The baby's early."

"*Ja.* But she is healthy and thriving. Just a few more days at the hospital, then home. Our baby has reddish hair."

"Viking shield maiden."

"I'd prefer she pursue something modern, whatever she wants. Doctor, explorer. By the way, Siv said that she tried to get in touch with me with a message from Mamma. She never got through to the number I gave her. Then she went into labor. It's probably doesn't make a difference now after all that has happened, but Mamma was worried that Solveig was talking to someone who was looking for you."

Haugland stopped dead in his tracks. "The phone numbers at Pilskog's house."

"Exactly. The woman said she was an old classmate of yours from the university before the war. *Fru* Norsby said she was that woman. Sorting was forcing her to call."

Haugland had little time to digest this news. In the waiting room, there was a stir as people went out onto the *quai*.

"Time to get everyone on board," Haugland said. He helped Anna with her donated suitcase while she held Nils. Lisel took Lars's hand. By the train's steps, Haugland gave Anna a kiss. "Get some rest when you get home. I'll be down on tomorrow's train." Love you, he signed.

Haugland waited while they boarded and then waved to Lisel when she appeared at the one of the windows. Be good, he signed.

Bye. Lisel signed, then added her name sign for him: Troll hunter.

Haugland laughed. He continued to sign when Anna sat next to Lisel and the train started to move. He didn't care if others looked at him curiously. Signing to Anna was their secret language of love.

Signing had also saved her and the children. For which he was eternally grateful.

Chapter 90

After the train left, Haugland hurried back to the center of town. From there he would go see Tommy and Margit at the hospital. All around him Constitution Day activities continued as the afternoon grew warmer. Families sat outside in cafés and *bakeris* where the bright Norwegian flags stirred gently in the breeze. Children dashed around. The only hint of snow from two days ago was a lone pile pushed up against the yellow wooden wall of one of the buildings. It was fast melting. The snowstorm and the hunt for Sorting seemed ages ago.

I should be feeling free. The trial is over. Instead, Haugland felt restless. Incomplete. He walked by the Ravnkloa Landing where fishing boats could come in with their catch. He looked for Sverre Haraldsen's fishing boat, the *Marje*. It was gone, back to the islands. Haugland won90dered if he would ever see the Haraldsens again. Melancholy settled on him. He tried to chase it off by focusing on the festivities around him.

Trondheim was an ancient city. As he passed the old two- and three-story wooden buildings and their brick-red or brown-tiled roofs, he realized he never had a chance to explore the city. During the German occupation, he had either been smuggled in to meet with local resistance groups, was running from the Gestapo or was in their hands and Rinnan's. As he made the turn onto Munkgaten and saw the ancient cathedral of Nidaros in the distance, he paused. The massive cathedral had survived centuries of fire, the Reformation, war with the Swedes, and the German occupation. The people of Trondheim had defied any attempt to Nazifiy it. It stayed as strong as King Haakon had been during the war, Norway's personification of steadfastness. *My all for*

Norway. King Haakon had been crowned there. Nidaros promised hope and a future.

A group of schoolchildren waving flags darted around him on the wide sidewalk, their parents and teachers following them. Haugland waited for them to pass, then continued on until he was up on the cobbled Torget. Olav Tryggvason's statue high up on its pedestal overlooked crowds of people mingling and visiting stalls set up for the national holiday. It was a sight to cheer anyone. *Why not me?*

How could such a beautiful city hold such evil? The Germans wanted the area for strategic reasons: access to the North Sea, shipping, and the rich ore mines south of the city. The Gestapo, the SS and SD troops and Rinnan made it a place of horror with its mass executions, round-ups, and arrests that sent people to Rinnan, Falstad Concentration Camp, or to German concentration camps never to return. Haugland rubbed the stump of his finger and shook off the feeling that he would never get over what they did to him.

As he crossed the huge circle, he looked to his right. The Phoenix Hotel—the Gestapo's first headquarters—was on the edge of the Torget. Just down the block was the Mission Hotel, the Gestapo's permanent headquarters, the one Haugland knew so well after he was arrested. Rinnan and some from his gang were being held there during the trial. *Is he in my cell?* It would serve the monster right.

At the last minute, Haugland decided he would walk that way and then head over to the hospital. He had faced Rinnan. Except for one last thing, it was time to move on.

Haugland arrived at the hospital twenty minutes later. After speaking to a nurse at a reception desk, he made his way upstairs to the second floor. As he entered the open ward, he spotted Tommy sitting by a bed in the center of the room. Haugland was relieved to see Margit sitting up and engaged in an animated conversation with Tommy. A curtain on a metal stand separated them from the bed on the other side.

"*Hei*," Haugland said as he came up to the front of her bed.

"*Hei*. Take a chair," Tommy said. He nodded at the wood chair by Margit's head.

Haugland sat down. "It's good to see you are well enough to give Tommy a piece of your mind."

Margit laughed. She smoothed down the blanket around her and smiled. "I'm doing much better, *takk*. You look as battle-worn as I am. That's some bruise on your eyebrow." Margit gingerly shifted against the pillows at the elevated head of the bed. She sighed. "I'm glad to know Anna and the children are safe. You are safe."

"And you are safe. I—"

"No regrets, Tore. I'm so glad that I was there. How is Anna doing?"

"She's not showing it, but I know she is having difficulty with how things turned out."

"As she should," Tommy said. "It's difficult killing someone under any circumstance."

Margit nodded in agreement. "I admire her bravery so much."

Haugland visited with his friends for a while. He was relieved to hear Margit was making good progress. She would be released next week. He did not broach the subject of her losing the baby. Instead, he shared what had transpired in Fjellstad after their return from the attempt to capture Sorting; how the villagers grieved for Helmer, how the Stagg family embraced Anna. "I know that meant a lot to Anna. She has mixed feelings about her time there."

Margit reached over to Haugland. "She met you."

"*Ja*, she did."

"Lars said you both got a good send-off to the trial. Sounds like the whole village showed up."

"We were surprised. It gives me a sense that everything will turn out all right."

Haugland grew quiet. Margit was right. He was battle worn. Finally, he asked Tommy where Pilskog was.

"He's down the main hall, then to the left in a private room, though I'm not sure it's all that private. There's a police officer outside his door. Once when I was out in the hall, I thought I saw *Inspectør* Barness go in there. You plan to talk to him about your father's journal?"

"He could answer some questions I have." Haugland cleared his throat. "There is something else I'm trying to figure out." Haugland switched to English in case someone in the next bed was listening. He knew Margit spoke English, too. "Those notes. There were three."

Tommy leaned over the bed. "Weren't there four?"

"Yes, there were four. The last one was the odd one out."

Tommy quickly reminded Margit of the notes sent to Haugland before the trial. "Does it matter now with Sorting dead?" he asked.

"Maybe not, though I wouldn't be surprised if *Inspectør* Barness is working with the prosecutor's office in trying to figure out how such notes got out of Vollan Prison. It could be a network, not just the jailer who was arrested for helping Sorting and Skele. It's a matter of the security leading up to my testimony at the trial." Haugland rubbed his chin. "Sorting worked so hard to keep me from testifying—even down to escaping and kidnapping Anna. He is gone, for sure, but those notes were specifically designed to discourage me from testifying against him."

"Something's still bothering you."

Haugland sat up straight. "I told you about the phone numbers found at the Pilskog farm. One was for Ella's *konditori*. The other to my mother's house. Before Lars left on the train, he told me he was finally able to talk to his wife at the hospital in Oslo. Siv told him she had tried to reach him here in Trondheim a few days ago. I think the contact Lars left for her was Axel's phone number. She never got through to leave a message."

"What was so urgent?"

"My mother was concerned that my sister Solveig was speaking to someone who was looking for me. A woman. That person could have been Bette Norsby under duress."

Tommy looked alarmed. "Do you do think your sister knew about your location and gave it away?"

"That's awful, Tore," Margit said.

"My sister is ill. She's often not in her right mind. She hates all Germans for what they did to her and her family in Telavåg. She hates even someone like Anna who is half-German and grew up in America. Solveig could have given away my location just to spite Anna, though I don't know how she knew."

Haugland shrugged, making his arm ache. "I don't know. Maybe she didn't think about the consequences—how it would affect me."

When he spoke, Haugland felt that sense of melancholy again settling on him again. He closed his eyes. He remembered the last time he had seen Solveig. It was the morning of the day they fled from Oslo. He saw her briefly in the hallway at the family home. She was looking at a painting and weeping.

"Solveig," he said. "What's wrong?"

Haugland's sister turned and looked at him with wide, sad eyes. Like she was seeing through him. She backed away and went down the hall. When Haugland came up to the painting, though he had never seen it before, he knew it was a scene of Telavåg. He also knew who the painter was by the brush strokes. His beloved *Onkel* Kris. Haugland cocked his head to catch the sound of Solveig's heels as she went around the corner toward the *stue*. He did not follow. Telavåg, he thought, will always be between us.

Chapter 91

Anna sat on the train with Nils asleep in her lap. Lisel sat beside her, playing with a new doll *Fru* Nissan had given her. Lars sat across from Anna reading the latest copy of the *Andresseavisen* newspaper. They were alone in a second-class compartment car and she relished their privacy. She was exhausted from the exertions of the past week. She wanted to get to Oslo and go to bed.

Anna looked out the train window and watched the landscape pass. Rising toward the vast and rugged Dovrefjell through the mountains of the Trollheimen region south of Trondheim, spring was evident in the dells and hills that followed the river. Cows and goats were out grazing. Anna could almost hear the clanging of their bells. Only the tops of the highest mountains were covered in snow.

Jens had told her about the time during the occupation when he took the train down to Kvam to meet Lars. He went disguised as a school-teacher. The ride had gone smoothly until the train began to struggle going to the summit at Hjerkinn. He discovered German agents on board. The train was stopped at Kongsvoll, a popular ski area before the war. Everyone had to disembark and be questioned while the SS searched for saboteurs. Carrying excellent forged papers, Jens safely resumed his trip after standing several hours in the freezing fog and drizzle. Undiscovered, he got off at his destination hours later. Now, as they approached the same station, Anna wished Jens were with her to point out the things he knew about the area. She had never taken a train through the center of Norway. She had always lived on the coast near Bergen.

"Want me to show Lisel around the train?" Lars asked Anna.

"Would you like that, Munchin? Would you like to go with *Onkel* Lars?"

Lisel nodded that she would like that.

"That would be nice, Lars."

Lars got up and took Lisel's hand. "Will you be OK, Anna?"

"*Ja*. I just want to get home. Right now, I'll rest and watch the scenery." Anna gently smoothed Nils's hair. He barely stirred, except to suck on a finger. "Will your friends still be there?"

"Do you mean Polsen and Øyen?"

"*Ja*."

"*Nei*. With the trial over, I felt there was no longer any danger. Everything at the house should be back to normal." Lars stepped to the compartment's door and slid it open. "We'll be back in a little bit." Lisel hopped out and then they were gone, leaving Anna to her thoughts and the clickity-clack of the train as it rose to the summit.

Back to normal. Will I ever be back to normal? She had no choice but kill Skele to save herself. She shot Sorting to save Jens. Now all she saw were their bloody faces. *Was that normal?*

Anna ran a finger over her wedding ring. Like all Americans, she wore her wedding ring on her left hand. Jens wore his on his right hand. He said it was the Norwegian custom, but he couldn't do it the American way because he was missing some of his ring finger and it would fall off. It was like him to make light of a serious issue concerning his health.

Thinking about him made her smile and gave her hope. She remembered the time she found him stripped to his waist in her spring house at the Fjellstad farm. He had been sent by the Fjellstad resistance committee to work for her in exchange for her fields. She had no idea who he really was, but seeing him like that had shocked her. There was more to him than a simple deaf-mute fisherman. Now she knew that body so well. She flushed, thinking about their recent lovemaking.

Anna leaned against the window. "I never got the chance to tell you how proud I was of you at the trial," she said out loud. "So proud." She watched the landscape become increasingly rugged. The rhythm of the train and passing images made her sleepy as the great Dovrefjell engulfed them. She rested her head on the headrest and closed her eyes.

***

Anna and Lars arrived in Oslo in the early evening. As they walked through the old train station crowded with people still in a patriotic mood, Lars helped Anna with the children and her suitcase. Outside the tall stone building, they stopped at the curb.

"Are you sure that you'll be all right going to the house alone?" Lars asked.

"We'll be fine. Conrad has arranged for someone to meet us. You need to go see Siv and your baby daughter right away. Aren't you pleased?"

Lars's broad smile told her that he was. "Nevertheless, I'll wait until you're on your way. I can always catch the next trolley."

A few minutes later, a black sedan pulled up. A middle-aged woman got out. "*Fru* Haugland?" The woman identified herself as a teacher from the Deaf School. "I'm *Frøken* Anja Torkelsen. Pastor Bonnevie-Svendsen asked me to take you home."

"You are very kind. It seems so out of your way."

"Not at all. My family lives not far from you. I've been loaned the school car for the rest of the holiday weekend. My turn to use my gas ration card." She opened the trunk of the car. "You can put your suitcase in here." *Frøken* Torkelson opened the passenger door to the front seat and invited Anna and children to sit there. "What is your name?" she asked Lisel. "Would you like to sit by your momma?"

Lisel shyly said her name. "*Ja.*"

Anna was relieved Tørkelson did not react when she heard Lisel's name. It was German.

Anna turned to Lars after he closed the trunk. "*Tusen takk* for coming with me."

"I would do it again and again. I should be thanking you for what you do for my brother." He took Anna's hand. "I hope you know how much the family loves you. I think even more now after what you went through and for how you supported Tore at the trial. Just being there helped him more than you will ever know." He kissed her cheek. "Take care of yourself. Get some rest. The worst is over. Mother will be so happy to see you." He nodded at *Frøken* Torkelsen who was on the driver's side of the car. He helped Anna into the front seat, a long-cushioned bench.

"Good-bye," Anna said as he closed the door. The car pulled away and they were off.

Twenty minutes later, they arrived at the Haugland home.

"What a pretty place," *Frøken* Torkelsen said as she parked the car, but left it running. "Is anyone home?"

"My mother-in-law is supposed to be here. *Takk* for the ride and conversation." On the way, they had talked about the Nordstrand Deaf School and what it took to be a teacher of the deaf. *Frøken* Torkelsen was impressed that Anna could sign fairly well.

Frøken Torkelsen helped her with her suitcase and placed it on the porch. In the golden sunshine of the Nordic evening, the house and gardens looked welcoming.

Have a restful night, the woman signed. Anna smiled and signed back, *Takk.*

The hallway into the Haugland home was dim and empty. Anna supposed that everyone was in the kitchen or the study. She told Lisel to go look for *Bestemor* Inga. When she came back and said no one was home, Anna hefted Nils up on her hip and started up the stairs with the suitcase. On the door to their room, a note was tacked on the door. Anna put down the suitcase to read it. It was from Inga Haugland.

"Gone to see the new baby. Food in the pantry."

Anna started to open the door when she heard a click behind her. She turned around. Solveig, her sister-in-law, held a gun.

Chapter 92

Haugland couldn't miss where Pilskog's private hospital room was located. A uniformed Trondheim police officer stood outside the recessed entryway. Another man wearing a suit and high collar, whom Haugland suspected was from Borstad's office, leaned against the wall on the other side of the hallway. When Haugland came up to the police officer, the man stopped him.

"Can't go in there," he said.

"It's OK," Inspektør Knut Barness stepped out of the recess and offered his hand to Haugland. "It's good to see you again. I didn't get a chance to talk to you before your testimony, but I'm relieved that Sorting and Skele were stopped before they caused further damage. How is your wife?"

"Doing well enough."

Barness turned to the police officer. "You can leave for a short break, Anders. I'll be here with *Herr* Haugland. You too, Iversen. I'll be in touch with the prosecutor if I learn anything else."

The two men left and disappeared down the main hall.

Barness removed his wire-rimmed glasses and wiped them clean with a handkerchief. "Now, we can talk. I commend you on your testimony."

"You were there?"

"*Ja*. All five hours of it. Very powerful. I think you nailed Rinnan, but I suspect it wasn't a pleasant five hours under the barrage of all those lawyers. Especially, your details about what happened to you in the Cloister. I don't know if you know, but I've been down there. I was part of the team gathering additional information for Rinnan's indictment. A nasty, haunted place."

Haugland agreed that it was, but he wanted to get beyond the trial. He needed to see Pilskog. "How is Pilskog? Can he talk?"

"He can talk. I interviewed him extensively this morning along with a counselor from the war crimes office. His hoard of German luxuries has struck a note with former resistance groups. They want to know about his dealings with the mines. They feel he got off light the first time. We've also discovered a possible connection to Skele and his black-market dealings. I've put out an arrest warrant for his wife."

"When will Pilskog be released?"

"Not for some time. He has extensive injuries to his internal organs."

"But can I see him? It's very important." Haugland explained Pilskog's connection to the University of Olso. He took out his father's journal. "My father, Jens Nils Haugland, taught in the Geology Department at the university. He was an early opponent of the attempt to Nazify the university. In the fall of 1940 when *Reichcommisar* Terboven began to crack down on the university, my father started to list professors and people in industry who were colluding with the Germans or the *Nasjonal Samling*. Then he was arrested."

Haugland opened the journal to one of the pages with lists. He showed Barness how each name had a note next to it. "I only found out about this journal just before I had to hightail it up here. A friend of my father's had kept it hidden all these years. Most of my father's papers were destroyed when he was arrested." He pointed out the note about Pilskog:

I'm beginning to distrust Aage's position on the faculty acquiescing to German dictates. Seen with NS men. Possibly Gestapo.

"May I see?" Barness asked.

Haugland gave the journal to Barness who flipped through the pages of lists with great interest.

"You ever meet Pilskog?"

"He came to my parents' home on a couple of occasions. I was in college at the time." Haugland asked for the journal back. He pulled out the letter drafted to the rector of the university. "My father was concerned that Pilskog might be informing on Jewish members of the university faculty and medical school."

Barness frowned. "That is pretty early in the occupation, but there were similar efforts in Trondheim to identify Jews in the community. It was one of the reasons I left the police force and fled to Sweden. I had no desire to be in the Nazified police force."

"Before Milorg and Sivorg got involved, there were individuals helping their Jewish friends and colleagues to get out. Pilskog may have been giving away secret hiding places."

Barness read the half-finished letter. "This is disgusting."

Haugland took back the letter and inserted it into the journal's back pocket.

"All right, you can see him, but you have to tell me everything he says. I'd like to get photographs taken of those lists. They might be useful for future investigations. Most members of the NS have been disciplined, but there could be names that have gone undetected."

Barness opened the door to the hospital room and invited Haugland to enter. He closed the door behind Haugland once he was inside.

For a moment, Haugland studied Pilskog who looked half asleep. The man was in an elevated position with an IV dripping into his arm. Without his glasses, Pilskog's face looked as worn and as pale as the white pillow behind his head. Lines on his forehead and around his eyes were etched in pain. Not so *Herr* Professor. Haugland had mixed feelings about him. From what Anna told him, Pilskog had helped her and he apparently was kind to Bette Norsby—but the quisling had much to account for.

Haugland walked over to the metal-framed bed and sat down on a chair next to Pilskog. The movement made Pilskog open his eyes.

"I wondered when you would come," Pilskog said in a whispery voice. Haugland had to cock his head to hear him better.

"You were expecting me?"

"*Ja*. As soon as Sorting said his hostage was your wife." Pilskog grimaced. "Is she all right?"

Haugland said she was. "Do you know who I am?"

"*Ja*. *Professor* Haugland's youngest son. Tore, right? I thought you were killed."

"A ruse." Haugland decided he'd let Pilskog talk, let him get comfortable. He was surprised, though, that Pilskog knew something of his history at the start of the occupation.

"I'm glad to know that she is all right. It's been a nightmare. The boy, too?"

"*Ja*."

"Sorting said that you were an intelligence officer in the Resistance. Is that what you did during the war?"

"*Ja*. Sometimes I was rooting out people like you."

Pilskog's face turned gray. He asked for water. Haugland poured him a glass and handed it to him. Pilskog's hand shook as he drank.

"*Takk*," Pilskog said when he gave the glass back to Haugland. He laid his head back hard on the pillow. It took a moment for his color to return to its former pasty white.

"How well did you know Sorting?" Haugland asked when Pilskog was more composed.

"Never met him before in my life."

"But you knew Skele."

Pilskog nodded his head. "An unfortunate acquaintance."

"Unfortunate acquaintance or not, you seem to have done fine for yourself during the war." Haugland took out the black journal and opened it to the page where Pilskog was listed. "Do you know any of these names?" Haugland handed Pilskog his glasses.

Pilskog read them quickly. "Whose journal is this?" he asked in a low hoarse voice.

"Speak up." Haugland tapped his left ear.

Pilskog repeated the question in a loud voice that seemed to strain him. Haugland answered that it was his father's. Pilskog swallowed hard and looked away.

"Did you betray my father?"

Pilskog jerked his head back. "*Nei, nei.*"

"But you were pushing for some sort of agreement with the Germans on how the faculty should teach under Nazi rules. Something my father opposed." Haugland took back the journal and slipped out the letter from the pocket. "Or was it because of this?" He opened it and held it in front of Pilskog's nose. The man became still.

"As I recall," Haugland went on, "one of my father's friends was a Jewish doctor who taught at the Medical School in Oslo. I remember coming home during the first summer of the occupation and finding him visiting with my father in my father's study. *Doktor* Moritz looked uneasy when I interrupted their conversation. A few days later he disappeared. Fortunately, I learned after the war that he had been safely delivered to a group in Sweden where he and his family remained during the occupation."

"I'm glad to hear it."

"He was one of the lucky few. The *Nasional Samling* had already compiled a list of all Norwegian Jews. Two years later, most on that list were deported to Auschwitz and died or were killed at Falstad. Did you help the police?"

To Haugland's surprise, tears began to roll down Pilskog's cheeks. "I never intended any harm. I only made an inquiry into a Jewish man my daughter was seeing. My wife objected."

"Don't blame your wife. You have your hands in all of this." Haugland stood up. His stomach was churning with disgust. "I don't believe you about my father."

"I was only trying to survive, to keep my family safe."

"To your great benefit while others suffered."

"It wasn't easy. The German authorities were always pressing. Especially at the mines."

"I don't care."

"I promise you, I did not betray your father." Pilskog choked on his words, his voice pleading. "We were colleagues. Please believe me."

Haugland wanted to get out of the room as quickly as possible, but a nagging thought made him ask about the phone numbers at the house. "Where did the phone numbers for my parents' home come from?"

Pilskog took off his glasses and wiped his eyes. "Sorting had them." He sniffed back tears as he put them back on.

"How?"

"I think Skele had a contact outside the jail. Got information on you in the first place."

"Someone called the house. My mother said it was a woman."

"Sorting forced *Fru* Norsby to make that call. He said that is how he knew you were in that fishing village on the coast. Then he made me make a call to Fjellstad. Some man Sorting knew there eventually called back and confirmed you were there."

As Haugland listened, a heavy, depressing weight fell on his shoulders. The worst kind of truth unfolded as he realized that his sister Solveig was the one who had given away his location. Bugge Grande had only added the possible location of Anna's cabin.

Then Haugland remembered Sorting's words *"I don't know what you're talking about,"* when he asked him about the final note. With a sinking heart, Haugland knew that it was Solveig who had put the note into Nils's hand.

Chapter 93

On Haugland's second attempt to reach the family home in Oslo, the operator told him she was sorry but the line appeared dead. She then apologized. "Some parts of the city are still under reconstruction from Allied bombing two years ago. Sometimes the lines are unstable."

"Can someone check?"

"It's Constitution Day."

"Of course. *Takk*." Haugland held the phone in his hands and frowned.

"Can't she get through?" Tommy asked in English. He had caught Haugland as he came out of the hall that led to the private rooms and was now with him in the ward doctor's office.

"No. Something's wrong. The line is dead, but I don't believe it's a coincidence. I think it's been cut."

"Would your sister do that? Cut the line?"

"It's something I don't want to believe. But I'm positive Solveig is the one who put the fourth note into Nils's hand. Anna and our children are in danger."

Haugland hung up the phone. He went over to the window of the doctor's office. Down below, a woman entered the main entrance carrying Norwegian flags and flowers. Further out in the park in front of the hospital, families walked among the trees. On the furthest side of the park was the *Hjemme for Døve*, where Haugland's friends and family had gathered earlier in the day.

Haugland picked up the receiver again and asked the hospital operator for an outside line. Once he was connected to the telephone company, Haugland asked the operator to call his brother, Alex in Toyen, near Oslo. When that proved fruitless, he turned to Tommy. "I need to find out when the next train to Oslo leaves."

"That won't be until this evening," Inspectør Barness answered in decent English when he came into the room.

"That's too late." Haugland tried not to panic. His mother was supposed to be at the house. If the phone line was cut like he thought, she could be in danger, too, though he couldn't imagine Solveig would hurt their mother. Still, Inga Haugland was a practical woman and wouldn't have called Siv if she wasn't worried about Solveig talking to a stranger looking for him. Knowing that it was Sorting looking for him...

"When does Anna's train get in?" Barness wondered.

Haugland put the phone on its cradle. "In about five and half hours. Conrad has arranged for someone from the *Hjemme for Døve* in Norland to take them to the house."

Out in the hallway, someone had turned up a radio loud enough for Haugland to hear it clearly. Some nurses stopped to listen. King Haakon VII was giving a Constitution Day speech. It was full of inspiration and hope, a celebration of being free from German oppression for a full year. Haugland was not feeling hopeful.

Tommy came over by Haugland. "Are Lars's men still at the house?"

"No, Lars didn't think it was necessary since the trial was over. He let them go."

"Damn."

The King was finishing up his speech. Haugland and Tommy stopped to listen along with Barness. When the speech was over, some out in the hallway clapped and began singing the national anthem, *Ja, Vi Elsker Dette Landet.*

Haugland did love his country, but right now it was still unsettled as the Legal Purge continued and people sought some sort of equilibrium in their hard-won freedom.

Tommy looked thoughtful. "Didn't Lars come up by military plane?"

"He did. Axel picked him up."

"There you are." Tommy turned to Barness. "I don't know anyone in the military here, but you know Axel. Can Tore get a flight?"

Barness said he would get in touch with Axel.

A couple of hours later, Haugland was on a military flight to Oslo. It would cut off four hours from a train trip. Perhaps he could reach the house before it was too late.

***

For what seemed like the hundredth time in three days, Anna had a pistol aimed at her. Except for the unpredictable terror in the basement at the Undset farm, she had learned to judge Sorting's actions when he pointed a gun at her. The look in her sister-in-law's eyes, however, was unreadable. Anna knew that she must remain calm.

"*Hei*, Solveig. Is everything all right?" Anna pulled Lisel to her. "Do you mind if Lisel goes into our room?"

"*Nei*. Stay where you are. I want you to come into my room. With the children."

"Are Tine and Barne there?"

Solvieg didn't answer, which worried Anna. Instead Solveig waved the gun at her. Lisel cringed and hid behind Anna.

"Move," Solveig finally said and began to back down the hall to her room.

Anna hefted Nils on her shoulder and did as she was told. "Where is Inga? Where is your mother?"

"No talking. Go sit in that armchair."

Anna had never been in Solveig's room before. The room was decorated in a soft blue, a calming color. It was a pretty place with flowery drapes, a vanity, and a bed. On the right side of the room, an armchair was set next to a small reading table. As she walked to the armchair, Anna realized that Solveig had a nice view of the patio and gardens from a multi-paned window that looked out over them. One of the side windows was opened on the left. Anna recalled seeing the drapes open and close when the family first gathered after they arrived in Oslo from America. Had Solveig been spying on her? *How long ago that seemed.*

With Lisel holding tight to her dress, Anna sat down. Lisel climbed in next to her. When Nils began to fuss, Solveig looked at him with distaste. "Are you going to feed him? I never got a chance to wean Tine. They took her away."

"I'm so sorry, Solveig. Telavåg was a terrible war crime. How awful to have your children taken away. I can't imagine it."

Solveig stepped over to the open window. "Bloody Germans. They blew up our houses. They killed and killed. Our cows. Our men. Then took the remaining men away. My Ole." Solveig looked sharply at Anna. "You're just one of them. *Tyskertøs.*" Solveig pointed her gun at Anna. It shook in her hands. "You took Tore away from us. My baby brother. Hasn't he suffered enough?"

"Mamma, I'm scared." Lisel's small, frightened voice drew Solvieg's attention.

Solvieg nodded at Lisel. "She's Norwegian. I knew her father long before you knew him. Did you enchant Einar, too?"

What Solveig said didn't make any sense to Anna. By Solvieg's logic, Lisel would be pure Norwegian. *I'm not a German whore.* Anna tried to change the subject. "Where is Inga? I thought she would be here."

"She went to see the new baby. My Tine and Barne are with her." She looked at Lisel. "She can go to her room."

"Go, Lisel," Anna said in a steady voice. "Wait for me. Wait for Pappa Jens."

Lisel got up and ran.

"Who is Pappa Jens?"

"Your brother, Tore. I call him Jens."

"Huh." Solveig waggled the gun at Anna. "Go lock the door."

"Why? I'm not going to run."

"Lock the door."

Anna got up holding Nils in her arms. He held onto the front of her dress, but turned to look in Solveig's direction. Anna wondered if she should risk running out, but if Solveig fired, she could hit Nils. She shut the door and turned the key in the lock hole.

"Now bring the key here." She held out her hand.

Anna gave it to her and sat down in the armchair with Nils. Solveig put the key in her dress pocket.

Solveig leaned against the window sill. "Why did Tore run away in the night?"

"You know why. Someone wanted to hurt your brother. One of Rinnan's men. That man didn't want him to testify at the trial." Anna attempted to keep her voice conversational, but her heart was pounding away. Staying calm was hard. Anna took a deep breath.

Solveig squared her shoulder. "I wouldn't hurt Tore. I love my brother. I only wanted to hurt you. To make you go away. That's why I put the note in the crib."

The note. This news nearly stopped Anna, but she went on. "But you did hurt him. He was nearly killed by that Rinnan's man because you told him where Jens was."

"I don't know this man."

"His name was Odd Sorting. Jens was going to testify against him and Rinnan in Trondheim."

"This Sorting tried to kill Tore?"

"*Ja.* He almost succeeded." Anna sat up. "Do you know who stopped him? I did. I shot him dead."

Solveig wiped her forehead with the back of the hand holding the gun. Remembering what Margit had taught her, Anna wondered if a bullet was in the chamber. Solveig's action made her nervous.

For the first time since Anna was forced into the room, Solveig studied her. "You're lying," Solveig said.

"I am not. Jens—"

"Stop calling him Jens."

"All right." On the vanity near Solveig was a picture of a tall man holding a large salmon with his fingers in its gills. The man wore a fisherman's cap and rubber overalls. "Is that Ole?" Anna asked.

"Don't say his name."

"I'm only asking. I love my husband, too. And my children. Just like you."

"*Tyskertøs*. You are not like me." She waved the gun at Nils. The baby looked at her with wide eyes, then smiled. He patted a chubby hand on Anna's breast. "Tine was that age when they took him away. I wonder if Nils will remember me."

"What?" Something in Solveig's voice sent a chill down Anna's spine. She realized for the first time how ill the woman was. *She's looking through me.* Anna pulled Nils close to her.

"Mamma says Nils looks like Tore when he was a baby. I see it, too. I wish Tore didn't make a baby with you. I can't stand the idea. It makes me sick, but maybe I can start all over again. I could sing to Nils, tell him stories all about his father and what it was like waiting for fishing boats coming back full of their catch. Our big bonfires on St. Hans Day on the beaches. And St Lucia in Telavåg. The candle lights were so pretty." Solveig aimed the gun at Anna. "Give him to me."

When Anna refused, Solveig rushed Anna and hit her head with her gun. The pistol discharged with an ear-splitting bang, the last thing Anna heard as she slipped unconscious to the floor.

Chapter 94

It was late in the evening when Haugland finally arrived at his family home. The military flight, though bumpy, had made good time. He was arriving two and a half hours after Anna should have arrived with the children. Tommy had arranged for one of his former Milorg friends to pick him up at the airport miles north of Oslo. Now in the golden light of the sun that would not sleep for another five hours, Haugland carefully surveyed the grounds. He had specifically asked to be let out before the house, so he could go through the pine forest. As he stood at the edge looking down on the patio, he noticed that there were several cars parked out in front. One was his mother's old car. He didn't know the others. *Maybe it's not as bad as I feared.*

Something moved in the window over the patio. When the figure turned, Haugland saw that it was Solveig. On a second look, he saw to his horror that she was holding Nils. She was singing to him. As he gripped her sweater front, he kept turning his head into the room. *Where was Anna?*

Solveig turned back to the opened window as she bounced him. When she shifted Nils onto her shoulder, Haugland saw that she had a gun in her right hand.

"Christ," he said outloud in English. He immediately pulled back into the trees. Going deeper into the pine woods which still held patches of hard snow, he was glad their thick branches would partially hide him. He crept by the patio wall and around to the back of the house. When he felt it was safe, he went down the stone stairs onto flagstones in front of the kitchen door. Here his mother kept boxes of herbs she brought out for the summer months. Nothing was planted there yet. He looked around, then went through the unlocked door.

The kitchen was dark, but out in the lighted hallway, Haugland could hear voices murmuring. *Stop. Think. Who is here?* His mother's car was here. He cocked his head. Was that his brother Alex speaking? He stepped to the hallway door. A shadow of a figure appeared on the wall at the far end. Someone was coming down to the kitchen. Haugland pulled back, wishing that he had his gun on him.

"I'll check the pantry," Alex Haugland was saying. He started when Haugland stepped out with a finger to his lips. "Tore, how did you get here? Thank God."

"What the hell is going on? Where's Anna?" Haugland looked beyond Alex, then started down the hall.

"Tore, wait."

"I'm not waiting. Did Solveig hurt her? Solveig has Nils and a gun for God's sake. Where the Devil did she get it?"

"We don't know." Alex looked as distressed as Haugland felt.

Haugland hurried down the hall to the grand staircase that led to the upstairs bedrooms. He took the stairs to the landing two at a time. As he turned to go up higher, Lars appeared at the top of the stairs. He cautioned Haugland to be quiet. When Haugland was up on top, he looked down to the right to Solveig's room. Inga Haugland was sitting on a chair looking weary and forlorn. She jumped up when she saw him.

"Let's go into your old room," Lars whispered in English. "We can talk here." As he gave Inga his arm, he added, "I wasn't expecting you until tomorrow."

"I found out Solveig was responsible for that last note. Axel Trafjord got me on a military flight."

"Jesus." Lars's face blanched.

"Oh, Tore," Inga put hand on her mouth and shook her head back and forth.

Haugland pulled his mother to him and hugged her. "How long has this been going on?"

"About two hours,"Lars said. "Mamma came home and found Lisel crying in your room. She went to a neighbor to call my apartment. The phone line was cut, it turns out."

"Tell me Anna is all right."

"Seems to be. I can hear her talking through the door."

"And Lisel?"

"The neighbor has her." Lars paused. "She said there was a loud bang."

Haugland swallowed. Just as when he realized Sorting had Anna, he felt like he was falling down a dark hole that would require all the strength he had left in him to climb back out. "I'm going to talk to Solveig."

"Tore, I don't think she'll listen. She hasn't listened to either Mamma or me."

"She has to." When Nils started to cry, Haugland's decision was made.

Outside the door to Solveig's room, Haugland tried the glass handle knob. The door was locked. He looked back at his mother who was standing along the rail that overlooked the stairwell. He pointed to her hair and made motions about her hair pins. I need two, he motioned. She pulled them out and quietly brought them over.

Haugland knocked. "Solveig, this is Tore. May I come in? I just want to see if you are all right."

There was a rustling sound. "I can't come to the door."

"What if I were to open it on my own? Remember the game we played when I was a boy? I was lucky to have such a wonderful big sister."

Silence.

"Let's see if I remember. Is that all right?" Haugland fashioned the bobby pins in a way that would work as lock picks. He looked at Lars and his mother, then put the pins into the lock. Within seconds, the tumblers turned. He turned the door knob and stepped in.

It took all of Haugland's training not to make a sound when he was all the way into the room. Next to Solveig's bed, a lamp lay shattered, shards of its porcelain base scattered across the *dyne*. Anna sat on the floor next to an armchair. There was blood on the side of her temple. Solveig sat precariously in one of the opened side windows holding Nils. When the baby saw Haugland, he pumped his arms up and down and started to whimper.

"Solveig, how did I do? Remember the time I picked a way into Bestemor's pantry up at the *seter*? We found all her lingonberry jam." Haugland kept his focus on his sister, maintaining a smile that hid his worst fears. With his right hand, he signed to Anna, one-handed, You OK?

Ja, Watch her. She thinks N-I-L-S is hers and O-L-E's.

Do you want to run?

Nei.

"Stop," Solveig blurted out. "Stop that finger talking."

"All right. Can I come over? I just want to see Nils."

Solveig watched him suspiciously, then her face brightened. She adjusted the baby in her arms. She held the gun under her left arm. A military service revolver. "Isn't he sweet? We're waiting for Ole to get home."

"Is that what this is?" Haugland came a little closer. "Has he been out for cod or herring? I didn't see his nets."

"It's May. He'll be going for herring." Solveig leaned in. "He has to be careful. There are German patrols."

"I know he'll be careful." Haugland sensed that Lars was near the door. Mother not far behind. Anna was carefully moving onto the armchair.

"Don't move," Solveig shouted at Anna.

"It's all right. My friend is just tired."

"Your friend?" Solveig looked puzzled.

"*Ja*. It looks like she bumped her head. She just wants to sit down. We don't want our guest to be tired."

"I thought she was—"

Haugland didn't know how long he could keep this up. He frantically sought a way to get Nils away from Solveig without her shooting the gun. "When do you think Ole is getting home?" As soon as he said that, Haugland knew he had made a mistake. Solveig's eyes filled up with tears.

"He's not coming home," Solveig said in a dull voice.

"Solveig," Inga said coming into the room. "Why don't you let Tore take Nils? I think he needs a bath. You can have him back—"

"*Nei.*" She aimed the gun at Haugland, her finger resting on the trigger. "He's going with me."

"With you?" Out of the corner of his eye, Haugland saw Anna move off the armchair and crawl around to the side farthest away from Solveig. It was enough to distract Solveig. Haugland leaped at his sister, grabbing her gun and pushing it high above her head.

"Lars," he shouted as Solveig's position on the window sill became tenuous. "Grab Nils."

For a moment, both brothers struggled, but eventually Lars was able to get Nils away from Solveig as she wailed and punched Haugland in his face. His sister's strength surprised him, but then his left hand was still healing. The gun went off with a loud report, hurting Haugland's bad ear as the bullet went into the ceiling.

"Let me die. Let me die!" Solveig screamed and slowly forced the gun down so that it was close to their faces. When she struggled to point it at herself, Haugland felt the two of them verging over the edge of the window.

"*Nei, nei, nei.* Don't, Sister." He twisted and finally got the gun out of her hands. He threw it down to the ground below where it discharged again when it hit its hammer.

Solveig bent back and closed her eyes. Her hair flew out behind her as she began to tumble over. Haugland grabbed her around her waist and strained to pull her back in. At the last moment, he felt Lars pulling on his belt. Together, they pulled Solveig back into the room.

Haugland didn't let her go. He held his trembling sister, his heart pounding at the close call. He told her he loved her. That things would get better. He found himself weeping with her. *Telavåg*. All the hurt done to his family there. All the hurt done to countless others throughout Norway. He didn't think he could take it anymore.

Down below Haugland saw a black car marked POLITI slowly come up the road and park outside. Another followed. Holding Solveig tight, he walked her away from the window. Alex joined him and helped her to the bed. Once a howling Nils was safe in Anna's arms and both of them out of the room, Lars shut the window.

For a short moment Solveig continued to fight Haugland and Alex, but she suddenly went limp and frowned. Her glazed eyes cleared. "Tore? Alex?"

Inga came in and sat down on the bed. "Mamma," she whispered and then closed her eyes. A lone tear strayed down her wet cheek.

"I'll stay with her," Alex said to Haugland. "You go see to Anna."

"And I'll talk to the police," Lars stepped away from the window and followed Haugland out.

***

Downstairs, in the hall by the study, Anna leaned against the wall holding Nils. He had stopped crying and put a thumb in his mouth as he rested his head on her shoulder. His small compact body scrunching against her gave her comfort. She bit her lip when Haugland came up to her.

"Anna," he said softly. He cupped her head in his hands and kissed her forehead. "Let me clean you up." He took a handkerchief out of his pants pocket and smoothed away the drying blood on her temple where Solveig had struck her. "Did she hurt you in any other way? Lars said she held you in there for two hours."

"*Nei*. But I just never knew what she would do to Nils. Sometimes she talked so sweet to him. Other times—she was talking to herself and her dead husband." She leaned into his chest. "It was awful."

"You're safe now. She won't ever hurt you or Nils again." He paused. "Promise me you won't leave me over this. Please...I need you."

"I need you, too. "

For a moment, neither spoke. The last half-hour had been harrowing. They had survived, but at what cost? Eventually, they drifted into each other's arms with Nils between them.

Anna pulled back from him. "What made you leave so early from Trondheim?"

"It was something Pilskog said that made me realize that Solveig was the one who sent the fourth note. I got down here on a military plane."

Anna put a hand on her mouth, trying not to weep. "I'm so glad. Solveig admitted that she was the one who did it."

"If I had figured it out the first time I found the note, this never would have happened to you and our children."

Anna stepped back and went into the study. Haugland followed and closed the door. Adjusting Nils on her hip, Anna sat on the edge of the sofa.

"You did nothing wrong, Jens, but I can't stay here anymore. I want to go away. It's not just the five years of occupation and everything that has happened in the last week. Right now, it's my own sense of guilt. Every time I look around, I feel so guilty for all the havoc that has been heaped upon this country. *Mea culpa, mea culpa.* My German side feels blame for everything. How could this happen? Why are Germans so cruel? I'm not cruel."

"You're not cruel."

Anna sighed. "I just don't understand how decent German people could be so swayed by one man that they became vile themselves and contaminated the rest of the world. Your family was torn apart by the occupation: your father imprisoned, your brother shot, your sister, and uncle destroyed at Telavåg. Every time they see me, they will be reminded of what happened *to them.* After what has happened today, I can't pretend that things will get better. There will always be a rift in this family."

Anna kissed the top of Nils's head. "I'm so weary from the war, Jens. The Legal Purge. I feel there will never be justice for what happened to you or to me." Her voice was close to breaking.

Haugland caressed her cheek. "I know, love. I'm weary, too. We can go somewhere else, but so many places around Oslo were bombed out. It will be hard to get a decent place. The farmhouse in Fjellstad can't be rebuilt yet because I have no money, so we can't go there," he answered softly. "Besides, I'm not sure if you want to return there." He cleared his throat. "We could emmigrate to America. To take up your uncle's offer. I can finish school there while you live with your relatives. We could start over."

Anna switched to English. "You would do that? You would leave Norway?"

"Yes." Haugland rubbed his hand over the stump of his finger, something Anna recognized recently as a way he gathered his thoughts. "Norway is broken. Jobs will be hard to find. I don't know if an ex-intelligence officer with bad hearing and a Swastika brand on his rear end could get one."

"Jens..."

"As soon as things are settled here, I'll look into emmigrating."

"What will happen to Solveig?"

"I'm sure she'll be put in a hospital. We'll get the best care for her."

"And your niece and nephew?"

"I don't know." His eyes hardened. "I know this. Solveig can't take care of them. She may never be able to take care of them. And my mother is growing too old to do it on her own."

Anna nodded. "I'm sorry, Jens."

Lars knocked on the door. "How is Anna doing?" he asked.

"She's managing." My strong woman, he signed to Anna.

"And Nils?" Lars asked.

"A little traumatized, but he's settling down." Haugland brushed the baby's nose which made him smile a gummy grin.

"The police are bringing Solveig down. "

"I'll come out, Lars."

"Why don't you wait, Tore? They are taking her straight to the hospital. It might be best."

"*Nei.* I'm coming out. She is our sister and no matter what has happened, I will do whatever I can to help her." Haugland looked at Anna. "Will that be all right with you?"

Anna put a hand on his shoulder. "Jens, of course you have to go," she said, trying hard to keep her voice level. "It's the right thing to do."

Haugland took her hand and kissed it. His voice was thick when he spoke again. "Beautiful Anna. I know what it cost for you to say that. I'm so sorry. Yet, that is why I love you. Why I survived this past year, this past week. Conrad keeps saying that it's Providence we met. Maybe it is. I promise to do my best to give you the life you've wanted and deserve."

Anna pushed him to the door. "I'll be waiting."

BOOK 4

Det er aldri så galt at det ikke er godt for more

It is never so bad that it is not good for something

~ Norwegian saying

Chapter 95

Four months later, on a sunny September day, Tore Haugland returned to the family home one last time. His books and other belongings had been moved out some time before, packed for their long trip or given away. Tomorrow, he, Anna, and the children would board a steamer bound for America.

Ever since he announced to his mother that they were emigrating, he had been preparing for this day with a mixture of excitement and sadness. He was not just going to America; he would be on the other side of that country in Seattle. So far away. He knew his mother worried that she might never see him again. It filled him with guilt as it had only been a year since he showed up alive after capitulation. *All through the five years of occupation she thought me dead. Now I'm going away again.*

At the glass doors to the study, Haugland paused to watch her. Inga was dusting a shelf full of framed photos. When she turned sharply to the patio doors, he could see Lisel and Nils playing outside. Nils had pulled himself up to the chair where Anna sat. He was dressed in a little sailor outfit with a cap that was tied down under his chin. Lisel skipped around the chair holding a pinwheel. *My family. And the grandchildren she would miss growing up.*

Haugland checked his watch. They hadn't much private time before the rest of the family would gather to listen to an announcement on the radio. When Inga turned back and put a hand on one of the shelves to support herself, he decided to go in. He took a deep breath before he opened the door.

"Mamma."

"Tore." Inga offered him a cheek to kiss when he joined her. She picked up one of the framed family photographs. "Do you remember this trip?"

"*Ja.* Our trip up the Sognefjord. I was seven, wasn't I?"

Inga smiled. "What a collection of young folks. I honestly thought I would never get you all to settle down."

"At least we aren't all squinting into the sun. Or seasick. Per was." Haugland laughed. "Look at Pappa. Always smoking his pipe."

Inga patted his arm. "You were all good children. Solveig, too. Just like Lisel and Nils. Just like their cousins, Tine and Bjarne." She swallowed hard. "Must you go?"

"*Ja*, Mamma. I need to break free, start a new life. Maybe even a new identity. I must do this for myself and Anna."

"We tried to make her feel welcomed."

"I know you did. She knows you did. It's better this way. Even if Solveig improves, it's better this way."

She turned to him and brushed a strand of hair off his forehead. "You look so much like my brother Kristian. Dark and handsome. Like him, you are also kind and resourceful. Yet, I don't think you know your own strength of character, dear son: how loyal you are, how quick to act and do the right thing. I'm so proud of you..." Inga stepped away. Her voice broke. "Now you are going away from me again, maybe this time forever."

"Mamma, I'll write. I might be able to call," Haugland's voice softened. "And when I can, I'll come home to see you. They're talking about increasing air flights between New York and London. It will make things easier getting here." He cleared his throat. "This new offer I have from Seattle is just the ticket for me. I can finish my studies there and then stay on to develop a new Scandinavian studies program.

"This is what you want, isn't it? To teach and study."

Haugland smiled at her, then grinned impishly. "And fish."

"Oh, Tore..." Inga chuckled, then cleared her throat. "I have the puffin painting," she said lightly. She picked up a package wrapped in brown paper and gave it to him. "And something else." She gave him a little blue book. "It has short prayers in it and poems. Your father read it secretly when he was in prison. It will give you strength and direction."

"*Tusen takk,* Mamma." He put his arms around her and hugged her close. "I'll take good care of them."

Haugland and Inga both turned when Nils began to cry after falling down outside. Anna picked him up and soothed him with a kiss and a hug.

"She's a lovely woman," Inga said as she stepped away. "A good daughter. I like that she's considerate of me, but even more she gives me great joy that she has made you happy." Inga began to weep softly. "And now I love her more because I understand the deeper truth—that without her love, you might never have recovered from your injuries. You might never have made it over the mountains into Sweden. Tommy Renvik said so." Inga wiped a tear away. "There is too much pain in this house. It isn't right that it should fall on her. It isn't fair, so I want you both to go with my blessing."

"That's what I hoped you would say." Haugland turned away to compose himself. "It won't be easy," he finally said, "but I am better off than most emmigrants. Her family is sponsoring me. All my papers are in order. I'm being classified as a war bride. Isn't that funny?"

Haugland straightened up when he noticed that Anna had gathered the children and was coming inside. At the same time, the hallway doors opened and Lars Haugland, his wife Siv, and Alex Haugland came in.

"It's time," Lars said. "Is the radio turned on?"

Inga waved her hand to the wood-framed radio set on a small table.

"I'll get it," Alex said. While his brother turned on the dial, Anna join Haugland.

"This is it?" Anna asked as she put an arm through one of his.

"*Ja.*" Haugland smiled wanly at her, then stiffened at the sound of the radio as it crackled on.

Suddenly, Haugland felt as though the world was slowing down. Everyone was moving at a snail's pace. Their words slurred. His heart began to pound. *Why now?* The radio made the same sound as his old wireless transmitter when it sought its frequency. The ticking clock's steady beat on the bookshelf morphed into the sound of dripping water.

"I'm sorry. I can't stay here and listen. Mamma, would you take the children?"

"Jens?" Anna looked alarmed.

"Don't you want to sit, Tore?" Lars asked.

"*Nei.* I need to go outside. I'll listen outside. " He rubbed his temple to smooth out a growing headache.

"I'm coming with you," Anna said. She gave Nils to Siv. "Lisel, stay with *Onkel* Lars and Bestemor."

Haugland stepped through the French doors and out into the clean morning air. He took a deep breath to steady himself. Up in the spruce tree that he had climbed in as a little boy a waxwing bird hopped from branch to branch.

Anna came out and stood beside him. "This is hard for you, isn't it?"

"Harder than I thought it would be."

Anna took his healed hand, now free for good of its half-glove. She gently squeezed it. "Then, we'll listen together."

The radio made a sputtering sound, then cleared. Someone turned up the volume so Haugland had no trouble hearing an announcer from Trondheim. In hurried, low tones the man made a quick introduction of the setting.

Haugland didn't need a description of the place. It was the courtroom at the *Tinghus* where he testified against Rinnan a lifetime ago. He pulled Anna to him. Her presence always calmed him.

He turned his attention to the radio broadcast. There were rustling sounds and the scraping of wood chairs as the court apparently rose and then sat down once the judges were seated.

A cultured voice came on the air and began to speak. "After deliberations held behind closed doors, a judgment has been found." The speaker paused to clear his throat. "The accused Number 1, Henry Oliver Rinnan, is sentenced to death for crimes against the criminal code number…"

The clerk continued in a flat voice for more than a minute, calling out the numbers of the various charges for which the court had found Rinnan guilty, but Haugland was no longer paying attention. Those numbers were flesh and blood. They represented all the victims of the ruthless actions by Rinnan and his gang against the Resistance and the ordinary people of Vikna, Selbu, Fjellstad, Lillehavn, the Haraldsens, and hundreds more over the four and half years he terrorized the region

Haugland turned and watched his brothers and mother sitting around the radio. They were all crying, tears rolling down their faces. He knew it was because finally there was justice for his brother, Per, executed four years ago. Rinnan would be shot for that along with the dozens of other actions, but Haugland wondered if he would ever feel right. He felt numb.

Anna cocked her head at him. "Justice is done, Jens. For you and for Einar. No one will mourn Rinnan. Sorting, too. We will forget them both." She stroked his arm. "Are you now torn about going to America? Leaving your mother?"

Haugland looked down at her. "*Nei.* She is strong. They are all strong and I know they will be fine."

He let go of Anna's hand and walked farther away from the house. His mother's cat had spotted the waxwing and was slinking toward the spruce tree. A slight breeze stirred the flowers in the garden. A normal day. Autumn was setting in. He wondered what fall looked like in the northwest corner of America. He turned to Anna. Her golden hair lifted in the breeze. Her eyes blazed with strength and love. Beyond her, in the doorway, his mother stood.

Det vil helst ga golt. Everything will work out all right

GLOSSARY

fjell	mountain
frøken	Miss
Fru	Mrs.
God dag	Good day
God natt	Good night
Hallo	Hello
Hei	Hi
Herr	Mr.
Hilsen	A salutation at the end of a letter Jøssing patriot
knottgenerator	a WWII era wood-burning furnace that fueled a car or bus
konditori	pâtisserie or confectionery shop, also serving as a cafe
lille jente	little girl, term of endearment
landhandel	general store
middag	dinner or meal during the middle of the day
nei	no
Onkel	Uncle
quisling	Traitor
razzias	raid
stue	living room
Tante	Aunt
takk.	thanks
tusen takk	thank you
Vaer så god	There you go.
Vær så snil	please

AUTHOR NOTES

When I first began my research for this sequel to *The Jossing Affair*, I recalled the memoirs of several heroes in the Norwegian Resistance. They told of their dangers and grand adventures, but I was also struck by what they did after the war. In one case, a famous resistance fighter, Max Magnus, struggled with alcoholism. Another, Joachim Ronneberg, the young leader of the heavy water raid, went into the public television. Famously, two young men went on one of the greatest twentieth century adventures of all, the voyage of Kon-Tiki.

In May 1945, ordinary Norwegian citizens wanted to get back to some of sort of normalcy. But first, after repatriating the 260,000 German soldiers and the 72,000 Russian POWs remaining in the country, they would have to relive the atrocities of the past five years of occupation carried out by Germans and in some cases, their own countrymen. Beginning in the summer of 1945 war criminal trials began across the country. One of these *quislings*, was Henry Oliver Rinnan.

There are two historic stories going on in *The Quisling Factor*: the war crimes trial of Norwegian Henry Oliver Rinnan, a real-life monster who worked with the Gestapo in Trondheim, Norway, and the tragic story of Telavåg.

First, Telavåg. The tragedy at this fishing village in 1942 was one of the great war crimes of WWII in Norway. On April 26, 1942, shots were exchanged between Gestapo officers and two Norwegian agents (SOE) in the village of Telavåg. Two Gestapo officers and one Norwegian agent were killed. The surviving agent was tortured, then executed. In retaliation to the killing of the Gestapo officers, on April 30, 1942 all the men in Telavåg aged 16 to 60 were arrested. Some of the men were executed on the spot, the rest rounded up and sent to Sachsenhausen. The next day, May 1, the remaining population was arrested. Telavåg was razed, the fishing boats blown up.The women and children were put first on a prison boat, then held in a school for three years. Some of the children were separated from their mothers. There was a scheme to separate the older children from the mothers and send them to different orphanages in Eastern Norway. Their ultimate intended destinations remain unclear. The mothers and children were eventually reunited in August, 1945.

Second, the trial in 1945 of Henry Oliver Rinnan, Norway's Number Two war criminal. Born in Levanger, Norway, he was recruited by the Gestapo in 1940. His independently run Gestapo unit known as *Sonderabteilung Lola* infiltrated the resistance movement. The Rinnan gang was responsible for the death of at least a hundred people in the Norwegian resistance and the British SOE, for torturing hundreds of prisoners, for more than a thousand arrests, for compromising several hundred resistance groups, and in some cases, for deceiving people into carrying out missions for the Germans.

Rinnan tried to flee Norway on Liberation Day, May 8 1945, but was turned back by a blizzard on the Swedish border. He was captured and held in Trondheim, then tried on April 13 1946 along with twenty-six members of his group in the first of two trials. It took six hours alone to read the indictments against him. In the end forty-one members of Rinnan Banden were convicted and sentenced. Rinnan was sentenced to death for personally killing thirteen people. He was executed February 1, 1947, immediately cremated and buried in an unmarked grave in Levanger.

Websites:
*The Story of the tragedy of Telavag
The North Sea Museum https://bit.ly/3d9PVKt
*Rinnan Trial records
Norwegian National Museum of Justice https://justismuseet.no/
*Forsvarsmuseet Rustkammeret
http://forsvaretsmuseer.no/Rustkammeret

ABOUT THE AUTHOR

Janet Oakley writes award-winning historical fiction that spans the mid-19th century to WW II. Her characters come from all walks of life, but all stand up for something in their own time and place.

Her books have been recognized with a 2013 Bellingham Mayor's Arts Award, the 2013 Chanticleer Grand Prize, the 2014 First Place Chaucer Award, the 2015 WILLA and 2018 Silver Awards, the 2018 Will Rogers award for romance, and the 2016 Goethe Grand Prize.

When not writing, Janet demonstrates 19th century folkways, including churning some pretty mean butter. She is also active in the CCC Legacy organization, supporting efforts to recognize the work of the Civilian Conservation Corps contribution to state and national parks as well soil reclamation during the Great Depression.

In addition to historical fiction, J.L. has also written mystery novellas set in the Hawaiian Islands and has been published in anthologies and magazines. *The Quisling Factor* is the sequel to *The Jøssing Affair*

You can find her at https://jloakleyauthor.com

Her award-winning books can be ordered from your favorite Indie Bookstore or on Amazon at https://amzn.to/31Cyu34

Made in the USA
Monee, IL
16 July 2020